THE NAVARRE

CHANGE OF LEADS

Book One
The Lost Shoe

A.K. Brauneis

A.K. BRAUNEIS

First Printing: 2019
Printed and bound in the USA
ISBN 13:978-1-7335920-0-0

Two Blazes Artworks
1938 Bartl Drive
Camano Island, WA 98282
USA

www.twoblazesartworks.com

Front cover art and design by A. K. Brauneis

Dedication

To my husband, Paul. Though often shaking his head at my chaotic creativity, he has always been there with his love and support throughout this whole process. Love you, Babe. You're the best thing to come into my life.

To Peter Elstrom. Deuel. Though gone from this Earth for many years, he was, back then and still is now, my creative inspiration.

Acknowledgments

Where would I be without the westerns? Movies, TV, books, they were all my sanctuary, my private world where I could go anytime and disappear into a world filled with fun and adventure.

Jimmy Stewert, Audie Murphy, and Ben Johnston, to name only a few who kept my eyes glued to the screen. Wagon Train, Wanted Dead or Alive, High Chaparral, Lancer, and my all-time forever favorite, Alias Smith and Jones. Westerns were abundant when I was growing up, and I'm sure I watched every single movie and most of the TV series that were out there.

Charlie Russell. Oh my, what an influence he had, and still has, on my creative endeavors. Attending the Out West Art Show in Great Falls, Montana has become one of the highlights of my year.

Max Brand was my favorite western author, and though I read books by others, his were the ones that kept me coming back.

Today, I watch most of the new western movies that hit the silver screen, giving my support to a genre that has lost its way but is struggling to make a comeback. At the very least, these more recent westerns have been entertaining, but there are a few that stand out as gems: Silverado, Dances with Wolves, Appaloosa, Open Range, Hostiles, and yes, I did enjoy Cowboys and Aliens.

I thank all these creations, and the many people that helped in their production for giving me a love that has lasted a lifetime. Now, here I am, writing my own western series, and enjoying every minute of it.

For those people in my life now who have helped me along the way I would like to thank:

S. Whyment for her support and contributions towards character development.

Stephanie Haenicke for the many hours she dedicated to proof-reading all the various versions of this manuscript.

Eric Hotz for his technical support. For someone, like myself, who is computer illiterate, his advice and assistance has been invaluable.

Also, to the various on-line writing sites that offered me a safe place to get my literary feet wet and for helping me realize when it was time to move on.

And, of course, my writing critique group, 'The Hard-Nosed Zealots'. This group has shown me so much support and encouragement, both in fine-tuning my manuscripts, and in weathering the stormy waters of self-publication. You're a great group of ladies.

Thank you.

Table of Contents
Change of Leads: The Lost Shoe

CHAPTER ONE
THE REUNION

Wyoming Territory. Summer 1885

Two men rode in companionable silence as the shadows of the warm day lengthened into late afternoon. They made good time after leaving Medicine Bow, but now, it dragged for the younger member of this partnership, as he became aware of the other's subtle scrutiny. Finally, Jack could stand the pressure no longer, and, despite knowing from experience what was likely to happen, he just had to ask.

"I can hear ya' thinkin', Leon. Ya' might as well put us both outta your misery and tell me what's rattlin' around in that over-active brain 'a yours."

Napoleon Nash grinned.

"Well, since you asked . . ."

"Uh huh."

"I was just thinking . . ."

"Yeah, I know."

". . . You need to get another hat."

"What?"

"You did ask." Leon's dark eyes sparkled with mischievous delight.

"Yeah, and I'm regrettin' it, already."

"Oh."

A strained silence settled between them.

"All right," Jack relented, as Leon knew he would. "Why do I need another hat, when the one I'm wearin' is fine?"

The impish smile returned. "It's the wrong color."

"The wrong color?"

"Yes. I mean—think about it. My alias is Peter Black, and I wear a black hat. Your alias is Mathew White, but you wear a brown hat. The way I see it, you either need to change your alias to Brown, or get a white hat."

Jackson Kiefer darted his partner a biting look, then he shook his dark blonde curls and brown hat with long-suffering patience.

Change of Leads: The Lost Shoe

"This is what you've been sittin' there, mullin' over for the last five miles? Jeez, Leon. I know you have a hard time, puttin' that brain 'a yours ta' rest, but why can't ya' just appreciate the peace and quiet for a change? It's a nice day, we got money in our pockets, and there ain't no posse chasin' us. Relax."

"I am relaxed," Leon insisted. "I think it's—"

Jack's black gelding chose this moment to take a wrong step. He stumbled, then recovered in one quick movement. But it was enough to end the bantering, and both men pulled their horses up.

"What was that?" Leon asked. "It's not like Midnight to trip over nothing."

"Yeah." Jack dismounted. Taking hold of the gelding's near foreleg, he lifted the foot. "Dammit. The shoe's gone."

"What? We just had them both shod. How could he be missing a shoe already?"

"How should I know?" Jack griped, as he went around to the other three feet. Shoes were still attached to those hooves, but Jack stood up, shaking his head. "That smitty did a lousy job. All 'a them shoes are missin' nails. No wonder they're fallin' off."

Hearing this, Leon dismounted and checked his mare's footwear. She still had all four shoes intact, but they wouldn't be for long. Leon stood up and gave the liver chestnut hide an assuring pat, but he was not pleased.

"That bastard. I guess he spotted us as drifters and figured he could get away with a cheap job. I didn't pick up any more shoe nails, either. I figured we were good for a while."

"I tell ya'," Jack complained, "I'm half-tempted ta' go back and force that smitty to redo 'em. At gunpoint, if necessary."

"It would be fun, wouldn't it?" Leon grinned. "Oh well. Remember what the governor said, *'Stay out of trouble.'* Other than the trouble he sends us into, that is."

Jack barked a laugh, shaking his head. "I wonder if those pardons he's offerin' us in exchange for workin' for him, are worth it, 'cause he sure is takin' his time in givin' 'em to us."

"Yup, I know," Leon said, as he remounted "Still, here we are. Come on. We'll take it slow to the next town and get this seen to. And, as you pointed out, we do have money in our pockets."

Jack grumbled something unintelligible but re-mounted his gelding and followed his partner while keeping Midnight to the softer parts of the trail.

***

An hour later, after checking the identity of the local sheriff, they left their horses at the livery stable along with instructions for the smitty. They then found themselves with an afternoon to kill. Assuming it would be too late to carry on once the horses were ready, they decided to book a room at the hotel and wash some of the trail dust off before checking out the local watering hole.

They strolled along the boardwalk with the outward appearance of a casualness that neither one of them felt. The knowledge that there was still a hefty reward for their capture hanging over their heads always made them anxious when they returned to this territory that they had once called home. To the unobservant passer-by, they were two young men, enjoying the warm and pleasant summer afternoon. But, upon closer examination, it could be noted that their eyes constantly scanned their surroundings, with every nerve and muscle ready for action.

They climbed the steps to the hotel entrance, feeling safe in their anonymity when the one thing they always tried to avoid, happened. They were recognized.

"Mathew. Peter. Hey, boys!"

Jack and Leon stopped in their tracks. Leon even had a hand on the door, preparing to push through when the dreaded summons sent tingles of shock down their spines. But there was also a measure of relief that countered the fear of being recognized, as their accoster used their aliases and not their actual names.

Jack's blue eyes narrowed, and his right hand instinctively dropped to the handle of his gun, but it went no further. Then both men grinned in recognition of the man who ran across the street toward them.

"Cameron."

"Hey, Cameron. What are you doin' here?"

Change of Leads: The Lost Shoe

"Howdy, boys." Cameron Marsham stepped onto the boardwalk, smiling broadly, and everyone shook hands. "What a surprise to find you two in these parts. How are you doing?"

"Oh, same as usual," Leon told him, his deep dimples dancing with delight.

"Just tryin' ta' stay outta trouble," Jack responded.

"What about you?" Leon asked. "We thought you folks moved to Denver."

"We did. But, well, it's a long story. I'm in town looking over some breeding stock for our ranch in Colorado. Which way you fellas headed? If you have time, why don't you swing by our place for a few days? The girls would love to see you. Actually, I should be calling them young ladies now. You won't believe how they've grown."

Leon and Jack exchanged quick smiles. What Caroline and Penelope might look like now, all blossoming into their own, took over their imaginations. Then, realizing that it was their father who stood before them, they forced themselves into the present and focused again upon their friend.

"Another ranch, Cameron?" Jack asked. "Thought you were goin' back ta' teachin'."

"I did," came the matter-of-fact response, then he sighed and smiled. "Well, we've gone through a lot of changes these last few years. Come on. I'd love for you to see the place, since you two boys had a hand in us getting it."

"We did?" asked Leon.

"How was that?" Jack asked, at the same time.

"Well now, that's just another thing I can tell you about when you come visit," answered Cameron, a smug look on his face. He knew their curiosity was up.

Jack and Leon exchanged a look. They shouldn't do it, but they both wanted to.

"All right Cameron," Leon said in response to the rancher's hopeful smile. "Give us a chance to get some of this trail dust off, then how about we buy you a beer while you give us directions, and we'll consider it."

"Is that the best I'll get?" Cameron asked, his smile broadening. "You'll be in for a treat—and a surprise."

Leon's dimples deepened, but he wouldn't budge. "We'll see."

***

Early evening found the two ex-outlaws seated at a quiet table in the hotel restaurant, tucking into a private supper of pot roast and fixin's.

Cameron had departed an hour earlier without having received more than the original ambiguous response to his invitation. Leon wanted to give him more, but the need to discuss this with Jack before giving a concrete answer took priority. Even though Leon and Jack had such a strong connection that others swore they must be joined at the hip, something this important needed to be vocalized before a decision could be assumed.

"What do you think?" Leon asked after a quick scan of the café to be sure of their privacy. "Is it smart?"

"Smart?" Jack queried around a mouthful of roast. "Since when have we ever been accused 'a bein' smart?"

"Yeah, but we had good reason for staying away."

"What was them reasons again?"

Leon narrowed his dark eyes at his companion's deliberate obtuseness.

"The Marshams are like family to us, Kid. You and I both know that the law knows this and could use it against us." Leon smiled as the use of the nickname produced the desired result.

Jack visibly bristled. "No need ta' get proddy, Ole' Man. You know darn well that a fella in his thirties ain't no kid, so stop callin' me that. Besides, I know what you're worryin' about, but it's been years."

"Yeah, it has been. But that doesn't mean it couldn't still be dangerous—for us and for them. Showing up there again could bring a whole lot of trouble down on them."

"But we ain't showin' up there again," Jack pointed out. "This is a whole new ranch in a whole different territory."

"Yeah, you have a point."

The two men sat in silence while they continued with their supper, each lost in his own thoughts, but thinking the same thing.

"Still," Leon mused, "it would be nice to see them again."

"Sure would."

"And Jean is an excellent cook."

"Sure is." Jack grinned, knowing that Leon was coming around to seeing this differently.

"I mean, what harm would it do, really?"

Jack knew when to keep his mouth shut, or at least otherwise occupied. The best person to talk Leon into doing anything, was Leon himself.

***

The next morning, standing outside the livery while they got their horses ready for travel, both men felt he growing excitement and anticipation of a long overdue reunion.

It took several days to ride to the Marsham ranch, and in that time, Leon noticed that his dark, liver-colored mare, Karma-Lou, was becoming more and more irritable. Instead of moving along at a smooth, ground-covering jog-trot, she insisted on prancing around, swishing her tail and tossing her head while constantly playing with her bit. All of this made for an uncomfortable ride. More than once, she flattened her ears and took a swipe with her teeth at ole' Midnight.

Midnight, always the gentleman, did his best to avoid these unprovoked onslaughts. But when Karma squealed and tried to swing her hindquarters around to kick the kind-hearted fellow, Jack laid in a loud protest.

"Leon. Come on."

"I know," Leon felt the mare move her hindquarters, and he blocked her with his leg to prevent her from kicking the gelding. "Cut her some slack, Jack. She's coming into season, and you know what she's like when that happens."

"Yeah, I can't help but know, can I? And poor Midnight has lost more hair to her teeth than he sheds out every spring."

"She's just a little testy."

"A little testy?" Jack harrumphed. "For her, 'a little testy' is kickin' down the stable door, headin' for the nearest farm, jumpin' their fence, and spendin' all night eatin' their corn. I'm surprised she ain't colicky."

"She only did that twice," Leon reasoned. "And the farmers were quite reasonable about it, once I paid them off."

"I donno, Leon," Jack shook his head. "I know she's saved your skin more 'n once with that untyin' knots trick, and on her good days, she really is somethin' ta' behold. But, I got ta' admit, there are times I wanna shoot her."

Leon smiled. "Yeah, but you love her." He never had, and never would, admit to Jack that he had come close to doing the same thing, himself.

Jack snorted. "Just keep her outta kickin' range, will ya'? With my luck, she'd miss Midnight and kick me. All I need is a broken leg 'cause of some 'testy' mare . . ." Jack's grumblings trailed off into his own thoughts.

Leon simply smiled.

***

Arvada, Colorado

Once having crossed the border from Wyoming into Colorado, the boys relaxed some, but they were still careful to stay away from the larger towns. The Marsham ranch was within a few days' ride of Denver, but since that town was the home base for a couple of noted detective agencies, the partners stayed clear of it. They easily found lodgings in smaller towns until they were able to make the last leg of their ride to the ranch.

The approach to the Rocking M was quite the opposite of what it had been four years ago, when running from a posse and lost in a blizzard, they had fortuitously stumbled across the Marshams' previous property. Even covered in snow, it was obvious that the ranch had been bleak and unprofitable. The house itself, though neat and clean, had seen better days, and the '*Welcome*' sign which greeted visitors to the homestead looked as old and worn out as the property it was attached to.

This new ranch was green and lush. White-fenced pastures lined the well-kept road that led to an open yard. There sat a friendly, two-story ranch house with a wrap-around porch, and flower beds hugging the front of the structure. There were two large barns, with paddocks leading off them, a bunkhouse, and a large, well-kept vegetable garden off to the side.

Change of Leads: The Lost Shoe

When all was said and done, it was an impressive package. The fellas rode down that pleasantly shaded roadway, and into the yard, feeling relaxed and welcome.

As they approached the front of the house, a large, tan-colored mutt padded around the side of the structure and barked at them, his tail wagging. Then, two hairy tornadoes scrambled around from behind, yapping their heads off and causing such a commotion that Karma stopped in her tracks, pinned her ears upon them, and started blowing.

Midnight, who was more experienced than his counterpart, sent them a glance and then dismissed them.

Leon gave his mare a reassuring pat, and dismounted. Jack followed his example as the front door of the house burst open and two more tornadoes in skirts flew down the steps toward them.

"Peter. Mathew," they shouted in unladylike glee. "We've been waiting for you. We thought you'd never get here."

"Wow. Girls, look at you." Leon exclaimed, as excited female teenagers tackled them both with hugs and kisses, interspersed with a stream of questions.

The dogs were underfoot now, yapping and woofing, wanting to be a part of the festivities.

Both Midnight and Karma backed up a step or two, not sure they wanted to be a part of anything.

"My, but you girls have grown up," Jack observed. "You're turnin' inta' real fine young ladies."

"We still ride and shoot," protested 16-year-old Penelope. "We only wear dresses because Mama insists on it when we're not helping Papa with the stock."

"I don't mind wearing dresses," announced the older sister, Caroline. "We are ladies, after all."

Leon and Jack exchanged glances and smiled. They were indeed ladies; in all ways that mattered to two young men whose only solace was the brothel. Still, these young ladies were like sisters to them, and they had to keep on reminding themselves of this fact.

"Girls, girls. Let the fellas breathe."

"Hey, Cameron. How are you?" asked Leon, as they shook hands.

"This is a nice place ya' got here," Jack complimented him. "A real step up from the last one."

"Yup. And I have you boys to thank for it."

"That's what you said before," Leon's eyes turned suspicious. "I think there's a story to be told there."

"Sure is," Cameron agreed. "Why don't you come on in and relax. Jean is putting together a fine lunch for us, and we can get caught up on all the news." He waved at his hired hand, who was just coming out of one of the barns. "Hey, Sam. Take these fellas' horses and get them settled in, will you?"

"Sure thing, Mr. Marsham." Sam smiled as he took the horses off their hands. "That's a real good lookin' mare ya' got there, mister."

Leon smiled.

Jack rolled his eyes.

While Sam, the horses, and the dogs headed toward the main barn, everyone else went up the porch and into the house.

The atmosphere was bright and airy, with a comfortable sitting room to the right, and a large dining area to the left. From the sounds and enticing aromas, it could be assumed that the kitchen was straight ahead. The table to the left of them was already laid out for lunch, and the boys thought about how hungry they were—again, when Jean appeared in the hallway.

The ex-outlaws lit up with pleasure upon seeing this kind woman whom they had come to feel such a bond with. There was something different about her, something subtle, that neither man could quite put their finger on. But whatever it was, it was a good thing, as she looked happy and welcoming.

"Oh, boys," she greeted them with a warm smile. "Look at you. You've hardly changed a bit."

"Hello, Jean." Each man took turns, giving her a warm hug and a kiss on the cheek. It really was good to see her.

"Now you sit down," Jean told them. "Girls, come help me. We have coffee or sweet tea, and a fine lunch ready. The girls made their special apple pie, just for you."

"Great," said Leon, his lips stretching into a wide grin.

"Yup," agreed Jack. "I been really lookin' forward ta' this."

***

Ten minutes later, everyone settled in to enjoy the spread laid out for lunch. As the meal progress, Cameron relayed the surprising turn of events which had enabled them to purchase such a profitable piece of property.

"That's the long and short of it, boys. We were prepared to get re-established with what little savings we had left, when out of the blue, the bidding war started. It seems that two wealthy gentlemen from back East had rather romanticized impressions of the 'Wild West' and wanted to buy a little piece of it. When word got around that Napoleon Nash and the Kansas Kid had been captured on our old place, well, they tripped over each other to see who could offer the highest price."

Leon and Jack stared at Cameron, mouths open in disbelief.

Leon was the first to speak. "But—we escaped. It's not like it was "the place" where Nash and Kiefer were finally "brought to justice". We're still at large, to carry on with our thieving ways."

Cameron shrugged, smiling. "I know. I thought they were crazy. But the price we finally got for that patch of dirt set us up very nicely. We moved to Denver and I got a job teaching. But, as it turns out, none of us were really happy there."

"That's for sure," Jean said. "I missed hearing the birds in the mornings, and the quiet afternoons out on the porch. Living in town had its advantages, but I think we all missed the open spaces."

"So, when this place came up for sale," continued Cameron, "we decided that if I still taught school part-time, we could afford to hire some help and maybe make a go of it. Goodness knows, the girls were ecstatic over the idea."

"I missed saddling up one of our own horses and going for a ride on our own property," commented Penelope. "None of the other girls in town were interested in that. They were more concerned with boys and gossiping. And Papa says that my numbers are good enough, I can start helping out with the business end of things here on the ranch."

"Well now, that's real promisin', Penny," commented Jack, obviously impressed. "We've come across a few ladies who ran their own businesses. And they did real well with 'em, too."

Penelope brightened. "Really? The other girls in town just laugh at me and say that it's not proper for a girl to want to go into business. That I should get married and have a family." She gave a sneer of contempt.

"No reason you can't do both," Leon said. "Why, some of the ladies we know . . ." His voice trailed off as he glanced at Cameron and Jean, realizing he might be overstepping the boundaries.

Jean smiled. "That's quite all right," she assured him. "Cameron and I have always encouraged the girls to go after what they wanted and not be too concerned about what other people thought." Then she sent a pointed look to her daughters and added, "You can be ladies and still pursue your dreams. Just be aware that it might be difficult managing both a career and a family. You might have to make some tough choices, girls."

The girls weren't too concerned about tough choices.

"What do your lady friends do in their businesses?" Penny asked.

"Well, let's see." Leon's thoughts turned to Geena, but a woman who ran her own saloon and gambling hall didn't seem appropriate for this group.

"There's June," suggested Jack.

"That's right," agreed Leon, thankful to his partner for coming up with a more appropriate example. "Now, June had a great sense for money and business. She came into some funds and was all set to open an establishment where people could go and have a fine dinner and watch theatre, at the same time."

"Really?" asked Jean. "What an unusual choice for a woman. Was she able to do it?"

"As a matter of fact, she did," said Leon. "She met a young German fellow named Paul, who just happened to be an excellent cook . . ."

"A married man who's a cook?" Penny laughed. "Whoever heard of such a thing?"

"Well now, there's the pot calling the kettle black," Jean pointed out. "Just a few minutes ago, you were complaining that people put you down for wanting to do something different with your life. Now, here you are, doing the same thing to someone else."

Penny hung her head and looked sheepish. "Yes, Mama."

"Yup," Jack carried on. "They made a good pair. With his cookin' skills, and June's head for business, they put together a real fine place."

"Then there's Constance," mused Leon. "She runs a mercantile in Sweetwater."

"Of course, there's Josephine," added Jack. "We've known her for years and she never did get married."

"Nope," Leon agreed. "Came close a couple of times, though."

"Yup, real close." Both men smiled at the memory of Josey.

"Then, there's Elspeth Parks," continued Leon, as he leaned back and smiled in memory of all these lovely ladies, "who was into banking."

"Banking?" Jean asked.

"Yes," Leon confirmed. "Her husband died and left her with the business. Most people said that she was the one running it anyway, so it was no surprise when she simply took it over."

Penelope contemplated this option. She'd never thought of going into banking.

"And we'll never forget Gabriella," said Jack, then instantly regretted it, as Leon's expression became somber.

Jean also noticed the change in Leon's countenance, and she knitted her brow. "Was she someone special?"

"Ah, well, yeah, you could say that," Jack murmured, He wasn't sure where to go with this, now.

Jack's eyes were on his friend, hoping for some indication. But Leon sat quietly, looking at the table, deep in his own thoughts. Jack decided that the damage was already done, so he might as well go for broke.

"Gabriella was kind of a private detective, among other things. She's done undercover work up in Canada, and for Wells

Fargo, Pinkerton, and The Bureau," he explained. "We locked horns with her on more 'n one occasion, while we were still in our previous line 'a work, ya' might say."

"That's interesting," Cameron said. "I didn't realize those detective agencies hired women."

"They do, on the sly," Jack said. "At least Wells Fargo, and The Bureau, but Alan Pinkerton openly hired women. It wasn't until he died, and his two sons took over that they stopped. They would still hire independents though, and Gabi can be real persuasive when she wants ta' be."

Caroline, who had been uncharacteristically quiet throughout the conversations, now perked up with interest. "She was a detective?"

"Ah, yup," Jack confirmed, still a little uncomfortable with the subject, knowing that he had probably cut Leon to the quick. "A real bright and gutsy lady, too." He smiled at some of the memories that came flooding back. "I tell ya', there was times she had us so riled up, we was both fit ta' be tied. But she had class, that's for sure."

Jean smiled while watching Leon. "I have a feeling she did more to Peter than just get him riled."

Leon looked up from his musings. He and Jean locked gazes for a moment, then he smiled. She knew.

Caroline, unaware of the underlying drama being played out around her, focused on the one thing that caught her interest.

"She's actually a detective?" she repeated, her excitement rising. "And you know her? Can I meet her? Do you think she would talk to me? Do you think she would tell me how to become a detective?"

"Whoa, hold on there," Jack held up his hands against the onslaught. "I thought you liked bein' a lady."

"Well, I do." Caroline insisted, her eyes shining. "But we've just been saying that a woman can be a lady and still follow her dreams."

"And it's your dream to become a detective?" asked Leon.

"Oh brother." Cameron and Jean rolled their eyes at one another. "You have no idea," Cameron continued. "Any detective books she can get hold of, anything to do with the law and the justice system, Caroline is right in there."

"She wants to go back East to study law, if we can find a ladies' college that will teach it," said Jean. "Law is a profession exclusively for men, so it's been difficult."

"Gettin' inta' law, is one thing," said Jack, "but becomin' a detective, that can be a dangerous line a' work, dealin' with all sorts of unsavory individuals. It's kind 'a like bein' an outlaw. The flip side of the same coin, ya' might say. Once ya' get locked into that kind a' life, it's difficult ta' break away from it. Ya' might find that it ain't quite as glamorous as ya' think."

"Yes, I know." Caroline sighed, undeterred. "But, if you know a woman who is already a detective, it can't be that dangerous. And maybe she could help get me going in the right direction. Can you get in touch with her?"

Leon and Jack exchanged glances. Both were hesitant.

"I don't think that's a good idea," Jack commented.

Disappointment damped Caroline's enthusiasm.

"You have to understand, Caroline," Leon explained. "Mathew and I are still wanted. We can't just 'get in touch' with those agencies and not expect some dire consequences to come of it."

"Oh, yeah. I forgot." she deflated.

"On top of that, she's not working as a detective anymore," Leon continued. "She and the Pinkertons had a falling out; a, ah, well . . . there was a . . . a conflict of interest, you could say. Her life has moved on; she doesn't even do work for Wells Fargo anymore."

Caroline frowned. "A conflict of interest? What does—?"

"Caroline," Jean interrupted. "Why don't you get some more of your special apple pie from the kitchen?"

Caroline slumped. "Yes, Mama."

And then it happened. That silent communication between two people who know one another so well that words aren't necessary. Just a glance between the partners, and a whole conversation took place.

Cameron and Jean exchanged looks, and smiled. The girls were oblivious.

"There might be someone we could get in touch with," offered Leon, even though he was still hesitant.

Caroline stopped and sat back down, instantly forgetting about more pastries.

"Yeah," continued Jack. "Someone in the Wells Fargo Detective Agency."

"Really?" Caroline perked up.

Another exchange of glances followed by a shrugging of shoulders.

"His name's Frank Carlyle," stated Leon. "He's a strange fellow, but very good at what he does. Oddly enough, he's a friend. And we do have a way of letting him know when we want to see him, without causing a stir. He might be willing to help you get started."

"That would be great," Caroline was ecstatic.

"You boys have another friend in Wells Fargo.?" Cameron was incredulous.

"Yeah, well," Jack explained. "It kind'a has ta' do with the deal we made with the governor. And we've helped him out of a scrape once . . ."

"Or twice."

"So, he's kind'a willin' ta' help us out, occasionally," Jack continued. "Above and beyond what the governor expects of him."

"If it doesn't threaten his career," commented Leon.

"Or get in the way of his social life."

"What little social life he has."

"Ya, but he keeps tryin'."

"True," Leon conceded. "He's an odd one, that's for sure, but brilliant. I came up against him once, when we were still on opposite sides." His eyes darkened with the memory. "Well, let's just say I wouldn't want to go through that again."

Jean frowned. "And he's now your friend?"

Leon returned to the present. A tight smile twitched his lip and he shrugged. "We worked it out."

"Yeah," Jack growled, "by him pistol-whippin' ya' just ta' make a point."

Leon shrug. "It's time you let that go, Jack. Water under the bridge, and all that."

"Oh dear." Jean looked from one partner to the other. "Do you think he's the kind of man we want helping us?"

"Oh, sure," Leon smiled with confidence. "Frank's a real gentleman, as long as you're not an outlaw."

CHAPTER TWO
THE ADD-ON

A quiet, barely audible sound came from a back room, off the kitchen. All heads swiveled that way.

"Oh, it sounds like someone is awake," announced Jean, and she got up to leave the table.

Both Jack and Leon sent a questioning gaze toward Cameron, but he just smiled.

"You boys like some more coffee?" he asked.

"Ah, sure."

"I'll get it," said Caroline, and she headed for the kitchen.

Jean returned, carrying a small, cooing bundle, wrapped in a blanket.

Both fellas got to their feet and gazed down upon the infant in Jean's arms.

"Oh my . . ."

"Oh ho, Cameron," Jack grinned. "You said you had a surprise, but we sure didn't expect this."

"No, neither did we," said Jean, as she smiled. "We thought we were all done with child-rearing, then suddenly, this little fella showed up."

"How old is he?" Jack asked.

"Just about six weeks," answered Jean. "Here, Mathew, why don't you hold him."

"Ahh . . ."

"Yeah. Come on, Mathew," said Leon, as he grinned. "Puppies and kittens adore you, so you shouldn't have any trouble with a baby."

Jack sent his partner a scowling look while he was shuffled into his chair and the blanketed bundle settled into his nervous arms.

Leon sat back down, but he leaned over Jack's shoulder, looking at the baby, with his face split in half by a huge grin.

Caroline returned with the coffee pot and filled everyone's cup. Then she settled into her chair and nibbled on a pastry.

Penny watched Jack, her gaze intense, with thoughts of going into business delegated to the back burner of her desires.

"What's his name?" Leon asked, as he continued to smile down at the infant.

"Elijah Cameron," Jean informed them. "Or Eli, for short."

Leon lifted his smile to Cameron and Jean as he settled back in his chair again. "He's a fine-looking boy. Congratulations."

The proud parents smiled and passed a loving look between themselves.

Then, all eyes were on Jack. He relaxed once he realized the baby wasn't likely to break in his arms. A huge smile broke over his face and there it stayed.

Cameron had a vision of a small boy at Christmas time, finally getting the present he had always wanted. It took the rancher by surprise.

Jean, on the other hand, had been no fool in handing the infant to Jack. With all the stories she had heard over the years about the notorious Elk Mountain Gang and its infamous outlaw leaders, once she met the men themselves, she knew they were nothing like what the tabloids made them out to be. They'd made some bad choices, certainly, and got themselves onto the wrong side of things, definitely. But they worked hard to turn their lives around, and they were both basically good men.

But, especially in Jack Kiefer, she sensed a gentle and caring soul, which was in drastic contrast to his reputation as a dangerous gunslinger and cold-blooded killer. She wasn't quite sure how to reconcile these two very different versions of the same man, but sometimes you can over-think a thing. She trusted her own instincts and had no qualms about handing her infant son to him.

In the meantime, Penny continued to watch Jack with bright eyes that took in everything. A quiet, knowing smile played upon her lips.

If Jack had had more experience with teenage emotions, he would have taken note of that look and quickly made his departure to parts unknown. As it was, he was so intent on this new little human being in his arms, he was oblivious to all the other thoughts swirling around him.

It seemed that Eli was also quite interested in this new person in his small world. Bright brown infant eyes locked onto bright blue adult ones, and little hands tapped against a lowered chin and played with smiling lips. Then, that same little hand clasped tightly onto a finger and a huge yawn escaped from the tiny mouth.

Jack laughed. "Aw, Leon. One day, maybe. Huh?"

Leon smiled. Visions of them being able to put all this running behind and settle down with families of their own were not far from his thoughts, either.

"I know, Jack. Maybe one day."

Penny's smile grew even broader.

***

Finally, the extended dinner was cleared away. Jean excused herself from the gathering and retreated with Eli into the nursery to feed him and put him down for another nap. The girls got busy cleaning up in the kitchen and argued over who was going to wash and who was going to dry.

Thoughts of supper were the last thing in anyone's mind, and the three men contemplated moving to the porch to enjoy a drink in the fading afternoon light.

Then, the serenity of the moment was shattered by loud, raucous horse squeals, the splintering of wood, and Sam yelling obscenities from across the barnyard.

Jack sent a suspicious look in his partner's direction. "Leon . . .?"

Leon gave an innocent shrug, and all three men headed out the front door and down the porch steps.

***

Across the yard, in the paddock where the horses had been put to enjoy their own lunch, Karma was in the middle of a temper tantrum. Ears flattened against her neck, mouth gaping open and emitting more, angry, guttural squeals, she had poor Midnight pinned into the corner of the paddock. With her hind feet, she reigned vicious kicks upon that kindly soul, as though he were the knacker man himself, coming to claim her.

Fortunately, most of the kicks missed their mark, but she still succeeded in hitting the fence a few times, splintering the wood and knocking some rails down.

Midnight did everything he could to avoid the onslaught and scrambled out of her line of fire.

In the meantime, Sam, having grabbed a driving whip, jumped what was left of the fence and yelled at the mare, cracking the whip to move her away.

To add to the ruckus, the three dogs, who had been quiet all afternoon, were now right in the thick of things They barked and yapped in their excitement but only succeeded in getting underfoot.

"Dagnammit, Leon," Jack yelled, as they both ran forward to assist Sam in separating the horses.

"Well, I told ya', she was a little testy," Leon countered in defense of his mare. "Midnight must have said something rude to her."

Jack sent him a nasty glare as they grabbed halters and proceeded to get their horses under control.

Once Leon had Karma in hand, he led her to the far end of the paddock and kept her walking around in a small circle to calm her down. Meanwhile, Jack gently ran his hands over his gelding to make sure he was all right.

"What set them off?" Cameron asked his hired hand.

"I'm sorry, Mr. Marsham. I guess I just weren't thinkin'. I never thought she might be in season. I was bringin' Gambler in for the night when that mare started actin' up. 'A course, Gambler got all hot and bothered, so I got him into his stall before he killed me. Then I hear all hell break loose out here. I got back as quick as I could. Again, I'm sure sorry about that."

It was at this moment, when a deep, stallion-sized bellow came from within the barn.

Karma's head went up and she answered with a loud, shrill whinny that caused her whole body to vibrate.

Leon grimaced in pain.

"Well, don't worry about it," said Cameron. "You better get in there and tend to that stallion. We'll get the fence fixed in the morning."

"Yessir." And Sam disappeared into the barn.

The three dogs were quite proud of themselves for getting things under control, and happily followed the young man, content in the knowledge that they had done their job.

Cameron smiled at his guests, each in their respective corners, attempting to sooth their horses.

"That was quite a show," he commented.

"Yeah. Sorry about that, Cameron," Leon apologized, sheepishly. "She can be quite a handful, sometimes. We'll be happy to fix the fence in the morning for you. It's the least we can do."

Quiet grumblings came from Jack's general direction.

"Don't worry about it," said Cameron, and he dropped into his 'school teacher' persona. "Sam's a great hand with the livestock, and the dogs love him to pieces, but he's young and sometimes doesn't think. He wants to go to town tomorrow morning to see his girlfriend, so having to hold off on that to fix the fence will be a good reminder for him. When you're handling a stallion, you must always be aware of your surroundings, or you'll get into trouble. A couple of hours delay won't kill him." He glanced at Jack. "How's your gelding?"

Jack was rubbing Midnight's ears while he spoke gently to him. Midnight responded with half-closed eyes and a quivering upper lip.

Jack glanced up and shrugged. "He's fine. He might be a little sore tomorrow, but that's all."

"Well, you fellas will have to stay over another day. Why don't you take them to the other barn and get them settled in for the night? In the meantime, I'll get us some drinks to have on the porch. I think, after this, we could all use one."

The partners, leading their horses, picked through the litter of splintered wood that had once been part of a rather sturdy paddock. They entered the barn and found themselves in a large, solid structure, with eight box stalls, and a well-supplied tack room.

Six other horses already occupied stalls, and though they were busy munching dinner, they showed interested in who these newcomers were. Though a couple of them laid their ears back, in a *'Don't even think, you're touching my grain.'* kind of attitude, a couple of the kinder souls perked their ears and nickered a welcome.

Two empty stalls, across the aisle from each other, presented themselves, and the boys led their horses into them. There, they found that water, grain, and good, rich hay had already been supplied. Leon gave Karma a final pat on her dark, liver neck, then left her stall. He closed the door behind him and leaned back against it with his arms folded, anxiously watching Jack.

The barn was light and airy, and smelled of fresh straw and sweet hay. The only sounds were those of the swallows settling into their nests up in the rafters, and of the horses munching their grain and giving the occasional contented snort or stomp of a foot.

Normally, this setting would have been a comfortable and relaxed one, but this time, it felt strained and heavy. Jack stayed in the stall with Midnight to assure himself that his horse was all right and settled enough to eat.

"Jack?" No response. Leon sighed. "Come on, Jack. I know you're mad at me."

"Yeah, I am," Jack answered quietly, not turning to meet Leon's eyes, while he continued to stroke his horse. "Or, maybe just more scared. Midnight might'a got hurt real bad."

Leon sighed again and lowered his head. He didn't know what else he could say.

Jack brightened and straightened up. "Just give me some time and a good shot 'a whiskey," he said, as he gave Midnight one more pat, then left the stall. "I'm sure I'll get over it."

Leon grinned, relieved.

Leon was fonder of this mare than he had ever been of any other horse, but the friendship of Jack Kiefer mattered more to him than anything else possibly could.

Though still feeling a little moody, Jack returned the smile.

They headed out of the barn and over to the porch where Cameron was waiting with the afore-mentioned drinks

***

The next morning, Sam Jefferies got up bright and early. He was quick to get Gambler out to the pasture with his own group of mares, so there would be no further issues with another accidental encounter.

Once the stallion was secured and out of sight, Sam returned to the main barn and turned Karma and Midnight loose in one of the smaller grass paddocks, where they could spend the day grazing. After making sure that the two groups of horses were settled, Sam began to fix the broken rails of the original paddock fence.

Jack, taking whatever opportunity that might arise to stay finely tuned, set up some tin cans by the far barn and busied himself with target shooting.

Penny stood behind, off to the side, watching in amazement as Jack executed his fast draw and repeatedly massacred the tin cans. When all the cans had jumped wildly off the fence in rapid succession, Penny went out and helped her friend collect them and place them back in position for another beating.

"How come you only fired five shots?' Penny asked. "I recognize a six-shooter when I see one."

"Never leave yourself on empty," Jack replied. "Ya' never know who might be watchin' ya'."

"Oh, yeah. I guess I never thought about that."

"You want to have a shootin' contest?" Jack asked, cocking a brow in her direction.

Penny smiled at him. "No way," she answered. "Even with a rifle, I could never out-shoot you."

"Smart girl . . . or, I should say, smart lady."

Penny smiled, pleased he'd noticed that she wasn't a little girl anymore.

Jack was oblivious. "In a competitive world, ya' gotta do your research. Part 'a playin' the game is knowin' who your opponent is."

"I'll keep that in mind."

Jack smiled. "Good." A flash of movement, five instantaneous cracks from the revolver, and the five cans met their maker.

***

Leon stood on the front porch, leaning against the main post by the steps. A small smile fluttered about his lips as he watched Jack practice. It didn't matter how many times he watched his partner shoot, it still amazed him.

Jean came out, holding Eli, and stood beside Leon, watching the target practice.

"He really is fast, isn't he?" she commented. "That's one thing the tabloids say about him that's true."

Leon's smile broadened. "Yup, he is fast. Fastest I've ever seen. And he's just playing now. You haven't seen him when he's really serious."

Jean's jaw dropped, and she stared at Leon. "He's faster than this? Now that really would be something to see."

"Well, that's the problem." Leon's smile turned impish. "When he's serious, you don't see it."

***

Sam finished mending the split rail fence by mid-afternoon and was quick to get the wagon hitched up, so he could head to Arvada

Cameron decided that since Sam was going to town anyway, he might as well pick up some supplies and save them from having to go later in the week. It would slow Sam down a bit, and the young man was in a hurry, but when the boss said to do something, well, you better take the time to do it.

It wasn't a long drive to town; a little over an hour at most, at a steady jog-trot. Still, Sam felt pressured to make up for lost time and the extra errand. As soon as he rounded the bend and out of sight of the ranch house, he pushed the horses into a hand gallop and kept them at that pace all the way to the outskirts of town. He did show enough common sense to pull the horses down to a reasonable trot when approaching the main street, but there was still a sense of urgency about him, and the horses tossed their heads and fought the bits in response to it.

Oblivious to the horses' agitation, Sam kept them going past the small family homes that lined the street on the way to town, including the home of his girlfriend. He didn't even look sideways as the team and wagon clattered past her front door and carried on into the commercial area, fully intent on his own business.

The horses tried to stop by the mercantile store, but Sam slapped the lines against their rumps and kept them going. They passed the feed store, hotel, train station, and saloon, and he gave no signs of pulling the team up. It wasn't until they arrived at the telegraph office that he finally pulled the lines and brought the antsy team to a halt.

He hopped down from the wagon, tied the horses to the hitching rail, and went inside.

The telegrapher glanced up from his work and smiled a greeting to his customer.

"Good morning, Sam. How's everyone out at the Rocking M?"

"Howdy, Clayt," Sam answered. "Everyone's fine."

"You wanna send another telegram?"

"Yes, please."

"Well, here you go," Clayt handed Sam a pencil and paper. "That sure must be an important job you're waitin' to hear about."

"Yeah, it is, Clayt. Real important."

"Uh huh. Does Marsham know you're thinkin' of moving on?"

"No," Sam snapped, then realized his rudeness and toned it down a bit. He smiled. "No, he don't, Clayt. And it ain't a sure thing yet, either, so don't you go sayin' anything."

Clayt raised his hands in surrender. "Wouldn't dream of it. Ya' gotta understand confidentiality if ya' wanna stay in this business."

"Yeah. Good. Thanks." Sam nodded, and with another smile, he took the pencil and paper to the side table where he composed his message in private.

He made it short and to the point, not wanting to waste money on unnecessary words:

'To Deputy Marshal Morrison. Rawlins, Wyoming. Contact has been made. S.J.'

CHAPTER THREE
OPPORTUNITIES

Wyoming, 1872

Sam Jefferies was ten years old the day his father died. His family lived in a quiet little house, in a quiet little town, close to the Wyoming-Montana border. Mr. Jefferies was the sheriff in that town for all young Sam's life. Sammy, with his mother and father, had basked in the glow of friendship and respectability that had been theirs, mainly due to his father's firm, but fair, interpretation of his duties. Thomas Jefferies was an honorable man, and the residents of Rocky Point, Wyoming couldn't have asked for a better sheriff.

But the unthinkable happened. It had been a cold, clear autumn day, with just a small dusting of snow on the ground, when a group of peaceable-looking men rode into town and brazenly robbed the small bank of $800.00.

The outlaws would've been content to keep to a sedate pace back out of town, but the assistant bank manager had different ideas. As the thieves started on their way, Mr. Peterson ran out of the bank, yelling his declaration, and attracting the attention of everyone within earshot.

The outlaws, true to their nature, kicked their horses into a gallop and headed for the outskirts of town by the shortest possible route.

Naturally, Sheriff Jefferies was alerted by all the commotion. Responding to the ruckus, he hurried into the street to assess the situation and, running around the corner of the general store, was promptly mowed down and trampled into the hard ground by the pounding hooves of the stampeding horses.

The town was in shock. No one could believe that such a terrible thing had happened, not in their town. Sam and his mother were devastated. Merle Jefferies was so grief-stricken at the loss of her husband that she became homebound and partially bedridden in her despair. Sam tried his best to tend to his mother, but he was much too young for that responsibility, and it fell to their kind and supportive neighbors to tend to the young widow and her son.

In time, the town recovered and carried on. A new sheriff was appointed. He was a fine, upstanding gentleman in his own right.

Merle Jefferies gradually got back on her feet and, with the small pension she received as the widow of a law officer killed in the line of duty, she was able to stay in their small home and raise Sam.

The outlaws were never captured, the money never returned, and the death of a good man never vindicated.

Sam Jefferies grew up with a mission burned into his heart and soul: that good, honest folks should be able to live their lives and raise their families without fear of assaulted. They should be able to work hard and prosper, and not lose their savings to thieves and con men.

Indeed, by the time Sam had grown into his late teens, he was determined to do everything he could to see that every man who rode the outlaw trail paid for the misery he caused, and justice would be prevailed upon him.

***

Wyoming 1882

When Sam was twenty, the Wyoming Marshals Department offered Thomas Jefferies' son the very opportunity he needed to carry out his mission. He was to become friendly with the Marsham family, become their employee and gain their trust, and possibly even their friendship. Then simply to wait.

Marshal Morrison was certain that sooner or later, those two most notorious of outlaws, Napoleon Nash and Jack Kiefer—a.k.a., the Kansas Kid—would come calling. And when they did, all Sam had to do was send a telegram and sit tight.

Sam did just that. While in town waiting for the reply to his message, he carried on with his errands as expected. He stocked up on the supplies that Mr. Marsham had requested, and even spent some time with his girlfriend to not arouse suspicions.

When the expected telegram finally arrived, it congratulated Sam on his good work and instructed him to carry on as he had been. As well as watch and listen, if the need arose, Sam was to do whatever necessary to keep the outlaws from leaving, which was the most important task of all.

Driving back to the Rocking M that afternoon, Sam felt a sense of guilt over his duplicity with the Marsham family. They were solid, hardworking people, and they had always treated him fairly and with respect. Not to mention, the eldest daughter, Caroline, was a fine-looking young woman, and Sam immensely enjoyed watching her figure walking away.

Still, they were friends with outlaws, even to the point of harboring them from the law, and that was not acceptable. Sam was determined to see Nash and Kiefer brought to justice, so he hardened his heart, stayed focused on his goals, and ran the risk of becoming just as smooth a liar and con man as the criminals he sought to bring down.

***

Rocking M Ranch, Colorado 1885

Jack took full advantage of the warm, sunny afternoon. He leaned back in his chair, feet propped up on the porch railing with his hat pulled down over his eyes. He was sound asleep.

The three dogs also took advantage of the lazy day and lay stretched out in shady spots on the porch.

Penny had gone inside to help her mother tend to Eli, so Leon decided that now was as good a time as any to ask Caroline to join him for a walk around the property.

She was pleased to accept.

"Where would you like to go first?" she asked, as they walked across the yard.

The two smaller dogs, not wanting to miss an opportunity for a walk, jumped up to join them. Rufus, being an older gentleman, decided to keep Kiefer company.

"I could show you the creek where we go fishing. Or we could saddle a couple of horses, and I could show you the new foals and calves up in the north pasture."

"I just wanted us to go for a walk and have a talk," Leon admitted. He smiled and offered her his arm, which she gladly, albeit suspiciously, took.

"Talk about what?" she asked him, with a sideways glance.

He began with a sigh. "I've been thinking about the conversation yesterday concerning your choice of careers, and I admit I'm a little concerned."

"But Mama and Papa are supportive of it, and you said you would introduce me to your friend."

"I know, I know. And I will. But first, I want to make sure you understand what you could be getting yourself into."

"Yes, I know," Caroline rolled her eyes. "It's dangerous. I'd be associating with criminals. It's not a job for a woman—"

Leon remained serious. "Yes, to all of the above."

"But you know a woman who did it. You said so."

He sighed again, he was treading on treacherous ground. He didn't want to come across as preachy or condescending, but he felt the need to impress upon her the gravity of her choice.

"To be a successful undercover detective, you must be able to look a person straight in the eye and lie to him. You must, in all sense and purposes, become what they are, to fit into their lives and be convincing. In fact, you have to be worse than the people you're trying to bring down, just to stay alive. Do you think you could do that?"

"I suppose I might have to do those things, but it would be for the greater good. Wouldn't that make it all right?"

"I've heard law officers—some of them, anyway—justify their actions that way. They reason that because the law is on their side, it condones the deceptions and brutalities they use to apprehend a criminal." His smile was rueful. "I suppose I could be prejudice in this matter, but I don't buy it. Injustice against another person, is just that, whether the man behind the gun is wearing a badge or not."

"But injustice is exactly what I want to stop," Caroline argued. "Take you and Mathew, for instance. You've been working so hard toward your pardons, and you don't seem to be any closer now than you were three years ago. It's not justice at all that the law still hunts you after all this time. You've been trying for so long to go straight, but the law won't let you. I want to get in there and make things better, because that's not right."

"Well, of course I'm going to agree with you on that. But there are other ways you can fight that battle without putting your own life in jeopardy." His expression clouded for a moment, and he gently squeezed her hand. "I care about you, Caroline, and I'd hate to see anything bad happen to you."

This time, it was Caroline who sighed. Why couldn't Leon understand how important this was to her?

Leon saw her frustration and decided it was time to change the subject. "What about the young men in your life? I admit, I'm surprised you're not married by now."

"Oh, don't you start on that, too."

"What?"

"This thing about getting married. Most of my friends are married now, and those of us who are not, are considered somehow 'beneath' those who are. The only one who seems to understand, is the doctor's wife. She was older than I am, when she got married. She didn't want to marry a rancher, either."

"What's wrong with a rancher? I thought you liked this life style. Your father's a rancher, and he's one of the finest men I know."

Caroline was silent as she considered this truth.

"I suppose, if I could find someone like Papa, I would consider it," she admitted. "But there's not many men like Papa around. I'd rather stay a maiden than marry beneath me."

Leon laughed. "A man is only beneath you until you fall in love, then suddenly he's the most magnificent creature who ever walked the Earth. You're right to be picky, but you can't tell me a pretty lady like you doesn't have any suitors."

Caroline smiled. "Oh, yes, there have been some, and I've certainly noticed Sam looking my way on occasion. I must admit, it's been fun to tease him a little." Her smile broadened as she put her other hand on Leon's arm. "But you know you're always going to be the first love of my life."

Leon barked out a laugh. "Oh, Caroline, you really are turning into a little flirt."

"Oh, it's all in good fun," she said, patting his arm. "You know that." Then she rolled her eyes. "Not like Penny. It's so embarrassing, watching her swooning over . . ." She stopped herself and brought a hand up to her mouth. She blushed.

Leon smiled. "Swooning over Jack, weren't you about to say?"

"Oh, my goodness," Caroline was mortified. "I can't believe I said that. Penny'll kill me if she finds out. Oh, you won't tell him, will you? Penny'd be beside herself, if he knew how she felt." Then a terrible thought occurred to her. "You don't think he already knows, do you?"

"What? Jack? Able to tell when a young lady's sweet on him?" Leon chuckling that deep, sexy chuckle Caroline remembered so well. "I think even Jack would pick up on that, sooner or later."

"Now you're teasing me," Caroline accused him. "Please don't tell him, okay?"

Leon smiled, and patted her arm. "Don't worry. I won't say anything." He pulled her into a friendship hug and kissed her on the forehead.

They heard the horses trotting into the yard and looked up to see Sam driving the fully-loaded buckboard over to the second barn.

All three dogs barked a cacophony as they scrambled toward the wagon, tails wagging at the return of the hired hand.

Sam, uncharacteristically, ignored the dogs because he noticed the two people at the other end of the yard. He was surprised and couldn't prevent the scowl that flashed across his face at the sight of that outlaw hugging a decent woman.

Leon smiled at what he took to be a young man's unnecessary jealously. He released Caroline and walked her back to the front porch.

Once there, Caroline went into the house to help her mother get supper ready.

Leon walked up beside Jack, who was awake now and leaning against the porch post, with a far-a-way look in his eyes.

"What are you thinking, Jack?"

Jack came back to the present and sent his partner a whimsical smile. “Oh, just how nice it would be to put down roots and stay here. Be part of a family again, ya’ know?”

“Uh huh,” answered Leon. “Would be nice, wouldn’t it?”

“Sure would.”

“But you know we can’t do that, right?”

“Oh yeah, Leon. I know. ‘Course, nothin’ ta’ prevent us from comin’ back for a visit, now and again.”

“That’s true. As long as it’s not too often.”

“No, no, not too often. Just special occasions, like the 4th of July.”

“Uh huh.”

“And Thanksgivin’.”

“Yup.”

“And Christmas. Sure would be nice ta’ spend Christmas with a family again.”

“Sure would.”

“And Easter . . . and the girls’ birthdays. We can’t miss Eli’s first birthday. That wouldn’t be right.”

“No, sure wouldn’t.”

“Then there’s my birthday, and yours. I wonder when Jean’s and Cameron’s are. Oh, and of course, their anniversary.”

“Jack?”

“Yeah?”

“I think supper’s about ready.”

“Oh.

***

“Wow, that was just as good as I remembered it,” Jack commented as he pushed his plate away. “I can’t imagine why we stayed away for so long.”

Leon patted his full tummy, contentment turning his eyes dreamy. “We convinced ourselves that our memory was playing tricks on us. That nothing could actually taste this good.”

Jean shrugged off their compliments. “Now you’re being silly,” she accused them, yet smiled with pleasure anyway, “but I’m glad you enjoyed it.”

“Nope, not bein’ silly,” Jack insisted.

"Meant every word," Leon concurred. "I don't know how you do it, especially with everything else you have to deal with. You're an absolute marvel." He grinned the ultimate impish grin as he noticed Jean blushing.

"That's very kind of you," she said, graciously. "I hope you'll be sticking around for a few more."

The two visitors locked eyes. It certainly was tempting.

While everyone had seconds of dessert and another round of coffee, Jean loaded up a tray with a full plate of dinner, dessert, and coffee, and handed it to Caroline.

"Here, take this out to Sam, please. He got back so late from town, I expect he's still out there putting the supplies away. I'm sure he's quite hungry by now."

"Yes, Mama," Caroline answered, as she took the tray and headed for the front door. She flashed a smile in Leon's direction, and he smiled back at their private joke. Obviously, poor Sam was in for some more teasing.

Jean returned to the kitchen and began the cleanup. Penny was busy tending to her young brother, so Jack excused himself from the table and joined Jean in the kitchen to help.

"Oh, yes. Thank you."

"It's the least I can do after you have made us feel so welcome," he answered. "It's been a real good break for us, ma'am."

"What's with this 'ma'am' stuff?" Jean laughed. "You're family here, you know that."

"Yes, ma'am . . ." Jack stopped himself and laughed. "Sorry, Jean. I guess my folks taught me to do things a certain way and some of that learnin' went pretty deep."

Jean stopped what she was doing and smiled up at the soft-spoken, handsome young man. Again, she found herself in conflict over what she felt for the person she had come to know, and the outlaw she had heard so many bad things about.

"Your folks would be very proud of you," she said. "You're a fine young man, and don't you let anyone tell you different."

Jack smiled. "No, ma'am . . . ah, Jean. I surely won't."

Change of Leads: The Lost Shoe

Penny interrupted them when she came into the kitchen trying to hold on to a grumpy little wiggly worm named Elijah.

"Mama, I can't get him to settle," she whined. "He always goes down right away for you. What's the matter with him?"

Jean turned from the dishes and dried her hands. "Well, did you go over the list the way we discussed?"

Penny rolled her eyes. "Yes." Her focused changed as she fought to hold onto her baby brother, while he twisted and turned, screaming his protest. "What do I do with him? He won't listen to reason. Tending to babies is a lot harder than it looks."

Jean smiled through her son's screaming, and in her quiet, calm manner, took control of the situation.

"He's been fed?"

"Yes."

"You've changed his nappy?"

"Yes."

"He's all clean and dry. He's not cold?"

"Yes." Penny's frustration rose. "I did all that."

"What else is on that list that you're supposed to do, before you put him down, after he's eaten?"

"I don't know."

Jean sighed. A mother's job is never done. "Have you burped him?"

"Oh." Penny's response said it all. "No."

Jean nodded. "Try that next."

"Yes, Mama." Penny slumped. "I'm never going to get the hang of this. How did you manage it with two?"

"Just don't worry about it," her mother suggested. "It'll come in time."

Jack leaned against the counter with a certain amount of detached humor as he watched this exchange.

"Just think of it as an opportunity for practice, Penny," he said. "By the time you have your own family, you'll be a real pro."

Penelope beamed with pleasure. She hoisted her brother onto her shoulder and headed back into the nursery to continue with her practicing.

Jack closed his eyes and grimaced as soon as the words left his mouth. "I think I should have just kept quiet. I know I said exactly the wrong thing."

Jean sparkled at smile at her embarrassed guest. "I think you made Penny's day."

"Oh, no. I'm going to have Cameron after me with a shotgun pretty soon, if I'm not careful."

Jean laughed and gave him a pat on the arm. "Don't worry about it. We've all had to suffer through first crushes, and most of us survive them. Give her time. She'll get over it."

"I sure hope so," then, thinking he might be giving the wrong impression, he did a quick back-step. "Not that Penny wouldn't make some fella a fine wife. I just think she could do a lot better than an old, ex-outlaw for a husband."

"Oh, I don't know about that." Jean's smile turned coyish and, taking the coffee pot, she headed into the dining room with the intention of sitting down and having a cup.

Jack leaned back against the counter and sighed heavily as he ran his hands over his face and through his blond curls. He knew Jean was just teasing him, but this was a balancing act he was not used to playing. He shook his head with a groan, pushed himself away from the counter, and headed into the other room to join everyone else.

***

When Jean and Jack left to clean up, Cameron and Leon found themselves sitting at the table on their own. Both were relaxed and enjoying a second cup of coffee.

"Are you sure you have to leave tomorrow?" Cameron asked. "Penelope and I have to go to school in the morning, but Caroline and Jean will be here. You know the two of you are always welcome."

"Yes, I know," Leon said. "It's been really nice, visiting with you folks again. And I know Jack would like to visit a while longer, but we can't stay in one spot for too long. You know that."

"Yes, I guess, I do. It must be hard on you fellas, having to stay on the move like that, all the time. It must get lonely."

"Hmm, yeah, it does." He sighed and ran his hands through his thick brown hair. "We keep hoping it won't be for much longer, but I don't know. Jack and I are the only ones sticking to the deal. We keep on doing whatever the governor asks of us, but year after year, we're no closer to getting the pardon he promised. The governor's playing games with us. Besides, I suppose he's got us right where he wants us, now. We're not robbing banks anymore, or making the railroads look foolish, so the big wigs are happy with him, which means President Cleveland is happy. Everybody's happy.

"He also has two experienced and motivated thieves to do whatever dirty jobs he doesn't want to be personally connected with. We're under his thumb. He knows it and so do we."

"What else can you do?"

Leon shrugged. "I don't know. Just keep on trying, I guess. We do have friends with some clout, who are putting pressure on the powers that be, but in the meantime, every day is a risk. Every day without the pardon is one more day that could be our last. We could end up in prison for twenty years . . . or worse, if there is anything worse than twenty years in prison."

Cameron knitted his brow, then leaned across the table, as though getting in closer proximity of the younger man would give his words more impact.

"Listen to me, at least in prison, you still have life, and as long as you have life, there's hope. You just said yourself, there are people who care about you two and who know about the deal the governor made with you. We will not just sit back and forget about you, do you understand? If you find yourself with a choice to make, do not chose death over prison. Do you hear me?"

A chill went through Leon. He felt like a small child again, being reprimanded by his father for some misdeed or selfish word. But at the same time, his respect and affection for this man grew tenfold. He choked down his emotion and smiled, feeling embarrassed.

"Yeah, Cameron. I hear you. Thanks."

"Good. Now, would you like a shot of whiskey in your next cup of coffee?"

***

Caroline walked into the dusty barn, carrying the tray of food.

She could hear Sam in the feed room, stacking the sacks of grain he had brought back from town. She set the tray of food down on one of the hay bales, then promptly sat down beside it and waited for Sam to finish what he was doing.

The three dogs, instantly picking up the scent of food, were all attentive. The two smaller ones, Peanut and Pebbles even went so far as to jump up on the hay bale, beside their young mistress, and did their best to look cute.

Sam came out of the feed room, bare-chested and sweating from the exertion. He saw Caroline sitting there and his eyes widened

"Oh. Miss Caroline." He moved to where he had hung his shirt and pulled it on over his head.

Caroline smiled shyly. But she quite enjoyed the view and was sorry he had been so quick to cover it up.

"Mama thought you would be hungry by now, so she asked me to bring this out to you."

"Oh, yeah." Sam smiled nervously. "Your mama is a fine woman, and I sure am hungry. Thank you!" He picked up the tray and looked around for another bale to sit on. The dogs' attentions followed the food.

Sam spied another bale close at hand and promptly sat down and began to eat. He broke up the biscuit, sopped it in some of the gravy, and threw each dog a dripping piece relevant to their sizes.

"It's no wonder the dogs are so fond of you, if you keep tossing them table scraps," Caroline said. "You're going to make them fat. And Papa says you let them sleep in the bunkhouse with you, too. You're spoiling them."

Sam shrugged. "It's cold out at night and they don't have much fur on to stay warm, especially the little ones. And a few treats, here and there, won't hurt them. Besides, with all the running around they do here, there's not much chance of them getting fat."

"I suppose you're right. I certainly noticed the hard work is good for you," Caroline mumbled.

But Sam still heard what she said and smiled with pleasure. She sure was pretty. With those brown eyes and long blonde hair; she was a treat to the eyes.

He took another mouthful of food and started chewing, looking at his plate. He felt the need to say something to her, but did not know where to start. Finally, he just started.

"Are those two fellas going to be here much longer?"

Caroline frowned with disappointment. "No. I think they're going to be leaving in the morning."

"Oh." This got Sam's attention. "Do you think they'll be back again?"

Caroline brightened. "Oh, yes. Peter said he was going to introduce me to a detective he knows at the Wells Fargo Detective Agency. Their home office is in San Francisco, but they have a smaller office, in Denver."

Sam looked puzzled. "He knows a detective at Wells Fargo?"

"Yes. Isn't it wonderful?" Caroline was excited. "Then I'll be able to go inside the agency and see how it all works, maybe even get a job there or something. Wouldn't that be grand?"

Sam wasn't smiling. Things were not at all going according to plan.

"Maybe it's not my place to say, but I think you should be a little more careful around those two."

Now it was Caroline who wasn't smiling. "What do you mean?"

"I saw Mr. Black giving you a hug out there this afternoon, and I don't think that it was very appropriate, is all."

Caroline shot to her feet. "You're right about one thing. It's certainly not your place to say. We've known them for years and I would trust either one with my life." Then, in a huff, she stomped out of the barn and returned to the house.

The dogs felt uneasy with the changed atmosphere. When Caroline left, they were torn between going to support their mistress and staying where the food was. Peanut and Pebbles decided to keep their eyes on the gravy. Rufus, being older and wiser and not inclined to eat much anyway, got up and padded after his distressed human.

Sam's shoulders slumped, as he continued to eat his supper. He sure had messed that up.

***

Caroline stormed into the house just as Jean and Jack sat down to relax with some coffee. It was obvious that the evening's drama wasn't over yet.

"I hate men," Caroline fumed, as she headed for the staircase that would take her up to her room. "Men are so stupid, every single one of them. I'm never going to get married!"

The ranting continued as she stomped up the stairs, completely oblivious to the fact that Eli's nursery was right under the staircase, and her stomping echoed loudly in his room. Within seconds of Caroline entering the house, Eli screamed at the top of his lungs, and Penny burst out of the nursery, a picture of anger and frustration.

"Thanks a lot, Caroline," she yelled up the stairs. "I finally got him to sleep, and then you go and wake him up. The only stupid one here is you."

Cameron and Jean both sighed and pushed themselves away from the table.

"Here we go again," Cameron stated. "Girls. Settle down! What in the world got this started?"

But Penny was already up the stairs after her sister. Their loud quarreling reverberated throughout the house.

Rufus stopped at the front door, knowing, and perhaps grateful, that he wasn't allowed inside. He turned and headed toward his favorite spot on the porch to lie down and soak up the last of the evening sunshine.

Jean came to her feet. Turning her back on her cup of coffee, she hurried into the nursery to work her magic on the youngest member of the Marsham family.

"Oh, my goodness," Cameron mumbled as he stood up and headed for the stairs. "Welcome to family life, boys."

Leon and Jack sat at the table, nursing their coffees and listened to the sounds of battle emanating from the various levels of the ranch house.

"Leon."

"Hmm?"

"I'm beginnin' ta' think it's a good thing we're leavin' in the morning."

Leon smiled and nodded in agreement.

CHAPTER FOUR
COMPLACENCY

The next morning, Leon and Jack were still in the room they had been sharing for the last couple of nights. It was a large, airy room, with a double bed and windows that opened out onto the pasture where their horses had been turned out during the day. It was on the main floor, right next to the day nursery, but fortunately for the guests, Jean always took little Eli upstairs to their own room each night.

The fellas were busy packing their saddle bags in preparation for leaving, but Jack dragged his heels. Leon felt the need to nudge him a little or they would never get on the road.

"Come on, Kid. You knew we couldn't stay for long."

Jack frowned. He hated being called 'Kid' and knew that Leon only did it when he was setting the younger man up for a lecture.

"Yeah, I know, Old Man," he snapped back. "But it's gonna be real hard, havin' ta' eat your cookin' again after Jean's fine suppers." He emphasized his irritation by punching an innocent pair of socks into his saddlebags.

Leon smiled, taking the griping in stride. Silently, he agreed.

"What do ya' think?" Jack asked, intent on changing the subject. "Are we gonna get in touch with Frank and ask him about Caroline?"

"I suppose," Leon answered. "I tried to talk Caroline out if it again, but she's adamant that it's what she wants. Maybe the best thing to do is just to let her see, first-hand, what it's all about." He smiled wickedly. "If anyone can deter anyone from becoming a detective, Frank can."

Jack laughed, his mood lightening up. "Leon, has anyone ever told you that you have a devious mind?"

"Yes, Jack. I believe you have, on several occasions."

A quick survey of the room convinced them that they had everything, and they headed out to the porch. Once arriving there, however, it looked as though Jack might end up getting his wish.

Change of Leads: The Lost Shoe

Cameron and Sam stood at the foot of the steps in quiet conversation until Cameron noticed the fellas coming out.

He turned to Jack, apologetically. "I'm sorry," he said, "but when Sam went into the stable to saddle your horses, he noticed your gelding was lame. Maybe you should go in there and look at him."

"Oh." Worry flooded Jack's eyes. "Thanks, Cameron. I will."

***

Jack squatted down beside Midnight's off foreleg, feeling the swelling in the tendon.

"I'll say he's lame. A lot of heat in there." He straightened up with a sigh, and gave Midnight a pat on the neck. "It looks like Karma got a good kick in, after all."

"I could always loan you one of our riding horses," Cameron offered. "You expect to be back this way in a month or two, anyway. You could always pick him up then."

Jack appreciated the offer but didn't feel right about leaving his trusted mount behind. If he and Leon got into a pinch, he needed a horse under him that he knew and who knew him. His very life could depend upon it.

Leon remained quiet; his renewed guilt over his mare's behavior put a knot in his gut. He was antsy to get on the road, but he also understood his partner's reluctance to leave his horse behind.

"How long do you think it'll take to heal?" he asked Cameron.

"It's hard to say. It depends on how bad the bruising is. It could take a couple of weeks."

The partners groaned. Even Jack knew they couldn't hold off leaving for that long.

Sam saw his opportunity slipping away. He had to keep these men here.

"It shouldn't take that long, Mr. Marsham. If we keep him quiet in a stall, and if I can get some ice from the icebox to wrap around that leg, I'm sure I could have the swelling down in two or three days. You'd have to ride him easy, though, not put too much strain on it."

Jack looked at Leon, "What do ya' think?"

Leon hesitated. He knew he'd feel the same way if he was faced with leaving Karma behind, but his itchy feet were acting up and he wanted to be on the move again. He was just about to diplomatically suggest that Jack take Cameron up on the offer of a borrowed horse, when a voice from the barn door stopped him.

"Oh, please stay." It was Penny. "What harm could a couple of more days do?"

Jack and Leon exchanged another look. Now they were in a pickle.

Cameron smiled at them. "You know you're welcome to stay. And if you get really bored, I can always put you to work."

"All right," agreed Leon, conceding defeat. "I suppose a couple more days won't kill us." Then he gave Jack a serious look. "But then we go, whether Midnight is better or not. Agreed?"

"Agreed," Jack answered with a relieved smile. He gave Midnight another affectionate rub on the neck and looked at Sam. "You sure you can get that swelling down in a couple of days?"

"Yes, sir, Mr. White," Sam answered with a relieved grin of his own. "I'm positive."

***

As is often the case, the day turned out quite different from what the partners expected when they got up that morning.

Cameron and Penny went into town together in the single horse dogcart. Him to teach and her to learn—hopefully. Penny had put forth a brilliant argument that since their guests were going to be staying on a few more days, and who knew when they would all get together again, that it would make sense for her to stay home from school to help entertain.

It was a good effort, and her parents were impressed with the amount of thought that had gone into it. Nevertheless, a disappointed Penny still ended up accompanying her father to town.

Jean and Caroline got busy with the daily household chores, so Leon and Jack were left to keep themselves occupied throughout the day. This did not prove to be difficult.

Change of Leads: The Lost Shoe

Jack was concerned about Midnight's welfare, and when he spied Sam packing ice from behind the house to inside the barn, he hurried to join him.

Inside the stall, Jack held onto Midnight's head, petting him and scratching him behind the ears, which was a treat the big gelding particularly enjoyed.

Meanwhile, Sam did his best to wrap an ice-filled burlap sack around the swollen tendon.

Midnight was not happy with this treatment. He tossed his head and pulled away on more than one occasion.

"Whoa, easy, old friend," Jack soothed him and continued to stroke his neck. "I know it ain't too pleasant, but it'll feel better soon."

"You're real fond of this horse, aren't you?" asked Sam, from his position on the floor.

"You better believe it. This old boy and I have been through a lot together. Wouldn't trade him in for nothin'."

"It's good to have that," said Sam. "I noticed your partner is awful fond of that mare, too."

Jack rolled his eyes, as he often did, when Karma was mentioned. He glanced at the mare where she stood in her stall across the aisle.

Karma, who always seemed to know when she was being referred to and was in no doubt the comments made were all complimentary, pricked her ears and gave the two men her best countenance.

"I swear, I can't understand why," Jack admitted. "That mare can be a real headache sometimes, even when she ain't in season."

Sam smiled as he continued to massage the ice around Midnight's tendon.

"Yeah," he agreed. "Mares can be like that sometimes. Me, I like dogs. Always have. I miss havin' my own dog."

"Yeah? Did ya' have a dog as a kid?"

"Sure did. Best friend a boy could ever have."

Both men glanced out the open stall door at the three dogs stretched out in the aisle, overseeing the operation.

"Yeah, me, too," Jack mumbled, going back in time.

“Where did you grow up, Mr. White? Somewhere around here?”

“Oh, no,” Jack told him. “We both grew up in Kansas.”

“Really? What brought you out this way?”

“Oh, well, lots ‘a things.” Jack stroked Midnight’s forehead. There was something about standing in the stall, spending time with his horse, that made Jack relax. Perhaps a little too much. “We both lost our folks in the Border Wars, and then we just started driftin’, and takin’ odd jobs, until we found ourselves out here.”

“Oh,” said Sam. “That’s a shame. About your folks, I mean. I lost my pa when I was quite young, too. But I still have my ma, and we did all right.”

“Where do you call home, Sam?”

“Wyoming.”

A chill went through Jack, but he pushed it down and ignored it. He was sure it was just the mention of that territory that sent his nerves to tingling. Besides, many people were from Wyoming. He was sure it didn’t mean anything. Still, he thought it might be best to change the subject.

“So, I hear you have a girlfriend in town.”

Sam smiled. “Yeah. Maribelle. She’s real pretty. We’re going to have supper this evening.”

“Yeah? You sound like you’re kind’a serious about her.”

“I suppose I am. Why you askin’?”

‘Well,” Jack frowned. “It’s just that I noticed you spending a lot of time talkin’ ta’ Caroline. It seems ta’ me that if you’re courtin’ one gal, ya’ shouldn’t be thinkin’ ‘a courtin’ another one at the same time.”

Sam froze. Damn. Had he blown it? Having a girlfriend in town was a believable cover, and Maribelle was pleasant enough company, but nothing more. He hadn’t even thought that showing interest in Caroline might compromise his integrity in the eyes of these men. Did Kiefer suspect something? Being in the barn, tending to the horse had made him too relaxed, and he stopped thinking about what he was saying.

Now, it was time to start thinking again. Get back on track.

He smiled and shrugged his shoulders, thinking on his feet.

"It's not like Maribelle and me are betrothed or anything. You can't blame a fella for looking around before he makes his final choice, can you?"

"No, I don't suppose so," Jack had to admit.

Damn. He could remember being twenty-one and hopping from one bed to another, without any thought or concern about the feelings of his various bedmates. He had assumed they were all in it for the fun, too. So, no harm done. Now, a twinge of guilt pricked at him. Here he was, well into his thirty's, and he was still doing the same thing.

But now, suddenly, he looked at the equation from the other side of the bed. This time it was Caroline who stood the chance of getting her feelings hurt.

Jack had a hard time digesting this new revelation. He always felt the pull to protect a lady who needed a helping hand. It never occurred to him that he could be the one they needed protection from! He felt an unreasonable desire to grab Sam by the scruff of the neck and shake some decency into him. Then he mused, maybe it was himself he needed to slap some sense into, instead.

"I just don't want to see Caroline get hurt, is all."

Sam looked up at him, suddenly all serious. "No, Mr. White. Neither do I."

Leon showed up at the barn door and interrupted this uneasy conversation. "Hey, Matt, come outside. I want to talk to you for a minute."

"Okay, hang on."

"No, that's all right, Mr. White," Sam told him. "I think that's enough of a cold pack for now. I'll come back and do it again after lunch. In the meantime, I got chores ta' get to. And after that, Mr. Marsham wants me ta' take that stallion up to the south range ta' turn him out with the broodmares. So, you're good to go."

"Okay, Sam. Thanks for your help," Jack told him, as he removed Midnight's halter and joined his partner.

The sun felt warm after the coolness of the barn and Jack soaked it in. It was going to be a fine day.

"What's up?"

"Nothing, really," Leon answered casually. "I was just thinking that since Midnight is laid up and all, I might ride into Arvada on my own and send that telegram to Frank."

"Yeah, okay. You want me to borrow one of the horses here and come with ya'?"

"No, that's okay. To be quite honest, I'm feeling all pent up and restless. I need to get out and blow off some of the cobwebs. You know how I get when we're holed up in one place for too long and there's no poker."

Jack grinned. "Yeah, I know. You go ahead. I got enough to do here with Midnight, and I'll probably help Sam get caught up on his chores, since it's 'cause 'a my horse, he's gotten behind. Besides, I think Karma could do with a stretch of the legs, too. She was gettin' kind'a restless in there."

"Okay. See you in a couple of hours. Stay out of trouble."

"Yeah, yeah."

***

Leon left the main road into town and flew at a full gallop across open country. Karma felt her oats and wanted to run. As soon as Leon turned her head toward freedom, she let loose a squeal of pleasure and gave Leon a little buck, just for the fun of it, then lit out, full speed ahead, for parts wherever.

After three years of riding this mare, Leon still hadn't gotten over the thrill of her full-out gallop. He was relieved that Jack hadn't pressed coming with him, as he felt the need for some time alone. Sending a telegram to Frank was just a convenient excuse. Now, all the restlessness and worry that had been building up inside him, slipped away, and he laughed into the full force of the wind.

Karma picked up on his joy and, snorting, she flung her head in response, then executed a quick change of leads and picked it up another notch. She loved it when her human let her go like this, just the two of them, flying over the countryside together.

Not to misunderstand her, she had become quite fond of Midnight over the years. Many a time it was his steadying presence that helped to calm her nerves when unexpected things happened. And they did seem to happen a lot, in this transient life of hers.

But there were times when she found his patience and understanding toward her and to all things around him, downright boring. Both man and horse had need of a serious adrenaline rush.

Eventually, as Leon felt Karma start to show on her own accord, he settled back into the saddle and eased her down to an easy lope, then a trot, and finally, to a walk. Karma mouthed the bit a couple of times, then set out on a loose rein at a comfortable swinging gait and looked around to take in the scenery.

Leon had no idea where they were in relation to the ranch, but that didn't matter. He rapidly got his bearings, then casually made his way in the general direction of town, thinking that he should at least send the telegram, since that was his excuse for leaving the ranch in the first place.

Leon was still worried, though not with the pent-up, stressful worry that had been building in him all morning. He hoped that by getting out here, just him and Karma, he could clear his mind and settle some of the nagging questions that had been taking hold.

Watching Jack that first day with the Marshams, when he was holding their new son, had affected Leon more than he realized. It had awoken disturbing memories along with doubts that had settled on him soon after they had been offered the pardons. Until now, he had pushed those feelings back out of the way and hoped they would simply disappear. No such luck.

The question of what they would do with their lives, if and when the pardons came through, still lingered. On the rare occasion when the subject came up between them, Jack laughed about it and proceed to name a series of the most ridiculous and unlikely professions that two single men in their mid-thirties would ever consider doing.

But Leon knew, first and foremost, that Jack wanted a family. He wanted to put down roots, have a home and a life he could call his own. Coming to the Marsham's brought that yearning to the surface again. Over the last few days, Jack snatched moments, here and there, to help with the care of Eli, assisting whoever with the bathing and the dressing. Jack played with Eli when the baby was awake and rocked him to sleep when playtime was over. And he always looked happy doing it, so content, even, that it made Leon worry.

Leon didn't think he could settle into that kind of life. Not now. He'd tried it once, with a woman whom he thought he'd loved, but it had turned to disaster. His heart had been shattered, and he swore, he would never go down that road again.

Oh, it hadn't all been her fault. She'd wanted him to leave his outlaw life behind, settle down and have a family with her. But it didn't work out that way.

He was consumed by a restlessness he didn't understand. Oh, he grew tired of the fugitive life, for sure. Always sleeping with one eye open, never knowing when a peaceful morning was going to blow up in his face. But two or three days in one place, and he needed to get going again.

The only thing that seemed to calm him enough to stay put for a longer period was a good book or a good poker game. It was only then his mind was occupied enough for him to relax. Sometimes he felt it was his mind that was his biggest enemy. Sure, his ego loved it when he could out maneuver a posse or effortlessly rule over a poker game, just for the fun of it. His flashes of genius, that dazzled anyone around him into awed submission, were like candy to his psyche. It was an addiction he needed to keep feeding to feel alive, to feel he was actually worth something. Without his incredible mind, he was no different from any other worn-out ex-outlaw with nothing to show and nothing to offer.

But he couldn't turn the damn thing off. Constant impulses of information bombarding his senses, twisting and turning into schemes and plans, and what if's and why not's. He had learned how to settle his mind to some degree at night, so usually he could sleep, but even that wasn't a guarantee.

How did Jack do it? Even in the middle of the day, he could stretch out anywhere, pull his hat over his eyes, and be asleep in minutes. And there Leon would be, up and pacing. Pace, pace, pace. It drove Leon nuts. It seemed the only way he could relax at all was to keep moving or to keep his mind focused and calculating on something—anything—to distract him.

Change of Leads: The Lost Shoe

So far, Jack had been happy to follow along whenever Leon got restless and had to hit the trail again. But what if Jack married and settled down? Would that be the end of their partnership, their friendship?

Leon's throat tightened at the thought. Could he go on? Could he face a life without Jack by his side? He needed his partner's calming influence, his quiet, down-to-earth common sense, just as Karma had come to depend on Midnight's steadying support in times of stress.

The possibility of Jack moving into another life, a life Leon could not emulate, scared him more than death itself. So, he simply chose not to think about it. Until they were sitting around the lunch table with the Marshams, and Jack sat there, holding an infant in his arms, with a smile on his face that lit up the room.

Leon was stressing himself out. No questions answered, no doubts relieved. He pushed these thoughts out of his mind and decided to just enjoy his day out with his favorite girl. He pushed Karma into an easy lope as they headed toward town. Maybe he'd even be able to find a poker game.

***

Jack felt a sense of relief as he watched his partner ride off. He could feel Leon's stress building; something was bugging him, and Jack couldn't, for the life of him, figure out what it was. Maybe some time on his own and the distraction of a good poker game would help Leon sort out whatever had him worried. But Leon was so 'high energy'. It was no wonder the man was as skinny as he was; he burned calories in his sleep.

Still, Jack did feel bad about the forced delay. Not because he felt it was his fault, but that he was secretly glad for it. He was sorry his horse was in pain, of course, but not sorry for some more time with the Marshams.

He was surprised with how much he enjoyed being part of a functional family again. And, admittedly, the talk with Sam earlier, about where they had grown up, had stirred some deeply buried memories and longings, things that Jack usually didn't want to think about. Yet, now, and in this place, those thoughts bubbled to the surface and weren't going away any time soon.

Jack had to admit he was getting tired—tired of life on the run, of waiting for the governor to follow through on his agreement. Five years now and still no sign of those pardons coming their way. Just how long were they supposed to carry on like this? It wasn't so bad when they had money, could stay in a decent hotel and sleep in a bed—two beds, if possible.

But being out in the elements, sleeping on the ground in all kinds of weather. Geesh. They'd both gotten sick doing that. And as they got older, the more often it was going to happen, until maybe one of them wouldn't recover. Jack didn't like being sick, and, dagnammit, he did seem to have a predisposition toward phenomena that he was none too comfortable with. Winters on the run were getting harder to face with each passing year.

Jack sighed and ran his fingers through his curls. For the second time that morning, he found himself caught up in a train of thought that was getting him nowhere. He went back into the barn to see if Sam needed help with the chores.

***

The rest of the day went by quickly, but uneventfully. Jack iced Midnight's leg a couple more times throughout the afternoon and he was pleased with the progress. Another day of rest and ice should bring the tendon back down to normal, and they could be off and gone.

By late afternoon, Cameron and Penny had returned home from their day of education.

Sam completed the final chore of the day by cooling out and bedding down their harness horse, then scurried off toward town for his anticipated rendezvous.

Jack got himself cleaned up and settled in to join the family around the large table for supper.

Jean entered the room with a pot of stew and, right away, she noticed that one place was still empty.

"Where's Peter?"

"He went ta' town ta' send a telegram ta' that detective friend of ours," Jack answered, as he passed the fresh buns to the ladies.

Caroline smiled with anticipation of what the answer to that telegram might be.

"I know that," Jean said. "But that was this morning. He should have been back ages ago."

"Oh well, I wouldn't worry too much about him, ma'am . . . I mean, Jean. If he's found himself a good poker game, he may not be back 'till mornin'."

"Really?" she asked. "He doesn't stay up all night, does he?"

"Yup. He's been known ta' do so."

"Well, he'll definitely be hungry when he gets back, then. I'll save him some supper, or breakfast, as the case may be."

"Is he really that good at poker?" Cameron asked. "I hear it's a very difficult game to master."

"Yeah, it is a difficult game," Jack agreed. "And there are an awful lot 'a bad players around who refuse to acknowledge it. I'm not too bad a player, but Leon, now he's a natural. He has a way of readin' people, and of keepin' track of all the cards. Once the deck has been dealt out, he never forgets the order of 'em, and because 'a that, he knows what players should have what hands." Jack grinned in admiration of his partner's abilities. "It's a real amazin' thing ta' watch."

Jean smiled, remembering a similar conversation she'd had with Leon while they were on the front porch, watching Jack practice his fast draw.

"Isn't it a rather dangerous pastime, though," asked Cameron. "It doesn't happen here in Arvada, too often, but we do sometimes hear of these games getting a bit out of control."

"Yeah, it can. There are too many sore losers who would rather accuse the winnin' player of bein' a cheat than admit they were beat, fair and square. But Leon is too good a player. He don't have ta' cheat."

"How does that help him, if somebody accuses him of cheating?" Caroline asked, suddenly all concerned for the safety of her friend. "Couldn't he get into trouble?"

"Yeah. But usually I'm there ta' watch his back," Jack confessed. "I know I ain't there tonight, but like you just said, Cameron, there ain't too much trouble in Arvada."

"No, not usually. But I hardly think the small games we have here would interest your partner if he's that good a player."

"Leon uses poker to relax, just as much as he uses it for income."

"Income?" questioned Jean. "A risky way of earning your income, isn't it?"

Jack smiled. "Not for Leon. His skill at the poker table has put food in our bellies and a pillow under our heads more times 'n I care ta' keep tally of. He's that good."

Cameron and Jean exchanged glances. It still seemed risky to them.

"Do you think you could teach me to play poker?" Penny asked of Jack.

Jean snapped, "Don't even think it, young lady."

Jack mumbled, "I don't think that's a good idea."

"Over my dead body," was Cameron's take on the issue.

"Well, I just thought because I'm so good with numbers . . ." Penny mumbled.

Caroline snickered into her stew and received a scathing look from her younger sister.

***

After supper, Cameron and Jack sat on the porch, enjoying a cup of coffee, when Leon and Sam returned from their entertainment in town. They rode up to the barn and dismounted, each apparently pleased with the outcomes of their endeavors. Sam offered to take both horses in to feed and bed down, so Leon came over to join the two men on the porch.

"Sam's a pretty helpful young fella," Leon commented, as he pulled a chair over to sit beside Cameron. "He's a good hand with a horse, anyway."

"Yes, he is," Cameron said. "I think he'll make a fine foreman on a large spread someday, once he gets some more experience under his belt."

"So, how did it go?" Jack asked his partner. "Did you send the telegram?"

"Oh, yeah," Leon answered, all smiles and good humor. "Didn't receive an answer yet, but we can check again before we leave." He pulled off his hat and ran his hands through his long hair, pushing it back off his forehead.

A frown flashed across Cameron's face when, for the first time, he noticed the white scar just below Leon's hairline. It was a solid scar, made by a deep graze, and Cameron wondered why he had never noticed it before. Then he reasoned that it was well hidden underneath Leon's long hair and could only be seen when he pushed it back that way.

It's odd how you can know something, but not acknowledge it, until it slaps you in the face. Of course, he was aware that these two men were Napoleon Nash and Jack Kiefer, but he had never really considered the dangerous lives they must have led and were still leading. No wonder they were so cautious all the time and loath to stay in one spot for too long. Leon was lucky that bullet hadn't killed him.

Cameron was still processing this new realization when Jean joined them on the porch, carrying two cups of coffee.

"There you are," she said, when she spotted Leon. "I thought I heard your voice out here. I brought you a cup of coffee."

"Oh, thank you." Leon stood up to offer Jean his chair, which she gladly accepted. He dragged another one over and, once seated, took the proffered beverage and gave himself a moment to savor its aroma before indulging in a sip.

"There's some supper for you in the kitchen, if you would like something," Jean told him.

"Oh, yes." Leon smiled broadly. "I will, thank you. Just give me a minute to unwind."

"You're back early," commented Cameron. "Your partner here, gave us to believe you could be gone for the night."

Leon sent a smile over to Jack. "Did he?"

"Well, I know what you're like when ya' get into a poker game, Leon."

"Yeah, I suppose you're right."

"None to your liking this evening?" Jean asked him.

"Oh, on the contrary," Leon's eyes sparkled, still wound up with the thrill of the game. "I think I did quite well." He sent another huge smile to his partner. "I guess I would still be there, but the poker shuts down kind of early here, and then, what do you know? I ran into Sam as he was coming out of the telegraph office, so we decided to head on back here, together."

"That was fortuitous," commented Jean, though she fleetingly wondered who Sam would be sending a telegram to. He usually wrote letters to his mother.

The two girls, having finished with the cleaning up, came out to join the group on the porch. Leon and Jack surrendered their chairs to the ladies and found comfortable perches on the porch railings.

"All sounds quiet in there, Penny," Jean said. "Did you have more success with Eli, this evening?"

"Yes,' Penny beamed, and smiled at Jack. "I think I might be getting the hang of looking after babies."

Jack and Leon exchanged quick smiles. Even they knew it wasn't that easy.

"Did you get the telegram back from your friend?" Caroline asked Leon, all eager for some news.

"No, not yet," Leon answered, but seeing her disappointment, quickly continued. "But that's not too surprising. He's probably out on some assignment or something. He knows how to get in touch with us. Don't worry, Caroline. I'll set something up for you, if I can."

Caroline smiled her thanks.

***

At the barn door, Sam stood in the fading light, watching the group of people on the porch. He listened to the light banter and laughter coming from their direction and his jaw tightened in irritation.

He couldn't understand it. How could these people be on such friendly terms with the outlaws? Didn't they understand what those men were capable of, and the numerous crimes they'd already committed?

Riding back from town in the company of that slick con man, Sam had to muster all his self-control to not draw his gun on the man and arrest him, then and there. Nash had been so elated, so sickeningly pleased with himself, over card-sharping the hard-working citizens of the town out of their week's wages.

Change of Leads: The Lost Shoe

Sam had been infuriated, and it was all he could do to smile and laugh along with the outlaw, pretending to be happy for him. Sam was frustrated at having to hold off; to stand there and listen to young Caroline laugh and talk with him, as though he were entitled to her admiration.

But, if there was one thing his father had taught him, it was the importance of sticking to a plan. If you are a member of a group, and a junior member at that, you did what you were told, and you stuck to the plan.

So this is what Sam did to the best of his ability. He knew that Marshal Morrison was getting everything in order, that all the paperwork would be taken care of and out of the way, so nothing hindered bringing those two highwaymen to justice, once they were arrested.

The trap was being set, and Sam Jefferies was determined to be there and see it sprung.

***

The next morning, Jack arose bright and early. He was dressed and just strapping on his holster when Leon rolled over, stretched, and peeked at his partner through sleep-heavy eyes.

"Wha' ya' doin'?" he mumbled. "Is early."

"Yeah, I know," Jack replied. "Go back to sleep. I just wanna check on Midnight and see how the swellin' is. If'n he's lookin' good, maybe we can head out this morning."

"Hmm . . ." Leon pulled the blanket over his head and rolled over, fully intent on taking Jack's advice.

In the kitchen, Jean was already up and putting the coffee on.

"You're up early," she commented when Jack appeared. "Breakfast will be a while, but the coffee's almost ready."

Jack smiled. "Sounds fine, Jean. I won't be long. I just wanna check on Midnight."

He stepped out into the crisp, sunny morning and made his way over to the outhouse first, and then into the barn. Upon opening the door, he was met with numerous nickerings and stamping of feet. Every horse's head in the place turned toward him in anticipation. He must be early, he mused, if he was getting out here even before Sam came to do the morning feeding.

Not wanting to keep everyone waiting, Jack climbed up into the loft and dumped a fair share of hay into each stall. Everyone seemed content with this, and the barn was soon filled with the sounds of happy munching and contented snorting.

Jack set the pitch fork back in its place, jumped down into the aisle and entered Midnight's stall to see how things were going. He gave the big, dark gelding a rub and scratch on the neck. "How ya' doin' this mornin', old friend?"

Midnight snorted an acknowledgement but continued to munch.

Jack knelt by the injured leg and ran his hands down the tendon. He sighed in disappointment. The injury was much improved, but there was still some heat and swelling in there. He knew they wouldn't be going anywhere that day. Again.

"How's he doing?"

Jack just about jumped out of his skin.

Then Midnight jumped in reaction to his human jumping. The gelding snorted out an indignant blast, gave the intruder a dirty look, and settled back to his hay again.

Jack straightened up and turned on his partner. "Geesh, Leon. You should know better than to sneak up on me like that."

"Oh, sorry," Leon responded with a smile that suggested he wasn't sorry at all.

***

Leon'd had every intention of going back to sleep, but sounds of the household stirring and the aroma of coffee brewing had succeeded in dragging him the rest of the way awake.

His activities of the day before, though exhilarating at the time, had left him burned out and exhausted. Morning came much too early for his liking. He sat on the edge of the bed, wearing only long-johns and undershirt, then he yawned and stretched again as he rubbed the sleepiness out of his eyes.

For decency's sake, he pulled on his trousers, then his socks and boots, and left the room. As he headed for the front door, he had said good morning to Jean.

She smiled at him over her first cup of coffee, thinking that he looked like something the cat had dragged in—if cats were allowed in the house. She would take some coffee out to them in the barn, if they didn't come back soon.

Like his partner before him, Leon headed to the outhouse first, then made his way to the barn. The coolness in the spring air helped to wake him up, and he regretted leaving his shirt behind. He allowed a minor shiver to run its course and consoled himself that they wouldn't be outside for long.

"Is he fit to ride, today?"

"Naw," Jack said, as he pulled out his revolver and checked the chamber. "It's gettin' better, but it's still swollen."

Leon frowned. "I really don't think there's any call to shoot him."

"Ha, ha, Uncle. I thought I might get in a little target practice before breakfast, is all."

"Oh." Leon's face dropped. "Can't that wait until after breakfast, Jack? I don't think my head could stand it before nourishment."

Jack slipped his colt .45 back into its holster and sent his partner a reprimanding look. "Well, whose fault is that? Just how much did you drink yesterday?"

"I know, I know," Leon grumbled, still looking bleary-eyed. "It's nothing that ten or twelve cups of coffee won't cure."

"Come on. Let's get some food inta' ya'," Jack suggested, walked past Leon, heading for the barn door.

Leon smiled through his sleepiness. He hurried to catch up and put a hand on his partner's shoulder as they stepped out into the sunlight.

"Geesh, Jack, you're usually the one who's gotta eat first."

"Uh huh."

And then the rifle shot broke through the early morning quiet.

CHAPTER FIVE
THE TRAP

Rawlins, Wyoming, 1885

Rick Layton took pride in the fact that he was the best shot with a rifle in all the county. Whenever there was a shooting contest, he won. Whenever there was a rogue cougar taking out too many calves or foals, the ranchers hired him to track it down and take care of it. Whenever Deputy Marshal Tom Morrison had need of some trustworthy and capable men for a special job, Rick was always first on his list. Therefore, it came as no surprise to Layton, when Morrison got in touch and told him to be ready to move out at a moment's notice. Something good was in the air, and Rick, with his trusty and well-oiled '73 Winchester 44-40, was definitely going to be needed.

Two weeks previously, Morrison had received a telegram from his informant. It stated that two men, by the names of Peter Black and Mathew White, would be dropping by the Rocking M Ranch sometime in the near future, and that was all Morrison needed to know to start getting preparations under way. He began by contacting the three men who had the talents and the tenacity to understand the plan, and to carry it out to its conclusion.

Along with Layton, there was Alex Strode, who, though not as handy with a rifle as Rick, was as good a tracker, and Morrison wanted him along, just in case the quarry escaped the trap.

The third member of the party was one of Morrison's regular deputies, Mike Shoemacher, who had no special abilities other than he was big and could look menacing without even breaking a sweat. He also had a brain under his hat, and was not an easy man to con, which was a strong asset, considering who they were going after.

Once Morrison had his three men organized and standing by, he went to the county seat and paid a visit to the honorable Judge Henry Jackson to arrange for warrants and extradition. These papers gave the marshal the lawful right to enter another state or territory, arrest the outlaws, and return with them to Wyoming.

There, they would finally be brought to account and face trial for their numerous crimes.

Marshal Morrison left no stone unturned. Knowing that timing was everything, he didn't wait for the news telling him that the outlaws had arrived. He gathered his carefully chosen posse together, boarded the specially ordered train, and began chugging and clanking their way to Denver, as fast as the engine could haul them.

His local deputy would be on the lookout for another telegram from Arvada, Colorado, and when it arrived, to send it on to the telegraph office in Denver. Morrison would be waiting there to receive it.

Once that telegram arrived, things got serious. Everything hinged on Sam keeping the two outlaws from leaving the ranch without them getting suspicious that something was in the works. If that part of the plan had been up to Morrison, he wouldn't have used him. Sam was a good lad, but he was young and inexperienced, and could easily give the game away without even knowing he had done it.

But Sam's father had been a much-liked and respected lawman, and the people funding this little operation wanted to give Deputy Sam Jefferies a chance to prove he was the man his father had been. Morrison just wished they would do that on a plan that wasn't quite as volatile or potentially profitable as this one was.

Nash and Kiefer were anything but stupid. The slightest hint of a setup, they would be gone, and so would any chance of ever laying out a trap like this again. This plan had been over a year in the making, but it was a one-time, good deal. No second chances. It had to work.

***

From Denver, the posse took a stagecoach to the small town of Salt River, which was ten miles outside of Arvada. Morrison didn't want to announce their arrival to anyone in Arvada, in case someone in town got word to the Marshams, inadvertently or not, and that included the local law enforcement. Morrison didn't know the sheriff of that town and didn't want to take the chance that the man might be an idiot. The less anybody knew about their plans, the better.

That evening, Morrison sent one more telegram to Sam, letting him know, in as few words as possible, in case the telegrapher liked to gossip, that everything was ready. Then, all Morrison could do was hope that Sam knew his job and not lose his nerve this close to the end.

Horses and a few last-minute supplies were purchased, and the small posse, minus Mike Shoemacher, who had his own special orders, made their way toward the Marsham ranch.

They made good time at first, but as the light started to fade, they slowed the pace to not cause injury to themselves or the horses. They all rode in silence; everyone's nerves were just a little on edge. It was close to midnight by the time they approached the ranch, and five miles out, they stopped to wait out the night.

They picketed the horses, but left them saddled and ready to go, just in case. The men wrapped themselves in blankets to keep warm in the chilly spring night air, and they settled in to wait for the first hint of dawn to make an appearance.

Nobody slept.

If it wasn't for the anxiety involved, the anticipation of dawn's arrival would have reminded the men of long-ago Christmas mornings, when the first light of day would bring happy surprises. But there was no telling what this first light was going to bring, other than relief that when it finally did arrive the men could get moving again.

By the time the sun peeked over the horizon, the posse members were in their positions around the Marshams' ranch house, waiting for anything to start happening.

Alex settled into a spot by the barn, furthest from the house, but with a clear view of the yard and the front porch.

Rick and Morrison hunkered down behind the woodshed and water well, which gave them a side view of the porch, but a clear view of the barn, closest to the house. All the strategic points were covered.

Just as the sun was clearing the horizon and warming itself up for another pleasant spring day, the front door of the house opened. A man with curly, dark blond hair, came onto the porch and down the steps. He headed for the outhouse.

"That's Kiefer," Morrison whispered.

"I know," Rick murmured.

"Just let him carry on. We have to wait until they're both in the open."

"I know."

Jack came into view again and made his way into the first barn.

The men waited.

About ten minutes later, the front door opened once more, and a dark-haired, disheveled man, staggered his way down the steps. He, too, headed for the outhouse.

"There. That's Nash."

"I know."

"Damn," Morrison said. "Why couldn't they come out together? The longer this takes, the more complicated it could become."

They sat quietly, watching while Leon make his way from the outhouse to the barn. They waited, hearts thumping and nerves jingling.

"Damn." Morrison chewed his lip. "Come on. If anyone else comes out of the house now, this whole thing could be a wash. If either of those girls are anywhere near your line of fire, you cannot shoot."

"I know," Rick snarled. *'Dammit, why can't Morrison shut up and let me focus? I know what I have to do.'*

Then, what seemed like an eternity later, Nash and Kiefer came out of the barn and headed back toward the house.

Kiefer came out first, but Nash was close behind. He hurried to catch up, placing a hand on his partner's shoulder. They were talking, smiling in good humor, and completely unsuspecting of anything amiss.

Rick took a deep breath and lined the target up in his sights.

"Do you have him?" Morrison whispered.

"I have him."

"Take your shot."

Rick moistened his lips, held his breath, and then slowly squeezed the trigger.

Leon felt the shock of the impact go through his partner's body as the bullet slammed into Jack's right shoulder.

Jack grunted softly, fell over into Leon's arms and then started to go down.

Leon grabbed him and went to the ground with him, trying, unsuccessfully, to cushion his fall.

Pandemonium broke out.

Leon couldn't decide if time sped up or slowed down. He was hardly aware of the sudden eruption of activity around him: of people shouting and running, the dogs barking from some distant, far-away location. A baby screamed. But Leon and Jack were in a bubble all by themselves, where time had no meaning and the world stood still.

Jack gasped, fighting to breathe.

Blood was everywhere. It spread across the front of his shirt like river water overflowing its banks, turning the blue material into a sopping, sickening mess. It seeped out from where Jack was lying, escaping from the exit wound in his back. It pooled upon the dry, dusty ground and soaked into the knees of Leon's trousers.

Jack's right arm lay helpless by his side, but his left hand clutched at Leon's shirt, hanging on for dear life.

Leon was terrified. In his mind's eye, he was sure he had never seen so much blood. *'Oh, dear God. Please stop the bleeding!'* He leaned over his friend, his hands grasping the saturated material of Jack's shirt, causing blood to seep through and paint his fingers, while he desperately hung on to his partner. If he could just hold on tightly enough, then maybe Jack wouldn't leave him.

"Un . . . uncle . . ." It was hardly more than a gasping whisper.

"Yeah, Jack." It was all Leon could do to push the words out. There was no breath in his lungs.

"I'm sorry . . ."

Leon knitted his brow. "What have you got to be sorry about?"

"Should . . . have been . . . more careful."

"Aww, Jack, no. This wasn't your fault. We both got careless."

"Napoleon . . ."

"Yeah, Jack."

"Gonna . . . pass out . . . now."

"Yeah, Jack. Okay."

Jack's eyes rolled back, and his body relaxed. His left hand released its desperate hold on Leon's shirt and dropped down onto his chest.

With that intimate contact broken, the bubble surrounding them burst open. Leon's senses were instantly assaulted by the noise and confusion of the activity around them, and he became aware of the lawmen surrounding him.

Then Penny, skirting through the circle of guns and oblivious to her own safety, knelt by Jack's head, clutching at his shoulders. Jean came right behind her. She knelt across from Leon and, with desperate hands, began stuffing padding and cloth into the wound to slow the bleeding.

Penny sobbed, rocking herself and pleading with all her soul, "Please, don't die. Please, don't die."

Then, the inevitable. A hand grabbed the back of Leon's undershirt and an authoritarian voice cut through to his senses.

"Napoleon Nash, you're under arrest. Get your hands up where I can see them. Now!"

Leon was in shock. The words meant nothing to him. He looked to Jean with eyes asking for help. She smiled at him and touched his hand. That small contact enabled his mind to focus, and to tell his fingers to release their grip on Jack's shirt. He automatically went to wipe them on his own shirt, to clean off the blood, but quickly thought better of it, when the cold steel of Morrison's revolver pressed harder against the back of his skull. He left his hands bloody and raised them for the marshal to see.

"Good," Morrison congratulated him. "Now, put them behind your head and stand up."

Leon did so, keenly aware of the two rifles aimed directly at him, at such an angle to hit him, if fired, but conveniently miss the marshal. He felt rough hands manhandling him, starting at his boots and working their way up. First one lock pick was discovered in his right boot, another in his left boot, and then a third, neatly tucked away in the waistband of his trousers.

Morrison laughed. "My, my, Mr. Nash. You're a walking mercantile store, aren't you? Do you have one hidden behind your ears, or how about up your shirt sleeve?"

Leon felt no need to comment. He stood quietly, despondent, looking at the two men with their rifles aimed at him. He noticed Caroline standing back from the main group, being comforted by Sam. He could hear the dogs, quieter now, but still letting out the occasional woof from inside the bunkhouse. Birds chirped, and flies—or was it a bee—buzzed around them. He felt the marshal grab one of his wrists and then the other. They were pulled down behind his back, and the handcuffs snapped on. He was numb. He didn't care.

Penny's terrified voice cut through his haze.

"He's not going to die, is he, Mama? Please, don't let him die."

"Well, now, Penny, we are going to do everything we possibly can to make sure that doesn't happen, okay?"

Jean's words and tone were quiet and comforting to keep her daughter calm, but when she looked up at Leon, the worry and fear in her eyes reflected what was in his own. They both knew that saving Jack's life was anything but a certainty.

Cameron came out of the house and hurried to them, carrying a blanket. He put a hand on his wife's shoulder and knelt beside her.

"I've laid blankets and some pillows on the large table. If we can get him onto this blanket, then maybe we can carry him inside and settled there without causing him too much distress."

Jean nodded, then she and Penny spread out the blanket.

Cameron stood up and sent a glare to the marshal. His nerves were on edge, not only because of his friend, lying in the dirt, but because of the obvious risk that this posse had placed upon his family. He shuddered to think about one of his daughters getting caught up in the gunfire.

"Why are your men just standing around? Why hasn't someone gone into town for the doctor?"

"Calm down, Mr. Marsham," Morrison suggested. "That's been taken care of. I left one of my men in Arvada, so he could get the doctor out here, first thing. I want the Kansas Kid incapacitated, not dead. They both have too much to answer for."

"This man could bleed to death by the time the doctor gets out here," Cameron shot back at him. "There was no need to shoot him in the first place. You had them cornered. You could have easily just walked in and arrested them without all this bloodshed."

Morrison bristled at the assault. "On the contrary, Mr. Marsham, The Kansas Kid is too damn good with that handgun. I had no intention of giving him the opportunity to use it. He's a killer, and he's dangerous. The sooner you and your family realize this, the better off you'll be."

Cameron fumed, and though he was normally a calm and sensible man, the marshal had seriously rubbed him the wrong way. He was preparing to counter Morrison's accusations, when his wife drew his attention back to the immediate problem.

"Cameron, help us."

Jean and Penny were attempting to roll Jack onto his side, so they could slide the blanket under him, but they were having a hard time doing it.

Cameron turned away from the confrontation and knelt to help.

Ten minutes later, with Cameron, Rick, Alex, and Sam each grabbing a corner of the blanket, they had Jack inside the ranch house and settled onto the layers of blankets on the table.

Morrison gave Leon a slight shove to follow, and the girls brought up the rear. Once inside, the marshal indicated one of the chairs that had been pulled away from the table, for Leon to sit in.

Jean immediately took charge.

"Caroline, you know where I keep the laudanum for your papa's headaches?"

"Yes, Mama."

"Please, go and get it. And bring some more padding and towels from the storage. Penny, go see to your brother."

"But, Mama—"

"Don't argue with me, young lady. Just do it."

With a quick, heart-wrenching look at Jack, Penny did what she was told. However, no one specified exactly where she was to see to her brother. Within minutes, she was back in the living area with Eli in her arms and doing her best imitation of a mouse in the corner.

Caroline returned with the required supplies and helped her mother remove the sopping, red paddings, and replace them with clean ones. It was hard to tell if it was doing any good. The bleeding had been staunched to some degree, but the necessary jostling that had taken place, to get Jack into the house, had set things to flowing again. It wasn't long before the new dressings were just as bloody as the previous ones.

Leon felt sick. How long was it going to take for that doctor to get there?

Alex was in the process of unbuckling Jack's gun belt and pulling it out from under him, when the wounded man groaned and was suddenly awake.

Jack looked around and could only see strangers standing over him, and panic slowly started to rise.

"Leon?"

"Yeah, Jack. I'm here," Leon answered, scrambling to his feet to go to his partner's side.

Morrison was having none of that and sent him back to his chair with a quick gesture and a hard look.

Leon sat back down with a scowl on his face, feeling that a battle was imminent.

Cameron moved forward and put a hand on Jack's leg. "It's all right. We're here."

Jean was beside Jack, speaking softly to him, hoping to keep him calm and maybe get some laudanum into him. It wasn't a strong painkiller, but at this point, anything might help.

Jack would have none of it. Nothing was familiar to him, and that pain in his shoulder was driving him mad. Panic swelled, enveloped him, and then exploded. He started to fight.

"Leon!"

"No, Jack, don't. I'm here!"

Change of Leads: The Lost Shoe

Leon was on his feet again, ignoring Morrison this time. But the marshal grabbed him and pulled him back.

"No." Leon was furious. "Let me go to him. I can calm him down. Uncuff me."

'You can stay right where I put you," Morrison snarled back

"I'm not going to go anywhere," Leon pleaded in desperation.

Finally, after what seemed an eternity, Morrison reconsidered. He dug out the keys to the handcuffs and unlocked one bracelet, leaving the other in place.

As soon as Leon felt himself free, he was at Jack's side. He shoved one of the deputies out of his way and while grabbing his friend by his good shoulder, placed his other hand across the bloodied chest. Leon shook him, trying to break through the panic, trying to get his attention.

"Jack, Jack. It's me, Leon. I'm here."

The change was miraculous. As soon as Jack heard his partner's voice and could see his face, he calmed down.

"Leon?"

"Yeah, Jack." Leon went weak with relief. "It's me. I'm here. You can relax, okay?"

"No," came the whispered, but urgent demand. "Run, Leon. Run."

Leon gave a rueful smile, as he glanced around at the stern faces and bristling guns surrounding them.

"No, Jack. It's too late for that. We're done."

Jack groaned in disappointment and closed his eyes as he laid his head back down on the damp blanket.

Leon sighed and ran his hand through Jack's hair, stroking him, coaxing him to relax and stay calm. He was only dimly aware of the stickiness of the blood in those blond curls.

"Peter?" It was Jean.

Leon looked at her.

"Peter, see if you can get him to take some of this. It's just a mild painkiller and sedative, but it might help."

Leon nodded and took the small bottle from her. He put his hand behind Jack's head and lifted him up.

Jack opened his eyes.

"Here, Jack. Try to swallow some of this."

"What's it?"

"Just something to help with the pain. It's okay."

He pressed the bottle to Jack's lips, and he took a sip. He snorted and made a face.

"I know," Leon said. "It's probably bitter."

"Yeah."

"It'll help, though. Okay? Take some more."

Leon got a few more sips into Jack before the injured man made it clear that he'd had enough. Leon laid him back down again, and with a small smile of thanks, returned the bottle to Jean.

Leon felt wrung out.

Jack was so weak, and that panic attack had sucked away even more of what little strength he had left. The top blanket was damp with blood, and even though Jean repeatedly changed the dressings on the wounds, the white cloths continued to turn red as the blood seeped out.

Leon used a clean patch of his shirt sleeve to wipe his face and was surprised to find tears on his cheeks. He closed his eyes with a sigh, and again wondered how much longer that doctor was going to be. Just how long could they hold on?

He looked at Jack and was surprised to find those brilliant blue eyes staring at him, clear and bright, and as focused as they'd been the night before.

"Uncle Leon, do you really think we should be doin' this?" Jack asked him, in a clear and strong voice. "You know my pa will tan both our hides, if'n he finds out."

Leon was taken aback. His mouth opened, but it took a couple of beats before he could stammer the words out. "Yeah, Jackie. Don't worry about it. Everything's all right."

Jack nodded and smiled a smile of trusting innocence. He closed his eyes and laid his head back down. A sigh escaped him.

The room was heavy with silence. Even Eli had stopped crying and laid nestled in his sister's arms. He knew the world was on hold.

Leon felt hot tears burning behind his eyes. *'I'm losing him. I'm losing him, and there's nothing I can do about it.'*

The sound of horses galloping into the yard broke everyone out of their trance.

The doctor had arrived.

CHAPTER SIX
THE DOCTOR

On this chilly, but promising, spring morning, Doctor David Gibson had been enjoying his first cup of coffee, and had gone into his office to review his list of patients for the day. He hadn't been at it for long when his wife, Tricia, entered his office and announced that they had a visitor. David entered the living room and found himself in the presence of a mountain of a man, wearing a deputy's badge.

"Ah," David commented, trying to get over the illogical feeling of intimidation that was simply based upon the man's shirt size. "What can I do for you, Mr. . . .?"

"Shoemacher, Mike Shoemacher."

"Well, ah, nice to meet you, Mr. Shoemacher. What seems to be the problem, today?"

"Shooting. Out at the Marshams' place."

"What?" David wasn't often caught off guard. "My goodness. How long ago?"

"I don't really know for sure."

"You don't know?" David rushed around, gathering together all the items he would need on such a call. "Do you have any idea how serious it is?"

"If he's still alive, I guess it's serious enough," commented the deputy. "You don't need to worry too much about it. It's just an outlaw our marshal cornered out there at the ranch. It's not like it's one of your townsfolk. If things went as planned, that gunny should still be alive, but ya' never know. Sometimes they do stupid things when they're cornered and get hit worse than he should'a. If that's happened, he could already 'a bled to death by now. Still, it's not too likely; it's not often the marshal's plans go awry. Best if you come out, anyway, just in case."

David was slack jawed for a moment. He couldn't believe the callousness of this man. Surely even an outlaw deserved more regard than what was being displayed here. The deputy spoke about the cold-blooded, calculated shooting of a man as casually as a hunter discussing the tactical killing of a buck.

Change of Leads: The Lost Shoe

The doctor gathered everything he needed, grabbed his standby carpet bag containing bandaging and wound dressings, and then hurried into the kitchen, where he gave his wife a quick kiss on the cheek.

"I'm sorry, Tricia. No time for breakfast, I'm afraid."

"Yes, I know. I heard." She was accustomed to him running off to some emergency or another, and often, in the middle of the night. This was nothing new for a doctor's wife. "I'll expect to see you when I see you."

David flashed her an appreciative smile then dashed out the door and down to the livery for his horse. He considered taking the buggy instead of riding but decided that a horse under saddle could move a lot faster than one hitched to a cart.

Rudy, his trusty gelding, was also accustomed to the unscheduled, mad dashes out to wherever. The little chestnut stood quietly, but at attention, while David attached the various pieces of luggage to the rigging.

Leading the animal out of the livery, David mounted and settled into the saddle amongst all the other accessories tied to it.

Shoemacher calmly sat his horse while the doctor got prepared. He found the whole procedure humorous and, in his mind, totally unnecessary.

Then, they were on their way, heading out of town at a gallop toward the Rocking M Ranch.

***

David entered the ranch house, carrying some of his supplies, with Shoemacher following him, lugging the rest. The doctor sent a quick look around the room and his gaze took in and processed everything in an instant.

The Marsham family, he already knew, so it came as no surprise that Jean was tending to the patient. Cameron assisted where he could. The two girls stayed out of the way, tending to their brother, and Sam stood against the wall, looking ashen-faced. The other men were strangers to him.

"I take it you're the doctor?" Marshal Morrison asked him.

"Yes. What have we got here?"

"Rifle wound in the shoulder," Morrison informed him. "Bullet went in the front and out the back. He's lost a lot of blood.

If you can save him, I would appreciate it. The law wants him dead or alive, and if he survives this, he'll be facing most of his life in prison. He might just prefer it if ya' left him alone. But I want him alive, and I expect you to keep him that way."

The doctor was tired of this callous attitude being shown by the lawmen, and he sent a scalding glance back at the marshal.

"If you'd wanted the man alive, Marshal, then why shoot him in the first place?"

"That's my business," Morrison responded. "All you have to do is get on with yours."

David felt his hackles rise but choosing not to waste any more time on a pointless argument, he hurried to the man lying on the table. He took off his jacket as he went, and had his sleeves rolled up in preparation before he arrived at the patient's side. He placed his bag on the table, next to the patient's legs and indicated, with a look to Shoemacher, where he wanted the rest of his supplies set down.

"Hi David," Cameron greeted him. "It's sure good to see you."

Jean smiled a greeting then got out of his way.

David nodded to them and began examining his patient. Within moments, he took in all the information the man's physical condition could tell him.

"How long ago did this happen?" he asked.

"A little over an hour, now," Cameron informed him.

Leon couldn't believe it. An hour? Is that all? It seemed like an eternity since he had gone out to the barn to talk with his partner.

David nodded. "Was he lucid? Did he know what was going on?"

There was a beat of silence. No one really knew how to answer that one.

Again, it was Cameron who spoke up. "Yes and no. He panicked at first but calmed down when he saw his partner. Then he sort of . . . well, he . . ."

"He went back to when we were kids," Leon finished.

"Ah," David acknowledged. "He regressed."

"What's that?" Leon asked.

"What you said. He went back to childhood memories."

"Oh. Is that normal?"

"It happens sometimes," David answered, not wanting to mention that it usually did not bode well.

David then took a moment to assess the man who stood across the table from him. One look in those dark-brown eyes told him all he needed to know. The worry and the strain were evident, and the amount of smeared blood on his person, from the tips of his dark hair all the way down to his boots, indicated that he had been in close and constant contact with the stricken man. This was a friend or family member who needed to be treated with as much sensitivity and care as the patient, himself.

"What's your name?" David asked him.

"What . . . oh, ahh, Peter . . . no . . . Napoleon Nash. Ah . . . Leon"

David cocked a brow. He hadn't expected to hear a name he would recognize. He'd heard faint rumors that the Marshams were on friendly terms with the outlaws, Nash and Kiefer, but in the three years he had known the family, there had never been any hint of it.

If these men were Napoleon Nash and the Kansas Kid, that would explain why there were so many guns present, and why the lawmen were being so cautious. But for now, all David cared about was treating an injured man and acknowledging the concerns of his friend. Who these two men were and what they had done, were not relevant to him.

"My name is Dr. David Gibson," he introduced himself to Leon, "and I'm going to do everything I possibly can to save your friend."

Leon gave him a weak smile. "Thanks, Doc."

"I'm going to need you to help me with some things, though. Are you up to that?"

"Of course."

"What are you two talking about?" Morrison demanded. "Speak up, so's we can all hear what you're saying."

David sent the marshal another nasty look and then brought his attention back to his patient.

Leon took an instant liking to this young doctor. Leon didn't trust easily, but David Gibson felt like kin from the instant he'd walked through the door. It was obvious this man was highly intelligent, and Leon could relate to that. But also, the doctor did not suffer fools or bullies lightly, and Leon suspected he may have found himself another ally.

With David's assessment of the patient completed, he got to work, explaining things as he went. He took a pair of heavy scissors from his satchel and began cutting away Jack's shirt and undergarment.

"Okay. We need to get these clothes off him, so, Leon, if you could pull the cloth away, as I'm cutting. Yes, that's good. Jean, get in there with the padding and stop that bleeding if you can. Okay, lay him back down. We need to pull this sleeve off, away from the wound here. Good. Jean, some more padding, please. Good. Don't throw that shirt away; we need to hang on to it until I'm sure none of the material has stayed inside the wound. Cameron, could you pull that carpet bag over here and get me some more padding? Caroline?"

Caroline jumped, startled out of her fear trance.

"Could you heat up some water, please? But not too hot. Just so we can wash some of this blood away."

"Yes, all right," Caroline answered and hurried into the kitchen.

David sent a glance to Penny. She sat in an armchair, rocking herself and cradling Eli in her arms. She hummed softly. In her numb mind, she did it to keep her baby brother quiet and still, but she was really doing it for herself. David decided to leave her be.

The doctor took a small glass bottle out of his satchel and popped the cork.

"Okay, Jean. I need you to let me get at the wound."

Jean removed the padding from Jack's shoulder, and blood instantly started to seep out. David poured some of the clear fluid into the wound, and immediately it began to froth and fizz until it absorbed into the flesh.

"Is that Carbolic Acid?" Leon asked.

"Yes. It'll clean and disinfect the wound. It's a good thing he's unconscious, otherwise, it would hurt like mad. Jean, if you could clean up that blood again. Thank you. I need to examine the wound, to make sure there is nothing foreign in there. You'll have to keep it clean, so I can see what I'm doing. It won't be easy, but do the best you can."

"Yes, all right."

David brought out some small forceps and with gentle hands, spread open the lips of the wound.

Jean did her best to wipe away the blood as it emerged, without hindering David in his examination.

David inserted the forceps into the wound and then focused intently on feeling for any change in the resistance, or any sound of metal on metal. Anything to suggest an object inside.

Leon couldn't help but be fascinated, as he watched the man working.

He was an artist, no doubt about it. His long, slender fingers gently probing, examining, searching for anything that wasn't what it should be. And all the while, as his fingers were busy, his eyes glanced here and looked there, making sure the physical symptoms did not change, that the patient's coloring hadn't paled further, or the rhythmic breathing hadn't slowed any more.

Leon felt like an ignorant fool beside this man, and for once in his life, he was thankful for it. Here was someone who could help.

"Okay." David took a deep breath and straightened up. "There's nothing in there. It's clean."

Caroline showed up a little sooner than expected, with a basin full of water.

"Mama had heated some water for breakfast, so it was already there," she explained. "I just had to find a basin to put it in."

"Good," David answered her. "Well done. If you could put it on that chair, beside Leon."

Caroline looked at Leon and did as she was instructed.

"Thank you, Caroline." Leon smiled at her.

She gave a weak smile back, then put a hand on his shoulder and stayed close.

"Okay, Leon," David continued. "Here's a cloth. If you could wash him down, get rid of as much of this old blood as you can. And then," he reached into the carpet bag and pulled out a towel, "you can dry him off with this."

Leon accepted his new duty, and soaking the cloth in the warm water, he began to gently wash his friend, removing the drying blood from his torso, and then his face and his hair. Then he moved down his left arm and continued to the hand. He did his best to remove the blood from under and around Jack's fingernails.

Caroline followed him with the towel, drying Jack off as they went.

Never once did it occur to Leon that he could have benefited from just such a sponge bath himself. All he could see was the blood on Jack.

Meanwhile, David pulled more supplies from his satchel. He sprinkled some white powder into the shoulder wound, watched it being absorbed, and then sprinkled some more.

"What's that?" asked Jean.

"It's morphine powder," David explained. "It's a powerful painkiller. It can also be taken orally, so I'll be leaving quite a bit of this with you."

Next, David opened a small case and took from it a curved needle and some suturing thread and began to stitch the lips of the bullet wound together.

Jean continued to sop up the blood as it appeared, but the more David closed and stitched the wound, the less blood there was, until finally it stopped flowing altogether.

Both David and Jean took a deep breath and relaxed for a moment. David checked on Leon's and Caroline's progress, and seeing that they were about done, prepared for the next step.

"All right, Leon. We need to get your friend onto his side, so I can examine the exit wound. I don't want him lying fully on his chest, so you'll have to support him. Here's a clean pad to put against the shoulder wound and keep pressure on it, but don't support him there, just keep a light pressure. Use your own body if you must but block him from rolling onto his chest. Okay?"

"Yeah, okay, Doc. Here, Caroline, come over to my other side. Use your body to support his hips, all right?"

"Yes, okay."

This was the second time David had noticed the familiarity between Napoleon Nash and the eldest Marsham girl. In fact, the whole Marsham family appeared to be on intimate terms with these outlaws. This would certainly give some credit to the rumors he'd heard. It was obviously no coincidence that these men had ended up here, at the Rocking M, and if there was opportunity, he was curious enough to want to ask about how a family so respected in the community could have become acquainted with outlaws. In the meantime, back to business.

"Okay, Cameron. Help me roll him onto his side. Easy."

They got Jack rolled over quickly, and gently. Leon and Caroline got up and sat on the table, to support the wounded man and prevent him from rolling over too far. Then David and Jean began the procedure all over again.

David's jaw tightened, and he subtly shook his head when he got a good look at the damage the bullet had done when it exited his patient's body. He relaxed his features and reminded himself not to do that. It tended to give the wrong impression and elevate the worry and stress level in the patient's family members and friends, who might be present.

Again, David poured on the carbolic acid. Jean kept the area as clean as she could while David put his magic fingers back to work, determining the internal damage done to the shoulder.

"Yeah," he said to himself. Then he explained. "The bullet went through the shoulder blade and shattered it. There's going to be a lot of bone splinters in there. I'm not going to be able to remove them under these conditions, and he's probably too weak to survive such a lengthy procedure, anyway. We can deal with that later, preferably in a hospital when he's stronger. In the meantime, the arm and shoulder are going to have to be completely immobilized. There's no telling how much damage has been done to the nerves and muscles. He'll probably never have full use of this arm again."

Leon groaned. Jack wasn't going to like the sound of that.

David got his forceps again and began searching inside the wound. Within seconds, he smiled and pulled out a piece of material.

"Here, Cameron. I think this is part of the undershirt. Can you check it with the hole in the garment, and see it if matches?"

"Sure." Cameron took the saturated piece of material and went over to where they had laid out Jack's shirts.

In the meantime, David went back to probing for the second piece of material from Jack's outer shirt. He was optimistic that he would find it, but then he froze, and a look of concern flashed across his face.

"What?" Leon asked him.

"He's stopped breathing."

"What?" Leon's energy shot up. "Do something. Get him back!"

The dynamics in the room changed in a flash. Penny, leaving her brother to sleep in the armchair, ran over to stand by her sister while Jean and Cameron came back to the table.

The lawmen, who had all been insisting on indifference, now tensed and went on alert, unable to avoid getting caught up in the stress of the situation.

Leon came off the table and shook Jack, frantic to get some sign of life.

"Quickly," David commanded. "Get him onto his back. Cameron, Napoleon, pull him up to the end of the table until his head just tips back over the edge. Do it now. Quickly."

It was David's turn to get up on the table. He checked Jack's positioning, making sure that his head was tilted back just enough for his mouth to open, so the air passage to his lungs was unhindered. He took the chance of causing more damage to the shoulder by lifting both of Jack's arms over his head. He saw the sutures he had just put in place, start to tear. That was second priority now. He had to get this man breathing again.

David put his hands together, palms down, one on top of the other. He placed them in the middle of Jack's chest, just below the breastbone and then pressed down. He released and pressed down again. He performed this action repeatedly, putting his whole body into it and breaking out into a sweat with the exertion and the stress. He stopped, put an ear to Jack's chest and then to his mouth, listening, praying there would be some stirring of life.

Nothing.

Back to the chest compressions.

Leon was beside himself. His hands came up, clutching at his hair as the forgotten handcuffs dangled from his left wrist. He felt his chest and throat tighten up again, and tears burned behind his eyes to spill out and roll down his face. He thought he was going to explode.

"Come on," he heard his own voice yelling from off in the distance. "You're a doctor. You're supposed to save people. Save him. Get him back."

"I'm trying," David hollered, unable to believe he was losing this man. He couldn't lose him, not now. They were so close. *'Come on—breathe.'* Another quick check, listening, praying for any response.

Nothing.

Back to compressions.

Cameron moved to stand by Leon and put a supporting hand on his friend's arm.

Leon struggled to breathe; he gasped, perspiration mingling with the tears and blood on his face.

"Oh God, Cameron. No," he whispered. "What'll I do without him? Come on, Jack. Come on. Breathe. You can't give up, now. Come on."

Finally, Jack gave a barely audible sigh and took a breath.

The doctor pounced on it. An ear and a hand went to Jack's chest. Yes. Something was happening. Back to compressions, desperate to keep it going, like stoking a barely flickering flame on a windy, wet night.

Jean stood with her children and hugged them close in moral support.

Everyone in the room, except Jack, was now holding their breath, waiting with strained anticipation, grabbing on to that little bit of hope.

David continued to work.

Pump, pump, pump.

Stop, ear to the chest.

Yes. It was getting stronger.

Pump, pump, pump. Stop, ear to the chest. Pump, pump, pump.

David sat back on his heels, waiting, watching, and seeing if Jack could continue breathing on his own. Then, yes. There it was. The slow, gentle rise and fall of his chest. Jack was breathing again.

There was a collective sigh of relief. Everyone felt weak in the knees.

"Okay," David said, as he climbed down from the table. "That's obviously it for today. He needs time to rest and get some strength back. Marshal, if one of your men could find that bullet and see if the remaining fabric came out with it that would save me from having to go into that wound again."

"Yeah, sure," Morrison agreed. "Sam, go see if you can find it. It's probably embedded in the side of that barn."

"Okay, Marshal," Sam mumbled. He locked gazes with Cameron then snapped his eyes away as he headed out the front door.

Cameron wasn't sure what had happened there. His mind was so exhausted from the events of the morning, it couldn't grasp the significance of the exchange between Sam and Morrison. But the alarm bells were sounding, and the seed of suspicion was planted.

Morrison continued. "We'll have to borrow your buckboard, Marsham, so we can get Kiefer into town."

Everyone looked at Morrison in disbelief.

"This man isn't going anywhere, Marshal," said David. "Didn't you hear me? He needs rest. The only moving he's going to be doing is from this table to a bed, and that's it."

"It's too risky to leave him here. He's dangerous."

"He's hardly dangerous now, Marshal," David shot back. "He's not even conscious. You can leave a man here to guard him, if you feel it's necessary. But if you try to move him in a buckboard now, you will kill him. That is not an educated guess. It's a guarantee."

"Fine," Morrison snarked. "But he will be under guard, and I want to see the room where he'll be kept. I want to be sure we can make it secure."

"I'll show you, Marshal," Cameron offered. He gave Leon a reassuring pat on the shoulder and took Morrison into the room under the staircase where Leon and Jack had been sleeping during their stay at the ranch.

CHAPTER SEVEN
FORK IN THE ROAD

Leon felt all done in. He had to get outside for some air or he was going to faint. He placed a hand on Jack's shoulder to reassure himself that his skin was warm and that there truly was life in his friend's body. Leon smiled, then met David's glance. A silent *'thank you'* and *'you're welcome'* passed between them.

Leon, forgetting that he was in custody and was supposed to stay put, headed for the front porch to give himself a chance to recuperate.

David turned back to his patient. With Jean helping, he pulled Jack down from the end of the table, and they focused on getting him cleaned up and the shoulder immobilized.

***

Leon stood alone on the porch. He tried to take all this in, but he was numb. He didn't know what he was supposed to feel, what he was expected to feel. But tears still pooled in his eyes and occasionally rolled down his cheeks. He didn't seem to be able to stop them, and yet, he didn't feel like he was crying.

'I must be crying, so why can't I feel it?'

From the corner of his eye, Leon saw a blurry image of Jean as she stepped through the front door. She had noticed Leon leave the group and stagger out to the porch. Calling Caroline over to help David, Jean wiped her hands on a towel and followed her friend outside.

Leon turned away from her, feeling embarrassed.

She smiled at his discomfort and put a gentle hand on his arm.

He still wouldn't look at her. "I'm sorry," he finally said.

"Don't be silly. We all know how important Mathew is to you, how close the two of you are."

Leon nodded, his throat tightening even more. Of course, now he felt like he was crying. Couldn't come on him when he was alone—no. Had to be when Jean was present. His embarrassment grew, but he decided to ignore it.

"He's the only family I have still with me," he whispered through a strangled throat.

Jean squeezed his arm. "No, Peter, that's not entirely true. You know Cameron and I both think of you and Mathew as family. The girls love you like brothers. Well, at least Caroline does. Penny seems to have other designs. We'll always be here to support you, no matter what happens. You know that."

Leon smiled about Penny, then turned somber again. He raised his eyes and looked at Jean, straight on—tears be damned.

"We always seem to bring trouble to you and your family, Jean. Why would you be willing to put up with that?"

"Isn't that what families are for?"

Leon smiled again. "What? Bringing trouble, or putting up with things?"

"Both."

They laughed a little. But then Leon turned away and gazed off into the distance, worry returning to his brow.

Jean's heart went out to him. She felt she had to give him something to hold onto, so she decided to divulge a piece of knowledge that she had originally planned on keeping to herself.

"Well, I have it on good authority that Mathew can't die right now, so you don't need to worry about him so much."

Leon turned a skeptical eye her way. "Really."

"Yes. Penny made me promise not to tell Mathew, but she never said anything about not telling you, so here it is. About three years ago, shortly after we moved to Denver, Penny came to me and told me that she'd had a premonition."

"A premonition?"

"Yes. She said that she was certain we would be seeing you boys again because she and Mathew were bound together in this life; that the two of them had something important to accomplish."

"Hmm. Does she know what that something is?"

"No. It wasn't that specific. But she has herself convinced that it's of a romantic nature. I have a feeling it's something more than that."

"And does she get these often?" Leon asked, his skepticism beginning to shift to interest.

"No, not often. But when she does, they usually come to fruition. I can't explain it. Neither can she. She just knows. So, you see, Mathew can't die, not right now, because then he wouldn't be here to help Penny accomplish their goal—whatever that's going to be."

Leon sighed, as he reflected. His mother had often spoken of premonitions and being able to converse with the spirit world. He believed in them as a young boy, but as he grew older and more cynical, he wrote them off as simple fairy tales. Now, here was this woman, whom he loved and respected as much as he had his own mother, telling him the same thing. He still wasn't convinced that he believed in premonitions, but the possibility of it did give him some hope.

"Where the hell is Nash?" Morrison's booming voice broke the trance, and the softness of hope burst under the pressure of reality.

A quieter response came from one of the deputies. "He's on the porch with Mrs. Marsham. We're keeping an eye on him."

Leon took a deep breath as he straightened up and composed himself. He swiped both sleeves over his eyes and face and hoped that it would clean away any sign of tears. Jean was one thing, but Leon promised himself something, right then and there: The law was never again going to see him cry.

The front door slammed open. Morrison pounced on his prisoner, pushing him against the wall of the house and cuffing his hands behind him.

"Marshal, please…" Jean began, angry at the unnecessary show of force.

But Morrison simply glared at her, then dragged Leon along the porch and down the steps to get him away from moral support.

Alex and Rick followed the marshal to keep a closer eye on their prisoner, leaving Mike inside to guard the prisoner. Hardly a taxing job, just then.

Cameron knew the patient was in safe hands so long as the doctor and the two girls were present, so he decided to join the group outside. His regard for Morrison dwindled as the morning progressed and the rough handling Leon was receiving from the lawman convinced Cameron he had made the right choice.

Then Sam came running over from the barn, excited by his obvious success.

"I found the bullet, Marshal," he announced. "See? Here it is. And here's the piece of shirt with it. The doc ought'a be happy about that."

"Good work, son," Morrison said as he took the bullet from him and shoved it into his pocket. "And Sam, I meant to tell you, you've done a fine job here for us. Your pa would be real proud of you."

Sam's excitement disappeared. He looked uncomfortable as he avoided meeting the gaze of either Mr. Marsham or Leon. "Yeah, thank you, Marshal," he mumbled.

Leon and Cameron exchanged looks. Suddenly, it all made sense. All the little nuances which, on their own, didn't amount to anything, but put them together and there was a trap being laid. Sam showing up just when the Marshams needed a hand. Sam bonding with the dogs so they would listen to him and become used to being in the bunkhouse at night and out of the way. His steady girlfriend in town, even though he had been showing interest in Caroline. And then Jack's horse coming up lame, on the very morning the fellas had planned on leaving.

Leon's jaw and fists tightened, and the glare he sent Sam would have set the lad's knees to shaking, if he had seen it.

But a small gasp coming from the porch caused all heads to turn. There stood Caroline, staring at Sam, her hand to her mouth. She was stricken to the heart.

Sam started toward her, to say anything; to apologize, but Caroline ran back into the house.

Jean threw a shocked look at Sam, as she followed her daughter inside.

"Sam," Morrison got his attention. "Do you know which horse is his?" he asked, gesturing toward Leon.

"Yes, Marshal."

"Good. Go get it saddled up, will you? It's time we got this business over with. You two," he added, looking at Alex and Rick, "keep an eye on Nash, and don't let him out of your sight this time.

Apparently, I need to remind you that the main reason this pair hasn't yet been brought to trial is because every lawman and bounty hunter in the whole damn country underestimates this man. Don't make the same mistake again." He glared at Leon and then stomped into the house to get events going in the right direction.

Cameron moved over to Leon, very much aware of, and annoyed by, the scrutiny of the deputies. "I'm sorry about this, Peter. Obviously, Sam has been in on it all along."

"Yeah. I hope Caroline is going to be all right."

"It's been one hell of a morning."

"Hmm."

***

Inside the barn, Sam got Karma saddled and ready, but his thoughts were miles away. This wasn't anything like what he thought it would be. He had been so looking forward to the moment when the trap would be sprung, when Napoleon Nash and the Kansas Kid would finally be in custody. But it didn't go the way he imagined.

When he thought of outlaws, he always pictured them as ignorant, puffed up, brutal people, who didn't deserve respect or consideration. But these men were nothing like that.

Indeed, as Sam thought back to the time he had spent with Jack Kiefer, it occurred to him that under different circumstances, he might have come to like the man.

Nash, however, was another matter. Nash frightened him. Even now, when the outlaw was at a disadvantage and scared to the bone over the fate of his friend, Sam found him intimidating. It's odd; he thought Kiefer would be the intimidating one.

He cringed, as he remembered his arrogance of the previous evening, thinking that he would be able to arrest Napoleon Nash, all on his own. Thank goodness, he hadn't tried it. Nash would have taken him apart, and the whole operation blown.

They had all made that mistake, for even Morrison had cautioned them that during the set up and arrest, Kiefer would be the one to watch and to not let his quiet manner and amiability fool them. It was Jack 'Kansas Kid' Kiefer, who was the dangerous one; he was the killer. But once they were in custody, it turned out that

Nash was the one who would need watching, and not just because of his silver tongue.

"Capturing Napoleon Nash was like trying to grab a river trout with your bare hands," Morrison had cautioned them. *"If you were lucky, and everything went according to plan, you just might be able to snag him. But it was another matter to hold onto him."*

And Sam believed it. There was something in the man's eyes. He might be an outlaw, but he demanded respect.

He finished getting Karma ready then led her out of the barn.

Midnight watched them go and sent a little nicker after her. He wondered where she was going, and if he would be joining her. It would be good to get out on some grass, again.

Once outside, Karma spotted her human across the yard, and with head down and ears up, she walked toward him, leading Sam along with her. She hoped that maybe they could get out for another gallop like they had yesterday. That was fun.

She got up to him, nudged him and nibbled on his shirt. Leon smiled at her and spoke a quiet greeting but didn't touch her. Karma felt a little put out. *'What, no scratch on the neck? No head hug?'* She rubbed her head against his chest and gave him a stronger nudge, but still nothing. She began to sense something was wrong. He smelled funny. He wasn't responding to her the way he normally did.

Karma nibbled at the sleeve of his undershirt, then followed his arm around, behind him, and found the metal bracelet encircling his wrist. This was something she knew about.

Leon smiled as he felt her lips investigating the handcuffs, and then her warm breath and soft tongue moistened his hands. He knew there was nothing she could do to free him this time, but she sure was trying.

Her teeth nibbled at the metal links attaching the cuffs, but try as she might, she couldn't get a good hold on them. Every time she bit down on them, they slipped out of her grasp, and her teeth snapped together with a loud 'click'.

Sam watched the front door of the ranch house, thinking about Caroline, until the mare's behavior jolted him back to reality. Feeling he had not been paying attention to his duties, which included watching the mare, he made the big mistake of overreacting.

"Hey. Cut that out," he yelled at her and gave her a sharp jerk on the mouth with the reins.

Karma's face tightened with pain. She threw her head up and reared backward, pulling Sam with her for a few yards, before she broke free of him. Then, blowing in agitation, with her head and tail up, she danced sideways and galloped to the far end of the yard, before turning to see what was going to happen next.

Leon's nerves were on edge. He had already been thinking thoughts along criminal lines, where that little upstart of a lawman wannabe was concerned. Seeing the same man abuse Karma like that, was all it took to push him right over the edge.

With a snarl of pent-up anger and frustration, Leon ducked his head and charged, his right shoulder catching an unprepared Sam square in the midriff. Leon heard and felt the air explode from Sam's lungs, and then they were sprawled in the dirt, scrambling for the upper hand.

Within seconds, Alex and Rick, whose egos were still bruised from the chewing out they'd received, charged in and joined the battle. Sam was unceremoniously dragged out from under Leon and pushed to the side. The deputies then turned on their prisoner and began to kick and punch him into submission.

There's no telling how long the beating would have gone on, if Cameron hadn't been there. A gentle man pushed to his limit, Cameron's adrenaline surged, and he was in the middle of the fray before too many blows found their mark.

With the physique of a tall man who had done hard physical labor all his life, Cameron grabbed one deputy and then the other, easily sending them both sprawling toward the porch. Hitting the steps stopped their momentum and, coughing from the dust and indignation, they leapt up, ready to charge in for round two.

Leon, cat-like, rolled away and scrambled to his feet. With blood running from his nose and a split lip, he yelled his challenge and began his second charge.

Then Cameron was there. He took up a central position, with arms spread and palms out, keeping the three combatants apart through the sheer force of his presence.

He hollered, "Peter—stop." His palm turned into an accusing finger pointed at Leon, bringing him to an instant, raging halt. "You remember what we discussed about choices. You remember."

Breath ragged with anger, and adrenaline still pumped, Leon fought against Cameron's force of will. It seemed an eternity, but it was only a heartbeat, before Leon broke eye contact. He submitted to the older man at a time when he would never have submitted to any other.

Tensions relaxed as everyone backed off.

Sam still sat in the dust, hugging his torso and trying to pull air into his lungs.

Morrison was back on the porch, practically purple with anger.

"What the devil is going on out here? Do I have to be everywhere at once? Bloody hell. Can't you men even handle one prisoner in handcuffs?"

The two deputies, looking put out at being reprimanded again, glared daggers at Nash, who was beginning to calm down and get himself under control.

"Just a little misunderstanding, Marshal," Cameron answered him. "Things are under control now."

"Misunderstanding? Looks like the bloody Indian Wars, all over again. Sam, go catch that damn mare."

Leon jumped to it. "No. Cameron, please. Please. Don't let them take her. I gave her to you. Remember? Don't let them take her off this ranch."

"You got no say in this," Morrison yelled at the prisoner, as he came down the steps toward the group of men. "As soon as you were arrested, everything you owned became the property of the Wyoming courts."

"We're not in the Territory of Wyoming, Marshal," Cameron countered, "and, though I expect you have the proper paperwork to escort prisoners across the territorial line—"

"I do."

"—it still does not give you the right to seize property wherever you chose. You are in Colorado now, and that mare belongs to the Rocking M."

Alex was disappointed. As soon as he spotted the mare coming out of the barn, he had designs of bidding on her at the next sheriffs' auction. Now, it appeared, that wasn't going to happen.

"Fine," Morrison fumed. "Sam, go saddle up Kiefer's horse. Nash can ride in on that one."

Sam hesitated, still rubbing his chest. "Ahh, Marshal . . ."

Morrison turned on him. "What?"

"Kiefer's horse is lame. He can't go anywhere."

Morrison went into a slow burn. He glared at Cameron, as though all this was his fault.

"What is it with you people?" the marshal asked him. "This man," he pointed an accusing finger in Leon's direction, "is one of the most wanted outlaws in the Wyoming Territory. He's a cardsharp, a conman, and a thief. He has cost the banks and railroads thousands of dollars, and you're treating him like he's one of the family."

"Everyone makes mistakes, Marshal," Cameron reasoned. "Doesn't mean he can't turn things around, if he's given the chance."

Morrison scowled. "Don't give me that pardon nonsense. That's a rumor, at best. It was never offered and will never happen. That man is going to prison, and if Kiefer survives, he'll be joining him there." He turned to his deputies. "Alex, you stay here and watch Kiefer, and Nash will ride your horse into town."

Alex slumped. "Yessir, Marshal."

"I know we're all tired," Morrison told him. "As soon as Rick gets some sleep, I'll send him out to relieve you."

Alex nodded and headed up the steps and into the house.

"All right," Morrison continued. "Let's get this show on the road."

***

Caroline ran into the house, holding back tears until she could get somewhere private. She had been busy helping Dr. Gibson bandage Jack's shoulder, when Penny had decided Eli was drowsy enough to go back to his room for a nap, and then joined them at the table. It was obvious to David that Penny wanted to help but didn't know what to do. He smiled at her and got her to hold the dressing in place while he and Caroline wrapped the bandages.

At this point, Cameron and Morrison exited the bedroom and came over to the table.

"How much longer are you going to be with him, Doc?" Morrison asked.

His dislike for the man was so intense, David barely glanced at Morrison as he answered. "Not much longer. But I want to make sure he's as comfortable as possible, and that Jean has all the supplies she'll need until I get back out here."

"Fine, but hurry it up, will you?"

"It would help if your man could find that bullet."

Morrison snorted. He scanned the room, and then froze.

"Where the hell is Nash?" he bellowed and headed for the front door under a full head of steam.

"He's out on the porch with Mrs. Marsham," Rick answered, as Morrison charged past him. "We're keeping an eye on him."

David breathed a sigh of relief as the area emptied of everyone but his two young assistants and Mike Shoemacher. The deputy, at least, was sitting out of the way and staying quiet. David smiled reassuringly at Penny, again sensing that she was having a hard time dealing with all that was happening.

"You and your sister care a lot about this man, don't you?" he asked her.

She looked up at him through frightened eyes staring out of an ashen face. "Yes," she mouthed the word, but hardly any sound came out.

"Have you known him a long time?" David kept her talking, getting her mind focused and working again. Sixteen was awfully young to be dealing with something like this.

"Yes," Penny answered, her voice coming easier this time. "About four years. They came to stay at our ranch for a while. He's a good man."

"So, can I count on you and your sister then, to look after him while he's here?"

"Oh, yes," Penny was adamant. "I'll look after him."

"*We'll* look after him," Caroline piped in, not wanting to be outdone.

David smiled. "Good. Then I can rest assured that I'm leaving him in capable hands."

Both girls smiled.

"Caroline," David continued. "Could you step outside and see if anyone has found that bullet yet? I would feel a lot better about patching him up if I could be sure I haven't left anything behind in there."

Caroline smiled and nodded. She stepped onto the porch, just in time to hear the marshal complementing Sam on his "good" work.

David glanced up, surprised at Caroline's almost-instant return, but when he saw the look on her face, he realized that the errand was completely forgotten. Looking about frantically, and not even acknowledging David or her sister, Caroline ducked into the spare room where Leon and Jack had been staying.

Two beats later, Jean came in and not seeing her eldest daughter anywhere, sent a questioning look to the doctor.

David nodded to the bedroom door, thinking to himself that this ranch house was busier than the Denver train station on the 4th of July. He shook his head in mild bewilderment and put his attention back on his patient and his young assistant.

***

Jean moved to the threshold of the bedroom and stood for a moment as she watched her eldest daughter. This was certainly one of those hard lessons life tended to throw at the young and inexperienced. Everything hurts so much when you're young. Things like deception and betrayal are new emotions, with no coping built up yet to deal with it all.

Jean came in and sat down beside her daughter. She put her arm around Caroline, who, in turn, hugged her mother and cried into her shoulder.

"Oh, Mama. How could Sam do that? I thought he was our friend."

"I know, sweetheart, but he obviously thought he was doing the right thing."

"But he lied to us, pretended to be someone he wasn't, just to get us to trust him while he laid in wait."

"Well, that's what someone working undercover for the law does. Didn't you say that was acceptable, as long as it was for the greater good?"

"But, that's just to trap bad people. Not us. We're not bad people."

"But who's to judge that, Caroline? Who's to decide, who is good, and who is bad? To our way of seeing it, we're not bad people, and neither are Peter and Mathew. But to the law, they are Nash and Kiefer, and they are criminals. Using us to get to them was acceptable."

Caroline sniffed and wiped her eyes.

"I guess that's what Peter tried to tell me, and I couldn't see it," Caroline admitted. "I don't think I could ever do what Sam did."

Jean gave her shoulder a squeeze. "Try not to be too hard on him. We don't know what his reasons were, and I think he may already be feeling some regrets."

"A lot of good that does now," Caroline answered, bitterly.

"I know," Jean agreed, with a sigh. "I'd best get out there to help with Mathew. Penny looks a bit overwhelmed. You stay in here for a few minutes, if you like. Come out when you feel better."

"Yes, Mama."

***

Caroline sat on the bed, getting her thoughts sorted out. So much for being a detective. She was never going to treat honest, hard-working folks like this. Sam should be ashamed of himself.

From the other room, she could hear Marshal Morrison and Dr. Gibson discussing the bullet. Then Morrison and Mike hashed over their next move and how to make it. Listening to all this, she realized she didn't want to go into the common area while that marshal was there. She really didn't like him.

Taking a deep breath, Caroline wiped away the last of her tears and looked around the room. There was Leon's hat, setting on the dresser. She knew how attached he was to that black piece of felt, with the topaz Conchos. He would also probably be needing it.

Jack's hat was on the chair, but he wasn't going anywhere. There were their saddlebags, and a shirt she recognized as belonging to Leon, draped over the back of the other chair. All their meager belongings, looking sad and lonely, spewed out, just as they had been left earlier that morning.

Caroline's heart skipped a beat as she spotted Leon's holster and gun hanging off the same chair as his shirt. She had a wild, fleeting thought of grabbing his gun and forcing Marshal Morrison to release her friends. But then she realized, with a sinking heart, just how foolish that would be. Even if she knew how to use a pistol, she could never get the drop on all of them at once, and it would only create more problems.

Standing up, she went to the chair and affectionately ran her hands along the material of Leon's shirt. Looking around to make sure she was alone, Caroline picked the faded shirt up and hugged it to her chest, burying her face into its soft folds. Breathing deeply of his scent, she felt the tears start to come again.

Then she felt something that wasn't quite right. There was an object, slender and hard, neatly sown inside the collar. She looked around for something sharp and found a pocket knife on the dresser, along with some coins and a few other knickknacks. Using the point of the knife, she broke through the threads and pushed the object out, into her hand. It was a set of lock picks, bound together with a small piece of wire.

Once more, Caroline made sure no one was watching her, when she heard more commotion outside, including her father yelling at someone. That was unusual. She could count on the fingers of one hand how many times she had heard her father raise his voice, and it always portended trouble for someone.

Morrison started to curse, which dropped him even lower in her esteem and she heard him storm back out onto the porch again. Then the yelling began in earnest. She decided she had best wait until things quieted down.

Exhaling, she draped the shirt over the chair and grabbed Leon's hat, where she stealthily hid the picks, and after what felt like an eternity, made her way back out to the porch.

She saw her father walking away from them to catch the mare that was keeping her distance.

Sam moved Alex's gelding over to the porch, so Leon could move onto the higher step, reach up, and slip his foot into the stirrup. Then, with a couple of hands helping to steady him, he swung his other leg over the cantle and got mounted. And there he sat, looking a little dejected, while he waited for the lawmen to get organized.

"Peter," Caroline called quietly to him, and casually walked down the steps to stand beside the horse.

Leon looked down at her.

"I found your hat in the room, and I thought you might be needing it."

Leon smiled. "Oh, yes, Caroline. Thank you." He leaned over to her, so she could put it on his head.

While he was down there, almost face to face, she showed him the lock picks and then slipped them inside his boot.

Leon bit his lip. He wasn't sure if this was a good idea or not. Then they both jumped when Morrison came out of nowhere.

"Here, here, young lady," the marshal took hold of Caroline's arm and pulled her back up onto the steps. "Best stay away from him. Even handcuffed, he can be dangerous, and I wouldn't want to see anything happen to you."

Leon and Caroline exchanged small, knowing smiles. As if Leon would ever do anything to hurt her.

Then the lawmen, including Sam, all mounted up.

Leon mouthed a silent *'goodbye'* to his young friend. He sent a disparaging look toward the house, wishing for one last look at his partner, but knowing it was not to be.

Then they rode away.

Sam held back a moment, hoping to say something to Caroline, but she avoided his gaze, turned, and went back into the house.

Sam hung his head and kicked his horse after the departing posse.

Leon heard Karma whinny for him and her cries broke his heart. But he did not look back. Everything and everyone who mattered to him, were there, at the Rocking M Ranch, and he was being forced to leave them behind.

Would he ever see his beloved mare again?"

Would he ever see his partner again?

The first answer that came to his mind, scared him more than prison itself.

CHAPTER EIGHT
IT BEGINS

The ride to Arvada was one big blur to Leon. He had so many other things on his mind, he was hardly aware of Morrison leading the procession. The halter rope attached to Leon's horse was firmly wrapped around the marshal's saddle horn, and Leon felt just as docile and omnipotent as the animal he was riding.

Mike rode at Leon's right, with the rifle casually cradled in his left arm, but ominously aimed at the outlaw, nice and handy, just in case. Sam rode along on Leon's left, trying to remain inconspicuous.

Leon hardly noticed.

What he was aware of was the set of lock picks inside his left boot. What he was thinking about was what exactly he intended to do about it. He could leave them there until he was safe within the confines of a cell. Once the handcuffs were removed and everyone had settled for the night, he could retrieve the picks and make his escape. He had done that very thing so many times in the past, it was like clockwork. Still, he hesitated this time, being faced with a new situation. If he escaped from the jail cell, what would he do then?

Previously, Jack had been with him, waiting for Leon to save the day, or hiding out in some pre-determined place, anticipating his arrival. But this time, Jack was seriously wounded and unable to go anywhere.

Sure, Leon could easily escape, but where would he go? He would have to leave his friend behind. Leon wouldn't be able to lay in wait and retrieve him later because the law would be waiting for just that kind of action. And what about their pardon? Leon could escape, lay in wait, and maybe, with luck, grab Jack later. But what of all those years of being at the governor's beck and call? Both of them, risking their necks, doing the jobs that no one else would or could do, all in hopes of being granted their pardons. Had it all been for naught? Was it just a pipe dream?

The best Leon could do, if he made a run for it, would be to head to Mexico and hope that Jack survived his wounds and get his pardon on his own. That would be a long-shot, since Leon making a run for it would probably cancel out any chance Jack might have to get that pardon. Leon's own freedom could end up costing Jack twenty years. Damn. Damned if you do, and damned if you don't.

He decided to fall back onto plan B: When in doubt, wait and see what happens.

Leon felt eyes upon him and he glanced over to meet Sam's inquisitive gaze.

The young man ducked his head and turned away, afraid to meet that dark, accusing stare.

Leon sneered in disgust. That lad was going to have to develop a thicker skin if he planned on making a living by knifing people in the back.

His mood was bitter, and he didn't mind sharing it.

"Sam," Morrison called to the young man. "Ride on ahead and let the sheriff in Arvada know we're coming."

"Yeah, all right, Marshal." Sam pushed his horse into a lope, relieved to get away from the outlaw, and to have something useful to do.

***

Forty minutes later, the small posse jogged into town and turned in at the hitching rail in front of the sheriff's office. Much to Morrison's disgust, a group of citizens had spotted them riding in and began to follow, pointing and mumbling to themselves along the way. By the time the mounted group made it to their destination, there was quite a crowd gathering.

This was exactly what Morrison had hoped to avoid. How had word gotten out? He scowled to himself, then decided to ignore the populace and just get on with the business at hand.

The three lawmen dismounted, and Leon swung his right leg over the horse's neck and slid to the ground.

Mike grabbed hold of him and, pulling him around the horses, headed him toward the steps leading to the office. All of them tried to ignore the numerous comments bombarding them from the growing crowd. It was futile.

"Yeah, that's Nash, all right," came one comment from the on-lookers. "I was in a bank they robbed a few years back."

'Jeez, another eye witness. Had we really been that flippant about our identities?' He sighed. *'Yes, we had. Young and foolish and arrogant.'*

"That's Napoleon Nash?" came an incredulous voice. "Why, he's a skinny little fella. With a name like 'Napoleon', I always thought he would be bigger than that."

"What do ya' mean?" another observed. "He's skinny, for sure, but he's got some height to 'im. He's taller than you, Shorty. I think he's taller than Ole' Bonipart hisself, if'n I ain't mistaken."

"Who's Bonipart?" came a gruff grumble. "And what the hell he gots ta' do with Nash?"

This query was met with looks, but the conversation moved on before enlightenment was offered.

"My God. There's blood all over him," a newcomer exclaimed.

"That would make sense. I heard one of 'em took a bullet. Looks like it was Kiefer."

"That's Napoleon Nash? Damn. I was playin' poker with him all yesterday afternoon. Wow. I'm never gonna forget that game now."

'*Yesterday afternoon?'* Leon thought, as he was dragged into the sheriff's office. *'That was only yesterday?'*

Once inside the office, Morrison glared at Sam.

That young man stood behind the desk, taking refuge with the local deputy. Unfortunately for Sam, the deputy was just as young as he was, and completely awestruck by their new prisoner. The honorary posse member wasn't going to get any help from that quarter.

"I'm sorry, Marshal," Sam piped up before Morrison started in on him. "Somehow, everybody already knew you were bringing at least one of them in here today. That crowd was gathering before I even arrived."

Morrison calmed down and his craggy face grimaced a small smile. His nerves were on edge, dealing with these outlaws, and he knew he had been taking it out on his men. Everybody needed some rest.

"I know, Sam," the marshal answered him. "I think it was that big mouth of a livery man who let everyone know something was up. It's all right. Just don't let any of them in here for a visit." He glanced around the office and frowned. "Where's the sheriff? I would have thought, he'd want to be here for this."

"Ah, Sheriff Jacobs is out of town right now, attending his niece's wedding," answered the local deputy. "Ah, my name's Palin, Sir. Ben Palin. I'm in charge here until the sheriff gets back." He swallowed and sent a quick glance in Leon's direction. He did not want to be in charge of such an important prisoner.

"Oh, that's just great," Morrison complained. "About the only right thing that has happened on this venture, is that we actually captured Nash and Kiefer."

'Speak for yourself,' Leon thought. *'As far as I'm concerned, that's about the only thing that hadn't gone right.'*

Morrison sighed and gave in to the inevitable. "All right. Deputy Palin is it?"

"Yessir."

"Show Deputy Shoemacher, here, where to lock up the prisoner, and then both of you return here so we can go over the details and get the paperwork out of the way."

"Yessir, Marshal."

"All right, Marshal," Mike responded. "C'mon, Nash. This way."

Mike escorted Leon to the heavy wooden door that led into the cell block, and then waited for Ben to grab the keys and get the door open.

There was nobody else in the cell block that day, so Ben swung open the door to the cell that was closest to the entrance. Mike casually pushed the prisoner inside.

Leon stood there, his back to the cell door, and took in his new lodgings with a heavy heart. There was only one bunk in this cell, running lengthways along the far wall, and aside from the chamber pot in the corner, that was about it. There wasn't even a window.

The cell at the far end of the aisle had a window, and Leon could hear people out there, talking and laughing. He even caught his name being mentioned a couple of times. But that only served to depress him more.

Change of Leads: The Lost Shoe

Leon heard the cell door swing shut and clang into place. He turned and looked at the large deputy.

"Ah, Mike? What about the cuffs?"

"Sorry, Nash," Mike answered. "Morrison has the keys. You're gonna have ta' wait for him."

Leon slumped in disappointment. His shoulders ached, and it would be nice to at least get the cuffs off. He watched as the two men exited the cell block, and that heavy, wooden door closed and then locked behind them. Leon was very much alone. He sighed, feeling a little sorry for himself. He went to the bunk, sat down, and pushed back into the corner. He closed his eyes with the hope that he might get some rest and collect his thoughts. That didn't happen.

As soon as his eyes closed, he heard the rifle shot, again. He felt the tremor go through Jack's body, and then Jack falling back over and into him. Blood everywhere. Penelope pleading, *'Please don't die. Please don't die.'*

Leon jerked himself out of it. It had been bad enough going through that once; he didn't want to re-live it. Unfortunately, now that he was alone, and things had quieted down, worry over his partner's fate took hold of him, and he wasn't going to be allowed to think about anything else.

***

After what seemed an eternity, but had only been half an hour, the heavy wooden door opened, and Morrison came into the cell block. He unlocked the cell door and entered.

"Okay, Nash," he ordered. "On your feet. Turn around."

'It's about time,' Leon thought, while he did as instructed. *'Finally getting these damn cuffs off.'*

But to Leon's surprise and disappointment, the cuffs were not released. Instead, Morrison started another methodical search of Leon's person. The marshal started at the prisoner's neck and shoulders, and slowly worked his way down.

Leon felt anxiety seep into his gut.

"Another search, Marshal? Surely you don't think—?"

"Quiet."

Leon closed his eyes. He knew the marshal would find it; Morrison was being too thorough not to. Leon thought, regretfully, that he should have shaken those picks down further, so they could fall over and rest under his foot, inside the boot. But he had wanted to keep the tools handy, easy to get at in case he needed to retrieve them quickly. Now, he knew he was going to lose them, altogether.

Sure enough, Morrison finished with the right leg and started down the left. As soon as he slid his hand inside Leon's boot, he froze. Sliding the lock picks out, he stood up, and Leon tensed.

"Well, now, isn't this interesting?" Morrison commented. "Where did you get this, Nash?"

Leon smiled, his nerves jingling. He was more than a little aware of the sheriff's close proximity behind him. "You missed that when you searched me the first time."

"You're lyin', Nash. I searched you thoroughly, and I didn't miss anything. The three I took off you this morning are still with me. So where did you get these?"

"Honest, Marshal. You simply missed it—"

The sucker punch to Leon's kidney put him into the floor before he even realized he'd been hit. He lay there on his side, gasping for air as the pain radiated out from the point of impact.

Morrison stepped around in front of him, and squatting, shoved the lock picks in front of his prisoner's face.

"Where did you get it?" Morrison asked again, then he paused as a thought occurred to him. "It was that Marsham girl, wasn't it? The oldest one, Caroline. She slipped it into your boot when she came to say goodbye to you, didn't she?"

"No," Leon gasped. "Like I said . . . you just . . . missed it."

Morrison stood up. The kick that landed in Leon's ribcage caused his senses to dim, but the nausea forced him to remain conscious. He pulled both knees up to his chest, as he fought to breathe. Pain filled his senses.

"Don't play me for a fool again, Nash."

Leon vaguely heard the cell door open and then clang shut, again. He was left alone, laying on the cold cell floor, gasping for air.

***

Change of Leads: The Lost Shoe

Ben Palin knew all about Napoleon Nash, and the tricks that outlaw had up his sleeve, and he found it difficult to relax with such an infamous prisoner in his custody. When he heard footsteps outside, he hoped it was Morrison or one of his deputies coming back to assist him. But the handle on the front door rattled as the person tried to enter, and, finding it locked, started knocking.

"Ah, who is it?" Ben called out.

"It's Doctor Gibson and Cameron Marsham," came David's voice. "I want to come in and check up on the prisoner."

"Oh, ah . . . just a minute."

Ben hurried to the door and unlocked it to let the two men inside. He did an anxious scan of the boardwalk and, finding it empty, breathed a sigh of relief. He pushed the door closed and locked it.

Cameron and David exchanged glances.

"A little nervous, Ben?" Cameron asked him.

"You better believe it. I'm not supposed to let anybody in here, or even go into the cell block unless it's a dire emergency. I wish Sheriff Jacobs was here."

"Sheriff Jacobs wouldn't have left you in charge if he didn't think you could handle anything that came up," Cameron assured him.

"Yeah, but I don't think he foresaw this."

"You're doing fine, Ben," the doctor assured him. "We brought some clean clothes for Mr. Nash, and I want to check him out. He took a bit of a beating out at the Marsham place. I need to make sure he's all right."

"Oh, I don't know," Ben said, biting his lower lip. "Marshal Morrison said …"

"Marshal Morrison is not in charge of this jail, Ben. You are," David countered him. "And being the town's doctor, I have authority over you and Morrison when it comes to the welfare of a prisoner."

Ben looked like he was faced with a conundrum.

The doctor smiled to put him at ease. "Don't worry about it. We won't let your prisoner escape. And you know Sheriff Jacobs would approve."

"Yeah, I know," Ben nodded. "All right. I'll let you in."

He retrieved the keys and opened the wooden door to let the two men inside. One look in the first cell and everyone was up in arms—again.

"God dammit, Ben," David snapped at him. "What happened in here? How long has he been like this?"

"I don't know." Ben stepped forward and unlocked the cell door. "Morrison was the last one in here, and he told me to stay out."

David and Cameron rushed into the cell. They were down beside Leon in an instant.

"Oh, my goodness. What happened?" Cameron asked him. "Are you able to sit up?"

"No." David stopped him with a touch. "Don't move him, Cameron. Not yet." He then turned to Ben. "Get the keys to these handcuffs, for goodness sakes. What the hell is Morrison thinking, leaving him like this?"

"I don't have the keys, Doc," Ben admitted. "Morrison's got 'em."

David fumed. "Dammit. They haven't even cleaned him up. Ben, go get water and soap—lots of it. And keep it coming. And towels and some extra blankets. And bring in some drinking water as well. Go."

His orders given, David then turned his full attention to Leon.

"Okay, Napoleon. Where do you hurt?"

"Everywhere," came the tight reply.

"You're going to have to be more specific than that," David told him. "Where does it start?"

"My right side, front and back."

"Okay. Just try to relax."

David gently pulled Leon's blood-stiffened undershirt up and away from his right side. Both Cameron and David sucked their teeth when they saw the deep, dark bruising that was already developing on Leon's torso. They nicely competed with the bruises that were there from the earlier assault. David examined the ribcage and applied a very gentle pressure against the lower ribs. But, as subtle as the exam was, Leon tensed and gasped in pain.

"Easy," David eased off. "Just relax. I won't be long."

Done with examining the ribs, David then concentrated on the bruising on Leon's back, feeling around the area, and applying gentle pressure only where he needed to. Leon closed his eyes and tried to block out the pain, but he wasn't having much luck. He finally broke down and started to protest.

"Ow."

"Sorry."

"*Ow.*"

"Sorry."

"You're not sorry, Doc, so stop saying you are."

David smiled. "Okay. You have a point. I don't like hurting you, Napoleon, but I need to be sure there is no serious damage inside. I want to feel confident you're going to heal up all right, since I don't know how long I'm going to be able to keep you under my care."

"Yeah, okay."

David finished with his examination and straightened up.

"All right. That kidney feels tender and bruised, but I don't think it's damaged. I wouldn't be surprised if one of your floating ribs has a hairline fracture in it, but it hasn't snapped. It'll cause you some pain for the next few days, but it ought to heal all right. However, having said that, if you start to cough up blood, or you see any when you use the chamber pot, you let me know, right away. Do you understand?"

"Sure, Doc."

"I mean it, Napoleon. It's important. Don't play heroics, or the tough guy, telling yourself that if you just give it some time, it'll go away on its own. I know what young men are like, when it comes to seeking aide. And a few older ones, too." He sent an accusing glance directed at Cameron. The rancher chose to be looking elsewhere at that moment.

"No, don't worry, Doc," Leon said. "If I see anything like that, I'll let you know."

"Good." David was satisfied. "Now, do you think you can sit up on your own?"

"No. I've already tried. The pain shoots through me, and I can't breathe."

"All right. Cameron, if you can give me a hand, here."

"Sure."

"If you can get hold of him on that arm, and I'll pull him up with this one. Then we can get him into a sitting position. Leon, I'm going to straighten your legs out in front of you, then we'll pull you up. Don't do anything, just stay relaxed. Let us do the work, okay?"

"Yeah, fine."

"Okay, Cameron. You ready? All right, up you come."

Leon found himself in the seated position without too much fuss and bother. He still hurt like the dickens, but the sharp pain he expected, never struck, and his good opinion of this doctor increased with each encounter.

"Okay, that went well," David commented. "Now, your bunk is right behind you, so the next step is to get you sitting up on it. I'm going to bring your knees up now, to get you into position, so just relax." That done, David and Jesse both stood up, and each grabbed hold of an arm. "Just like before, Napoleon. Don't you do anything. Let us do the work. Okay, Cameron. Ready? Here we go."

And, just like before, Leon found himself now sitting on the bunk, and the world was looking a whole lot better.

David and Cameron sat down on either side of him.

David frowned. "Now, if we could just get these cuffs off, we might start making some progress."

"I see you have your medical bag with you," Leon observed. "Do you have anything long and slender in there? Something that might resemble a lock pick?"

Cameron and David exchanged looks, and David smiled.

"Yes, I think I just might."

David retrieved his bag from where he had dropped it by the cell door. He sat back down on the bunk, opened his bag, and rummaged through it until he found another small case. He opened that case to reveal a set of probes of various lengths and thicknesses for Leon to choose from.

They weren't exactly like a lock pick, not having been designed for that use, but Leon spied one that ought to do the job. David pulled it out for him.

"Now what?" David asked. "I'm quite proficient at using these tools for what they were designed for, but I've never picked a lock in my life."

"That's all right," Leon assured him. "I can pick a lock with my hands tied behind my back." He smiled at his little joke. "Just put it in my hand. That's right. Now, direct the end of it into the key hole for me. Good."

Leon started to take a deep breath, then stopped short at the pain it caused. He released the air that was in his lungs and closed his eyes, easing himself into a relaxed state. Normally, he would use two picks to manipulate a lock, but this lock was small enough, he was sure he could manage with just the one. He focused his mind on the lock and the tool in his hand. He smiled with pleasure, despite his pain, when he felt himself in familiar territory. He pictured the inside of the lock in his mind. He knew exactly where the end of the pick needed to be, and just how much pressure to apply to seduce the lock into opening for him.

Both Cameron and David watched silently, mesmerized by the artist at work. His long, slender fingers barely moved. Everything was precise and delicate, and then, 'click'. The one cuff surrendered.

Leon's smile broadened.

Cameron was amazed. He felt like he was gradually saying 'goodbye' to Peter Black, and just beginning to scratch the surface of Napoleon Nash. No wonder Morrison was so jumpy.

"Easy does it," said David, as Leon tried to bring his arms around in front of him. The muscles in his shoulders were so tight and sore, they protested at the sudden movement, and Leon's jaw tightened with the pain. "Just bring them around, slowly. Then work them a little, until they ease up. There you go. That better?"

"Yeah." He started to take a deep breath and was reminded of the pain caused by the last attempt to fill his lungs, and decided it wasn't such a good idea.

He moved his neck and shoulders around a bit, until the stiffness in them eased, then he placed his hands on his lap and unlocked the second cuff from his wrist. He allowed the offending manacles to slide to the floor.

"How is Jack doing?" he asked David.

"As well as can be expected. He's resting."

"Yeah, but—he's still breathing, right?" Leon needed to hear the reassurance.

"Yes, Napoleon, he's still breathing. Plus, he has three lovely ladies who are more than happy to tend to his needs. He'll be well looked after."

Leon nodded, feeling relieved.

Loud banging and clanking came from the outer office, which was followed by Ben, who carried a pitcher of water and a cup. He preceded another young man, who came into the cell block sloshing buckets of water while trying to keep hold of all the other paraphernalia associated with a sponge bath.

Leon's relief disappeared.

David brightened up. "Oh great. Bring it all in here, boys. Ben, pour out a cup of water for him, please. Hello, George. How are you, today?"

"Fine, Doctor Gibson," Ben's friend answered, but his eyes never left Leon.

Leon slumped. *'Wonderful. Another awestruck youngster. Hopefully, he won't be sticking around.'*

"Where's Marshal Morrison, Ben?" David asked, as he took a pouch from his bag and poured a small amount into the water cup. "I'd like to have a word with him."

"Ah, I think he said he was going to set up travel arrangements and then get some sleep." Ben didn't like being put on the spot and was already worried about what was going to happen when Morrison got back and found that Ben had not obeyed his orders.

David's lips tightened with irritation. "If you see him, tell him to come talk to me"

"Yessir."

"Well, go on, off with you," David told them. "Get more water. We're going to need it."

Much to Leon's relief, the two young men disappeared.

"Okay, Napoleon; drink this. There's a dose of laudanum in there, and this should help with the pain.

"Oh yeah. Thanks."

Leon dutifully accepted the cup of water and downed it in one go. The medicine had a bitter taste, but he didn't mind.

Then David's next words set him on edge, all over again.

"All right. Let's get these clothes off you, and get you cleaned up."

"Ah . . . I can do that on my own, can't I?"

David sat back and sent him a smile. "Well, I don't know. Can you?"

Cameron decided to take the doctor's lead and sat back quietly, giving Leon the time he needed to come to the uncomfortable, but inevitable, conclusion for himself.

Leon sat for a moment, staring straight ahead. He looked from one man to the other, hoping for some reprieve. He didn't find any.

Showing a streak of stubbornness that would match his partner's, Leon tried bringing one foot up across his knee, so he could pull the boot off. No go. He barely got his knee half way up when pain shot through his torso, and he gasped for breath. He then tried using the boot heel on one foot, to assist in pulling the boot off the other. Damn. That hurt even more. He sighed and sat for a moment. There had to be a solution to this.

Finally, he changed tactics and attempted something simpler.

Slowly and carefully, and with a great deal of effort, Leon pulled his arms out of the sleeves of his undershirt. He tried to pull the shirt over his head, but pain shot through his chest and his lungs seized. "All right," he conceded, once he could breathe again. "Let's just get this over with."

Cameron and David both smiled and got down to business.

Washing Leon's hair proved difficult because he was unable to lean over the basin; water and soap were dripping down his back and over his face. Despite Cameron's efforts to keep the soapy water away, some still managed to seep into Leon's eyes, causing the prisoner even more discomfort.

Still, they managed to get the job done. They let Leon wash his own face, and he carefully dabbed at his split lip. It was sore, but not a bad cut, and once he had removed the dried blood from it, it was barely noticeable.

His two companions carried on, washing his arms, shoulders, and torso, being careful of his many bruises. The buckets of water were turning red faster than Ben and George could replace them.

It was at this point that Cameron noticed other injuries that were well-healed, but still apparent. Yet another scar from a bullet wound, under the left shoulder blade, was the worst that he saw, and probably the most life-threatening.

Still, the collection of scars from nicks, and slices, and close calls, told their own story of a life full of danger, and pain, and no way out.

Leon was acutely aware of his nakedness.

Many men liked to boast of the scars they carried and the close calls they had escaped from. But Leon wasn't one of them. He kept himself covered up, not wanting others to see his battle wounds. To him, they were an accounting of all his foolish choices and decisions, and his inability to keep himself, and those for whom he was responsible, safe from harm.

"My goodness," Cameron began before thinking it might be intrusive. "Just how many times have you been shot?"

Leon pulled his mind away from the pain and discomfort he was currently in and focus on Cameron's question.

"Including the grazes, or just the ones that had to be dug out?"

David and Cameron exchanged glances.

"And your partner?" Cameron continued.

"He's got his share."

Not wanting to delve any deeper, Cameron draped one of the dry blankets across Leon's shoulders, so he would not get cold, and they continued undressing their patient.

"Okay," David said, "let's stand you up, so we can get your trousers off."

Leon groaned. *'Please don't let Morrison walk in on us now.'*

He saw no way out of his situation, so reluctantly, he allowed the other two men to assist him to his feet.

Cameron grabbed another blanket and held it around Leon's waist to preserve some of his dignity, while David pulled the trousers and long johns, both stiff and unyielding with dried blood, down to the floor.

Leon held onto Cameron's shoulder to steady himself while he stepped out of the soiled clothing, and David continued cleaning him up.

Cameron, aware that what David was doing, even as a doctor, could cause extreme embarrassment to any grown man, engaged Leon in a distracting conversation.

"What in the world did you do to deserve such a beating? I know Morrison is a bit of a bully, but I don't think even he would have laid into you like this, without a reason."

Leon looked sheepish. "Yeah, well. He found another set of lock picks on me."

"Another one? I find it hard to believe that he missed one when he searched you."

"No, he got all the ones I had on me, at the time."

"Well then, how? Oh, don't tell me, it was one of my girls."

Leon smiled. "Okay."

"Oh, my goodness." Cameron groaned. "Well, it couldn't have been Penny. She was too distraught to follow through on something like that. It must have been Caroline. She's going to be hearing about this."

"I wouldn't be too hard on her, Cameron. She was just trying to help."

"Trying to help is one thing," Cameron complained. "But assisting a known outlaw to escape custody is quite another. If Morrison pushes this, both those girls could wind up in prison themselves, then where would we be? They're not children anymore." Cameron shuddered. "And now, you've received a sound beating because of her bad decision. She has to learn that there are consequences to making those kinds of choices." He sighed. "I don't know what it is about you and your partner. Those girls are usually very responsible and knowing right from wrong. But, as soon as you fellas show up, all their common sense goes out the window."

"Jack does seem to have that effect on the ladies," Leon smiled. "I can't imagine why."

Cameron laughed out loud.

"You devil. You know exactly why. And you're worse, because you don't do it intentionally."

"Do what?"

"My point, exactly."

Leon shrugged, a whimsical smile tugging at his lips. He couldn't help it, if the ladies found him and Jack irresistible.

Then his smile dropped, and he became serious again. He looked Cameron straight in the eye.

"Don't worry about your girls. They're both fine, sensible young ladies. When the time comes, they'll make the right choices."

"Hmm." Like many fathers, Cameron wasn't completely convinced.

"Okay," David announced, "I'm done here. Let's get you into those clean clothes."

"Oh." Leon was surprised. Cameron had done a good job at distracting him.

***

Half an hour later, Leon looked more like himself. He was comfortably dressed in black trousers and boots, and a light coffee-colored shirt. A dark-brown jacket lay at the foot of the bunk for when the evening turned chilly. His previous clothing would have to be discarded, since nothing was going to get those blood stains out.

Then, as if on cue, Morrison came storming into the cell block.

"What the devil is going on in here?" He took one look at Leon and his anger rose another notch. "And why isn't he in cuffs?"

David and Cameron stood up. Neither man cared for this marshal, and both were ready to do battle.

"What's going on, is exactly what I was wanting to ask you," David threw back at Morrison "What's the idea of leaving a man in that condition, alone and locked in a cell? He may be your prisoner, but I insist he be treated with a certain amount of humanity."

"Oh, you do, do you?" Morrison rounded on the doctor. "Well, I've said it before and, apparently, it bears repeating. Nash and Kiefer are dangerous men. They've yet to make it to trial because people like you treat them like they're honest, upright citizens. I intend to make sure this man goes to trial, and I really don't care if you disapprove of the way I go about it." He paused and glared at Leon. "Mr. Nash and I needed to come to an understanding as to my tolerance level for con games. Hopefully, we have reached that point."

Leon sent a weak smile back to the lawman, not feeling up to including himself in this discussion.

"I understand your concern, Marshal," David responded. "But, keeping a man's hands cuffed behind him, indefinitely, is borderline torture. I will not tolerate it as long as he is in my care."

"Fine," Morrison snarled. "We'll just see how long that's going to be."

David ignored the threat. "I also want to see a decent meal and a good deal more drinking water brought in here," the doctor continued. "I have a feeling he hasn't had anything all day."

"I'm really not hun—"

"Shut up," David threw back at Leon, so riled, he forgot about courtesy. "You're going to get some food into you, whether you like it or not."

"Ben, Sam," Morrison yelled, while still glaring at David. The two deputies appeared. "Get this cell cleaned up. Then go over to Molly's and ask her to prepare a meal for the prisoner."

"Yessir, Marshal," Ben answered.

He and Sam began to collect items from the sponge bath, and even did their best to wipe up any water pooling in various places on the floor. Sam could feel the hostility aimed at him as he entered the cell, and one look at the glare the prisoner sent him, warned him to keep his distance.

Ben, picking up on the animosity, took the danger zone duty, leaving Sam to take care of the parameter. He also collected the handcuffs that Leon had removed and returned them to the marshal.

"Are you going to be visiting with the prisoner for much longer?" Morrison's sarcasm ran deep.

"At least until I see he has had something to eat." David answered.

"And you?" the marshal asked Cameron.

Cameron sat down and folded his arms. "I have nowhere else I need to be."

Leon knitted his brow and looked at Cameron, as a thought occurred to him.

"That's just fine," Morrison answered. "I'll be in the office until you finally take your leave." He turned on his heel and stomped out of the cell block.

David breathed a sigh of relief. He collected his medical supplies and returned them to the bag.

Ben and Sam were quick to finish gathering the other items and made a hasty exit, both glad to get away from the friction.

Leon turned to Cameron. "Speaking of places to be, weren't you supposed to be teaching school today?"

"Oh, yes, I know," Cameron admitted. "With all the chaos at the ranch, I forgot about school until it was too late to do anything about it. By now, everyone knows what happened, so it won't be a problem. I'll be back at it tomorrow. There's probably no point in expecting Penny to attend class. I doubt she'll be able to focus on anything, other than Mathew, and I think Jean is going to need all the help she can get, looking after the baby, and Mathew."

Leon didn't answer. He felt guilty about the situation they had put their friends in. He also had no idea how to respond to Cameron's comment.

Understanding the predicament, David stepped up with an offer, as he collected the last of his supplies.

"I'll bring my wife out with me in the morning, when I go to check up on Jack. She will often help out with the care of my patients." He frowned, looking around the floor. "Have you seen that little utensil Napoleon used to open the handcuffs?"

Cameron joined David in the search of the bunk and floor for the missing item. Then, in unison, they stopped and looked at Leon.

The outlaw wore a sheepish smile while holding up the missing tool.

Both men sighed and sat back on the bunk.

David took the tool from Leon's fingers and returned it to its case.

"Sorry," Leon said. "Force of habit."

"Hmm." David nodded.

Neither man wanted to know when, exactly, Leon had snatched the tool, or where he had hidden it.

"I swear, you're incorrigible," Cameron commented. "I'm beginning to think you ask for the treatment you get at the hands of these lawmen. You certainly don't go out of your way to make it easy."

Leon didn't feel inclined to respond.

CHAPTER NINE
A NEW FRIEND

"Come on, Napoleon, you have to eat."

Leon looked at the plate in front of him. He hurt, inside and out, physically and emotionally. Every time he forced a forkful down his throat, his gut tightened into a knot and let him know the intrusion was not welcome. He managed to swallow half of what was on the plate, just to get the doctor to stop nagging him, then he drank some water and called it quits.

"Well, all right," David conceded. "I guess that's good for now. But try and eat some more later, will you? And drink lots of water."

"Yes, Doc. I will," Leon lied.

"Here." David retrieved a small pouch from his bag. "There's a few more doses of laudanum for you to take. Mix it in some water before you go to sleep, and again in the morning. It should help."

"Yeah, okay. Thanks."

Leon took the pouch and set it beside his cup.

"I better get home before my wife starts to worry," David said. "I'll drop in again, first thing tomorrow morning, to check up on you."

"Thanks, Doc. For everything."

David nodded and glanced at Cameron.

Cameron stood up. "I better be going as well. I need to get home before it gets too dark. I may not see you again before you leave. Is there anything else you need? Anyone you want me to get in touch with?"

"Oh, yeah," Leon said, now that Cameron had mentioned it. "Could you send a telegram for me?"

"Sure. I'll need something to write it on. David, do you have anything?"

David nodded. He opened his handy medical bag and pulled out a pencil and some paper. "Okay, go ahead."

"Send it to Sheriff Taggard Murphy, in Medicine Bow, Wyoming. Just—tell him what happened. He'll know what to do."

David finished writing down the information and handed the paper to Cameron.

"All right. I'll get this done, right away." Then Cameron put a hand on his friend's shoulder, and Leon looked up at him. "You remember what we talked about. You could be in for a difficult time, but I expect you to keep your word."

Leon nodded.

Then they were gone, and Leon found himself alone again.

He sent the dinner plate one last disgusted look and pushed himself further back on the cot. He settled into the corner, hoping to get some sleep. His body was so sore from the beatings, he didn't even bother trying to lay down. The laudanum was causing some drowsiness, so he decided to give a nap another try. Using the skinny pillow as a cushion for his head and shoulders against the wall, he managed to find a position that gave him some measure of relaxation.

He closed his eyes.

'He's stopped breathing.'

'What? Well do something. Get him back.'

'I'm trying.'

'Get him back. Get him back.'

Leon's eyes snapped open. He was sweating, and his heart raced. Then he jumped, surprised to see Morrison standing on the other side of the cell door, watching him. Leon closed his eyes and groaned, '*What now?*'

"On your feet, Nash. Come over here, up to the bars."

Leon sighed, then slowly eased himself off the bunk and walked toward the marshal.

"Put your hands through the bars," Morrison ordered, "one on each side. Good."

The marshal snapped the handcuffs onto Leon's wrists. He then unlocked the cell door, entered, and began a methodical search.

Leon suffered the indignity of it in silence, except for a small intake of breath when Morrison patted along his torso, not giving much concern for the tender bruising there.

Once he was done with Leon, he turned to the cell and did an efficient, thorough search. Including Leon's black hat, and the new jacket draped across the foot of the bed. Fortunately for Leon, he found nothing to cause him concern.

Spotting the pouch of medicine sitting beside the plate, Morrison snorted. He snatched it up and slipped it into his vest pocket, shaking his head at the naivety of some people; why bother wasting good medicine on an animal in a cage? He placed the plate and water cup on the floor outside the cell. That done, he came in behind Leon, unlocked one cuff and brought his hands behind his back.

"Oh, come on . . ."

"I don't mind bruising your other kidney."

Leon's jaw tightened. "No, that won't be necessary."

"Good. Keep your comments to yourself."

Morrison snapped the cuffs shut, and Leon started to step back from the bars. But, before he made it far, Morrison shoved him between the shoulder blades, slamming him into the unyielding barrier, causing him to flinch with pain. "Stay put. Don't move 'till I tell you. Understand?"

"Yeah."

Leon heard the cell door open and clang shut, as the marshal locked the prisoner in again.

"Now, you can move."

Leon backed off the bars and sent a glare after Morrison as the marshal walked toward the wooden door. Turning, the lawman smiled as he locked eyes with the outlaw. He was wearing Nash down; he could see it. He was winning this battle of wills.

Leon returned to the bunk and tried to settle into the pillow again. With his hands cuffed behind him, he gave up any hopes of getting any sleep. Chances of resting had been slim, anyway, considering how his mind had already sabotaged the effort.

On top of these obstacles, he felt angry and irritated over the way Morrison was treating him. He felt he didn't deserve such treatment. But then, he had to stop and honestly reconsider this assumption. His thoughts went back to what Cameron had said, about how he seemed to be asking for it, sometimes. How he was pushing the limit.

Change of Leads: The Lost Shoe

Leon realized, he'd always been flippant when it came to outwitting the law; it was a game to him. It was all so easy. With his brilliant mind and nimble fingers, he'd open safes and cell doors like a parlor trick being performed for the amusement of all.

But now, Morrison wasn't amused; he was fed up. He'd had it with Nash and Kiefer running rough shod over the legal system of the country, and it was time to get serious and do something about it. The marshal never pretended to be anything other than what he was: a law officer, determined to bring two outlaws to justice, no matter what it took or who tried to stand in his way.

What was getting Leon's goat, was the realization that Morrison wasn't a fool. And the marshal was right: Leon had been playing him for one, just like he always did. Only this time, Leon was up against a man who understood the way his mind worked, and was always one step ahead of him, blocking every move he made. Morrison was meticulously wearing him down, mentally and physically; beating him into submission.

A tingling of fear settled over Leon as he finally came to an understanding of whom he was up against. It wasn't the fear of going to prison, or the fear of never seeing Jack again; it wasn't even the fear of death. It was the fear of losing.

Napoleon Nash wasn't used to losing. He insisted there was always a way out, and his arrogance had never allowed him to seriously consider the possibility that there could come a time, maybe this time, that the way out would be blocked.

***

The chilly midnight hour found Leon up and pacing. His eyes burned with exhaustion, but his mind wouldn't let him sleep, and his aching body wouldn't let him rest. He impatiently awaited the coming of daylight, hoping it would bring news of Jack.

His partner was fighting for his life. For all Leon knew, he could already be dead, and it was driving him mad not being with him. He wanted out of this cell, not to run away and disappear, but to return to the Rocking M, to put his mind at ease, one way or another.

He stopped when he heard talking in the outer office.

Morrison's gruff voice was giving orders again. There was the jingling of keys in the lock and the wooden door swung open.

Morrison, along with his personal deputies, Mike Shoemacher and Alex Strode were dressed for travel, and the two deputies were armed with rifles to go along with their handguns. Something was up.

Morrison unlocked the cell door and all three entered, rifles at the ready.

The marshal unlocked Leon's handcuffs.

Leon clenched his teeth, as the muscles in his upper arms protested the sudden liberty. He found himself wishing for another dose of laudanum, if only to ease this particularly painful throbbing.

"If you have to use the pot, better do it now, 'cause I won't be giving you another chance."

'Well, that was diplomatic.' Leon forced his cramped arms to come forward. Then he considered his options and decided maybe it would be a good idea.

While Leon was busy with this little necessity, Morrison grabbed his prisoner's jacket and hat, and gave them both another quick inspection. Then, it was Leon's turn. Face first, up against the bars again, for yet another search of his person.

Leon was getting tired of this. Just where did the marshal think Leon would be getting any more tools of his trade?

Truth of the matter was, Morrison knew darn well that Leon would be clean. But every chance he had to let the outlaw know who was in charge, was going to be utilized. The prisoner was not to be given any leeway at all.

As soon as the search was completed, Morrison gave Leon his jacket. "Here. Put it on."

Leon did as instructed. "Little early for a ride, isn't it?" No one answered him. "Can I ask how my partner is doing?"

Again, no answer. But Alex Strode broke eye contact with him. This only increased Leon's worry.

Morrison held out his hand to Mike Shoemacher, and the deputy passed him a leather belt with manacles attached to it.

Leon had never seen such a contraption before, and he had a feeling he wasn't going to like it much.

"Turn around, hands up," Morrison instructed him.

Leon obliged. The belt was put around his waist and cinched up snugly behind his back.

Leon sucked his teeth as the belt applied pressure to his injuries. "Easy." But again, he was ignored.

Morrison turned Leon around, brought his hands down in front and snapped them into the manacles. He grabbed Leon's hat, plunked it onto his head, and promptly marched the prisoner out of the cell and to the front office.

Ben was there, sitting at the desk. He looked sleepy, but also relieved that these men were finally going to be leaving his town.

Morrison grabbed the pen that was on the desk, dipped it in the ink well, and signed the release form. Once this was done, the marshal officially took custody of the prisoner again, relieving Ben of any responsibility.

"Don't get too relaxed," Morrison told the local deputy. "You'll be getting the other one in here, just as soon as he's healed up enough to make the trip."

"Yeah, but by then, Sheriff Jacobs will be back," Ben said, "and it will be his problem."

Morrison snorted at the deputy's attitude and walked out.

Leon felt a rush of relief at what the marshal had let slip. Jack was still alive. That was all he needed to know for now.

The small group of men left the sheriff's office and headed toward the train station. Leon had expected to see saddle horses waiting for them outside, or at least a coach. It had not occurred to him that they might be leaving town by train, and in the middle of the night.

The doctor was not going to be pleased.

Morrison knew what he was about and because of this, there was no one else around, as he and his group took up position on the platform. In no more than five minutes, the headlight of an approaching train could be seen.

The engine chugged and hissed its way into town, going past Morrison's group, to slowly come to a halt alongside the depot.

The steam billowing from the engine mixed with the cool night air, giving the platform an eerie, ghostly atmosphere.

A conductor, carrying his own shimmering lantern, approached the four men.

"You Marshal Morrison?" the begrizzled employee stifled a yawn, his red-rimmed eyes looking beyond the marshal to the man in chains.

"That's right. Is everything arranged?"

"Yup. Just climb aboard, right here. There are some empty seats at the back, on this side." Rubbing a bony hand across his graying mustache, he looked again at the marshal's prisoner. "You sure he's secure? We got ladies and children on board here tonight. Don't really understand why you got to transport him by passenger train."

"Because nobody would expect it, that's why. And it ain't your place to worry about it, either. Besides, he won't be causing any trouble." The marshal grinned, the stubble on his chin pulling tight and standing out as he looked over at Napoleon Nash. "Will you?"

Leon's eyes were dark, but the smile he presented was warm and friendly; the epitome of innocence. "Not me, Marshal."

"What goes on, on my train, is my business," the disgruntled conductor replied, clearly unhappy with the situation, "but I know ya' got special permission, despite my misgivin's. Just you make sure he don't cause no trouble. I don't need that on my train . . ." and his voice trailed off as he traipsed away to continue his inspection.

Without giving the nosy conductor another thought, the lawmen, with their notorious prisoner, entered the dimly lit passenger car. Mike went first, followed by Leon, then Morrison, who kept his fist in the middle of Leon's back, shoving him forward. Finally, Alex brought up the rear.

After the cool night outside, coming into the confined space of the passenger car felt like stepping into a warm, encompassing blanket. The weariness and aftershock Leon had felt in his cell, doubled its intensity. His head swam, and he thought his knees might give way beneath him.

Glancing to the sleeping passengers, his weary eyes lighted onto a young boy, who snoozed in his father's arms. There was something familiar about him, as though Leon were looking at the childhood version of himself.

He felt a hitch inside. The child couldn't be any more than eight or ten years old, right around the same age he had been when his own life had started to go so wrong. The lad was small, and appeared young and vulnerable, nestled there, safe in this father's arms.

Leon's exhausted mind drifted back in time. He wouldn't have been much different from this boy, when his own family had been violently taken from him.

'How could a small boy, that age, take on the weight of the world and not be damaged by it?' And yet, Leon could remember not thinking of himself as a small, frightened boy, but as the uncle who willingly took on the responsibility of raising his younger nephew, who had also been orphaned on that terrible, fateful day.

Leon had tried to be a good provider, someone whom Jack could look up to and depend upon, and young Napoleon thought he was doing right.

The boy's wide eyes met Leon's, and then widened more.

'Is he afraid of me?' Leon flashed a quick, bright smile and did his best to pass the child a wave, in hopes of putting the boy at his ease.

The child ducked down but couldn't bring himself to look away.

Then Leon passed him, and the contact broke. He was directed into the middle set of seats and was grateful to be able to sit. To his bruised and aching body, the cushioned seats were like a warm, well-padded woman's soft embrace. Exhaustion threatened to take him over, yet he was afraid to close his eyes, not wanting to relive the nightmare of the previous day's events. But that didn't stop exhaustion from threatening to take over.

Morrison took another set of manacles from Alex Strode. Kneeling in front of Leon's seat, he snapped the leg irons around the outlaw's ankles. Taking the length of chain attached to the leg cuffs, he wrapped it around the metal bar under the seat and brought the loose end up and attached it to the leather belt.

Leon was secured. He didn't care. He was so tired.

Mike Shoemacher sat beside Leon, making a point of keeping his rifle handy.

Alex Strode dropped into the seats behind them. He hadn't had much sleep, having taken the first watch with Kiefer. Now, it was finally his turn to catch a nap.

Morrison sat in front of Leon, with his back to the prisoner, so he could keep his eyes on the other occupants of the car.

From the corner of his eye, Leon watched Morrison, deciding the man didn't look like he was planning on sleeping. Beyond the marshal, Leon again made eye contact with the staring youngster. He sent the child another quiet smile.

The boy's face hardened, and, to Leon, the dark-haired lad did something which seemed very prophetic. He pulled out a little toy hand gun, took careful aim at the prisoner, and pretended to shoot him.

Leon's smile deepened for an instant. It wasn't because he thought the boy's actions were amusing. On the contrary, he found them tragic. Tragic and symbolic of how far his life had gone wrong.

The loud whistle from the engine sounded, and as the train lurched into movement, Leon turned to look out the window and found himself staring into the dark brown eyes of his own reflection.

He read worry and sadness in them, but worse, he saw defeat. He closed his eyes. '*No, not defeat.*' Even in his state of exhaustion, he was not willing to concede defeat. Acceptance, maybe. Cameron had been right—again. There were going to be difficult times ahead, but maybe it was time to face up to them. Maybe it was time to stop running.

Leon sighed. *'Is this how it's going to end? All these years of avoiding the law, and now, ironically, here I am, on a train, being taken back to Wyoming to stand trial for . . . how many crimes? I've lost count.'*

He shifted in his seat, trying to find a level of comfort and yet was appreciative of his hands being secured in front of him, at last.

Mike looked hard at him. "Settle. It's a long ride to Cheyenne."

Leon nodded, then, avoiding the man's scrutiny, he returned to window-gazing.

'Maybe I need to look at this from another point of view. If this is the end of my life as an outlaw, undercover or otherwise, didn't that also mean it could be the beginning of a life as a free man? Turn the negative into a positive. Isn't that what I'm supposed to be good at? But Jack is right; I am a bit of a cynic. What about that other possibility, that one where I spend the rest of my sorry life in prison?'

And so, it began. His life was changing. Time to face up to a history of bad choices, and all he could do was hope he had the fortitude to carry it through.

The clackity-clack of the wheels, along with the rhythmic rocking of the car, had a mollifying effect on Leon. The exhausted eyes gazing back at him from the reflection began to glaze over. He leaned forward to remove his hat but was halted by the sharp pain in his ribcage.

He glanced at Mike. "Hey, Deputy, can you remove my hat for me? The brim isn't letting me sit back. Would you mind?"

"Fine." Shoemacher took the hat, but then he gave the rim and crown a thorough searching before plunking into Leon's lap. "The marshal's been real clear in his instructions."

Leon sent him a weak smile. "I'm sure he has. But don't you think that hiding a lock pick in my hatband is a bit obvious?"

Mike shrugged. "All the more reason to check it."

Leon added a sigh to his smile; lawmen showed such a lack of imagination. Besides, he loved this hat; especially the band. He had always felt a special connection to it. Now, caressing the small, ragged hole in the crown of the felt, the result of yet another close call, his thoughts drifted back to the day when that special equine red-head had come into his life . . .

Then, just as Leon wasn't thinking about it, sleep snuck up from behind and put his troubled mind to rest.

CHAPTER TEN
AWAKENING

Rocking M Ranch, Colorado.

Jack Kiefer hooted with laughter. He, his older brother, and Leon, his best friend, chased each other around the porch of the Kiefer farm house, taking turns at being the 'good guy' and the 'bad guy'.

Jack's toddler sister sat by the open front door, banging her toys on the floor of the porch as she laughed with delight every time the boys galloped past her.

The summer sun heated the porch, giving a more realistic flair to their game, but there was also a soft breeze whisping its way through the trees and grasses of the farmland, bringing with it the fresh scents of flowers and leaves and warm dirt. The windows of the home were all wide open to allow the breeze to flutter through the rooms and mingle with the warm, enticing aroma of baking bread and pies.

Mrs. Kiefer was in the kitchen, humming a tune to herself as she rolled out fresh dough. The sounds of her activity filtered out onto the porch, where the children played. They knew; soon warm bread with freshly churned butter would be their reward for keeping out from under foot. In the meantime, they played and laughed, and rejoiced at being young and full of energy.

Jack felt warm and comfortable. He was safe in this place and didn't want to leave it. This was home. But gradually, no matter how hard he fought it, the here and now started to fade. The comforting sounds of laughter, and of his mother's tuneful humming, started to mute, and Jack drifted away. He fought so hard to stay, to remain inside the warmth and the safety. But more and more, he was rising away from it, his consciousness becoming aware of the outside of his being, rather than the inside.

He could still feel the warm sun and the breeze coming through the window, and hear the birds singing to the summer day. There was the distant sound of a child cooing, and a woman humming.

Change of Leads: The Lost Shoe

The aroma of fresh baked bread still lingered, but it was all outside of him now, and what had been inside, what had been joyous and content, was gone. He had lost that warm, comfortable place that was home.

The humming stopped.

With that well-developed instinct of a mother, Jean discerned that her patient was finally awake. She made her way into his room.

He felt her sit on the side of the bed, and he tried to open his eyes, but he was so weak. He became slowly aware of a dull throbbing in his shoulder, and a muddiness to his brain that went beyond a hangover.

A gentle hand touched his arm, and he opened his eyes to slits, trying to focus. His lids felt heavy, and they didn't want to cooperate. Finally, the room stopped spinning, and he knew the face of the woman sitting by his side.

She smiled at him. "Mathew?"

"Hmm." His mouth felt dry; his throat tight.

The Angel of Mercy seemed to know this. She went to the night stand, poured some water into a cup, then lifting Jack's head, she pressed the cup to his lips and helped him drink.

Some got down his throat, some when down his chin, but he got enough to satisfy for now.

Jean put the cup back on the night stand and picking up the small towel that was there, she dried the little rivulet that had made its way down his neck and onto the pillow. She dried his mouth and then caressed his quiet face with her thumb.

She worried about him. This past week had been frantic, and she had been scared to death, every time she came into the room, that she would find a corpse, instead of a patient.

The doctor came out every morning, bringing his wife, Tricia, with him. He checked Jack's condition, helped with the first changing of the bandages and the cleansing of the wounds. He gave new instructions for the patient's care and left more medications and painkillers, including quinine, for the fever that had taken hold of Jack's body for the last three days.

Tricia stayed at the ranch for the day, helping Jean with the bathing and the bandage changing that had to be done at least three times a day. She helped the two girls with their brother, helped Jean with preparing meals, and helped with the all-round, general housekeeping chores. She was a blessing, since she knew a lot more about breaking a fever and keeping a wound clean, than anyone else in the county—except her husband. And even then, there could be some debate about that.

Late in the afternoon or early evening, David returned and did another check on the patient as well as give more instructions for his care and comfort. He and his wife usually stay for supper, then they'd head for home until the next morning, when they came out to do it all over again.

The first morning David and Tricia came to the ranch, David had been in a tiff. Jean couldn't remember when she had seen him that angry.

Apparently, Leon had suffered more rough handling at the hands of the marshal. David was tending to him and had returned to the jailhouse first thing that morning to check up on the patient and give him more laudanum, if necessary. But when he got there, he found the jail cell empty, and the posse, with their prisoner, long gone.

David had taken much of his anger and frustration out on Rick Layton, who happened to be on that shift to guard the unconscious man.

Layton took it all in stride. He knew that Morrison tended to rub people the wrong way. But the man got the job done, and right now, that was all that mattered. Let the doctor fume; it was nothing to him.

Sam did not have as thick a skin. He had been asleep in the bunkhouse at the time of the verbal bashing, and, therefore, had avoided the whole unfortunate situation. He preferred the night shift guard duty to avoid the Marsham family as much as possible. Caroline, specifically, made him feel extremely uncomfortable, and the less interaction he had with her, the better he liked it.

As the days went by, both men became increasingly bored with the guard duty, and found other ways to occupy their time. They generally tended to the outside chores, such as looking after the barns and the livestock, and leaving the household duties and care of the prisoner to the women. This arrangement suited everyone just fine. Everything got done, and nobody got under foot.

Finally, Jack's fever broke, and they'd all breathed a sigh of relief. But still, everyone knew that the open exit wound in his back needed a lot of care and attention to keep any infection at bay, and to encourage its healing.

David was anxious about those bone chips floating around but didn't dare do any probing while Jack was still in such a weakened condition. He hoped he would be able to get to them, eventually. That is, if Morrison didn't return and abscond with this patient in the middle of the night, as well.

On the afternoon that Jack had finally regained consciousness, everyone but Jean had been out, tending to other chores. Jean and the two boys had the house to themselves.

Eli was having a good day, which was normal for him. He was a happy baby and had been content to play and coo in his bassinet, between times of eating and sleeping.

When Jean heard Jack stirring, she judged that her baking could be left to carry on by itself for a while, and she came into his room to ease his fears. And her own.

She sat beside him, caressing his face, as he fought to open his eyes again.

"Jean?" It came out as barely a whisper.

"Yes. I'm here. You've had a fever, but you're doing better now."

"Hmm. Pneumonia?"

"No. Just . . . a fever."

He closed his eyes and sighed. She thought he was going back to sleep again, but then he jerked and forced his eyes open, one more time.

"Leon . . .?"

Jean hesitated. She didn't want to lie to him, but she didn't want to worry him with too much truth, either.

"He's . . . gone into town."

Jack nodded. He seemed content with that. He closed his eyes and was instantly asleep.

Jean continued to sit beside him, holding his right hand where it lay on his chest. Just being able to sit there and watch his steady, rhythmic breathing eased her concerns and gave her hope that he just might come through this, after all.

***

The next time Jack woke up, it was nighttime, and the house was dark and quiet. He lay for a while, trying to remember where he was, but without any visual reference, his mind couldn't put it together. He gradually became aware of light coming in under the closed door and tried to call out to see if anyone was up. Nothing came out. It was like he had to relearn how to use his vocal cords. He felt so weak. He really must have been sick. Something about a fever?

He worked up some saliva and swallowed to moisten his throat. He managed to croak an *'Ahh.'*, and then heard chair legs scrape on the floor and footsteps coming toward his door.

The door opened quietly, and the bright light from the lamp shone in, silhouetting a man's figure in the open doorway.

"Uws 'at?" Jack managed to slur out.

"It's Sam."

"Sam?" Things were starting to come back to him.

"Yeah." He came into the bedroom keeping the lamp turned low.

"Ow are ya', Sam?"

"I'm okay. How are you feeling?"

"Tired. Shoulder 'urts like fire. Pete's mare kick me, or somethin'?"

"No. Ah . . . I'm sorry, you're hurtin'. I don't know if I should give you anything so . . . Mr. Kiefer?"

Jack had fallen back to sleep.

***

The next time Jack awakened, it was the following morning. He could hear activity and people talking in the main part of the house. Jean's voice, he recognized. And there—that was Caroline. Then a strange voice. It sounded like a young woman, but he didn't know who it was. He tried to sit up, but that wasn't happening, and, oh man, his shoulder hurt. He couldn't move it. He brought his left hand over to investigate and found that his whole right arm was bandaged up tight against his torso, and there were layers of padding on his shoulder, both front and back.

He couldn't remember what happened; his brain was still foggy.

"Hello," he called out, still weak, but a better effort than his previous attempt during the night.

The voices and clatter coming from the kitchen area instantly quieted, and then there were two teenage girls fluttering about the bed.

"Mathew. You're awake."

"Mama said you woke up before, but we missed it."

"Girls. Be careful," Jean warned them. "Take it easy"

"Oh, yeah," Penny apologized. "Are you hurting, Mathew?"

"A little," Jack lied. He was hurting a lot. Then, aware that there was at least one stranger in the house, he added, using the alias, "Where's Peter?"

There was an awkward silence, and Jack noticed another man standing in the doorway to his room. He frowned. It wasn't Sam and it sure wasn't Cameron.

"Who are you?"

"I'm Rick Layton. I'm here to—"

Jean put a hand on Rick's arm to silence him. She couldn't help but think that the less Mathew knew of his true situation, the better. At least for now.

"Are you hungry, Mathew?"

Jack turned his attention back to Jean, but his focus was beginning to fade, and his concentration slipped away.

"Hungry?" he murmured.

"Yes." Jean moved to the bedside to pour him some water. "There's some soup simmering on the stove for whenever you feel up to eating anything." She took a small pouch out of her apron pocket and added some of its contents to the water.

"Hungry . . ." Jack wasn't sure what the word meant. "I don't know. Tired."

"All right. In the meantime, here's some water. It's important that you get fluids in you, so at least drink this."

Jean held his head up and put the cup to his lips.

The attempt was more successful this time, and Jack got most of the contents down his throat. It tasted bitter, but his body was craving fluids so much, he didn't care. He drank it, willingly.

Jean settled him back again. She placed her hand on his forehead, then his cheeks, and she smiled. The fever was gone.

Jack closed his eyes. Her hand felt cool and comforting, and he was back home again. His mother held him in a close hug, murmuring how much she loved her little Jackson.

"Is he going to be all right, Mama?" he heard Penny's voice from way off in the distance.

The answer was a soft murmuring that faded away.

And then he heard no more.

***

The next time Jack woke up, it was the evening of the same day—and he was *hungry*.

"Jean?" His voice was stronger, but still not much more than a loud whisper.

But Jean heard him and was at the door just in time to stop Jack from trying to sit up. "Oh, no, Mathew. Just wait. Cameron, can you come and give me a hand?"

Rick came forward to help, but Jean stopped him with a look, shaking her head. He shrugged and sat back down in the hallway to wait for Sam to relieve him.

Cameron came in from the dining room and joined his wife at the bedside.

"Well, good evening, Mathew. I was beginning to think you were going to sleep the whole month away."

"Have I been out of it that long?"

"Well, not quite. But it's been a while."

Cameron helped him to sit up while Jean rearranged the pillows, so he could lean back comfortably.

"Now," said Jean, "are you hungry?"

"Yes."

Jean's smile broadened. "Good. I'll get you some soup." And she headed for the kitchen.

Jack looked up at Cameron, who was thinking how worn out Jack was looking. He'd really been through the wringer.

"What happened?" Jack asked him. "I can't seem to remember anything."

Cameron smiled at him. "That's all right. We'll talk about it in the morning, when you're a little stronger."

"But where's Peter? Shouldn't he be here?"

"In the morning, Mathew. All right? We'll talk in the morning."

Jack was about to protest, but Jean showed up with a cup of soup, and its enticing aroma captured his attention.

Cameron took that opportunity to escape.

Jean smiled at his cowardice, then placed the cup on the nightstand, laid a towel across Jack's chest, and prepared to spoon him a mouthful of soup.

Jack frowned. "Ahh… can't I just feed myself?"

Jean settled back and smiled. "Well, I don't know. Can you?"

Jack accepted the challenge. Determined to accomplish this simple task on his own, he took the spoon in his left hand and dipped it into the soup. It felt foreign to him, like his arm wasn't going to do what his brain was telling it to. The spoon shook and refused to stay level as he attempted to transport the broth from the cup to his mouth. By the time the spoon reached its destination, there was very little soup left in it. Most of it was on the towel. Jack's frown deepened, but he was determined to try again.

Jean waited for him to come to the inevitable conclusion. She had tended to enough sick or injured adult males, to know that she couldn't push him. He would have to figure this one out on his own.

He dipped the spoon in again, and it started its shaky journey toward his mouth. This time, the utensil didn't even get half way when Jack's fingers weakened and lost their grip. The spoon with the soup, ended up in his lap.

Jack groaned. "Oh, all right. You win. But will you close the door? The last thing I need is for the girls to see me being hand fed like a baby."

"Mr. Layton. Would you mind closing the door for now?"

"Yeah, all right," came the reply from the hallway, and the door quietly closed.

"Now, who's Mr. Layton, again?"

"Mathew . . ." Jean admonished him.

Jack sighed. "Yeah, I know. In the morning."

***

Sam spent another long, quiet night, sitting in the hallway outside the bedroom door, trying to stay awake. In some ways, the night shift was the hardest to get through because there was absolutely nothing to do. He tried reading, but the light from the oil lamp was so inconsistent, it made that pastime nearly impossible. He tried writing a letter to his mother, but that proved to be equally as frustrating. Finally, he folded his arms, leaned back against the wall, and let himself doze.

He allowed his mind to wander and found himself thinking about the choices he'd made and the consequences of them.

'I sure hope I can make things up to Caroline. Geesh, she still won't talk to me. At least her parents are a bit more understanding, otherwise this duty would be impossible." He sighed. *'Still, I do like Caroline. I was kind'a hopin' . . . ah well, I don't suppose that's too likely now . . .'*

When Morrison told him to stay behind and share guard duty with Layton, Sam had been relieved. He had not been looking forward to escorting Napoleon Nash anywhere. Sam still found the man intimidating, and Leon made no effort to hide his disdain for Sam.

Jack Kiefer was a much more amiable person, even if he was what Morrison called a "cold-blooded killer". Sam couldn't help it; he found himself liking the blond outlaw, and he felt terrible that the man's life had been put in such jeopardy because of him.

'If either of the outlaws had to get shot, why couldn't it have been the dark-haired conman? That would have been a whole lot easier to live with.'

The young man sighed with boredom.

He spotted a spider creeping along the wall toward him, so, for lack of anything else to do, he gently plucked the arachnid off the wall and put it outside. He then returned to his chair, folded his arms and sighed again.

'Ho hum. I suppose I could think about what I'm going to do next. Kiefer will be strong enough to move to Wyoming soon, and then

I'll have some choices to make. It's a pretty fair bet that I won't be staying on here. Damn, and Caroline's so pretty, too . . ."

***

The next morning started early. Jean was up first and got the stove going. Her current routine consisted of heating up the water for coffee and for Jack's bath, then, while that was happening, she settled into the day-nursery with Eli and gave him his morning feeding.

This was Sam's signal to head out to the barn to care for the livestock and the dogs, who were always happy to see him. This was a nice bonus, considering the cold shoulder half the Marsham family gave him these days. After feeding the animals, he then headed to the bunkhouse to get some sleep. He always tried to head outdoors before Caroline came down, as he wasn't ready to face her yet.

Cameron and the girls would come down shortly after Jean and get breakfast going for everyone. It was Penny's job to take something out to Sam, since Caroline wasn't quite ready to face him yet, either. Sam was still in the 'doghouse' as far as she was concerned.

With the coming of summer, Cameron planned to head up to the northern pastures to check on the foals and calves. The yearlings needed to be separated from the herds, branded and sorted, and decisions made about their fate. Many of the animals would be heading to market soon.

It was a busy time of year and Cameron missed having Sam as a hand. But, obviously, Sam had a previous commitment, so most of the work was falling to Cameron, himself. Fortunately, with classes being finished now, and Jack apparently out of danger, the girls were both able and willing to accompany their father on a day of riding the range.

David and Tricia would be coming out later that morning, so Cameron waited until they had the doctor's diagnosis on Jack, before leaving Jean and Tricia shorthanded in looking after the household. There was a lot of juggling of chores these days.

Jack had been awake for some time and could hear the household beginning to stir, but he was in no hurry to announce his awareness. It was warm and comfortable in bed and, though his shoulder ached, it wasn't bad enough to cause him distress. His brain still felt muddy, so he assumed he was on quite a dosage of painkillers. But that was all right; he probably needed them. He lay there with his eyes closed and allowed his mind to wander.

He still couldn't remember anything about what had happened. *'Who is this Layton guy? And where the hell is Leon? And what exactly happened ta' me, ta' keep me stuck in this bed at the Marshams' ranch? This weren't no kick from a horse. I've been shot up often enough ta' know what it feels like, and this ain't no little graze, neither. Whoever done it, meant business. But, if that's the case, why ain't I in some jail cell instead 'a bein' nice and comfy here?*

A quiet knock on his door brought him out of his musings, and he forced his eyes open.

Jean entered, carrying a bowl and a towel, and placed them on the night stand while she helped Jack sit up. The fact that she could accomplish this without Cameron's help, was an indication of how much stronger the patient was this morning. While she rearranged his pillows, Jack protested his need for such attention. But Jean ignored him. She sat down and prepared to feed him, despite his lack of enthusiasm.

Jack groaned. "I'm really not hungry."

"Too bad," Jean responded, but with a smile in her voice. "Just eat a little. You need to get your strength up."

Jack nodded and swallowed the spoonful of oatmeal headed his way. He had to admit that once the warmth of it hit his stomach, his appetite picked up, and he was able to put away a good portion of the bowlful.

"That went well." Jean picked up the towel and made sure there were no dribbles of oatmeal on his chin. "Let's hope the next endeavor goes just as smoothly."

She stood up and left the room, leaving a suspicious Jack Kiefer wondering what the next endeavor was going to be.

A few minutes later, his worst fears were confirmed when Jean returned carrying all the items she would need for a sponge bath. She deftly closed the bedroom door with her foot and began to go about her business of setting everything up for the inevitable.

Jack grasped the blankets with his left hand, pulling them snugly up around himself in a defensive response to an uncomfortable situation.

"What are you doing?" he asked, though he knew darn well what she was doing.

"The doctor is coming out shortly to check up on you and change your bandages. You need to be cleaned up before he arrives." She put a hand on her hip and gave him her best 'stern mother' look. "You're not going to give me a problem with this, are you?"

Jack gave her his best 'charming scoundrel' smile. "I don't need a bath, Jean."

"Now, don't get all bashful." She raised an eyebrow. "You've been in this bed for close to ten days now. Do you really think this is the first bath I've given you?"

Jack groaned, and he felt himself blushing. Then an even worse thought occurred to him. "The girls weren't helping you, were they?"

Jean gave him a look. "Really, Mathew, of course not."

Jack sighed with relief.

Then Jean added, "I did need some help while you were unconscious, though, but then it was just the doctor's wife."

"Oh. The doctor's wife being older and matronly."

Jean smiled. "Well, actually . . . no. She's twenty-four and quite pretty."

Jack groaned again, his embarrassment growing.

Jean smiled at him, and he was beginning to think she was enjoying this.

"Oh, come on, now," she said. "You can't tell me that a young, handsome man like yourself has never been undressed in front of a lady before."

"Well, sure I have. Plenty'a times, but I didn't know them." He blushed even deeper as he realized what he had just said. "I mean . . . ah . . ."

Jean laughed. "I'm no maiden. Do you think I don't know about young men's appetites? Come on, let's get this done. We'll start out easy, and when we get to the more sensitive areas, I'll let you do that yourself. Okay?"

Seeing no way out of this, he agreed. Then, just like with breakfast, once he had accepted the inevitable, it was refreshing to get cleaned up.

Jean kept her promise and was discreet at the appropriate moments, and the bath was completed without Jack suffering too much more embarrassment. She even helped him to shave, not wanting him to cut his own throat, due to his still-weakened condition.

Jean's timing was impeccable. Just as she was cleaning up, they heard the dogs start a loud chorus of barking to announce David and Tricia's arrival.

***

Midnight and Karma, who were in the front pasture outside Jack's window, trotted and danced along the fence line, in their usual morning greeting to the arriving horse and buggy.

Jack admitted that seeing Karma in the pasture had put his worries at ease to some degree. If Karma was still here, then surely Leon could not be too far away.

Within moments, the new arrivals entered the house, and Jack heard Cameron and Jean greeting them.

"Good morning. Our patient is doing much better today."

"Excellent," Jack heard a man answer. "Is he eating?"

"Yes," Jean confirmed. "I've been able to get some food into him."

"Good." And then the owner of the voice entered the bedroom and greeted Jack. "Good morning."

Jack nodded a greeting. He was surprised at how young the man looked. Not exactly his idea of a typical country doctor. And Jean had been right; his wife was young and quite pretty. Jack's discomfort returned.

"I'm Doctor David Gibson," the doctor introduced himself. "This is my wife, Tricia. We've been tending to you these past couple of weeks."

"You've done a lot more than just tend to him," Jean said. "He saved your life, Mathew. I shudder to think what would have happened if he hadn't been here."

Jack nodded. "Ah, thank you." He couldn't think of anything else to say.

"You're welcome." The doctor smiled, putting on his bedside manner. "It was touch and go there for a while, but I'm glad to see you're looking so much better. I want to change your bandages and see how things are healing up. How does your shoulder feel?"

"It hurts."

"Yes. I'm not surprised. I'll leave some more morphine. It will take the edge off the pain and help you to rest. In the meantime, let's get these bandages off."

With help from Jean and Tricia, Jack sat up straighter, and David began to unwrap the bandage that secured Jack's right arm to his chest.

"Do you know what happened to you?" David asked, as he worked.

"No."

David nodded. "What's the last thing you remember?"

"Ah . . . it was early mornin'. My friend and I were in the barn. We were discussin' our travel plans. My horse was lame, so things had been delayed. Then, I woke up in here."

"Okay. You don't remember coming out of the barn, or anything that happened after that?"

Jack shook his head. "No."

"Well, I'm sure it comes as no surprise to you that you were shot. It was a Winchester 44-40."

Jack felt his heart sink. He knew that wasn't good.

David noted his subtle reaction to the news. "The entry wound is not too bad. I managed to get it cleaned out and stitched up without much trouble. But as the bullet entered your shoulder, it started to spin, and it tore up a great deal of muscle tissue and badly fractured your shoulder blade before exiting out your back. Okay, this is the last of the bandage coming off. Try to keep your arm still, all right? It's important that you don't move it."

Jack nodded.

Tricia helped to hold his arm in place, so her husband could continue with his examination.

Cameron, who had been doing some paperwork at the dining room table, could hear the direction the conversation was going and decided his presence in the bedroom might be desirable. Jack was not going to like what he would be hearing.

"Now, the exit wound is another story," David continued. "I cleaned it out as best I could under the circumstances. But you were in a great deal of distress, so I couldn't do as much as I would have liked. I got all the foreign material out of the wound, but there still may be some bone chips floating around in there. That may not be a problem, or they may gradually work their way out on their own. It would create an abscess and it would be painful, but manageable. However, another infection could set in, and we would have to open your shoulder back up and try to remove the chips surgically. You would have to be hospitalized."

Jack closed his eyes and groaned. This was not sounding good.

David hurried on. "In the meantime, we must keep this wound in your back covered, and very clean. It's wide open, as there was nothing left to stitch together. Do you understand?"

"Yeah, I think so, Doc. In simple language, this is gonna take a long time ta' heal."

"Yes, it is. And Jack, I'm sorry, but you may never get full use of this arm back. There was too much damage."

Jack's throat tightened. He was dimly aware that David had used his real name, but he had already concluded that this man knew who he was. Of course, it was the diagnosis the doctor gave him that put a knot in his stomach. He felt a hand on his leg and looked up to meet Jean's gentle eyes. He flinched, as David began to clean the wound in his back, but he welcomed the pain, and focusing on that helped him to bring his emotions under control.

"Are you sure . . . about that . . . Doc?"

"Well, there is always a chance that you could get a lot of your mobility back. But you will have to be diligent. As I said, it must be kept clean until it heals over, and then you can't move it while the bone is healing. After that, I know of some exercises you can do to get the flexibility back in the muscles and tendons. But I won't lie to you, Jack. It's going to be a long, difficult road." David sighed and, as an afterthought, added, "And I don't know how long you're going to be in my care."

Jack sat quietly for a moment while David finished cleaning the wound and began to re-bandage the shoulder. He felt weak and sick, and more than a little scared.

"Where's Leon?" He was met with silence. "Cameron? Where's Leon?" A tingling dread settled over him, and it felt like his lungs had collapsed. "He's not . . . dead . . . is he?"

"No," Both Cameron and Jean answered together.

"Well, then, where is he? His mare is still here."

"He gave Karma to us," Cameron informed him. "He didn't want the marshal to take her off this ranch. I guess he'd rather we keep her for him, instead of her being sold. As for where he is right now, I've been in touch with Taggard Murphy."

Jack nodded at the mention of their friend's name.

"According to him, your partner was taken directly to Cheyenne, Wyoming. Apparently, they have the most secure jailhouse in the territory, so that's where Marshal Morrison wanted him to be. He's had a preliminary hearing, but the judge did not grant him bail, even though I offered to put it up, and Sheriff Murphy guaranteed his presence when his trial date arrived. Unfortunately, it seems the judge felt it was too big a risk that Napoleon Nash would make a run for it."

Jack closed his eyes again. "Any word from the governor?"

"Not that I've heard, but it's early days yet."

David finished up his ministrations, and Jack settled back onto the pillows, feeling lost and wrung out from all this bad news. Leon must be going nuts and pacing a trench in his cell by now.

"How?" he asked. "How did . . . Marshal Morrison?" Cameron nodded. "How did he know we were here?"

"Apparently, he'd been planning this for a long time," Cameron explained. "He'd had someone watching the ranch for close to a year, just waiting for you and Peter to show up."

"Who?" Jack's brain was in a whirl. "Who could have been watching you for that long, without you noticing them?"

Cameron looked shame-faced. "I'm sorry, Mathew. It was Sam."

"Sam?"

Cameron nodded. "Apparently, he deliberately set himself up for me to hire him here, all with the intention of spying on us and reporting back to Morrison about everything that went on."

"Ah, geesh. He seemed like a real nice kid, too."

"Well, he is," Cameron responded. "If it makes any difference, he feels bad about the way things ended up and his part in it. I don't think Caroline is ever going to talk to him again, though. All of this has been hard on the girls."

"I'm sorry, Cameron. We shouldn't have come here."

"I think that's enough talk, for now." David had been watching Jack closely during this discussion, and his pale, clammy complexion made it clear that his patient was about done in. "Jean, would you mix up some of the morphine for him, please?"

"Certainly."

CHAPTER ELEVEN
CONSEQUENCES

Rick Layton arrived from town shortly after the Gibsons, but had gone unnoticed by everyone, except the dogs. When he entered the house, the two Marsham girls were sitting at the table, looking distressed, so Rick poured himself a cup of coffee and joined them, hoping he could help cheer them up. He didn't have much luck and soon it became apparent why, as he began to pick up some of the conversation drifting from the bedroom.

To say that Deputy Layton felt bad about shooting the Kansas Kid would be an overstatement. It had been the job he was hired to do, and he was darn good at it. So, no regrets. However, he did realize that, for some reason, this family considered the outlaws to be friends, and this was a difficult time for them. It was especially hard for the girls to know that their friend was having to hear such bad news, not only about himself, but also about his partner

Though Rick was not someone who would normally be welcome in their home, considering the role he played in their friends' capture, he was an officer of the law and was treated with respect. To their credit, the girls were trying their best. Sam was the one who got the brunt of their disapproval.

So, having been given the task of guarding Jack while he was still laid up, Rick did his best to fit into the routine of this household. Though Morrison had not suggested it, Rick tried to be as helpful as he could to the family he was intruding upon, and they seemed to appreciate his predicament.

Jack would probably be ready to move soon, but where he would ultimately end up, Layton had no idea. He knew Leon was in Cheyenne, so Jack would probably end up in Morrison's home town of Rawlins, to await his trial.

Morrison insisted on the two prisoners being kept apart, and little to no information was to be given to either one of them, concerning the condition of the other. "Keep them off balance," Morrison ordered. "If their minds are occupied worrying about each other, they won't be as inclined to think up means of escaping." It all sounded good, and maybe it would work.

Jean came out of the bedroom, smiled a greeting at the group around the table, and carried on into the kitchen. They could hear her making some preparations, and then she disappeared back into the bedroom.

Rick returned to waiting.

***

Jean handed the cup of medicated water to David, who added some more ingredients from his own supplies.

"Here, Jack," he said. "I want you to drink all of this. It'll help you sleep. And that's the best thing for you, right now."

He barely noticed the doctor, as he took the cup from his hand. "Yeah, all right, Doc."

He drank down the contents and settled into the bed again. He turned his head toward the open window and could just see their horses, Midnight and Karma, out in the field. They were contentedly grazing and enjoying one another's company.

Very quickly, his eyelids began to feel heavy, and his body melted into the mattress. He wasn't even aware of the other people leaving the room and closing the door, as the heavy sedative took effect. He continued to gaze out the window, unable to take his eyes off their horses. He could feel the warmth of the mid-morning sun, giving a promise of the hot summer days to come, while the soft, aromatic breeze fluttered through the curtains.

He was a child again, hollering with laughter, as he chased his older brother, and his best friend, around the porch, anticipating a treat of warm, freshly baked bread with creamy, churned butter, as he drifted off to sleep . . .

***

When Jack awoke next, he had no idea how much time had passed. Was it the same day, the next day, or a week later? There was nothing in his conscious mind that enabled him to judge the passage of time. He was confused, with some vague memory of bad news. There was a tightness in his throat and chest, an anxiety that weighed heavy upon him and grew as he became more and more awake.

There were no sounds outside his room and in his confused state, the silence was eerie and ominous.

He raised himself into a sitting position and was momentarily surprised at how easily he accomplished this. He pushed the blanket down, swung his legs off the bed, and found himself facing the open window. The first thing he saw was the two horses peacefully grazing in the pasture. He sat on the bed, watching them for a few moments. They looked so content, happy even, in the comfort of their shared camaraderie. It created an aching in Jack's heart, a yearning that he couldn't quite understand. All he knew was that he had to get out of here; he had to leave—*now.*

Carefully, he stood up, testing his legs and balance.

"Damn," he mumbled, as his head spun in different directions.

The dizziness caused him to take it slow, and with his left hand, he held onto anything that presented itself, as he made his way to the dresser. He saw his boots and hat by the chair, but no gun belt. He tugged open one of the drawers and his clothes were there, waiting for him. He took them out and sat down on the chair, breathing heavily and fighting the dizziness that wouldn't leave him alone. He felt cold and clammy, but he would be all right once he got some clothes on.

It was a slow process. Getting dressed, with just one good arm, had to be done in stages. He had to stop on a regular basis to quiet his shaking limbs and push the dizziness back from his brain. He needed to focus on what he had to do.

Finally, after an eternity, he had everything on to the best of his ability. He pulled his left arm through the sleeve of his shirt, but the right sleeve, he could only drape over his shoulder. He tried to button it up but couldn't quite manage the dexterity needed for what he would normally consider a simple task.

He forgot his hat.

Moving to the window, he managed to open it wide enough to maneuver himself over the sill and drop the short distance to the ground. He landed on his feet, but his knees gave way beneath him and he went all the way down. He landed sharply on his right shoulder, and gasped as the pain, like daggers, stabbed into his brain. Nausea reigned over him, and blackness threatened to envelop his senses. He lay on the ground, breathing heavily and fighting the physical symptoms that tried to prevent him from completing his task, whatever that task was.

The two horses stopped grazing and watched him with interest. They knew who he was, but he wasn't behaving normally, and that aroused their curiosity.

After a few minutes, Jack pulled himself to his feet and inched his way across the bit of yard separating the house from the field. He got to the fence and slid in between the planks, so that he was inside the pasture, and using the fence for support, he aimed for the gate that was next to the road.

The horses, thinking that he was going to take them into the barn for a good feeding of grain, followed him, then passed him and waited by the gate for him to catch up.

Jack spied the halters, with their attached lead shanks, hanging off the fence post. He took one of them off the post and turned to his horse as he grabbed a handful of mane to steady himself.

"Whoa, big guy." His voice was weak and distant. "You know me. We're just gonna go for a ride, okay?"

Midnight snorted and nuzzled into the shirt.

Jack gasped when the normally soft muzzle became a hard, probing club hitting against his shoulder, looking for attention. He pushed the large, black head away from him but still gave the neck a reassuring pat.

"It's okay. Just don't do that again."

With only the one good hand, it took some effort to get the halter onto Midnight's head, but he finally managed it. Midnight stood quietly while Jack looped the lead shank around his horse's neck and tied the loose end to the halter.

That done, he opened the gate and led his horse out.

He heard Rufus barking, and sure enough, Peanut and Pebbles were quick to join in.

Jack knew he had to get moving because the alarm had been sounded, and he wasn't going to get stopped now. He lined Midnight up against the fence, stepped onto the lower plank, and hoisted himself across his horse's back. He again grimaced with the pain, but that only drove him on further. He swung his right leg over, grabbed hold of the mane, and pushed the gelding into a trot, heading down the road and away from the ranch.

Jack was vaguely aware of someone yelling behind him, of the dogs barking, and then a rifle shot, and a woman screaming. He didn't hang around for any more. He leaned forward, against Midnight's neck, and tried to push him into a faster gait.

"C'mon, Middy, go. C'mon, boy . . ."

Midnight was nervous and confused. His human was not acting as he normally did, and it made him hesitate to pick up speed for fear that Jack would fall off.

Then Karma was beside him, and holding her head and tail up with this new adventure, she quickened the pace. Midnight joined with her, and together they took off at a gallop down the road and away from the yelling and commotion behind them.

It was all Jack could do to hang on. He had no control over where his horse was going, but they were going there fast, and that's all that mattered. All he had to do was stay on. He leaned against Midnight's neck, knowing that if he tried to sit up, he would lose balance and fall off. His right arm was trapped underneath him, but his left hand clutched the mane, the speed of the gallop making his eyes water, and the ground blur in their passing.

They must have continued for a few miles at that breakneck pace, but with Jack not encouraging him, Midnight gradually began to slow down.

Karma circled around and came back to him, preferring to stay with her buddy than continue to gallop on alone.

Jack lay motionless along Midnight's back, his face buried in the handful of mane that he still desperately hung onto.

***

The quiet, warm day was slipping into mid-afternoon when Jean and Tricia took a break from the gardening to settle down with some tea on the front porch.

"Oh, what a day," Jean said. "I am ready for a quiet evening."

"Yes." Tricia sipped her tea then leaned back with a sigh and closed her eyes. "At least supper is simmering. Thank goodness for left-overs."

Jean chuckled. "They do make life easier, don't they? I hope David won't mind the same meal two days in a row."

Tricia laughed. "David will eat anything that's put in front of him, especially after a long day. He'll be fine."

Silence took over the porch, until Tricia sat up and took some more tea. "When will Cameron and Caroline be back from checking the new calves?"

"Later this evening. We don't need to wait supper on them. As soon as David gets here, we'll eat. I know you'll both be ready for your own beds early enough."

"Yes." Tricia stifled a yawn. "I do hope Jack doesn't give you any problems during the night. I know David sedated him, but sometimes they still get restless."

"Don't worry about it. We'll be fine."

***

Sam and Rick were in the barn, discussing the game plan for that night and the following day, when Penny joined them. Her intent was to invite them to the porch for tea, but she was interrupted by Rufus breaking out into loud barking. The other two dogs instantly joined in, even though they'd didn't know what they were barking at.

Rick rolled his eyes. "Sounds like that old hound of yours has flushed out another rabbit."

Penny frowned. "No. This is a more serious bark. There must be someone coming."

"Hmm," was Rick's only response.

He walked out of the barn to check up on the cause of the commotion, but when he got to the yard and looked down the lane, he stopped with an uncharacteristic abruptness. What he saw made his blood run cold.

Cursing, he ran into the barn and grabbed his rifle. Sam and Penny, alerted by his agitated return, were quick to follow him back outside.

"What?" Sam asked. "What's the matter?"

"Damn that Kiefer. As soon as I get that bastard in my sights, I'm gonna kill him."

He ran into the middle of the yard, where he knew he could line up a clear shot, then brought his rifle to bare.

By this time, the two women on the porch were alerted and coming down the steps.

The dogs continued to bark their warning.

Penny, terrified by what Rick had said, ran, with heart in throat, after the deputy. She had no plan in mind and no idea how she was going to do it, but she was determined to protect her friend from further harm.

Jack was just getting going. Still at a trot and moving away in a straight line, he made an easy target, especially for a marksman like Rick. He lined Jack up in his sights, held his breath, and squeezed the trigger.

Suddenly, Penny was all he could see. He cursed again, and with a speed that only comes from reflex, he jerked the rifle barrel up just as the bullet exploded from the muzzle.

Jean screamed in a terror she had never known before, and she ran to her daughter. Penny collapsed on the ground in a semi-faint. All her strength had left her with the realization of what she had done, and what had almost happened. Rick was white as a ghost, his fear and shock coming out in anger.

"What the hell's the matter with you?" he yelled her. "I could have killed you." Then he ran for the barn to saddle his horse and get after the escaping prisoner.

Within minutes, Rick had his horse saddled and was swinging aboard. With one more angst-laden glance at the women huddled in a terrified embrace of skirts and sobs, he kicked the animal to a gallop and headed down the road in hot pursuit.

The first thing Rick thought, as he galloped down the road, was that he could use Alex's expertise just now. He was a much better tracker than Rick was. However, after he had covered approximately half a mile, Rick began to relax, as he realized that Jack was not going to be difficult to follow. The outlaw obviously wasn't thinking; he was simply running, in a straight line, down the only road.

After another mile of easily following the galloping tracks of the two horses, Rick pulled up and dismounted. He had noticed something else on the soft, churned up dirt of the road, and decided that it needed a closer examination. He squatted and put his finger to a small dot of dark moisture that had settled upon the dusty track.

Bringing his finger up for inspection, he smiled and shook his head. Sure enough, the tip of his finger was red; Jack had started bleeding again. This was going to be easy.

He remounted and carried on at a casual lope. He watched the ground in front of him, on the outside chance that Kiefer might gather his wits and make a sudden turn off the road and head for the hills. But it didn't happen.

On the contrary, it wasn't long before the hoof prints indicated a slackening of the pace, and Rick took his eyes off the ground and started searching the road ahead, expecting to make visual contact at any moment.

Keeping his rifle at the ready, he trotted around a bend, and then sure enough, he spotted the two horses up ahead.

They had decided that galloping on a hot day wasn't all that much fun anymore and were off on the side of the road, casually nibbling on some greenery.

Jack still lay on the back of his horse, his right arm pinned underneath him, and his left lying along the animal's neck, clutching a handful of mane.

Rick brought his horse down to a walk and slowly approached the two loose animals.

"Kiefer," he called, quietly. "Kiefer, can you hear me?"

There was no response.

Rick saw blood soaking into the back of Jack's shirt, where the wound had been irritated and started seeping again. He assumed that the wound in the front was doing the same thing.

He could already hear the good doctor fuming about this one. Rick slid down from the saddle, and keeping the rifle at the ready, quietly walked toward the two horses.

Both animals shot their heads up and stopped munching. They barely knew this human, and they were suspicious of is approach.

"Whoa, easy there, big fella," Rick soothed the black gelding.

Midnight arched his neck and blew heavily through his nostrils. Karma skittishly danced away from the man. Midnight started to join her, when Rick made a quick grab for the halter and stopped him in his tracks.

Jack started to slide off, so in a quick motion, Rick swung his right shoulder against the prone man and pushed him back into position.

Jack groaned quietly, and Rick shook him on the left shoulder.

"Kiefer, can you hear me?"

Jack's eyes opened to slits, but he didn't answer. He looked pale and was damp with sweat.

"If you can hear me, just hold on. I'm going to get you back to the ranch, all right? So just keep holding on like you have been, and everything will be okay."

Rick turned and put his rifle back in its scabbard, then untying the loose end of the lead shank on Midnight's halter, he organized the two horses, so he could get remounted. Once settled, he set off back to the Rocking M.

Karma watched them walk off, and with a snort and a toss of her dark red mane, she decided she might as well join them.

Rick pulled Midnight up to walk along beside his horse, so he could keep a steadying hand on Jack's shoulder. The deputy had calmed down considerably since his vow to 'kill that bastard', the next time he had the outlaw in his sights. He had been angry more at himself than at Jack, and now that the situation was back under control, he felt less retaliatory.

His initial anger had been justified, though, since he knew that Morrison would have his hide staked out in the sun, if he had lost his prisoner. With the boredom settling in from the extended, uneventful guard duty, Rick had fallen into the very trap that Morrison had repeatedly warned them about: Don't underestimate these two outlaws.

Jack was badly wounded and being kept under heavy sedation most of the time. He barely sit up on his own, let alone get on a horse.

Rick had become complacent and nearly paid a heavy price for it. Not only in the loss of their prisoner, but in very nearly shooting an innocent young woman, to cover up his mistake.

In hindsight, Rick realized he should have been more on his guard. With the news Jack had received that morning, it was only logical the man would be not only upset, but also scared to death at his own future prospects. Facing the real possibility of twenty years in prison, a crippled arm, and his friend and partner already incarcerated for who knew how long, it suddenly all made perfect sense that Jack would react unfavorably to the situation.

Rick grudgingly admitted to a certain measure of admiration for Jack's display of determination. The amount of morphine the doctor had given him should have knocked him out for a good twenty-four hours. Yet, somehow, he had managed to dress himself, crawl out an open window, mount his horse, and make a run for it. It didn't matter that he didn't get far or that he was running blind, with no real plan in mind. Just the fact that he had managed to get as far as he did, was downright amazing.

Rick was never going to underestimate Jack Kiefer again.

***

At the ranch house, Penny sat on the porch steps with her mother's arms around her. She had calmed down to some degree but was still quietly crying.

"I'm sorry, Mama. I'm sorry." She knew the terror her actions had caused. "But I didn't want to see Mathew get hurt again."

Tricia stood by them, shading her eyes as she gazed down the lane. "Here they come. It looks like Mr. Kiefer is unconscious. Thank goodness, David will be here soon."

Rick brought the horses up to the steps and dismounted. Tricia and Sam hurried over to them, then all gathered around Midnight and Jack, assessing the situation.

Jack still clutched the handful of dark mane, refusing, even after passing out, to relinquish his hold.

Rick tried to pry Jack's fingers open but was unsuccessful.

"Sam, get my knife out of the saddle bag, will ya'? It's on this side."

Sam rummaged through the bag, until he came out with a hunting knife that was tucked away in a sheath. He pulled it out and handed it to the deputy.

Rick commenced to cut through the long hair until he had Kiefer's hand free. Returning the knife to Sam, he pulled Jack off the horse. Sam scrambled to grab hold of Jack's legs as he came off, and both men carried the unconscious outlaw up the steps and into the house.

Tricia came right behind them, but it took Jean and Penny a little longer, as Jean couldn't quite bring herself to let go of her daughter. By the time the Marsham ladies had joined everyone else in the bedroom, Jack was laid out on the bed, his boots and the soiled shirt had been removed, and Tricia was assessing the new damage done to his shoulder.

She removed some of the bandaging but didn't want to do more than examine the situation and stop whatever bleeding there might be, until her husband arrived. A look at the blood-covered material she had pulled away, made it obvious that the injuries had been torn open again. Tricia pursed her lips. David was not going to be happy about this.

***

Twenty minutes later, when David drove the horse and buggy into the yard, he knew something was wrong. For one thing, there were three horses helping themselves to the pedals off Jean's rose bushes, and for another, the dogs were more agitated than usual in their formal greeting.

David tied his horse to the rail by the porch, grabbed his bag from the seat, and hurried into the house. He went into the bedroom, and his jaw dropped at the sight that met his eyes.

"Oh, good heavens. What in the world happened?"

Tricia looked up with relief.

David sighed and shook his head in dismay as he headed to the bed. "How did he manage to do that? I had him sedated to the limit. He should have stayed down until morning."

"Yeah," Rick said. "That's the mistake I presumed to make, as well."

"Okay, everybody out," David ordered. "Except you, Tricia."

"Yes, I know."

"And Jean, you know the drill. Some warm water and soap, if you would."

Jean nodded and left to attend to this, leaving David wondering why she looked so pale. Then he leaned over Jack and slapped him, sharply, across the face.

"Jack. Jack, can you hear me?"

Jack groaned and opened his eyes to slits. He blearily took in his surroundings then started a mild protest and tried to push David away from him. David pushed him back and held him down. Jack was too weak to carry on the fight.

"No, Jack. Settle. You've torn out all your stitches. I'll have to redo them. It's going to hurt, but I don't dare give you any more morphine. Just take it easy, and we'll get it done."

Fortunately for Jack, he simply passed out again.

***

During the procedure, Tricia filled her husband in on what had transpired. David became increasingly frustrated with the futility of the whole episode.

An hour later, everything was patched up, and the patient rested in bed as though nothing had happened. David sat by the bedside, sighing with disappointment and discouragement, while Tricia stood behind him with her arms wrapped around his neck. He patted her hand, taking comfort in her presence.

"Why did he have to do it?" he muttered, more to himself than his wife. "Why couldn't he just listen to me? All he's done is make things worse for himself."

"I know," she kissed her husband on the top of his head. "He was running scared. He probably didn't even know where he was going, or why. He was just running."

"Maybe I told him too much. Why do I have to be so brutally honest with everyone?"

"Don't start second-guessing yourself. You've always told your patients the truth, especially if it's bad. They need to know what's going on, if they're going to be able to deal with it."

"Yes, but not to scare them so much that they run themselves to death."

"Come on, David. You can't make choices for everybody else. You have to let him accept some of the consequences for the decisions he's made. There's a lot more going on here than just what you had to tell him."

"Hmm." David still couldn't help feeling somewhat responsible.

Both outlaws were proving to be quite a challenge. David came to the realization that their priorities were different from other people's, so their behavior tended to be desperate and unpredictable. Though he still didn't hold with Morrison's abuse of his prisoners, David began to appreciate the lawman's attitude.

A knock came to the door and Rick entered.

"Are you finished in here, Doc?"

"Yes, for now."

"Good." Rick proceeded to the other side of the bed. He took Jack's left hand, snapped on a set of handcuffs, and then attached the other end of them to the ironworks of the headboard. He smiled at David and Tricia, then walked out of the room.

He meant it; he was never going to underestimate Jack Kiefer again.

***

Early evening settled in. Those people who needed to return to town had long since departed. Rick gave Sam strict instructions to not—except under the direst of circumstances—release Jack Kiefer from the handcuffs. Even at that, the deputy felt some trepidation at leaving the outlaw in the younger man's custody. But Sam had not let them down yet, and it would be on that young man's head if he did so now.

Cameron and Caroline had not returned yet, but this wasn't surprising. They would have had a busy day, and there were still a couple of hours of daylight left. They would be home before dark.

The light supper that had been simmering was ready to eat, but after the stressful events of the day, no one was particularly hungry. Jean settled herself in her rocking chair with Eli for a few quiet moments on the front porch. She had a relaxing cup of tea by her side, her son cooing in her arms, and a peaceful, pleasant evening, to help wash away the fears of that afternoon.

Sam sat at the dining room table, writing a letter to his mother, while Penny finished up in the kitchen.

When Penny was done with her chores, she hesitated in the hallway, making doubly sure that the other occupants of the house had their attentions elsewhere. Satisfied, she crept, silent as a mouse, into Jack's room.

She stood for a few minutes, just inside the door and watched him sleep. Her pulse raced with the anticipation of what she intended to do. She couldn't believe how nervous she was. Her breathing quickened, and her heart beat so fast, she was certain it was going to jump up into her throat and strangle her.

She crept her way over to his bed, wiping her sweaty palms on her skirt. She almost wanted to call the whole thing off, but she knew she would regret it, if she did. If she was going to do this, now was her best chance.

She ran her eyes along his left arm, up to the hand laying, palm up, on the pillow, and took note of the shiny metal cuff encircling his wrist. She felt a strange stirring inside, and it scared her. That wasn't right, was it? To feel arousal over her friend being shackled? Everything she thought she knew about what nice girls felt, told her that this was a bad thing. But she couldn't help it. There was something exciting about it—something dangerous.

She was so nervous her teeth started to chatter. She decided, she better do it now, or she was going to faint. She knelt on the bed and leaned forward to look at Jack, straight in the face. She wanted to be sure that he was soundly asleep.

She thought of his brilliant blue eyes and his gentle smile, and then she leaned into him, closed her eyes, and gently planted her lips upon his.

The emotion of the contact took her breath away, and she had to back off for an instant or be strangled by it. She opened her eyes and gazed at his restful face and then leaned in and kissed him again.

She had more control this time, and she savored the moment, taking in his scent, feeling the tickle of his breath on her nose, the softness of his lips pressing against hers, and beyond them, the hardness of his teeth.

She lingered there for a heartbeat and then, gradually backed off. Her whole being tingled with the excitement of the moment, and the thrill of having accomplished her mission. She smiled softly and sat back onto the bed, gently caressing his right hand.

"What are you doing in there?"

Penny jumped, then sent a defensive scowl in Sam's direction. "Nothing. Just sitting with my friend for a while. Is that all right with you?"

"Well, yeah," Sam shuffled, feeling embarrassed. "You just should 'a let me know, is all. You don't know what he might get up to. He already tried to escape once. What if he tried it again, and took you hostage? You'd be in a real fine kettle then, wouldn't you?"

Penny sent him a look, as he headed back to the table to finish his letter. Then her countenance softened, as she turned her attention back to Jack. She took his right hand in hers and gave it an affectionate squeeze. The smile that returned to her face was heaven.

***

When Cameron returned home, he knew something was up. His wife wasn't inclined to discuss it, and he didn't push her. A lot of their serious discussions took place once the household was quiet, and they had the comfort of their bed and each other's arms to make the hard stuff easier. Cameron was willing to wait.

When the moment arrived, Jean began her narrative. She trembled with renewed fear when she recounted Penny's brash actions, but she pushed through until the whole story was told.

When she finished talking, Cameron didn't say anything. Jean knew he was taking time to digest all that she had told him. He would need to let his emotions settle before making any decisions about what the next step would be. Cameron was not the type of man who reacted on impulse, but react, he would. And, as head of the household, whatever decisions he came to, would be respected and carried out.

***

The next morning, Penny and Caroline were both aware of strain over the breakfast table. They felt a family discussion in the works. Penny knew her little over-reaction of the previous day was not going to go unnoticed, and breakfast was a difficult meal to get down, due to a knot in her stomach.

Caroline felt sympathetic to her sister's plight, but also selfishly relieved that she'd had nothing to do with the incident and was safe from the predestined lecture. Therefore, it was with some surprise and self-righteous indignation when she responded to her father's statement that she was also standing accused of misconduct.

"But, Papa. I was with you all day, yesterday. How could I have had anything to do with it?"

"I'm not referring to what happened yesterday, Caroline, but to a minor incident, of someone in this household slipping a lock pick to Peter."

The wind went out of Caroline's sails, and she turned a shade of pink.

Penny felt relief that not all of this was going to be on her. She gave her sister a small kick, under the table, and snickered into her oatmeal.

Jean sat quietly, letting her husband take the lead. She didn't envy him this unpleasant task and, though listening with concern, she busied herself with her own breakfast and keeping Eli occupied as he attempted to play with her spoon.

Cameron shook his head with regret, as he fingered his coffee cup. "Peter suggested I not be too hard on you, as you were only trying to help."

"I was," Caroline responded in a small voice.

"Help a wanted criminal escape legal custody—again." Caroline hung her head. "It was bad enough, four years ago, when you intentionally lied to that sheriff, and then deliberately obstructed their duty.

"The consequence of that decision was that you girls were nearly taken from us and put in a reform school."

The girls shared guilty looks but said nothing.

"We chalked it up to immaturity, that you were both still impressionable children, and, hopefully, had learned a valuable lesson. Obviously, we were wrong, because you are not a child anymore, Caroline. You are an adult. If Peter had decided to use that pick, and, in fact, escape custody, you could have been held accountable, and ended up in prison, yourself. That would have gone a long way toward you getting any sort of legal education, wouldn't it?"

"I didn't think of that," Caroline mumbled. "I'm sorry, Papa."

"Well, if you ever see Peter again, I believe he is the one you need to apologize to. He's the one who suffered the consequences of your irresponsible decision. To his credit, he refused to say who had given him the pick, but Marshal Morrison gave him a nasty beating, trying to convince him otherwise."

Caroline gasped in fear and guilt. "Oh, no, Papa. I didn't want that to happen. Is he all right? Was he badly hurt?"

"I believe it safe to say that he is still feeling the effects of it."

Guilty silence ensued.

Cameron turned his attention to his younger daughter. "Penny. What in the world were you thinking? You scared your mother half to death."

"I know." She began quietly then built up a head of steam. "But Deputy Layton said he was going to kill Mathew. I heard him say it. What else was I supposed to do?"

"Let him!" Cameron yelled for the first time during this discussion. "Better Mathew than you. And I'm pretty darn sure, if you were to ask Mathew about that, he would agree with me."

"But, Papa . . ." Penny looked up at her father, with tears in her eyes. How could she tell him that she loved Mathew? She couldn't stand by and watch him be killed, any more than she could chop off her own arm. She dropped her eyes again, and the tears ran over.

It broke Cameron's heart, speaking to his daughters this way, but he had to get it through to them, that they couldn't make rash decisions and expect everything to turn out all right. To soften the blow to them, he admitted to some guilt in the matter, himself.

"I invited them to come and visit," he said. "They were smart enough to stay away, knowing they could bring trouble with them and put us at risk. But I insisted, they come. For that mistake on my part, we have all paid a heavy price."

"No, Cameron—"

"Yes, Jean. It's the truth. And now, it pains me to say it, but if, by chance, either of those fellas decide to break legal custody and continue with this dangerous path they have chosen, then they will not be welcomed back into my home."

This statement was met with gasps of disbelief.

"No, Papa."

"You can't mean that."

Eli, though not understanding the words, did understand the emotions. He stopped playing with his mother's spoon and stared at his father in opened-mouth disbelief.

"But Cameron." Even Jean was upset by this decree. "I've assured both of them that we would stand by them, that they are family and would always be welcome here."

"I know." Cameron's tone held a sadness to it. "I've said as much, myself. And I'll stand by my word, if they choose to stop running; to stop and turn and face what is coming to them."

"But twenty years, Cameron . . ."

"I know. It's a risk, and I can understand their fear of standing trial. But they both made choices, and it's time they faced the consequences of those choices. Otherwise, the path they are on now can only end badly. Not only for them, but also for those close to them. I will not put my family in any further danger." Cameron paused and looked around at the three distraught faces, staring back at him. "The governor may still come through for them. Or, a judge and jury may consider their years of staying legal, even if they don't know about the governor's deal with them. They may be lenient."

Jean rolled her eyes. She didn't think there was much chance of that. Even Cameron wasn't hopeful about those possibilities.

"It seems a moot point, anyway," Jean said. "Since they are both now in custody and not likely to have any choice—"

Her observation was cut short by Cameron shaking his head.

"Jean, from what I have seen and heard these last couple of weeks, all those rumors and dime novel stories we've read about them, don't even come close to the real animal. I watched Peter pick open a lock in less than five seconds, with his hands cuffed behind him. And he wasn't even using a real lock pick. If he decided he was going to leave, there's not a jail in the country that could hold him.

"No. He has a choice, and so does Mathew. If those boys were our own, natural-born sons, we wouldn't put up with this nonsense from them, and you know it. If they care about this family and want the privilege of being a part of it, then it's time they faced up to the consequences of the choices they have made. They must allow themselves to stand trial."

***

"I did *what*?"

Jack Kiefer sat, fully dressed, on the bed, with his stocking feet stretched out in front of him. With the one arm bandaged tightly in a sling, and the other cuffed to the bed, he found himself so incapable of doing anything, he was bored beyond distraction.

To help alleviate the situation, Penny and Caroline had drawn chairs up around the bed and filled him in on his activities of the previous day.

Rick had also taken up residence and was leaning against the door jam, quite prepared to confirm everything the girls were telling their friend.

"No, I couldn't have done that," Jack said. "How could I have done that? I didn't do that, did I? I don't remember. How could I have gone out the window? I can barely stand up. Penelope, you did *what?* What did you do that for? You could have been killed. Don't ever do that again. Ohh, your father must be furious. This ain't right. No, no, this ain't right at all. I gotta leave. I gotta get outta here."

Rick, who had been silently listening in amazement to the running monologue, tensed with this last statement and prepared to do battle.

Jack, noticing this change in Rick's attitude, smiled sheepishly and quickly back-stepped.

"Ah, no, Deputy. I didn't mean it that way." His gaze dropped to the Winchester that had suddenly changed its position. "I didn't mean like 'escape'. I meant as in away from here, like, inta' town. To the jail, yes. Ahh, not escape, Deputy, believe me. I just meant . . ." Jack sighed and realized he was rambling. That was the problem with feeling better and having nothing to do. He was slowly going nuts.

Cameron appeared in the doorway and the atmosphere in the room changed. "Girls. Deputy. Would you excuse us, please?"

Penny and Caroline exchanged worried glances, then with quick looks at their friend, they got up and exited the room.

Rick had already disappeared.

Cameron came in and closed the door. He moved one of the chairs closer to the bed and sat down. Both men assessed one another.

"Well, Mathew . . ."

"Cameron, I'm sorry. You know I'd never intentionally do anything ta' put the girls in danger. I don't even remember any of it. I don't care if David says I ain't well enough ta' leave, I'll go. Right now. Rick can escort me into town. I'll do just as well in a jail cell and it'll be a lot safer for everyone here if I go. Besides, it'll be closer for the doctor ta' check up on me if I'm in town, and his wife won't have ta' come out here every day, and Jean and the girls can get back to their regular routine, and you won't have ta' worry about anything happenin' while you're away, and I'm sure you'd be quite happy ta' get Rick out from under foot . . ." Jack trailed off. He was rambling again.

"Are you done?"

Jack sighed. "I'm sorry, Cameron."

"I know. And yes, it would be better if you were in town." Jack nodded. "But I do care about what David says, and if he doesn't think you're ready for that move yet, then you're not leaving." Jack was about to protest, but Cameron cut him off. "On the condition that you don't pull another stunt like that, again."

"Of course, Cameron. I don't know what I was thinkin'. I wasn't thinkin'. I wasn't in my right head."

"I know. That's the only reason you're still here. Although it appears Rick is not prepared to take any more chances on you." He sent a quick look to the handcuffs. "I've noticed Peter can make quick work of a pair of those."

Jack smiled. "Yeah, he's amazin'."

"Which brings me to my other condition," Cameron said, and Jack stopped smiling. "You boys are family. You have been since you first stepped foot onto our property, four years ago. I don't really know how that happened, but it did. Maybe we represent something that has been missing in your lives. I don't know, but there it is: We're family. But members of a family have responsibilities to one another, to support one another through the tough times, and to take into consideration the choices we make, and the effect of those choices on the other people.

"I have every intention of helping you and Peter in every way I can that's legal. I offered to put up Peter's bail and I'll do the same for you, because I've chosen to trust that you respect me enough, you won't high-tail it and leave me holding the bag. I'll help with the lawyer fees, as much as I can. We've got some fine yearlings up there, and they'll bring a good price.

"But I offer this only if you hold to your end of the deal, and that is, you and Peter stop running, that even if the opportunity presents itself for you to break custody, you won't do it. It's time you boys faced up to this and got it dealt with, one way or another.

"You've both mentioned being tired of the running, the hardships, and the dangers of living this lifestyle. You're both understandably angry and frustrated with the governor's apparent duplicity on the pardon issue.

"Well, now it's time to call him on it and find out once and for all, where you stand. You do that, and, like I say, I'll stand by you in every way that I can. Are you agreeable to this?"

Silence.

"Perhaps you need some time to think about it," Cameron stood up, preparing to leave.

"No," Jack stopped him with the quick word. "No, Cameron. I was just tryin' ta' figure out how ta' express my gratitude. Leon is a lot better with words than I am. After all that has happened here, your friendship and support is far more than we deserve. For my part, I agree to your conditions. I can only assume that because Leon is still in custody, he's also decided ta' stop runnin'. You're right Cameron, as usual. You're right. It's time to face the consequences."

CHAPTER TWELVE
IN BETWEEN

Cheyenne, Wyoming. Summer 1885.

Leon's arrival in Cheyenne didn't cause much of a stir. This was a large city compared to the towns Leon and Jack were accustomed to visiting. Though they'd been to Cheyenne before, it was usually for special occasions. The Cheyenne Social Club for one. He smiled as he recalled the fun times they'd had there, but he doubted he would be visiting that establishment on this trip.

The city bustled. People came and went, hurry out of the train depot, hoping to catch cabs to take them on way. Quick glances to the man in shackles were done on the go, and nobody felt that his arrival was worthy of being late to an appointment.

Aside from one lone reporter from the Cheyenne Tribune, hoping for a photograph and story, no one else was even aware of who he was. Morrison had done a good job of keeping the outlaw's identity and arrival date quiet. It was only after the first reporter had gotten the scoop, did the others get wind of it and swooped in upon the justice building to get their own fingers in the pie.

They disembarked the train and went immediately to the waiting horse-drawn transport. From there, they were taken directly to the ground floor entrance of the large stone building that housed the jail, the sheriff's living quarters, various offices and of course, the impressive courthouse.

Even Sheriff Turner, who ran the office, had an air of sophistication about him. Of average height and build, he still stood out from the run-of-the-mill law officers of the average western town. With combed-backed hair, a neatly trimmed handlebar moustache and himself impeccably dressed in a full suit with waist coat and tie, he far outclassed Marshal Morrison and his entourage.

He was a man dedicated to his duty and ran his jail with a stern, but fair discipline. No time was wasted with the transfer of custody, and Leon soon found himself locked in yet another cell in what felt like the dungeon of the impressive structure.

Change of Leads: The Lost Shoe

Somehow, it didn't make any difference that this was the capital city of Wyoming, that the governor's mansion was just a few blocks away, and that the jail he was in was part of the most modern, up-scale courthouse in the territory. Nor even that the sheriff wore a suit and tie. From Leon's position, it was still a jail cell.

***

It wasn't long before Leon was bored. There was only so much reading a person could do, and besides that, he had already exhausted the supply of newspapers this city had to offer. Just to show how bored he was, he had even gotten tired of reading the news articles about himself. The prisoner paced a trench in the cell floor. Just because he wasn't granted bail, surely that didn't mean he was never going to get out of here. Leon'd had it with nothing to do.

Hoping to kill some time with a snooze, he heard the cell block door open, and a big brown eye peeked out from under a black hat. Over-lapping footsteps told Leon that more than one person had entered, and his hopes rose in anticipation of someone new to talk to. A cell door squeaked open then clanged shut.

"Hey, Deputy," sounded an articulate voice from the next cell, "when do I get to see my lawyer?"

"For a misdemeanor? You'll be seeing the judge in a couple of days. That's it."

"But I am totally innocent—."

"Yeah, yeah . . ."

More footsteps indicated the departure of the lawman, and Leon heard the new prisoner snort in disgust.

"Imbecile," the man grumbled, then added in a louder voice, "I should be given the chance to defend myself."

Leon assessed his new neighbor from under his hat. At first glance he appeared to be a man of means. His graying hair was longish, but oiled back, and his moustache was trimmed and neat. He wore a suit with a sparkly blue waist-coat, suggesting that he was a gambler by trade.

But then, upon closer scrutiny, Leon noted that the newly brushed suit had worn areas around the elbows, and the cuffs were scruffy. A gambler on a long losing streak, perhaps? Well, can't blame a man for that.

Leon removed his hat and sat up, smiling a greeting.

The new-comer cocked a brow then returned the smile.

"Good day, sir," he said. "My name is Sydney Hardbuckle, but folks call me Syd. Who might you be?"

Leon approached the partitioning bars and offered a hand for shaking.

"Leon. Good to meet you. What are you in for?"

Syd puffed up and strutted around his cell. "Those idiots at the saloon accused me of cheating. Can you believe that? Just because they can't handle losing to a superior player. Now I'm stuck in here for goodness knows how long, before they all come to their senses." His pacing increased, and his voice rose, as a finger made pointed statements in the air. "Why, I've traveled all over the West making my living in the gambling profession. I am skilled at the games of chance, and I challenge anyone to defy my talents. And they accuse me of cheating. How dare they?"

Leon bit a lip as he watched this spectacle. "Gambling man, are you?"

Syd stopped and frowned. "Yes. Isn't that what I've been saying?" He sighed and rolled his eyes; his companion was obviously obtuse.

"I like to play a game once in a while," Leon owned. "Perhaps the deputy would loan us a deck. It'll help pass the time."

"I have no money on me. Those thieves wearing badges took all my winnings. How do you propose we gamble without any money?"

Leon shrugged. "For the love of the game. And, like I said, it'll help pass the time."

Syd looked at Leon as though he were a dead rat the jailhouse cat had just dragged in.

"Well, 'Leon', what, pray tell, are you in for?"

"Oh, lots of things," Leon said. "I expect to be here for some time."

"Really." Syd was skeptical. "Have I heard of you? What's your last name?"

Leon's smile was subtle but wicked. "Nash."

"Leon Nash?" Syd frowned, trying find some significance in it. Then the penny dropped, and his eyes widened to saucers. "Napoleon Nash? Oh my. Yes, yes. I heard you'd been arrested, but it never occurred to me that we would be sharing the same cell block. But then, it never occurred to me that I would be arrested." He gave Leon a nudge through the bars and winked. "How grand to meet you. Yes, a game of cards between us would be a glorious thing. Perhaps I will even teach you some of my moves."

"Your moves?"

"Yes. You know, of course. Those little moves every gambler has up his sleeve for those moments when he finds himself in jeopardy of losing."

"Ohhh." Leon nodded, his hopes sinking. "You mean 'cheats'."

Syd puffed up again. "Indeed not, sir. I am an honest player. But, I say, from what I hear, you have quite the range of talents." His tone lowered to a whisper. "Are you planning a break-out? Surely this ridiculous jail can't hold you." His eyes narrowed to slits. "And you're the one who blew the safe at the Merchants Bank, aren't you? No one else has done that before or since. Let's say we break out of here tonight and go do it again, eh? Wouldn't that be something?"

"No, Syd, sorry. Can't do it."

"Well, why not? We can be a team. You did it once before, no reason why you can't do it again."

"A job like that takes a lot of planning. Besides, I don't do that anymore."

"Fine then," Syd huffed. "If you don't want me for a partner, all you have to do is say so."

He then turned and plunked himself down on his bunk, arms folded, and legs crossed. He knew when he was being shunned.

Leon's disappointment grew. It truly was an insult to be considered the cream of the crop, when this was the best the crop had to offer.

***

The hours dragged by. Between the racket caused by drunks brought in to the tank to sleep it off, and the insistent chatter of his neighbor, Leon was bombarded by a wall of unsolicited assaults upon his eardrums. This is what he got for starting up a conversation with a stranger before knowing what he was getting into. Even the thought of playing a hand or two of poker with Syd had been chased from his mind. It was obvious now that the 'professional gambler's' talents would offer nothing in the way of a challenge or even a distraction.

Supper time arrived. Leon had been pacing the cell and just happened to be standing by the front bars when the deputy leaned down to slide his tray of food along the floor and into the cell. Quick as a wink, without any plan or thought, Leon snatched the ring of keys from the guard's belt. Habit caused him to hide the evidence, as the deputy straightened up and left the cell block.

Leon stood there, stunned. He pulled the ring out from hiding and stared at it, as though not quite believing it had been so easy. The cell block was unusually silent, not even the scrapping of plates met his ears. Glancing over to the other inmates, he found every one of them staring at him.

"That's the way to do it," Syd whispered, his teeth grinning. "That's the Napoleon Nash I've heard tell off. When do we make our move? Tonight? Yes, that would be best, wouldn't it? Tonight, when everything quiets down."

Looking beyond Syd, Leon saw the other faces grinning in anticipation.

He tweaked a smile, shook his head and tossed the ring of keys into the aisle.

The whole cell block deflated.

"What the hell did ya' do that fer?" asked a nobody, three cells down.

"Yeah," griped another. "Just 'cause you don't wanna escape, the least ya' could 'a done is let us out."

"Geesh," Syd snarked. "The great Napoleon Nash. What a disappointment. And to think, I was excited to meet you. Just whose side are you on anyway?"

Leon shrugged, picked up his food and returned to his bunk, ignoring the grumbling and hard looks sent his way.

Two minutes later, the distraught deputy slammed into the cell block. Instantly his eyes lighted upon the key ring sitting in the middle of the aisle. Rushing forward, he snatched them up and counted all the keys. A sigh of relief followed, then a sheepish look at the inmates followed that. Nobody paid him any heed and, taking this as an indication of innocence, he left the block, re-attaching the keys to his belt as he went.

***

Night time was even harder than the day. Leon lay awake, listening to the snores of his cell-mates while he stared, wide-eyed at the ceiling. The one drawback of allowing an intelligent and devious mind to reach this level of boredom, was that it usually found a way to liven things up. Leon's mind was no exception. Just when he had reached the point of banging his head against the bars, he found a way to put it to better use.

The ease in which he had snatched those keys got him thinking. It would be harmless fun, seeing how many times he could do it without getting caught. Tomorrow he would put it to the test. Maybe even lay bets with himself about how often he succeeded over a specific amount of time. He smiled. Yes, this could be fun.

He wound up being amazed at how often he managed it, but, much to the dismay of his fellow prisoners, he always threw them back, or simply re-attached them when the deputy strolled by again.

Still, the law was getting suspicious. Keys don't simply fall off belts on their own. Even though nothing untoward happened, and the keys were always found, the deputies began to look at Nash with retaliation in their eyes.

So, the next time, just to stir the pot and divert attention, Leon slid the keys into Syd's cell, while Syd was occupied with a snooze. Then he sat back to enjoy the fireworks.

"Hey, Larry, Chuck. Get in here," Deputy Jim called to his cohorts.

The scraping of chairs and the running of feet preceded the entrance of the two other deputies.

"What is it?" Chuck demanded. "Somebody escape?"

Jim pointed into Syd's cell. "Lookie there. Either 'a you yahoo's missin' your keys?"

Chuck and Larry did a quick check.

"Damn," Larry said. "I didn't even know they were gone. Dagnabbit."

Jim unhooked his keys and opened the cell door.

Syd was more than just awake now. He stood up, staring at the keys on the floor as though they were a ghost come to haunt him. His eyes widened as the three deputies converged upon him.

"I didn't take them," he insisted. "It was him. It was Nash."

"Now, why would Nash snatch the keys, then leave 'em in your cell?" Larry asked.

"How should I know? There's no telling what that fool's gonna do. He's been stealing your keys all along, just for the fun of it."

"Why don't I believe you?" Chuck growled as they closed in.

"No. Honest. I wasn't me—"

Further protestations were drowned out by the reign of punches that knocked out the wind and loosened teeth.

When the deputies were done and gone, Syd held his gut and dragged himself back to his bunk.

"You dirty dog," he groaned at Leon. "That wasn't right at all."

Leon sent him an impish smile. "Sorry Syd. I really didn't think they would go at you that hard."

Syd's response was a louder groan as he settled himself down.

Leon returned to his own bunk, his impish smile morphing into one of satisfaction.

The other witnesses turned away, each taking note that maybe it wasn't a good idea to taunt Napoleon Nash, after all.

***

Eventually, Leon got bored with key snatching. Like most things, it was fun for a while, but once it stopped being a challenge, he gave it up, and his mind returned to running in circles. Little things irritated him and even those who had not witnessed the key incident learned to leave him alone.

One night, fed up with not being able to sleep, he grabbed his mattress in frustration and hurled it against the bars.

"Get me out of here! I'm going stir-crazy."

"Shuddup," came the response from the other side of the wooden door. "The last thing we're gonna do is let you out."

The sound of laughter filtered its way down to Leon's ears.

"Aarg. Damn you!" He yelled out his anger and shook the bars with all his might. They didn't even budge.

He punched them. "Ouch, dammit." He turned and leaned against them, as he ran his hands through his hair and gave his lip a thorough chewing.

Then his eyes narrowed. The lantern in the aisle cast its light into his cell and caught the edge of something in the rope supports for his mattress.

'Now, what do we have here?' With a furtive glance to his sleeping companions, he walked to the bunk. Running his hands along the ropes, he felt, then saw, three strands of sturdy wire that had been intertwined to repair the frayed braiding of the lattice.

A smile tugged at the corners of his mouth. If he couldn't manage to fashion a set of lock picks out of this, then he didn't deserve to be called a criminal genius. But, did he really want to?

'Well, why not? I could have some fun with it. Doesn't mean I'm going to actually break out.'

Making doubly sure that all potential witnesses were asleep, he worked the rope strands until he had two of the wire links free. Bending a small hook at the end of one strand proved challenging, but he finally had something that was to his satisfaction, and he only acquired two punctures on his fingers from the effort.

His smile was devilment itself, as he settled the mattress back down on its rope supports. He re-organized his blanket and pillow, lay down again and fell asleep.

***

The following night, Leon got busy. It took him a few minutes to get the feel of the cell door lock, but once he had it, he had it. The act of simply stepping out of his cell lifted a weight from his soul. He almost started to laugh, he was so giddy.

Looking around to see what mischief he could get up to, he spied the bucket and mop leaning up against the wall at the far end of the aisle. Grinning with glee, he padded past the snoring guests, took the bucket, still half-filled with water, and leaned it up against the block door. He then returned to his cell to await what the morning would bring.

***

Breakfast was announced with a crash and a splash as the wooden door opened, knocking the bucket and mop over, and sending water flowing down the aisle way.

"What the hell was that?" Deputy Larry came in with his gun drawn, expecting an ambush to be waiting for him. Then he saw the water creeping down the aisle and into the drunk tank. "Oh crap."

The drunks, in the tank across the aisle from Leon's cell, grumbled awake, then started cursing as water rolled into their space.

"Hey. What the hell . . .?"

"What kind'a joint are you runnin' here?"

Others simply groaned, and clutching their aching heads, turned toward the wall and wallowed in their misery.

Deputy Larry cursed a blue streak, and Leon could hear the boss, Sheriff Turner, giving the available deputies what for.

Once things had settled down, breakfast over with and the water mopped up, it occurred to everyone that it would have been impossible to leave the bucket leaning against the inside of the door, then still be able to exit the block without disturbing it.

This caused a certain amount of consternation, especially after the recent event of key-snatching. A thorough search of all the cells and prisoners was conducted, but no spare keys were found.

Turner scratched his head. Walking down the aisle, he stopped at Syd's cell and considered the gambler. His deputies insisted that this was the man who had been snatching the keys, but, much to Syd's relief, Turner didn't agree. He moved to the first cell and crossed his arms with a sigh.

"What are you playing at, Mr. Nash?"

Leon emanated innocence.

"It wasn't me, Sheriff. How could I have gotten out of this cell? You fellas did a real thorough search of me and this lovely abode. You saw for yourself that I don't have anything."

Turner chewed his lip as he considered his options. Something was going on, and it irritated the hell out of him that he couldn't figure it out.

Syd glared at his neighbor, knowing full well this was his doing and wondering how this was going to affect him.

***

Change of Leads: The Lost Shoe

The following night, Leon removed his makeshift pick from the rope lattice and, within seconds, had his cell door open. He went across the aisle to the communal drunk tank and unlocked that door. Leaving it ajar, he returned to his own accommodation. The pick was returned to its rightful place within the rope lattice, and Leon went to bed.

This time, it was Chuck who came into the cell block first. He opened the block door with some caution after the previous morning's escapades. Finding that nothing seemed amiss, he sighed with relief and walked in, carrying the tray loaded with bowls of oatmeal.

Then his blood ran cold. The tray clattered to the floor, oatmeal flying everywhere, as Chuck went for his gun. All the drunks, now recovered from their imbibing, were loose in the aisle, just waiting for the block door to be opened.

There was a yell of exuberance, and the prisoners made a rush for the opened door. Chuck didn't even get a chance to fire his pistol, and, letting out a yell of dismay, he back stepped through the threshold and slammed the door shut before the prisoners could get to it.

"Aww . . ." came the universal complaint from those on the loose.

"Take heart, fellas," Syd encouraged them. "They'll have to come back in here, eventually. You just have to be ready for them."

"Well," Leon cut in, "if you want my opinion—"

"We don't," Syd groused.

"I'd get back in the tank, before it's too late," Leon continued, ignoring Syd's rebuke. "You've lost your advantage of surprise now. Next time they come through that door, they'll be spraying buckshot all over the place. Personally, I don't need any more holes in me, just because you fellas messed up your chance."

In the office, the sound of Turner's raised voice, giving his deputies hell, could be heard resonating throughout the jailhouse.

"What do you mean, the prisoners are all loose?"

"Not all of 'em, Sheriff. Just the drunks."

"Just the drunks? Last I counted, we had five drunks in there, and you're telling me, they're all out of the tank?"

Leon could almost hear Chuck shrugging, as he continued with his line of defence.

"Yeah, but, they're just drunks—"

"Get the shotgun out of the rack. And make sure it's loaded."

Leon grinned. "See?"

The loose prisoners exchanged glances. One mumbled incoherently, a couple of others scratched their balls, and the fifth looked back at the door to the drunk tank as their only possible salvation.

All eyes jerked to the front, as the key was inserted into the heavy lock of the wooden door, and they heard the tumblers grind and clunk.

"Crap."

"Shit."

"Move."

There was a frantic scurrying of feet, as the miscreants dashed back into the tank, the last fellow slamming the door shut behind him, wishing he had the keys so he could lock it for real.

The lawmen burst into the aisle, shotgun out and ready for business. All eyes were glued upon them, as they came to a halt and looked around.

"I thought you said they were out of their cell," Turner accused Chuck.

"They were." To prove his point, Chuck walked to the door of the tank and grabbed hold of the bar.

He gave it a yank, but one of the prisoners had also grabbed hold of it and wasn't allowing it to budge.

Chuck frowned at him and, with a determined set to his jaw, tugged on the door a couple of more times.

"Let go."

He was met with a hard and tenacious glare from his opponent, who refused to comply.

Chuck grabbed the bars with both hands and gave the door a good haul, but the other four prisoners took hold from their side, and the door didn't budge.

"Dammit. Let go," Chuck yelled and, in his frustration, began a frantic shaking the door. "C'mon."

Turner, who'd had more than enough of this, strode to the bars and leveled the shotgun into the tank.

"Back off.".

One look at the double-barrels staring at them, and all five inmates released the door, just in time for Chuck to give it a final yank. He cascaded backward and collided with Leon's bars. Leon grabbed him, preventing him from falling, then pushed him, so he ended up stumbling right into the drunk tank.

"Shit!" Chuck found himself surrounded by inmates. He leapt back into the aisle, came up face to face with Leon again and jumped back from him. "Dammit." He grabbed the open cell door and slammed it shut. "Where the hell are my keys?"

He patted himself around his waist and back, frantically looking for the ring and not finding it.

Turner sighed, and taking the key ring from Leon's grasp, he handed them to Chuck.

Chuck's glare was daggers.

Leon shrugged. "You dropped them."

"Get that door locked," Turner order his deputy. He turned and surveyed the mess of oatmeal strewn all over the aisle. "Then you and Larry can get this mess cleaned up. It looks like our guests will go without breakfast this morning."

Ignoring the groan from the prisoners, the sheriff sent Leon a pointed glare.

"Jim," he ordered his third deputy. "Get the handcuffs. I don't care if you have to strip Nash naked, find out what the hell he's using to open these doors."

"Yessir, Sheriff."

Again, nothing was found. Every stitch of clothing was searched thoroughly, and even when the deputy removed the mattress and checked the ropes, nothing was visible. Leon had woven the lock picks so neatly back into place that not even a bloodhound on the scent could have found them.

"There's nothin' in here, Sheriff," Deputy Jim announced, when Turner came back for the results.

"You looked everywhere?"

"Yeah. Unless he swallowed it."

Turner looked at Leon, who stood, stark naked and cuffed to the bars. The idea of slitting the prisoner's gut open to check could be seen flitting across the sheriff's face. It was only there for an instant though and, much to Leon's relief, the lawman's kindlier expression took over.

"Fine, Jim. Let him get dressed, then cuff him to the bunk."

Leon's heart sank. "Aww, but Sheriff—"

"Shut up."

Turner turned his back on the prisoner and left.

***

"What do you think you're doin'?" Syd snarked, once the cell block was empty of lawmen. "If you're going to escape, just do it. Now we're not even going to get breakfast. And I'm hungry. Why make life miserable for the rest of us, since you're not planning on taking anyone else with you. Now we have to go through those damned searches every day."

"Be thankful they didn't strip you naked and cuff you to your bunk." Leon shook his cuff against the bars for emphasis.

"Yeah, the world is full of simple pleasures. Where the hell are you hiding those things, anyway?"

Leon shrugged. "I don't know what you're talking about."

***

As usual, it wasn't long before Leon became bored with his new toy. What was the point of displaying his talents if he couldn't take credit for them? He conveniently sat right on top of his hiding place, and knew he could get out of the cuffs any time he wanted, but, then what? They might end up taking him out of this cell altogether and put him someplace worse.

But frustration settled in. That night, Syd's words came back to haunt him. *'Maybe that faux gambler has a point. But then again . . . hmm.'* Leon stayed awake most of that night, his mind working to talk himself out of what his heart wanted to do.

The following morning, Syd had his time in court and was released. The old drunks were replaced by new drunks, or maybe, they were the same drunks in for another visit. Leon stopped paying attention. His mind was on something else, and he couldn't shake the thoughts he was having.

'Just for fun, let's see if I can make a pick strong enough to open that wooden door'

Then, just for fun, he did. Again, assuring that all possible witnesses were asleep, he removed the mattress, unwound the lock pick and released himself from the cuffs. Taking two pieces of wire, he bent a longer, deeper hook at the ends of both, then, using the strands of the unraveled rope to bind them together, he had himself a pick that should be able to handle the heavier lock.

He sat on his bunk, contemplating the tool.

'I should test it,' he frowned, still hesitant to go there. *'That would be taking an awful risk. Even at night, the deputy on duty is supposed to stay awake. I could chance it, of course. There's not many deputies I know that actually do stay awake all night. Still, this is Cheyenne. They might be different here. Hmm.'*

He continued to ponder, weighing the odds. His itching fingers so much wanted to tackle that lock, but something in his cautious outlaw mind nagged at the risk. And though he wouldn't admit it yet, now that he had a lock pick that could likely do the job, it was only a matter of time and circumstance before he put it to practical use. He decided to keep his secret safe and hid the pick under the mattress.

He re-cuffed himself to the bars and went to bed.

***

Soon after, the inevitable happened.

All it took was another night of only getting snatches of sleep, and Leon's mind began to wander. He started in on his usual worrying pattern, beginning with concern for his partner, then concern over what his future would hold, if he continued to lay about, letting others make his decisions for him. Then, just for something else to worry about, he'd worry about Taggard. But most of all, he always settled back on the biggest worry of all; about how he was going to get through another bloody, boring day in this rat cage.

Sitting up, he brooded and glared at the handcuffs. Within moments, he had his pick and the cuffs dangled harmlessly from the bar. He tried to settle again, hoping that now, being free from the cuffs, he might get some sleep. It didn't happen.

Then he was up and pacing a circle, as he flashed daggers are the other occupants.

'How could it be, that all the other men in this cell block can fall asleep with apparent ease, and I can't? I've got to stand here,

listening to their snores and grunts.' He paced some more, slapping the bars with each step. *'This is madness. What was I thinking, allowing myself to be contained like this? I have to get out of here. The governor isn't going to come to my rescue. He's been ignoring Taggard's inquiries for the past week.'* He let loose a sardonic snort. *'What agreement?'* He sneered, mimicking the governor's probable response. *'There's no agreement between Napoleon Nash and the Governor of Wyoming. Nash is going to stand trial and pay for his life of crime.'* Leon sighed, his hopes sinking as he finally acknowledged the truth of his situation. *'The banks and railroads aren't going to allow this to go any other way. Jack was right, and I've been a fool to believe otherwise.'*

Boredom and frustration turned to anger, and what had been playful distractions, now turned to serious business. He made up his mind that it was time to leave. He retrieved his makeshift lock picks from under the mattress, grabbed his hat and jacket, and within moments, had the cell door unlocked. He made a quick survey of the other sleeping lumps in their cots, then slipped out of the cell and headed for the door that separated the cell block from the office area.

'Now, if I'm as good a lock pick as I think I am' he gave a silent snort '*What do I mean, 'if'? I am good. I'll be out of here in half an hour.'*

He inserted the heavier wire and slowly felt his way around inside the workings.

The replacement to Syd's cell snorted loudly and rolled over.

Leon jumped, nearly dropping the pick.

"Dammit." He sent a visual dagger to the newcomer. *'Someone hasn't learned my rules yet.'* He set the pick back in the lock and started over. *'And he better hope, I don't stick around long enough to teach him.'*

Once he found his barings again, he inserted the second pick and used it to keep the inner latch pushed back, so he could use the heavier pick to push the tumblers open. This lock was going to be a challenge, even for him. Though he pushed the thought from his mind, he knew he was in dangerous territory. If he got caught now, his intentions were obvious, and he could be in serious trouble.

Sweat beaded up on his forehead and lip. He closed his eyes, slowing his breathing down to a mere hint of an intake, as he pushed his mind to settle and focus on the lock's release.

Just like with the cuffs, he pictured the inner workings of the lock as clearly as they would be upon a worksheet. He swallowed, took another calming intake of breath, and then pushed his advantage.

The first tumbler gave in to his foreplay, succumbing to him as a lover would to a skilled seducer. It groaned with its release then clunked open.

Another loud snort, this time from the drunk tank, caused Leon to tense, his teeth biting his lower lip. He glanced back to the cell as one of the drunks farted, woke himself from his slumber, then sat bolt upright, looking around in confusion.

Leon sat still as stone, his eyes on the drunk. But the drunk only scanned the block at his own eye level, then satisfied that nothing was amiss, he coughed and rolled back into slumber again.

Leon's nerves jingled, but he was too much of a professional for that to affect his performance. He began his gentle attack anew, massaging the center tumbler until he found the spot, then added just the right amount of pressure to bring about its surrender.

He cringed at the noise the release made, but no more inmates awoke. He smiled. Taking a moment to wipe the sweat from his brow and lip, he then inserted his instrument for a third time and began his final assault.

As though seeing the other two tumblers succumb to the master, the third one gave up the pretense of resistance and allowed Leon to have his way with it. The lock surrendered, and the door opened.

Leon took a deep breath, then slowly let it out through pursed lips. His heart, slowed throughout the violation, now pounded in his chest with the excitement of the conquest. He sat back, again wiping away the gathered sweat, as he allowed his body to relax and return to its normal state. Then he smiled. *'Ohh that had been so good. I do miss this.'*

Standing up, he peaked the door open to ensure he was alone. This had been a risk Leon needed to take. If the night deputy had been alert, in the front office, Leon would have been found out as soon as that first tumbler had released. Since no one had come to interrupt his play, he felt confident that he had this section to himself.

As he assumed, the office was well lit, but quiet. Leon tiptoed into the room and looked around to see if there was anything lying about that might come in handy. The rifles were all in their rack but locked up. He hesitated; a rifle could come in handy. Did he want to take the time? He removed the smaller of the lock picks from his jacket pocket and contemplated the tool.

It would only take a moment, less, even.

He glided toward the far wall, taking note of the safe as he went. He could have a hay day in here. The desire to get his hands upon the dial of that metal box was almost too much to resist.

His lower lip suffered another chewing. There could be money in there. He would need money and a rifle, if he was going to make this escape complete. Like a gambler addicted to the cards, he couldn't resist the challenge. Moving to the rifle rack first, he was just inserting the pick into the small lock, when someone coughing sent a shiver down his spine and into his fingertips.

He froze, looking back at the partially opened door leading to a second office.

'Damn. Somebody is in there. Of course, there is. How could I have assumed otherwise?' He looked back at the lock, with his pick thrust half way into it, and sighed with regret. Withdrawing it, he sent a longing glance toward the safe and bid them farewell

He glided to the front door and even had his hand on the knob, preparing to open it, when he was stopped by a nagging whispering memory in his head:

'I swear, Peter, you're incorrigible. I'm beginning to think, you ask for the treatment that you get at the hands of these lawmen.' Then, adding, even more, to his guilty conscience: *'Listen to me, Peter, there are people out here who care about you and Mathew. We will not just sit back and forget about you, do you understand?'*

Leon sighed. Where was this coming from? It didn't use to matter to him, what other people thought. What were they to him?

Now, suddenly, he realized that he did have people going out on a limb for him and Jack. He did have friends, and yes, family too, who were willing to sacrifice in order to stand by him. Taggard had done a lot for them and it wasn't his fault, if the governor reneged on their deal. Leon, making a run for it now, would probably put Taggard in a great deal of trouble.

And what about Cameron, Jean, and the girls? They'd done so much to help them and were still helping them. Leon felt the chill of responsibility concerning two young ladies who admired and respected him and had given their love and friendship willingly and without measure. Caroline and Penny only knew Leon as the good-natured saddle tramp who, with his partner, had stumbled, nearly frozen to death, upon the doorstep of their isolated ranch.

Even after the family had discovered the identity of their guests, their friendship had stayed true. With a shot to his heart, Leon wondered what they would think of Napoleon Nash now. What would it do to them, if he decided to throw all that away and disappear into the night?

With a sigh of regret, he backed off from the door, wishing in some ways that he could go back to being Napoleon Nash, the outlaw. Choices were so much simpler then. But the time had passed for that now. Despite all his efforts, he had developed a conscience. Turning, he stood for a moment, looking through the open door of the adjacent office where the deputy was doing his paper work. If Leon was very quiet, he could sneak back down to his cell and it would be like nothing had happened.

But then he heard the scrapping of chair legs on the wood floor, and he knew it was too late. The deputy walked into the main office, intending to get a refill for his coffee cup, when he looked up and found himself staring into the deep brown eyes of the notorious outlaw.

Leon gave him his most charming smile. "Howdy, Chuck."

The empty coffee cup clattered to the floor, and Leon found himself staring down the barrel of the lawman's revolver. Leon dropped his smile and raised his hands.

The deputy was on him in an instant, spun him around, and slammed him into the wall. Retribution felt good. A quick search revealed the make-shift lock picks, and the fun and games came to an end.

***

Leon spent the rest of the night with his hands cuffed behind him. He had his mattress to sleep on, if he could have gotten any sleep, but the bunk itself had been removed. Morning found him spread out at floor level, his eyes bleary from exhaustion, and his brain swirling with regrets and pointless ponderings.

The heavy wooden door opened, and since breakfast had already been served, Leon groaned, wondering what they were going to inflict upon him next. He was aware of someone entering the cell block and stopping right outside his cell. Another groan.

"Aww, Leon," came a familiar, but long-suffering tone. "What have you gone and done this time?"

Leon felt his heart skip at the sound of his friend's voice.

"Howdy Taggard." He struggled to get to his feet. A twinge from his bruised torso caused him to grimace, but he still managed to stand up. "Any word from the governor?"

"No." Taggard gave Leon a closer scrutiny and changed the subject. "You didn't sleep again, did you?"

"Oh, it's just so hard to relax with all the excitement going on around here," Leon puffed up with self-importance. "We almost had a jailbreak during the night."

"So I heard. You're not doing yourself any favors."

Sheriff Turner entered the cell block and unlocked the cell door. He beckoned Leon over and motioned him to turn his back to the bars.

"It seems you've had a reprieve, Mr. Nash," he said, while unlocking the cuffs. "Though, after your escapades of last night, I wonder at the wisdom of it. Turn around."

Leon did so, while giving Taggard a questioning look.

Turner snapped the cuffs in place again, so Leon's hands were shackled in front of him.

Taggard stepped forward to take charge of the prisoner. "I finally found you a lawyer who is willing to take your case," he said. "He went to the judge and convinced him that keeping you locked up in a cell 24/7, for the next three months, was inhumane. The judge agreed to a limited bail so you could get out for an hour every day, so long as you were shackled and in the company of a lawman at all times."

"Oh. Well, thank you."

"Uh huh. It's Mr. Marsham you really need ta' thank. He's put good money up on you, so there better not be a repeat of last night's escapades. I swear, Leon, if you make me regret this—

"No, no, I won't. Honest, Taggard, thank you."

"Fine," Taggard accepted the promise, knowing that Leon generally kept his word, once it was given. He accepted the handcuff keys from Sheriff Turner and escorted his friend to the exit.

"Where are we going?" Leon asked.

"I told your lawyer to meet us at the cafe," Taggard said in his low, soft drawl. "I figured you'd had enough of jail food by now and could do with a decent meal."

Leon smiled. "Oh, yeah. You're a good friend, Taggard."

"Uh huh. I'm surprised Turner is letting you out at all. What were you thinkin'? I thought you said you were prepared to deal with this situation."

"I know. I'm sorry." Leon was sincere in his apology. "I was getting a little claustrophobic in there, that's all. I had already decided not to go through with it when the night guard caught me." Taggard shot him a skeptical look. "Honest, Taggard. I was heading back to my cell, not out the door. Otherwise, I'd have been long gone by now."

Taggard had to concede that this scenario was highly probable. "Yeah, all right, Leon. I guess I believe you. You're too damn good at what you do to have gotten caught that easily."

Leon grinned. "Thank you, Taggard. That's a rare compliment, coming from you."

Taggard scowled, his dark, gray-flecked moustache curling up in irritation. "Dammit, Leon. Can't you take things seriously for once in your life? I get the feelin', the only person you're ever truly honest with is the Kansas Kid."

Leon dropped his flippant demeanor. "I am taking this seriously. I'm scared to death. But I have to deal with it somehow, don't I? And you're wrong, Taggard. Jack isn't the only one I choose to be honest with."

Taggard grumbled

***

They entered the café and Taggard led them to a table that was some distance from the other patrons so they could talk in privacy. The young waitress headed over to take their orders, and Leon tucked his hands under the table, feeling embarrassed about the cuffs.

Her smile was sweetness itself. "What can I get for you gentlemen?"

"I'll just have coffee," said Taggard, "but I think my friend here would like something more substantial."

"Oh, yes." Leon was adamant. "Coffee for sure. And just whatever you're serving for breakfast, will be fine." He flashed a grin at her.

She smiled and blushed. "I'll be right back with your coffees." And off she skipped to get them.

"Will you cut that out?" Taggard admonished him.

"What?"

"Oh, never mind." Taggard brightened and motioned to a young man who had just entered the establishment. "Here he is."

Leon stood up as the lawyer approached and shook hands with him.

"Good morning, Mr. Nash. I'm Steven Granger. I've been retained by Sheriff Murphy, here, to act on your behalf."

"Good," said Leon, as they both sat down. "I take that to mean you're my lawyer."

"Yes, Mr. Nash. I'm your lawyer." Granger frowned and wondered if he had made a mistake in agreeing to take this outlaw's case. The man didn't seem to be showing much respect or appreciation for his situation. "I see you're taking advantage of your reprieve from the jail. I hope you don't intend on abusing this privilege."

Leon smiled at the thought that an hour a day, instead of full bail, was to be considered a privilege. But he decided he'd better play the game, at least until he had this awfully young lawyer figured out.

"No, Mr. Granger, I don't intend on abusing it."

The coffee arrived, and the two cups were set down in front of them.

"Oh, hello, Steven." The waitress smiled at the new addition. "Would you like anything?"

"No, Betsy, that's fine. I'm just here on business."

She nodded, then glanced at Leon as he held the coffee cup up to his nose. With eyes closed, he inhaled the rich aroma of the freshly brewed beverage. It was then that Betsy noticed the handcuffs, and her interest was piqued even more, as she realized who this dark, handsome stranger was. It had been the buzz of the town when Napoleon Nash had been brought in to await trail, but it never occurred to her that she would be serving him in her café.

She moved off, a little lighter in her step, to retrieve his breakfast.

Taggard rolled his eyes.

Leon was oblivious. He took a sip of the hot liquid and, with his eyes still closed, savored its strong flavor before allowing it to finally slide down his throat.

"Ahh, coffee. That stuff they serve at the jail can only be described as colored water, or mud soup, depending on the time of day."

Betsy returned with a large plate covered with fried potatoes, scrambled eggs, bacon, sausages and ham, and plunked that down on the table in front of Leon. "Here's your breakfast, Mr. Nash," she said, her eyes shining with admiration. "I hope you enjoy it."

"Thank you," he answered, with a huge smile. "I'm sure, I will."

The smile he received back was radiant, then she skipped off again to tend to her other patrons.

Leon immediately dipped into the meal, and, despite the awkwardness of the handcuffs, made short work of it.

"So," Mr. Granger began, as he watched Leon put away his food. "I realize that Sheriff Murphy is a friend of yours, and that he arranged this meeting. Still, I have to ask. You have a right to privacy while discussing your case with me. Are you comfortable with an officer of the law being present?"

Leon glanced at his friend. "Yes. In fact, I want him here."

Granger nodded, glad that this little formality was taken care of. "I understand from Sheriff Murphy that you were hoping for a pardon from Governor Warren, thereby avoiding prison time for your crimes. Is this the outcome you expect from your trial?"

Leon took a swallow of coffee and considered his answer. "No, Mr. Granger. I don't think the governor is going to honor the deal he made with us. He would have stepped forward by now, if he was."

Granger nodded. "I'm afraid, I agree with you. Not only do you not have any written proof of this arrangement, but the deal you supposedly made was not even with the current governor. Chances of it standing up in court are slim."

"But it should be noted," Leon wagged his fork in the lawyer's general direction, "that Governor Warren has already taken advantage of the arrangement since coming into office. If he didn't intend to stand by it, why would he do that?"

"Taking advantage of the situation," Granger shrugged. "It probably never occurred to him that this scenario would come up during his tenure."

"What about the fact that in keeping with the arrangement, my partner and I have lived honest lives for the past five years, except for when we were doing little jobs for the governor's office? We've proved that we can do it—that we, in fact, are doing it. Sending us to prison to reform us would be redundant."

"Yes, we can go at it from that angle." Granger considered this. "It will depend on whether the jury believes prison is intended for rehabilitation or for punishment. There are many powerful people in the territory who wish to see you punished for your crimes. The fact that you have been inactive in your criminal careers for five years would be irrelevant to them."

Leon nodded. This was sounding much like what he had expected.

Betsy came by again to refill the coffee cups.

"Would you like anything more, Mr. Nash?"

"Yeah," Leon mumbled. "Keys to the handcuffs and a fast horse."

"Pardon me?"

Leon smiled up at her. "Never mind. This is a wonderful breakfast, Betsy. Just keep the coffee coming and I'll be a happy man."

Betsy smiled again and poured coffee into his cup. She started to move away to the other tables, completely forgetting about Taggard's empty cup, until he beckoned her over. She smiled apologetically at him, as she came back and refilled his. Then her eyes were back on Leon, and she would have spilled coffee all over Taggard, if he hadn't brought her attention back to her duty.

"Oh. I'm sorry, Sheriff."

"Uh huh."

"Would you like anything else?"

"No, thank you."

Betsy was still smiling at Leon, as she moved off to attend to the other customers. Taggard shook his head, but Leon wasn't even aware of the interplay going on around and about him. He had other things on his mind.

Granger waited until he was sure of their privacy, then continued. "Of course, we could always play on the sympathy of the jurors. The fact that you have stayed out of trouble, shows that your intentions of going straight were honorable. That you never killed anyone, and that you only went after the larger corporations, may have the general citizenry in favor of leniency. It's not likely you'll get off completely, but maybe a reduced sentence."

"How reduced?"

"Well, maybe ten years."

Leon groaned. "Ten years. It might as well be twenty."

Taggard was getting nervous. He felt for his friend, but they couldn't back out of this now. There was still a chance that the governor would come through for them. But if Leon lost hope, he might disappear and any chance for leniency would be out the window.

"Leon?" Taggard tried to pull him out of his musings. "Leon!"

"Yeah . . . what?"

"Come on, don't give up. It's early yet." Taggard tried to sound encouraging. "We still have time before your trial date. You and Jack did a lot of jobs for influential people over the years. We can get in touch with some of them and get their testimonies."

"Indeed." Granger was quick to grasp onto anything hopeful. "That would be a good place to start. Get me a list of names to contact and I'll see what I can come up with."

"There you go, Leon. That's something you can work on this afternoon." At least this was some progress.

Leon didn't look enthusiastic.

Taggard sighed. This was going to be a long summer.

CHAPTER THIRTEEN
CHANGES

Rocking M Ranch, Arvada, Colorado

"How are you feeling?"

"Bored."

"No, I mean your shoulder."

"Hurts."

"Come on, Jack. You've got to give me more than that." David and Jack locked eyes, brown onto blue. It only made Jack miss his partner even more.

"It just hurts, Doc. What do ya' want me ta' say?" Jack was frustrated. "I'm stuck here, chained ta' this bed. I can't feed myself. I can't go for a walk, or a ride. Damn, I can't even read. Leon would love that one. When are you gonna let me outta here?"

"You'd rather be in a jail cell?"

"At least in a cell, I could move around, tend ta' my own needs. This is maddenin'—and embarrassin'."

David sat back in his chair, crossed his arms, and surveyed his patient.

Jack stood on the far side of the bed, staring out the window at the two horses grazing in the pasture. His left arm was still cuffed to the wrought-iron headboard, and frustration emanated off him in waves. The man was about to blow.

David knew Jack needed something to distract him, to keep him occupied, but he was at a loss as to what to suggest. Rick refused to remove the handcuffs, and David refused to give Jack the go-ahead to move into town and away from this haven. The prisoner was strong enough for the trip, had been for some time, but David knew that Jack would not be getting the tender loving care in a jail cell that he was getting here. And right now, tender loving care was what that shoulder needed. David sighed. Heal the body, but let the brain go to hell?

"I know, Jack. I'll talk to Rick and see if I can convince him to let you out of this room for a while. Some exercise would be good for you, about now."

"Yeah, why don't ya' do that," Jack's tone was filled with bitterness. Leon wasn't here, so Jack figured he'd fill in for his partner. "Go talk ta' Rick. He'll be so sympathetic to my plight."

David nodded to himself, got up, and left the room. There was no point in continuing the conversation when his patient was in this kind of mood.

Sam snoozed in the chair by the bedroom door, waiting for Rick to arrive from town to take over the day shift.

David continued past him, and Jean handed him a cup of morning coffee.

Her smile was sympathetic. "How is he this morning?"

"Testy."

"Yes. I noticed."

"Is Rick not here yet? Running a bit late, isn't he?"

"Yes, a little. But he should be here any time now."

"How about Cameron?"

"In the barn."

"Good." David headed to the front door, still nursing his cup of coffee. It was time for a discussion.

***

Sure enough, Cameron was in the barn, cleaning stalls. With Sam on guard duty all night, and Rick being more diligent with his prisoner, some of the chores were getting neglected. So, for now, it was up to the boss to fill the gap. He smiled, as the doctor walked in, knowing something was up.

"Well, David. What's the prognosis this morning?"

"He's feeling the strain of his confinement," David said. "He needs to get out, blow off some steam."

"That's not surprising. He's normally an active man, not used to being cooped up like that."

"You know him better than anyone else here. Do you trust him?"

Cameron stopped what he was doing and considered the question. "Well, he gave me his word he would behave himself. Still, I don't think it would be a good idea to put too much temptation in his path. What did you have in mind?"

"I don't know." David sighed. "Even to get out and walk around the yard, brush his horse, do something. He thinks he's got lots of energy, but he'll tire out quickly enough. Some fresh air would do him the world of good, though. It might help to relieve some of that stress that's building up."

"Rick ought to be here any time, now. We'll see what he says."

***

Rick was skeptical.

"Who's to say he won't high tail it out of here the first chance he gets? We all know what happened last time."

"He wasn't thinking clearly the last time, Rick. You know that," Cameron reminded him.

"And now that he is thinking clearly, you believe he poses less of a risk?"

"He gave me his word."

"And you trust him?"

"Yes."

"I donno. As far as I'm concerned, he should be locked up in a cell by now. He's strong enough to be driven into town."

"Getting him out for some exercise would help him to regain his strength and heal faster. It's not healthy for him to be sitting around all day," the doctor said. "He's also getting the medical attention he needs out here. Once he's in a cell, who's going to be doing that? Ben?"

"Oh, come off it, Doc. You know darn well, both you and your wife will be over at that jailhouse every other hour to make sure he has all the comforts of home." Rick stopped, hesitant to divulge the next bit of news, but he would have to say it eventually, so he might as well do it now. "He's not going to be in your care for much longer, anyway, so you may as well stop worrying about it."

"What do you mean?"

"I got a telegram from Morrison last night. He's on his way back to collect Kiefer and extradite him to Wyoming. About bloody time, too."

David was livid. "Why didn't you tell me?"

"I just did."

"He's not up for a trip that long," David insisted. "Who does Morrison think he is? He snatches up my patients in the middle of the night and disappears over the border. Napoleon wasn't ready for a trip like that, and neither is Jack."

"Well 'Napoleon' made it, didn't he?" Rick's mood was no better than David's. "And Kiefer will, too. You keep making the mistake of assuming these men are your patients, rather than our prisoners. You have say over their medical care while they're here, but Morrison has say over where they go and when. Get used to it, Doc. You're not the one in charge here. Morrison won't be in town for a few days yet, so that's how much time you have to get your 'patient' ready for the road."

Rick turned and stormed out of the barn, leaving his horse standing in the middle of the aisle, wondering who was going to feed him breakfast.

David was livid. "Dammit. Dammit, dammit, *dammit*!"

"Well." Cameron put a consolatory hand on the doctor's shoulder. "How about another cup of coffee, David?"

***

Rick flew into a rage. Arriving at the second barn, he aimed a kick at an empty bucket and sent it clanging into the pitch fork leaning against the wall, which, in turn, crashed to the floor. Barn swallows, two cats, and three, previously snoozing, dogs, discreetly vacated the premises for a quieter resting spot.

Rick didn't notice them. He hated losing his temper, but he was so frustrated with this current situation, and Doctor David Gibson wasn't helping. As far as Rick was concerned, keeping the prisoner here, where he had to be constantly under guard, was wearing everybody out, and it wasn't doing Kiefer much good, either.

'One more day. One more day, and I'll take Kiefer into town, where he can sit in a damn cell until Morrison comes to collect him. Enough of this.'

Rick paced back and forth in front of the second barn, smart enough, even in his anger, to avoid going anywhere near the prisoner. He didn't want to lose it altogether and start using Kiefer as a punching bag.

Rick fumed and gnashed his teeth, then finally began to calm down. Kiefer was just as frustrated as he was, probably even more, and the deputy knew it. This forced inactivity was nearly at an end for Rick, and he, at least, got time off and could head back into town every evening for a beer and an occasional romp in the sack with some fetching wench. But the outlaw's forced confinement was just beginning, and it was going to get worse—far worse. So, maybe Rick should cut him a little slack.

'*But what if he made a run for it again? Marsham seemed to think that he wouldn't, but, what if he did? Dammit. Well, just keep your eyes on him. Don't let him out of your sight and keep the rifle handy. But, again, what if he makes a run for it? I'd have to kill him, is all. Finish what was started. Yeah, that would go over well with this group. Dammit.*'

Rick stopped pacing and stood staring back toward the house, chewing his lip.

David came out of the first barn, then stopped when he saw Rick, and the two men stood and stared at each other. Finally, Rick threw up his hands in defeat and walked over to the doctor.

"All right," he said. "You win. But just in the house and in the yard area. No getting on any horses. And tomorrow, I take him into town."

It wasn't everything David wanted, but he'd take it. "Agreed. Thank you. But tomorrow, I'll take him into town. He's still not strong enough to be riding that far. I'll take him in my buggy."

"Fine."

***

So, that's how Jack Kiefer spent his last day on the Marsham ranch as a relatively free man.

Before going to bed for the day, Sam brought the two horses in from the field, so Jack could spend time in the barn, brushing his gelding. If he got through that without collapsing, then maybe there were a few other things around the place he could do that weren't too strenuous.

Rick sat on the bale of hay, a coffee cup in his right hand and his rifle casually, but obviously, resting in the crook of his left arm. Other than the sounds of the brush as it scraped against the horse's hide, and the occasional soft murmurings from Jack to the animal, silence reigned.

It felt good to be out of the house for a while, and Jack found himself relaxing. It was a warm summer morning, and the barn smelled sweet and fresh. The sounds of the horses contentedly munching their hay and of the birds chirping in the rafters, couldn't help but wash away the frustrations of his confinement.

After a while, Jack snuck a glance at the deputy and thought that there'd be no harm in striking up a conversation with him. Rick seemed like an okay fella, even if he was a lawman.

"So, Deputy, where do you call home?"

"Wyoming."

"Were you born there?"

"Yeah."

"Really? Never moved anywhere else?"

"Nope. Born there, grew up there, live there."

"You married?"

"Nope."

"Is deputing your full-time job?"

"Nope."

Jack sighed. He stopped brushing his horse, and leaning against the animal's shoulder, sent Rick an exasperated look.

"Not much for talkin', are ya'?"

"What do you want, Kiefer? A blow-by-blow description of what's gonna happen to you, like the 'good doctor gives you?"

"Just tryin' ta' make conversation," Jack mumbled, and went back to brushing Midnight.

Silence reigned again.

Rick sighed and relaxed his stance. "Yeah, all right. I just can't decide whether to trust you or not."

Jack smiled. "You can trust me, Deputy. I ain't goin' nowheres." Then added under his breath. "Probably wouldn't get very far, anyway."

"I was married," Rick offered up the information. "She died though, in childbirth. Lost both of 'em."

"Oh. That's rough."

"Yeah, it was," Rick admitted. "But I got a nice little spread over there by Rawlins. It keeps me busy."

Jack nodded, sensing that Rick was not going to elaborate. "So, you don't work for Marshal Morrison full-time?"

"Hell, no. He calls on me for certain jobs, like when he needs a good hand with a rifle."

Jack stopped brushing Midnight and looked at the deputy. "You the one who shot me?"

Rick met those brilliant blue eyes that had just turned to ice, and he didn't back down. "Yes."

A strained silence settled over the barn. Rick didn't tense, didn't move a muscle, but he was ready and so was his rifle. Just let Kiefer make a move toward him. It would be his last.

Jack nodded and smiled, the tension easing. "You're good."

"I know."

***

Penny entered the barn, hoping to visit with Jack, and conversation between him and Rick came to a halt. She smiled at Mathew, until she saw Rick, then her smile dropped. She looked embarrassed and irritated, all at the same time.

"Oh, Deputy Layton. I didn't realize you were in here." Then added as an afterthought, "But then, where else would you be?"

Rick got the hint. "Yeah, all right." He stood up from the hay bale. "I'll be just outside, Kiefer, so don't even think about going anywhere."

Jack nodded concurrence.

Penny waited until the deputy left, then sat down on the same bale, sending her friend a melancholy smile. "Papa says you're feeling better today."

"Yeah, I am. Shoulder still hurts, but that morphine works wonders."

"Papa also says you're probably going to be leaving tomorrow."

"Yeah. I think that's the plan."

"I'll miss you."

"I'll miss you, too, Penny." Trying to lighten the mood, he smiled and gave Midnight a quick pat on the shoulder. "There is somethin' you and your sister can do for me, while I'm gone, if you wouldn't mind."

Penny brightened up. "Of course. Anything you'd like."

Jack's smile broadened as he recognized Jean in her daughter's words. "I don't suppose I'll be takin' Midnight with me, and he and Karma could really do with some regular exercise again. Do ya' think, you and your sister could start takin' 'em out for a run, now and then? It don't have ta' be every day, but a few times a week would be good for 'em."

"Really?" Penny stood up, her eyes sparkling with the new adventure. "That would be wonderful. We wouldn't mind at all, looking after your horses for you. That is, until you both can come back and get them."

Jack turned solemn. "It might be a while before we come back for 'em. You know that, don't you?"

Penny nodded, her smile fading. "Yes, I know."

"So, it would take a real load off my mind, and Leon's, too, if we knew they were bein' looked after proper. They ain't gun shy, neither. You and Caroline can practice your rifle shootin' from horseback, if'n ya want. Watch Karma, though. She can be a little skittish at times."

"I don't really want to shoot a rifle anymore," Penny admitted.

Jack looked confused. "Why not? I thought you and Caroline enjoyed your target shootin'. And, livin' out on a ranch like this, it's a good thing ta' know how ta' do."

"Yeah, but . . ." Penny hesitated. She met Jack's gaze for an instant, glanced at his wounded shoulder, then dropped her eyes altogether.

A shadow of guilt fell over Jack. He'd have given anything for the girls to not have witnessed that assault.

"I'm sorry, Penny. That must 'a been a terrible day for you and your sister."

"Yes." Penny's voice tightened, as she fought to control the sudden tears that threatened. "I was so scared. I thought you were going to die. I was so scared."

Jack held out his left arm to her.

Giving up the fight against the tears, she ran into his embrace and held on tight.

Jack held her as best he could, despite the pain it caused his shoulder. He stroked her hair and whispered soft assurances to her, feeling that he wanted to take away all her worries.

He could feel her body trembling, and her heart beating against his chest. He thought about how much she had grown in the past four years, how her head fit so naturally under his chin, as he held her tightly against him, trying to calm her sobs. He noticed she wasn't a little girl anymore; at seventeen, she was developing into a pretty, young woman. He felt an unexpected stirring inside that had nothing to do with wanting to comfort her. Then he felt ashamed.

He closed his eyes and sighed. *'What am I doin', thinkin' about her like that? She's family, like a niece, or a sister. And she's so damn young. I can't think about her in any other way but family.'*

He thought back to what she had done that day, when he was out of his mind and trying to run, how she had risked her own life to save his. It had scared him to death when he heard about it, but another part of him admired and respected her for her courage and determination.

'She better never try anything crazy like that again. I ain't at all comfortable with the notion of her dyin' for me.'

His protective instinct kicked up a notch, and he held her tightly in his embrace as he gave her a gentle kiss on the top of her head.

He opened his eyes and found Cameron staring at him.

A tingle of shame spread over Jack again, as the two men gazed at each other. The silence in the barn grew heavy, broken only by Penny's sobs that were gradually subsiding, though her hold on Jack did not loosen.

Cameron broke the silence. "Jean wanted me to tell you there's some lunch up on the porch, if you'd care to join us."

Upon hearing her father's voice, Penny pushed away from Jack, wiping the tears from her eyes.

"Okay, Papa," she said with a wet smile, and she walked over to him and gave him a hug before continuing to the house.

Once she was out of earshot, Cameron, not sure of his own emotions at this moment, pinned Jack down with paternal scrutiny. "Is there anything you need to tell me, Mathew?"

"No, Cameron. On my honor, there isn't."

"Okay. Come on up to the house and get something to eat." Then Cameron turned and walked away, following his daughter.

Jack stood alone in the barn for a few more minutes, guilt and shame turning his stomach into a knot.

***

Later that afternoon, Sam awoke and headed to the ranch house in search of coffee. The first thing he noticed was Rick, leaning back in one of the porch chairs with his feet up, and his hat pulled over his eyes. Not exactly a picture of the diligent guard at work.

Sam started up the steps, and noticing another serene figure to his left, stopped in his tracks with surprise. The sight that met his eyes was one that, in all his born days, he would've never expected to see: Jack 'The Kansas Kid' Kiefer, notorious gunslinger, was sound asleep in Jean's rocking chair. Nestled safe and content in the crook of his left arm was the infant, Elijah, who was also sound asleep.

Sam's expression turned quizzical. This particular outlaw was confusing his well-established vision of world order.

Cameron walked out the front door of the house. He took note of Sam's reaction to the peaceful scene on the porch, and he smiled. He beckoned the young man to join him for a walk in the yard.

Sam turned and followed the rancher down the steps, wondering what was up.

As soon as Cameron reached a point where he considered them to be out of earshot of the house, he turned and assessed the young man before him.

"Well, Sam," he said. "I know you have a job to finish here for Morrison. But I'm thinking you might have had a change of heart as to your choice of career paths. Am I right?"

Sam hesitated. How could Mr. Marsham know this? Sam hadn't said anything. Like most young men, Sam was unaware that the confusion and turmoil he had been suffering from the past few weeks, had been written, quite plainly, on his face.

"As you know," Cameron continued, "there are six, two-year-olds down in the south pasture that need to be rounded up, broke out, and sold, before fall. You're a good hand with the horses, Sam, and I need a good man here, to help with the work this summer. On top of that, you're young and strong, and you still bounce. I take a fall off one of those broncs, I'll hit the ground with a thud and then be laid up until next spring. So, I'm offering you a job here, if you want it. You get done with Morrison and decide you might prefer it here, well, you're welcome to come back."

Sam was speechless. He never would have believed, after what he had done, that Mr. Marsham would be willing to let him come back. He glanced toward the house, where he knew the three Marsham women were preparing the evening meal.

"Do you think Caroline will ever talk to me again?"

Cameron smiled. "I don't know. She certainly won't if you continue with your current line of employment. If you come back to work here, she may not have any choice but to forgive and move past it. Only time is going to tell on that one."

Sam hesitated then nodded. "Thank you, Mr. Marsham. I think I would like to do that. Maybe not permanent, but at least until I can figure out what else I might wanna do."

"Fair enough. But Sam, if you ever show disloyalty to me, or to this family again, you'll be off this property faster than you can wrap your bedroll. Is that understood?"

"Yessir, Mr. Marsham," Sam agreed. "I promise, you won't regret giving me a second chance. I won't let you down again."

"Fine. Now, you and Rick are welcome to join the family for supper this evening, since you'll all be leaving in the morning, anyway." Then added an afterthought, "Hopefully, we can all find a way to get along."

***

Later that night, when the household was quieting into slumber, Jean and Cameron lay in bed. Embraced in each other's arms, they discussed the most recent turn of events.

"What do you mean, 'you already knew'?" Cameron asked.

"Well, not 'knew' as such, but I had my suspicions."

"How?"

"All you had to do was see Penny light up every time Mathew came into the room."

"I never noticed anything."

Jean smiled and gave her husband an assuring pat on his chest. "That's all right, dear. You can't notice everything. That's why there's two of us."

Cameron groaned and ran the hand that wasn't wrapped around his wife, over his eyes.

"What are we going to do about this? What about Mathew? Does he feel the same way?"

"I don't know," Jean admitted. "I don't think he knows how he feels, right now. He has too many other things on his mind."

Cameron lay there for a few minutes, staring up at the ceiling. He thought it would be his eldest daughter who would be giving him these kinds of problems first.

"Well, it may all work itself out anyway. Mathew is leaving in the morning, and there's no telling when, or if, he'll ever be back here again. Not that I want to see him go to prison." He was quick to assure. "I just mean, a little time apart might be a good thing."

Jean smiled but kept her thoughts to herself. She couldn't help but remember Penny's premonitions and feel in her heart that there was much more to this than a teenager's crush and an outlaw's loneliness.

Time would tell.

***

Jack shivered with the early morning dampness. It wasn't that cold, but anxiety over the move to the jail was affecting him more than he expected. He leaned against David's surrey, feeling woozy from the small dose of morphine the doctor had given him to help ease the upcoming jolty ride into town.

Cameron came over and placed a hand on Jack's shoulder.

"Take care, Mathew," he said. "I'll get in to see you, once you've had a chance to settle."

Jack simply nodded. This was awkward; all he wanted to do was get the trip over with.

Jean was next. She gave him a careful hug, then a kiss on the cheek. "We'll keep you in our prayers. Be careful with that shoulder."

"Yes, ma'am."

Penny and Caroline approached him, each giving him a gentle hug and kiss.

"We'll miss you," Caroline said, "and I don't suppose Papa will allow us to come visit you in the jail . . ."

She turned a quizzical look to her father; whose expression showed a definite denial. She sighed and looked away, trying to hide her sadness at this parting.

Penny was still unable to hold back her emotions. An expression of frustration tightened her features.

"I'm sorry," she mumbled, through wet tears and a runny nose. "I shouldn't be crying. I hate it when I cry, but I don't want you to go."

"I know, darlin', but it's for the best. You'll see."

She sniffed. "I suppose."

He gave her a quiet kiss on the forehead, then Rick stepped in to move things along.

"C'mon, Kiefer," he said. "Let's get going."

"Yeah."

Caroline and Penny stepped back as Jack turned to the get into the surrey.

He looked wobbly, and David stepped forward to help him in.

"Just sit there, Jack," he said. "You'll be fine."

"Yeah."

David walked around to the other side and joined Jack on the seat, as Rick handcuffed Jack's left hand to the arm rest.

Jack looked down at the metal cuff as though it was a foreign thing, then he shook his head to clear the cobwebs. It took all his effort to smile at the family that had come to mean so much to him.

"Thank you," he mumbled. "For everything."

Cameron nodded, as he held his wife in his arms. Jean looked like she might start crying, too.

Jack was at a loss. *'Oh, let's just get going. This is downright painful.'* He sent the girls one more smile. "Don't forget to look after Midnight and Karma."

"We won't."

"Good bye, Mathew."

David picked up the lines and clucked at Rudy to move out.

The little horse picked up the trot and they headed down the roadway, with Rick and Sam riding shotgun on either side of the vehicle.

Much like Leon before him, Jack felt the heartache of leaving his horse behind. Moving past the field, he couldn't take his eyes off the two animals that were out there, contentedly grazing. They were completely unaware that the last connection to their previous lives was disappearing down the road.

To Jack, the severing of that tie held more foreboding than the clanging of a cell door closing. They weren't just horses; they were freedom.

Other than the occasional query from David about how Jack was fairing, and that man's noncommittal reply, silence reigned for the duration of the trip to town.

Even though he was surrounded by people, Jack had never felt so alone. Arriving on the main street, he hardly noticed the glances from curious onlookers. But as they got closer to the sheriff's office, it became difficult not to notice the attention he was getting.

Once word spread around town that the doctor was bringing in the Kansas Kid, it didn't take long for a crowd to develop at their destination. Everyone wanted to see the infamous outlaw.

Sheriff Jacobs was alerted by the assembly outside and stepped onto the boardwalk to receive the prisoner. He was instantly bombarded by a flood of questions.

"Is he really the Kansas Kid, Sheriff?"

"Yes, I suppose he is."

"So, he didn't die after all, huh?"

"He sure looks like death warmed over, though," came another observation.

"I hear he's the fastest gun in the West. Or, well, he used to be. Probably ain't no more. Ha."

That commented hurt. Jack sent the man the iciest stare he could muster through the morphine haze, and that was the end of the comments.

It didn't stop the group from standing and staring, though, and Jack felt particularly self-conscious when Rick unlocked the cuffs and hustled him, a little too quickly, out of the buggy. Jack stumbled and found himself in the humiliating position of leaning on Rick to avoid falling to the ground.

"Be more careful, please, Deputy," David suggested. "He is drugged, remember."

"Yeah, yeah," Rick grumbled but did show a little more consideration, as he helped Jack find his footing again, then escorted him up the steps and into the office.

Sheriff Jacobs stepped forward to greet his new tenant. "Well, Mr. Kiefer, I've been hearing a lot about you—and about your partner. You don't intend on giving us any trouble here, do you?"

Jack acknowledged the man through his light-headedness. Though stern in carrying out his duty, the middle-aged lawman had an open and friendly face, and Jack felt at ease in this man's company. This was a relief, as both Leon and Jack knew, the attitude of the person holding the keys made a huge difference in the quality of your stay.

"No, Sheriff," Jack said through his slur. "No trouble."

"Good. Ben, take him and put him in the first cell."

"Yessir."

Just as Mike had done with Leon, Rick, with Jack in tow, followed Ben into the cell block and pushed his charge into the same cell that had previously been occupied by his partner.

Jack took a couple of steps forward, and then stood there, swaying.

David sneaked into the cell, before Ben could shut the door, and grabbed hold of Jack's left arm to steady him.

"Aw, Doc," Ben complained. "Are we gonna go through this again? Marshal Morrison gave me hell, last time."

"Morrison's not here right now, Ben," David said. "And I just want to make sure the prisoner is comfortable before I leave. I don't think Sheriff Jacobs will mind."

"I donno . . ." Ben grumbled.

"Come on, Deputy." Rick sighed with resignation. "No point arguing with the doc over stuff like this. They'll be fine.

David smiled. "I'll call you when I'm done, Ben. I won't be long."

"Yeah, okay."

The two deputies left the cell block.

"Okay, Jack," David said. "The bunk is straight ahead of you. Can you walk to it?"

"Sure, Doc."

Jack took some steps forward, and between the two of them, he managed to get over to, and sit on, the bunk.

David did a quick examination of his patient; checking his pupils, his heart rate, and making sure there was no telltale blood on the bandages that would indicate a tearing from the bumpy ride. Everything seemed fine.

David sat on the bunk beside Jack and gave him some words of caution. "You haven't been formally introduced to Marshal Morrison yet, so, a word of warning: That man is a bully. You need to be careful around him, okay?"

"Careful?"

"Yes. Don't provoke him in any way. He won't hesitate to hurt you in the fastest, most efficient way open to him. In your case, that means your shoulder. Do you understand me?"

"Yeah." Jack tried to smile. "Be nice to Morrison."

David became frustrated, finding himself confronted with the same flippancy from Jack, as he'd had from Napoleon, when it came to the warnings concerning Morrison.

"Please, don't take this lightly, Jack. Morrison won't care how permanently he hurts you. If you provoke him in any way, he'll rip your shoulder apart just to make a point. Do you understand? The way it's healing now, there's a good possibility that you'll get much of your mobility back, but if any more damage is done . . . well, just don't provoke him. All right? You understand me?"

Jack met David's intense gaze and nodded. "Yeah, Doc. I understand."

"Good," said David, as he stood up. "Now, try and get some rest."

"Oh, I am so sick and tired of hearing those words."

"I can ask the sheriff to get you a paper or something to read. How's that?"

Jack considered it for a moment. "No. I think I'll try and get some rest."

David smiled. "Fine. I'll stop in and see you tonight."

Jack nodded and stretched out on the bunk. He was asleep before David left the cell block.

CHAPTER FOURTEEN
ADJUSTMENTS

Cheyenne, Wyoming

Getting out for an hour every day helped to ease his frustration, and going over the past few years, coming up with names for the lawyer, had given Leon's brain something to do. But he still couldn't shut things down at night. For over two weeks, he paced the cell—back and forth, up and down, figure eights, and infinity, only to settle on back and forth, once again.

Only total exhaustion finally allowed him to lie down and shut his eyes. At those times, he partially dozed, but even a light sleep was filled with stressful dreams and mournful forebodings, so they didn't offer him any real rest.

After one of their regular outings, Sheriff Taggard Murphy, feeling concern for his friend, approached Sheriff Turner.

"You need ta' get your town doctor in here to see 'im," Taggard said.

Turner leaned back in his chair and crossed his arms, considering the request.

"I was just thinking the same thing. I hoped that having something to do would make things easier on him, but he's getting worse." Making up his mind, he nodded and stood up. "Jim." Deputy Jim poked his head out from the back office. "Go get the doc, will ya? We need to get this matter sorted."

Jim frowned, wondering what 'this matter' was, but he knew to follow orders and, with a quick acknowledgment, headed for the street door.

***

Dr. Taff took one look at the prisoner. The red-rimmed eyes and sunken cheeks told their own story.

"You're not sleeping, are you?" he asked the inmate, simply to confirm what he already knew.

"No sir. I guess I have a few things on my mind."

"Hmm." Taff pursed his lips and returned to the front office.

He approached the desk, set his bag on it and removed a pouch of medicine.

"Give him a dose of laudanum every night, Sheriff. If that man doesn't start getting some decent sleep, he won't be fit to stand trial."

"Sure thing, Doc."

"Every night," Taff emphasized. "No skimping on it. I'll be back in a few days to see how he's doing."

"He'll get it. I probably should have got this sooner, but," Turner shrugged, "as I told his friend, I hoped that getting out once a day, and having things to focus on with his lawyer, would take care of the problem."

"Obviously, it hasn't."

"I can see that, Doc," Turner said, an edge coming to his tone at the reprimand. "He'll get the laudanum."

Taff gave a curt nod and left.

***

The first night Leon took the sleeping aid, he slept for fourteen hours. Once the drug calmed his thoughts, his body and mind were so exhausted, they didn't want to wake up again.

Taggard dropped by a couple of times to check in on his friend, only to find him laid out on his mattress on the floor with a thin blanket partially covering him. Only the slow, rhythmic breathing of deep sleep showed he was still alive.

When Leon finally came to, he was bleary-eyed and exhausted, but hungry.

Taggard escorted him to the café, hoping a healthy meal would cure Leon's fatigue. They sat at the same table in companionable silence while Leon nursed his coffee and yawned every two minutes.

Taggard didn't like the look of him at all.

Locking Napoleon Nash up in prison for twenty years would probably kill him. This was becoming obvious, and Taggard felt like his executioner. But what else could he do? They'd come too far for Leon to turn back now, and Leon was being stubborn about it, anyway. Something about an obligation—a promise made to Mr. Marsham that he wouldn't back out of. That's all he'd say.

"Come on, Leon. What do you want to eat?"

"I donno. Something hot and comfortable."

"Oatmeal?"

"Yeah, why not. Oatmeal."

Taggard gave Betsy the order, and within a few minutes, she returned with a large, steaming bowl.

She was shocked at the change in the handsome man. He looked exhausted, worn out. She hadn't thought being in a jail cell for a few weeks would do that to someone. She left the table feeling sorry for him, even though she hardly knew him.

Taggard watched his friend for a few moments while he sleepily nursed his oatmeal. Then the sheriff sighed and brought up a subject that he knew would not go over well. "Look, Leon, I'm gonna have to leave you for a while. Things to take care of back in Medicine Bow. The town can't run itself."

Leon's spoon paused as he sat, staring into the bowl. "I suppose." He sounded disappointed.

"You knew I couldn't stay here forever. I'll get back in a few weeks. In the meantime, you and Granger can hash things out between you, and get a plan of action going. Okay?"

"I suppose."

Taggard slumped, feeling defeated. "You'll still get out for your hour every day." He tried to sound encouraging. "There are plenty of deputies to escort you. Go for a walk around town or somethin'. Get your blood goin'."

"You're right, Taggard. I'm sorry." Leon tried valiantly to perk up. "I know you can't stay here indefinitely. You've got things to do. I just feel awful."

"I'll say," Taggard agreed. "I thought you figured out how ta' shut off your brain when you need ta' rest."

"So did I. Nothing's working. I need a new technique." He breathed deeply and sat up straight. He smiled at Taggard, and some sparkle returned to his eyes. "I'll finish breakfast and down a couple more cups of coffee, and then we'll go for a walk. You're right. It'll do me good."

Taggard smiled back, relieved.

***

The walk did help Leon. He took his jacket along and draped it over his handcuffs, so he wouldn't feel so exposed. He needn't have bothered, though, as many people in town already knew who he was, and he found himself nodding and smiling at many of the folks he passed on the street. It boosted his spirits to know that some people still thought kindly toward him. Unfortunately, it was the wealthy corporations that would have the final say in the matter.

By the time they got back to the jail, Leon felt much more like his normal self, which only made it all the harder to step back into his cage. Still, he allowed Taggard to escort him to the block just in time to witness Deputies Larry and Jim coming out of his cell.

Apparently, they had taken advantage of his absence by supplying him with another cot for his mattress. One without wire bindings, this time.

Leon sent them a smirk. "Aww, gee. Just when I was developing a rapport with the rats."

The looks the two deputies gave him were anything but amused.

Taggard grumbled, shook his head as he removed Leon's cuffs, then closed the door on him.

"I swear, Leon," he said. "You ain't helpin' yourself. If ya' cut these guys some slack, they might treat ya' better."

Leon leaned up against the bars and smiled at his friend. "Yeah. Someone else said something similar, not too long ago. Maybe I do need to change my attitude. But it's so much fun to needle them."

A familiar, but unwelcome, individual came into the cell block and approached Leon's cell. Leon lost his smile, and he moved away from the bars.

Morrison grinned as he noted the prisoner's reaction. "Good to see our lessons have paid off, Nash. You'll do well to remember them, considering where you're going."

Taggard felt himself bristle at this man's obvious malice. "That's hardly a forgone conclusion, Marshal . . .?"

"Morrison. And it's Deputy Marshal."

"Oh. Yes. Leon's told me about you."

Morrison smiled at Leon again. "I'm sure he has." Then he returned his attention to the sheriff. "And you are . . .?"

"Murphy. Sheriff out of Medicine Bow."

The two lawmen shook hands, though it was a mere formality. There was already no love lost between them.

Morrison sent a smirk toward Leon. "I stopped by to check on my prisoner before heading out of town. I'd heard he took advantage of my absence last week and was up to his old tricks. I wanted to make sure he's where he's supposed to be."

Leon sneered back, though kept his distance. "Leaving, Marshal? I thought you'd want to stick around for the festivities."

"Don't you worry about that, Nash. I'll be back in time for the trial. Wouldn't miss that for the world. In the meantime, though, I've got other fish to fry."

"Wouldn't be my partner, would it?" A darkness settled over Leon's features.

Morrison simply smiled and tipped his hat to Taggard before leaving the cell block.

Taggard released the breath he hadn't realized he'd been holding. "Geesh, Leon. I see what you mean about him. Jack better watch himself."

"Yeah. Do me a favor, will ya'? You hear anything about how Jack is doing, will you let me know? Nobody here's telling me anything."

"Sure. I'll get in touch with Mr. Marsham and pass on what I find out. You know, he's offered to pay part of your lawyer fees, along with your bail. That's some friend you've got there."

"Yeah, I know. He is that."

"Okay, Leon. I'll swing by and see ya' again before I leave town. Then, you and Granger better get down to it. Your trial date is gonna be here before ya' know it."

The friends said goodbye and Taggard left the cell block.

Leon was on his own, again.

He glanced around at the other prisoners, wondering if anybody new had arrived, but no, just the same dreary lot that had been present fifteen hours ago. No stimulating conversation there.

Leon went to his new cot and laid down, hoping to get a little sleep. But it was to no avail. Oh well. He'd take some laudanum for the night and get himself back on some sort of schedule.

After a few minutes, he sat up and glanced at the prisoner in the cell next to him. "Hey, Hank?" he called to the prone individual with the hat over his eyes.

"Yeah? What do ya' want?"

"You done with today's paper?"

In answer to the question, Hank grabbed the paper and shoved it through the bars. He then promptly returned his hat to its resting place and went back to snoozing.

"Thanks." Leon gathered up the paper, put it back in order, and settled in to read the news of the day. He managed to kill about fifteen minutes before realizing he'd been reading the same page over and over.

He gave up and tossed the paper aside in frustration. His brain was doing it to him again. It ran wild, like a team of horses charging downhill, and there was nothing he could do to stop it.

He sighed, ran his hands through his hair, then punched the mattress for good measure. He looked around the cell block, and sneered a smile at Carl, in the far cell, who was watching him have another meltdown.

Leon's eyes glazed over as his thoughts turned inward, and, without thinking, he stood up and started to pace.

***

Arvada, Colorado

Dr. David Gibson would not get caught flat-footed again. As soon as he finished his calls for the day, he disappeared into his home office and got his information organized. He skipped supper altogether, then, to further contribute to Tricia's deteriorating patience, he sneaked out the side door and headed for the main street..

Tracking down Sam was not difficult to do. There were only so many places a young man, stuck in town, would spend an entire evening. David's first choice struck gold. Pushing through the batwing doors of the saloon, he stopped and surveyed the room until he saw Sam, standing at the bar, enjoying a beer.

"Sam. How are you this evening?"

"Doc." Sam gulped his mouthful and acknowledged his companion. "I wouldn't expect to see you in here. You and your wife have a fight or something?"

"No, not yet." David's tone held a touch of foreboding. "I need a word with you and to ask a favor."

Sam looked apprehensive. "A favor?"

"Yes." David took out an envelope he had tucked inside his jacket and handed it to Sam. "I've gathered together all the records I have of Kiefer's treatment and medications. I've also added some of my own notes about what I recommend for his ongoing healing. If you could pass those on to the doctor who will be attending to him, I would appreciate it. Also, I've added some pre-measured dosages of painkillers, with instructions, for you to give to Kiefer, once you're on the road. Can you do that?"

Sam grimaced. "Why are ya' askin' me? Why don't you give it to Marshal Morrison when he gets to town?"

"Because I don't trust him, Sam, that's why. Marshal Morrison would probably consider it a nuisance and toss everything into the trash. But it's important, all right? Please. Will you do it?"

Sam fingered the envelope and chewed his lip while debating the pros and cons. Sam was afraid of Morrison; if the marshal found out Sam was doing the doctor's bidding, there'd be hell to pay. On the other hand, Sam liked Jack Kiefer and still had twinges of conscience over what happened. Maybe this would be a way to make amends.

He relented. "Yeah, okay. I'll keep it safe with my stuff and give it to Kiefer when Morrison isn't lookin'."

David smiled. "Thanks. It really is important."

They were interrupted by the barkeep, who ambled over, wiping his hands on a handy towel. He didn't like bodies taking up space at the bar if they didn't order anything. He was running a business, not a social club.

"C'mon, Doc. You're a good guy and all, but order something, will ya'?"

"Oh, yeah. Sorry, Bill. I'll have a shot of whiskey."

Satisfied, Bill supplied him with his drink, and moved off.

David took a small swig and followed it with a relaxing sigh. Sometimes a shot of something a little stronger than coffee helped to ease a stressful day, Or, in this case, a stressful month.

"What do you plan on doing with the rest of your evening, Sam?" he asked. "Going back to the Marsham place for the night?"

"Oh no. I need to stay in town for when Morrison arrives. He may want to leave right away."

"Yes." Bitterness seeped into the doctor's tone. "He tends to slip away in the middle of the night, which is why I wanted to see you now, instead of in the morning."

"I doubt he'll be here tonight. Maybe tomorrow. I think I'm going to drop by and visit with Maribelle this evening. Her folks kind 'a like me and, well, so does she."

"That sounds pleasant enough," David said. "Are you no longer interested in Caroline?"

"Sure, I am. But she's not too interested in me, right now. I figure, I may as well go where I'm appreciated."

"Sound thinking." David finished his whiskey and gave Sam a pat on the back. "I'll check on Kiefer one more time this evening, and then go home, myself. Goodnight."

***

When David got to the jailhouse, Sheriff Jacobs was making a fresh pot of coffee. He poured himself a cup, just as the doctor walked in the door.

"Hey, Doc. How ya doin' this evening?"

"So far, so good. How's Kiefer?"

"Quiet."

"Is he asleep?"

"Nope. Just quiet. He's nothing at all, like I expected."

"Hmm. Give him time. He might surprise you."

"Oh, I'll keep an eye on him, don't you worry about that. You want a coffee?"

"Sure, why not. Let me take one in for Jack, too."

"Okay. I'll grab the keys."

Jacobs handed the two coffees to David, got the keys from his desk, and the two men headed into the cell block.

Jack was stretched out on the cot, hat over his eyes. He appeared relaxed. He sat up as soon as he heard the cell door open and smiled at David as the doctor handed him a cup.

"Thanks, Doc."

"I'll be in the office," Jacobs announced, as he closed the cell door. "Give me a shout when you're ready to leave, Doc."

David nodded and sat down beside the prisoner. They both took an appreciative sip of their beverages.

"How are you feeling tonight, Jack? How's the shoulder after the ride to town this morning?"

"Not bad, considerin'."

"Good." David nodded. "I'll be cutting back on your morphine, so we'll see how that goes."

Jack became concerned. "Why? By how much?"

"I'll give you the same amount at night, so you can sleep. But, if you can put up with some discomfort during the daytime, it's best if we start cutting you back. I've given some to Sam, for you to take if it gets too much on the trip to Wyoming. But the less you take during the day, the better. Okay?"

"But why?" Jack felt an irrational fear at the idea of the painkiller being withdrawn. "Isn't it better to not hurt at all?"

"Not necessarily." David took note of Jack's anxiety and was more convinced it was time to back off.

"David? Why?"

David sighed and took another sip of coffee as he considered the best way to explain the dangers of the drug. "Often, with morphine, and other painkillers like it, if you keep taking it over a prolonged period of time, you'll start needing it, even when you're not in pain anymore."

"Well, why?" Jack was confused. "Why would you keep taking it, once the pain is gone?"

"It's a side-effect. You start to crave it. It's almost like, not having it causes pain, rather than relieving pain that's already there."

"Oh." Jack contemplated this information. "You mean, like someone who can't stop drinkin'?"

"Yes. Very much like that."

"Oh. That ain't good."

David smiled at Jack's predisposition to understatement. "No, it's not good."

The two men sat quietly again, drinking their coffee. A heavy silence fell over the cell.

"What's the matter, David?" Jack finally asked.

"What? Why do you think something's the matter?"

"C'mon. You're as bad as Leon when it comes ta' talking a blue streak. Now you're sittin' there with nothin' ta' say. What's wrong?"

David sighed again and took another sip of coffee.

Jack waited patiently. The similarities between this young medical man and Jack's partner were becoming increasingly apparent. Jack had opened the gate, and he was willing to wait and see if the doc went through it. After a couple of minutes, Jack was rewarded with a response.

"I'm worried about your injury," David said. "I don't know what kind of doctor is going to be attending you after you leave here."

"Yeah, but so what?" Jack asked. "It's healin' up fine."

"Yes, it is. I'm pleased with the progress. The human body is an amazing thing, and given time, can repair itself of some of the worst injuries imaginable. I once treated a young man who . . ." he hesitated, catching Jack's ironic smile. "Yeah, never mind. I'd prefer it if Morrison let you stay here until your trial date, so we could get started on exercises for you. But that's not going to happen."

"You worry too much, David. Either that, or there's somethin' else botherin' ya'."

"It's Morrison," David said. "I don't trust him. He doesn't seem to care about the welfare of his prisoners, as long as he gets them from point A to point B. How he accomplishes that doesn't matter to him. He knew that Napoleon was injured, and deliberately snatched him out of my care because he didn't like me giving my professional opinion. I know he's going to try and do the same thing with you."

Jack felt a tight knot hit his stomach. "What do you mean, 'Napoleon was injured'?"

David looked at Jack in surprise. "Didn't anyone tell you what happened?"

"No. Not to any real extent. What happened?"

David felt a twinge of regret. He thought Jack already knew what had happened to his partner.

"He 'provoked' the lawmen and was badly beaten up," David said. "Then, Morrison gave him a bruised kidney and a cracked rib while he was incarcerated here. I was concerned he may have suffered more serious internal injuries, but Morrison sneaked him out of town before I could be sure."

Jack groaned and leaned back against the wall behind him. "Oh geesh. And Leon keeps tellin' me, I'm the hot head. I don't get it. That ain't like him."

"Caroline slipped him a lock pick, and when Morrison found it, Napoleon wouldn't tell him who gave it to him. He paid a heavy price for his loyalty."

Jack rolled his eyes. "Oh, brother. Peas in a pod, those two. I'm amazed they actually get along. They're both stubborn as mules."

David smiled, thinking Jack had shown quite a stubborn streak himself, on occasion.

"Still, Morrison shouldn't have hit him so hard," the doctor continued. "Especially after he'd already taken that beating out at the Marshams' place for attacking Sam."

"He did what?"

David shrugged and nodded.

Jack shook his head. "I don't get it. Leon is usually very protective of himself. He's the one who's always holdin' me back from gettin' inta' fights." He smiled with reminiscence. "He's a thinker, more brains than brawn. Ya' know?"

"Yes. Well, we all act out of character when we're scared. Watching you die on the table and not being able to do anything about it, terrified him."

Jack looked at David, his mouth open. Disbelief emanated off him. "What do you mean, 'I died'? I'm here now. How could I have died?"

David shrugged again. "You stopped breathing, Jack. You'd lost a lot of blood, and your body gave out. If I hadn't done extensive studying of the resuscitation techniques, you wouldn't be here now. Even at that, it was very close."

Jack ran his hand over his eyes and through his curls, as this information sunk in. "Oh, geesh. Yeah, Leon would 'a lost it. Especially if he knew it was Sam who betrayed us."

David nodded. "He was reacting to the emotions of the situation, and not thinking clearly. Much like you did, when you climbed out the window under a full dose of morphine. The only difference is, Napoleon can remember doing it, but he was no less out of control than you were."

Jack nodded. "No wonder Jean was so concerned. Oh—and the girls. They were there throughout all of this?"

"Yes."

"Oh, no. Aww, poor Penny. No wonder she was so . . ." his thoughts went back to the previous day in the barn. Guilt washed over him again.

"It's not your fault, Jack," David said, misunderstanding where the guilty conscience came from. "Those girls rallied and were very helpful, to both me and their mother, when it came to looking after you. They obviously care a great deal about you—you and Napoleon."

"Yeah, I know." Jack stared into his coffee cup. "I can only hope we don't end up disappointin' 'em too much."

David knitted his brow and gave Jack a thoughtful look. "I swear, you and Napoleon are the oddest pair of outlaws I've ever known. Not that I know many outlaws, but what I've heard and read about you two, well, you're not what I expected. You both have an edge to you that I find hard to understand, but you're not malicious. In fact, you're the opposite. Makes me wonder why you chose the life you did."

"Well, it weren't so much a choice, as we sort'a fell into it," Jack said. "We've been tryin' ta' make things right."

"Yes, I know. Cameron told me about your arrangement with the governor, which is why he's willing to help you. Do you think you have a chance at it?"

Jack sat quietly for a few moments, staring at the floor. A hand went through the curls again. "I donno. We've been in custody, what . . . six weeks now?"

"Yes, about that."

"And still no word from the governor. I think we're on our own." Then he came off the bunk and paced the cell, feeling agitated. "I wish I could talk ta' Leon, find out what he's thinkin'. But still, no jail cell is gonna hold 'im if'n he decides he wants ta' leave. The fact that he ain't, tells me he's gonna see it through. Dammit." He whacked the bars with his fist. "I just wish I could talk to 'im."

"That's not likely to happen," David said. "Morrison's adamant about keeping you two apart, probably for that very reason; he doesn't want you communicating."

Jack scowled. "You're right, David. I haven't even met the man yet, and I don't like him."

"Yes. Sometimes dislike is a healthy thing. Just remember what I said and don't provoke him."

"I'll try."

"In the meantime, here's some morphine. If you want to mix it in with what's left of your coffee, I'll at least know you'll sleep tonight." He stood up and took a small packet out of his pocket and handed it to Jack. "I better get home to Tricia. I think she's going be a little steamed at me."

Jack smiled. "Trouble at home, Doc?"

"Oh, nothing we can't sort out. Besides, she's probably right. If you ever get married, Jack, just remember, when you have a disagreement, she's probably right."

"Okay, Doc. I'll keep that in mind."

"Goodnight. I hope to see you in the morning."

"Yeah, goodnight, Doc. Good luck."

***

It was a pleasant evening as David walked home from the jailhouse. Well into summer now, the nights were long and usually pleasant. And this night, with dusk starting to settle in, was one of the nicest. Unfortunately, the good doctor wasn't enjoying it as much as he would have normally, due to his twinges of guilt over the way he had ignored his wife.

He had been so wrapped up in getting everything prepared for his patient, and then making sure he got the information to Sam, before Morrison got to town, that he had shut Tricia out of his plans. He had even skipped out on supper, and that wasn't fair, since Tricia had taken the time to prepare it. Besides that, now he was hungry, but was probably only going to receive hot tongue and cold shoulder for dinner.

No doubt about it, David Gibson loved his wife. He had been new in town, still hadn't bought his little house, or opened his practice when he met her. His heart had known that this was where he wanted to put out his shingle, but his head was still trying to rationalize it. Meeting Tricia had clenched that decision for him.

Doctor David Gibson was about the same age as Jack Kiefer, but that was where the similarities between the two men ended. David was handsome enough, with those same dark-chocolate eyes Leon carried, but his hair was a lighter brown, and not as thick as Leon's wavy locks. He was taller than both Nash and Kiefer, measuring in at well over six feet. He was slim and long-legged, but despite possessing enough broadness in the shoulders to be masculine, he always felt awkward and gangly. Though he was unaware of it, he turned many a feminine eye in his direction, being a fine catch for a husband. Too bad he was already married.

He was born in Philadelphia and grew up in a loving, wealthy family full of doctors. It was a family tradition and completely taken for granted that any sons born in the Gibson line would pursue a career in medicine.

David was somewhere in the middle of six siblings and had done exactly what was expected of him by following his father, uncles, and brothers into medicine. Then, when it became time to set up his own practice, he did something that was unexpected, even shocking, to the whole family: he moved West.

Life as a doctor in Philadelphia was boring and predictable. David decided he wanted something more than that. Medicine certainly ran in the Gibson family, but David was given more than just the family heritage to choose a medical career; he was given a gift.

He was a natural healer. He had an instinct for it. He took everything he learned one step further, to expand beyond what was already known and turn it to practical use. He improved on old methods and techniques and seemed to see how and why something should work. He had a successful and lucrative career ahead of him. That he would eventually publish, was a given.

Then, out of the blue, he packed up and moved. Of course, his family was shocked. He was supposed to stay in Philadelphia, set up a practice within the family business, marry the girl next door, who was also from a long line of medical men, and become part of the Gibson family dynasty. Why in the world would he want to give all that up and move out to the middle of nowhere, to set up a tiny practice in a tiny town where all he could hope to work with would be cowboys and dirt farmers? How was he supposed to make a name for himself way out there?"

Fortunately for the people of Arvada and the surrounding area, David had his own ideas about what made a successful practice, and treating society ladies, suffering from a touch of the vapors, wasn't it. He made a side trip up to Arvada on his way to Denver and knew that he had found his place in the West. He bought a quaint little house on a quiet street, put up his shingle, and was open for business within the week.

That was three years ago.

He had been walking into the mercantile just as she had been walking out, and as soon as their eyes met, there was a connection.

Tricia Baxter had grown up on one of the numerous ranches in the area and had learned one important thing from that life: It wasn't the life she wanted. She was young, pretty, and intelligent, and she had no shortage of suitors, but they were all ranchers. Though it was fun to have her choice of dates for any of the social events, she wasn't taking any of their advances seriously.

Her friends teased her, good-naturedly, warning her that she was going to become a spinster if she continued to be so picky. Tricia's response was that she would rather be a spinster, than marry into a life she already knew would make her miserable.

When the tall, dark, and handsome stranger showed up in town, she was completely smitten. When she discovered that he was a doctor—well. That made the romance all the sweeter.

The courtship only lasted three months. Once they were married, David took his new wife home to his new house and introduced her to the realities of being married to a new doctor. It was a lot of 'new' all at once, and the first six months of married life, though joyous in many ways, was also trying on the young couple. They had made a lot of adjustments.

One of the things they always tried to have in their relationship was respect for each other. David knew his treatment of his wife earlier in the evening, had been anything but respectful. Though Tricia was understanding of the unpredictable hours of a medical man and was always willing to help in the care of a difficult case, these past six weeks had been hard on her.

Now that the patient had been moved into town and David no longer had to make the trip out to the Rocking M, Tricia had hoped for a quiet, romantic dinner at home with her husband. Then he disappeared out the side door, without saying a word.

As David entered their well-lit home, he tried to work out, in his own mind, what he was going to say to make things all right. But, as usual, as soon as he saw his wife sitting dejectedly in the kitchen over a solitary cup of tea, all his arguments went out the window.

"I'm sorry," were the first words out of his mouth.

Tricia looked at him with a long-suffering sigh, and, getting up, she moved over to the stove.

"I tried to keep your supper warm. I'm sure you're hungry."

"Yes, I am. But Tricia, please," and David crossed the space between them in quick strides and took her in his arms. He hugged her close, but her body remained tense. She was mad. "Let me explain, I'm not trying to justify my actions. It wasn't right, leaving here without a word. I just want to explain."

"Fine." She pulled away from his embrace, removed his plate from the stove and plunked it on the table, then sat down in front of her cup of tea.

David sat down and picked at his food, feeling awkward. "It's just that, well, I'm worried about Jack, and how Morrison's going to treat him. That shoulder is so close to healing well, but the next stage is crucial, and I'm afraid that if anything happens, or the next doctor to treat him doesn't know what he's doing, Jack could still lose partial use of it."

"I know you want what's best for your patients, David," Tricia said, "but sometimes you take it too far. You can't be in control all the time."

"I know that."

"Then why can't you let Jack go? There are other doctors, you know."

"Butchers, you mean." David stabbed the potato with his fork. "Most of the 'doctors' I've seen out here haven't got a clue what they're doing. They haven't even had any formal training; it's all guess work. It would be tragic if Jack lost the use of his arm now, after all we've done to get it healing properly."

"David, you saved his life. There's nothing tragic about that."

She hesitated, looking into her half-empty tea cup. She wasn't sure if she should bring up her next thought, as David might view it as a betrayal, but she also thought it was important, and he should at least consider the other side of the coin.

David knew there was more coming, and he waited, patiently. Tricia often had input that may not have occurred to him and her views were always welcome. Finally, he saw her make her decision, and she looked him in the eye.

"Did you ever think that maybe it wouldn't be such a bad thing, if Jackson 'The Kansas Kid' Kiefer lost the use of his gun arm?"

David was shocked. "Wh . . . what?" This thought went against everything he held true to his profession. "How can you say that?"

"David, think about it," Trish pleaded with him. "You saved his life. Isn't that enough? The man's an outlaw. What if you save his arm and he escapes custody, then goes back to his old ways and ends up killing someone? How would that make you feel, knowing that you might have been able to prevent it?"

"Aww, Tricia, no. That's too many 'ifs' to be plausible. What 'if' he gets his pardon and turns out to be a model citizen? Or ends up using his talents for upholding the law, instead of breaking it? We don't know how his life will turn out. Besides, there's no proof he's a killer. On the contrary, Napoleon Nash and the Kansas Kid are noted for avoiding violence in the jobs they've pulled. To suggest that he's going to turn around and start killing now, is completely unfair."

"David, I'm just saying, you've done enough. Let him go. Another doctor can take over his care. Once he's out of this town, he's out of your practice, and, therefore, no longer your concern."

David picked at his food, no longer hungry. He knew that to some degree, Tricia was right; he did tend to get too wrapped up with his patients. But on the other hand, how could she expect him to be complacent about handing over the care of a patient to another doctor, when the job was only half done? It was a dilemma, and one that he was having a hard time adjusting to.

"Yes, all right. You do have a point, to some degree," he said. "But a lot of what I was doing this evening, complies with what you're saying. There were certain things I had to do, to ensure the proper continuation of his treatment before I could feel at all comfortable with letting him go. Do you understand that?"

"Yes, David. Of course, I do. But next time, let me know. I had no idea where you were or what you were doing, and that's not fair."

"I know. And I'm sorry about that. I was so focused on getting it done, I wasn't thinking. I apologize. You have every right to be angry. But, don't expect me to not care about my patients, or give them less than my best, just because of who they are and what they may or may not have done. Agreed?"

Tricia smiled at her husband. "Agreed."

Later that evening, David discovered something else that every married couple comes to realize sooner or later: Make-up sex usually makes the argument worth having in the first place.

CHAPTER FIFTEEN
A REPRIEVE

Cheyenne, Wyoming

'Did they really think that one hour a day, outside of this tin box, was a privilege?'

Leon paced his cell.

Though the mild sleep medicine he took every evening allowed him some relief from the day-in/day-out mundane wakefulness, it only worked for five hours of every twenty-four. Afraid he might get addicted, or some such nonsense, the doctor wouldn't allow him to take more than that. What did that mean, 'addicted?' *'Addicted to what? Sleep?'*

All the other inmates of the cell block had been rotated out numerous times since Leon had first taken up residence, so he had given up trying to remember their names. If, by chance, he wanted the attention of any of them, it was with a resounding '*Hey you.*' Or, if that didn't work, an empty tin cup thrown against the bars usually got the desired effect.

The initial awe of being in the company of Napoleon Nash, generally wore off if the culprit was incarcerated for more than a couple of days. The constant pacing of the outlaw, and the cynicism that was the usual response to the most casual of inquiries, tended to keep everybody at a distance, and Leon was left alone.

When Morrison went to tend to his other "fish", he left Mike behind to tend to his special prisoner. The marshal didn't have much confidence in the local constabulary, especially after Leon's near escape early in his confinement. Morrison wasn't going to trust the security of his main catch to anyone other than his own proven deputy.

So, during the numerous occasions when Taggard wasn't in town, Mike became Leon's regular escort, and the two men at least attempted to get along.

"Hey Mike," Leon started, with an air of innocent joviality. "Sure is hot today. Aren't you hot?"

"It's the middle of summer, Nash. It's supposed to be hot."

"Yeah, but, there's the saloon right across the street. Wouldn't you like to have a nice, cold beer?"

"A beer?" Mike stopped and looked down at Leon from his towering 6'6" bulk. "You'd love for me to get drunk, wouldn't you?"

"No. No, no. That's not it at all," Leon gave the deputy a two-handed, shackled pat on the arm. "I was just thinking, a cold beer would go down really smooth, right about now."

"Uh huh. Fine. You want a beer, let's go get you a beer. So long as you don't mind drinking alone. I'm on duty."

"Oh. No, I don't mind," Leon was surprised it had been so easy and kicked himself for not trying it sooner.

Once inside the establishment, Leon felt a great deal of the stress of his confinement melt away. The smile he beamed was as genuine as it was rare, these days.

They sidled up to the bar, and Mike ordered and paid for Leon's beer. Once it arrived, Leon took in a mouthful and, just as he had done with his first cup of coffee at the café, he held onto the beverage and savored its tingling coldness before swallowing it down and taking a second mouthful.

How long had it been since his last beer? He couldn't remember. Pushing his brain to go back to the past, the scene gradually came into focus. It had been that afternoon in Arvada. That last time he had taken Karma out for a gallop. The last time he'd played a game of poker. The last time . . . Jack.

Leon sighed. He took another swig of beer and turned around to lean against the bar. There weren't many patrons in the establishment yet, since it was only late morning. But there was a friendly poker game going on at one of the tables, and Leon couldn't help but feel drawn to it. Without him even realizing it, the game, like a magnet, pulled him toward it, until he felt Mike's large hand on his shoulder, dragging him back to the bar.

"Where do you think you're goin, Nash?"

"Just one hand, Mike. What harm could it do?"

"What are you gonna play with? You don't have any money."

Leon smiled up at the deputy. "Would you spot me?"

Mike wasn't impressed with this idea.

"C'mon, Mike. Chances are good I'll double your money in one hand. And if I do lose it, I'll buy you a beer—next time."

Mike chuckled at the unlikelihood of that happening. Then he gave in to Leon's charismatic manipulations and agreed to spot him for one hand.

Leon approached the table, feeling a nervous excitement that hadn't touched his soul for many a moon, and he wondered where it came from. Still, it had been a while, and a lot had happened since he'd last played.

"Good morning, gentlemen," he greeted the players. "Would you mind if I sat in for a hand or two?"

"Oh, Mr. Nash."

"Of course. It would be an honor."

Much to Leon's surprised and mild embarrassment—not to mention, pleasure—a few of the players stood up and shook a shackled hand. A welcoming slap on the back made the acceptance complete.

"By all means, Mr. Nash. Have a seat."

"We don't play for big stakes here, but we do have fun."

"Great." Leon displayed a dimpled grin. "Thank you."

He sat down, then was surprised by Mike unlocking the cuff on his right hand, then re-snapping it onto the arm of the chair.

"It'll make it a bit easier for you to handle the cards," Mike responded to Leon's quizzical look. "Just—don't tell anyone."

The deputy found a chair close to his charge, but still positioned himself between the outlaw and the saloon exit, just in case. He was being more cautious than usual, now that he had allowed his prisoner some freedom, and he was thankful that Morrison was away on business. Turner appeared to be a competent, but more lenient lawman.

Once he relaxed a bit, he was pleasantly surprised to find himself being drawn in to the game and to discover that Nash's reputation as a talented poker player was not unwarranted. One hand stretched into two, and two into three, by the time Mike realized that the hour was more than up, and it was time to get his prisoner back to the jailhouse.

The deputy had enough poker etiquette to not interrupt the hand being played, but once that was done, and Nash was raking in the pot, he gave a quiet, discreet cough, and got to his feet.

A look of disappointment flashed across Leon's face, but he covered it up and smiled with honest sincerity at his fellow players. "Gentlemen, thank you. It's been a real pleasure. But my companion has indicated that it is time for me to return to my lodgings."

"Aww, that's a shame."

"Sure is. You brought our little game up to a whole new level."

Leon's smile broadened. "Thank you. Now, ah, I promised Deputy Mike I'd double his money for him, so if you gentlemen don't mind, I'll keep that amount and return the rest of my winnings to the pot."

"What? But, why?"

"Yeah, Mr. Nash. You won that, fair and square."

"Yeah, yeah, I know. But what am I going to do with it, where I'm going?" Seeing the gloom these words brought to the table, he quickly added, "Besides, I'd like to join you again, and I wouldn't want you to think I was just after your money."

His ruse worked. Everyone perked up, and there were smiles all around.

"Sure thing, Mr. Nash. Anytime."

"Yup. We're usually here every Friday morning for a game. You'll always be welcome to sit in."

Leon nodded, as Mike uncuffed him from the chair, and the two men made their exit.

Leon handed him the coins, as they stepped into the street. "Here, Mike. Everything I owe you and then some. Have a beer on me when you get off duty."

"I might just do that." Mike smiled as he accepted the coins. "I take it, this is going to be a regular stop on Friday mornings now, until your trial."

Leon smiled up at him. "Would be nice."

"Hmm. We'll see."

***

Sheriff Turner looked up from his paperwork, as the two men entered the office. "It's about time you showed up. I was about to send a posse out to look for you."

"Sorry about that, Sheriff," Mike said. "We were at the saloon. Everything's fine."

Turner got the keys from the drawer and headed for the cell block. "Try explaining that to Mr. Granger. He's been in here twice, looking for his client. Still, I suppose it won't hurt him to actually work for his fee on this case."

Leon had been back in his cell for an hour and was settled enough to read and comprehend one of the communal dime novels that was making the rounds, when his lawyer returned. Leon stood up and approached the bars, so they could confer in privacy.

"Any luck?"

"Some," Granger said. "Your Texas rancher friend, Mr. Coburn, got back to me. Says he's too old to make the trip here in person, but he'll get together with his lawyer and write up a testimonial. He also wired a tidy sum to help cover some of you and your partner's expenses. It seems you have no shortage of sponsors, Mr. Nash."

Leon was surprised. "Max sent money? Okay, now I'm convinced. We must be in real trouble."

Granger looked confused. "Is this a problem?"

"No. But, as the saying goes, Max will squeeze a dollar until the eagle screams. He's not known for his generosity."

"Oh." Granger nodded, then carried on. "Judge McEnroe is retired now, but he also agreed to send a testimonial. He commented that he would convey his greetings to the governor and remind him of an obligation owed . . . whatever that means."

"We did some work for the judge, so he knows about the arrangement we have with the governor's office."

Granger nodded his understanding. "Is there anyone else you can think of?"

Leon leaned against the bars, his chin resting on his crossed arms. He disappeared into thought.

"Hmn. Frank Carlyle, if you can find him, that is. I tried to contact him before we were arrested, and still haven't heard anything. He's either avoiding us, or out of the country. Ah, what about George Baxter? We did some work for him a while back."

Granger sighed. "You apparently have a lot of friends in high places, Mr. Nash, which certainly adds credence to your claim of working undercover for the government. But, I'm afraid none of them seem willing to come down and acknowledge you. What about people with whom you grew up?"

"You mean, who aren't outlaws?"

"Preferably. There must be somebody."

Leon's sigh was laced with dejection. "We didn't really make any friends at the orphanage. Most of my friends are more recent than that. I guess I've known Taggard the longest, aside from Jack, of course. There's Cameron. Oh, and Josey. We knew her from the orphanage." But he shook his head. "No, not Josey. She's a lady of dubious employment, if you know what I mean. Dragging her into this would only get her into trouble, as well.

"It seems our friends are either too high up to come down, or too low to come up. There are other lawmen that we know—in a good way, I mean—but acknowledging that they know us could put their own lives and careers at stake. So . . ." Leon slumped. "I'm sorry, Mr. Granger. Many of the people who might have some influence in the courts would be put into compromising positions. I can't ask that of them."

"I can see where this could be a problem. Even if we protect them from prosecution, their reputations would be irreparably damaged," Granger said. "We're quickly running out of time. You can bet, the prosecution is preparing a solid case against you, and I'm sure they're not having any trouble doing it. Anything you can think of, at this point, would be helpful. In the meantime, I'll continue to work on the sympathy pleas: difficult childhood, falling into stealing to survive, that sort of thing."

Leon nodded. The moroseness that had been alleviated by the poker game was settling back onto him again.

"Any word from Taggard?"

"He expects to be back in town next week. I'm sure he'll have some news about your partner then."

"Okay." Leon sighed, then he straightened up from the bars and turned back to his bunk and the dime novel.

Granger hesitated a moment before leaving, wishing he could say something more optimistic. But truth be known, trying to set up a solid defense for a known outlaw, who was in no position to deny his guilt, was a task that even the most seasoned of barristers would shrink away from.

Napoleon Nash had been too damn good at what he did.

***

Arvada, Wyoming

"Jack. How are you doing, this morning?"

Jack removed his hat from over his eyes and sat up. "Mornin', David. I'm okay. How are you?"

The doctor's eyes twinkled. "Great."

"Uh huh."

"Here's a cup of coffee for you. I thought you might like one."

"Yeah, thanks," Jack took the beverage. He thought it best not to mention he'd already had two cups.

"So, let's see that shoulder," David put his own coffee down on the floor.

Unwrapping the bandages wasn't quite the ordeal that it had once been, since the open wounds had nearly healed over. The stitches had been removed and everything looked good. If David had had more control over the situation, he would have treated this wound differently, but as it was, the open wound on the back had healed over, and though there was going to be quite a scar, it appeared healthy enough.

At this point, David was more concerned about what was going on inside Jack's shoulder. As much scarring as was showing on the outside, there was going to be just as much, if not more, on the inside. And that is where the problems would be.

If the doctor in the next town didn't encourage Jack to move and stretch those muscles, to break down the scar tissue, everything would seize up, and Jack would be left with limited use of the arm.

In the back of his mind, David could hear Trish suggesting that this would not be such a bad thing, but the doctor in David could not accept this. He knew he had to give Jack the best possible option that was open to him and encourage a complete recovery.

David gently removed the gauze that held the arm snuggly against Jack's torso, then removed the sling.

Jack hesitated, and brought his left hand over to support the right, not wanting to let the injured arm hang loose.

"It's all right, Jack," David said. "Give me your left hand. Take hold, like we're meeting for the first time and shaking hands.

Okay, now squeeze, tight as you can. Good. That's a strong grip you're got there. Now, do the same with your right. Squeeze, tight as you can."

The effort it took for Jack to give David a good grasp showed in the tightness of his expression and the paled complexion.

"Okay. That's going to need work," David said. "Just relax."

Still holding on to Jack's right hand, David slowly pulled the patient's arm away from his body. Jack tensed and gasped with pain. David brought the arm back to Jack's torso, then took hold of his elbow and pulled the arm up, creating much the same response as the first maneuver.

"Okay." David let Jack take the arm back to hold in protective custody.

Then, the good doctor really began his examination. He slipped his hands beneath Jack's shirt and started to massage his shoulder muscles.

It amazed Jack to no end, how David's slim, sensitive fingers could always find the most painful spot to start probing in. The more David searched Jack's shoulder and back, the less tolerance the patient had for it.

"Ow."

"Sorry."

"Ow."

"Sorry."

"If you're sorry, David, then stop doin' it."

"Sorry," David said, again. He smiled and sat down beside his patient. "I know it hurts. But I need to do it to see how things are healing up in there."

"Yeah, okay. So, how's it goin'?"

"Good, so far. I'm going to give you some stretches and exercises to do, though, and it'll hurt to do them. You're also going to need someone to help you with them. Maybe Sam. I don't know. I'll need to think on this for a while."

The outer door to the cell block opened, and Morrison came up to the bars of Jack's cell. An instant tension settled over the occupants.

"Well, it looks like the prisoner has healed up quite nicely."

"On the outside," David said. "Still a lot of internal damage. I'd appreciate it, if you would keep that in mind."

"Sure, Doc. Anything you say." Then the marshal looked directly at Jack. "Name's Morrison, though I'm sure you've heard enough about me, by now."

Jack sent him a cold smile.

Morrison ignored it. "Had a lot of trouble convincing your partner to behave himself. Am I going to have the same problems with you?"

"Oh, no, sir, Marshal," Jack said, quietly. "Leon's the problem child. I'm as meek as a mouse."

"Uh huh." Morrison turned back to the exit. "It'd be in your best interest to remember it." And then he was gone.

"Sheesh." Jack released the breath he had been holding.

David gave Jack a reassuring pat on the shoulder. "Yup. Watch yourself with him."

***

Later that morning, after David had finished with his rounds, he drove his horse and buggy to the jailhouse to check on Jack again. Unfortunately, when he entered the office, Sheriff Jacobs could only give him an apologetic smile and show him an empty cell.

"I'm sorry, Doc. Shortly after you left on your rounds, Morrison came in here and took possession of his prisoner. And Kiefer is his prisoner, so there was nothing I could legally do to stop him."

David entered the empty cell and picked up the remnants of the fresh gauze and sling he had reset Jack's arm with.

"Yeah." The sheriff leaned against the bars. "Morrison wanted him manacled securely. He couldn't really do it while Kiefer's arm was in a sling, so . . ."

"So, Morrison took the sling off."

"Yeah."

David sighed. He dropped the sling onto the bunk, then turned and walked out of the jailhouse without a word. He headed for the saloon. He was fuming and needed a drink. He knew Morrison was going to pull that stunt again, which is why he had taken the precautions he had. But it was still maddening.

David punched open the batwing doors and headed to the bar, but then he slowed down nearly to a standstill, and his jaw dropped in disbelief.

"Sam. What you doing here?"

Sam's head snapped up, and he sent the doc an agonized look. "Aww, jeez. I'm sorry, Doc. Morrison told me, he didn't need me to escort Kiefer to Wyoming. I guess he heard I was going to stay on at the Marsham's place and thought he was doing me a favor by letting me go. So, I'm sorry, Doc." Sam pulled out the envelope, with the instructions and the medications intended for the next doctor down the line, and handed them back to the medical man.

David took the envelope without a word—at first. Then his temper exploded, and he slammed his fist onto the bar.

"Dammit! That bastard did it to me again."

***

Jack tried to relax, but his shoulder ached, and having his hands shackled in front of him didn't help. The first thing he'd noticed when they boarded the train the previous day, was that Sam was not with them, which meant the morphine wasn't with them, either. This was bad news, as far as Jack was concerned. He was becoming more and more uncomfortable, and sleeping wasn't in the cards for this trip, at all.

Just like Leon before him, Jack had been shuffled onto the passenger car and escorted down to the row of three empty seats, with Rick leading the way. Next, came Jack with Morrison directly behind him, pushing him along with a hand on his back. Alex brought up the rear. Once seated, Morrison secured Jack to the seat with the leg irons, and everyone settled in for the long ride to Wyoming.

As to be expected, the other passengers were curious who the prisoner was, and why he warranted such a heavy guard. The questions didn't go unanswered for long.

Unlike with Leon, by now the news about the capture of those two notorious outlaws, had spread far and wide. It didn't take much to put two and two together.

Soon, the braver of the boys in the car, and then some from the other cars who had gotten wind of the celebrity on board, began to approach the armed men. Even just a glimpse of the outlaw would make for hours of bragging rights, once they got home.

Jack tried to be amiable toward them, but he was hurting, and it was taking quite an effort.

"Wow. Are you really the Kansas Kid?"

"Who would have thought you'd be on this train?"

"Where's Nash?"

"Is he on this train, too?"

"Are you really as fast as they say?"

"Can you show us your fast draw?"

"Is it true you're going to prison for twenty years?"

"Wow, twenty years. That's a long time."

"Yeah. I'll be in my thirty's by then. That's so old."

"Is the Elk Mountain Gang going to try and rescue you?"

"Wow. That'd be great."

Jack smiled at them, and tried to answer their questions, but they came rapid fire and most got drowned out by the next, so he eventually gave up. Then Morrison called it quits and sent the young boys packing, much to their groans, and complaints, and dirty looks at the lawmen.

Jack, who usually enjoyed talking to children, was relieved when they disbanded. Even the quick, shy glances from a couple of the young ladies in attendance, didn't alleviate his slump.

The train crossed the border into Wyoming shortly after noon of that day, though there was no indication from the landscape that such a transition had occurred. It was a typical sunny, summer day, and the train carried on at a steady, rhythmic chugging throughout the long afternoon.

Jack sighed with boredom. Even the minor distraction of an admiring glance from a pretty, young lady didn't alleviate the monotony.

He tried to ignore the growing ache in his arm, but the pain worsened with each passing mile. He looked out the window, hoping that watching the scenery fly by would give his mind something else to focus on, but the landscape was just as dry and monotonous as his mood.

Gradually, he began to recognize certain landmarks. This was a well-used track, and he and Leon would have stopped trains along here on a regular basis. A smile tugged at his lips, as each passing knoll, or thicket of trees brought back memories of successful train robberies, gone by.

They were some distance away from their usual haunts, as their hideout was situated further north, in the Elk Mountain range. But things would get too hot for them in that area, if they hit it too many times in a row. So, he and Leon had often come south to do some reconnaissance. They had even gone further afield than this, hitting Denver and other areas in Colorado, as well as going up north, into Montana, to take the law by surprise.

He and Leon would first scope out a new run, then call for the required members of their gang to come and join them for the selected hit. Completely unexpected and precise, those jobs had paid off well, and made the travel and planning worth the expense.

He smiled whimsically, as he remembered those days. He and his partner, scouting out the territory and planning where, along the route, would be the best place to stop their chosen target. Those had been good times. They had been in their hay day then. They'd been invincible; nothing could stop them. Leon was brilliant. Jack was fast. They had been young and reckless, and they'd loved every minute of it.

Jack sighed, feeling regret that those days were over and gone. Life had changed, and they'd had to make certain adjustments just to keep their heads above water. Now look at them, still adjusting just to stay alive and move forward. Although, right now, moving forward meant stepping into the abyss and hoping that, somehow in the darkness, they would both land on their feet.

Jack came back to the present as the train started around a bend, and he smiled again, remembering this area as their favorite ambush spot. It was perfect; the bend in the tracks was just long enough, so the engineer couldn't see the logs blocking the way until he was into the trap, but still with enough room to stop the train without endangering anyone.

On top of that, there was just the right amount of level ground to make room for the passengers to be safely disembarked and assembled while the outlaws went about their business. It was as though this spot had been designed, specifically, with outlawin' in mind.

Then, like déjà vu, the train slowed down. The screaming brakes against the metal wheels competed with the frantic whistles from the engine, as the people in the car looked anxiously around them.

The lawmen were instantly on the alert.

"What the hell is going on?" Morrison snarled, then was up in a flash, walking toward the head of the car. He disappeared through the door and out to the landing, to get a better idea of the situation.

Jack tensed, sitting up straighter.

"Stay seated," Rick told him, placing a cautionary hand on the prisoner's arm. "Alex?"

"Yup." Alex stood, rifle at the ready, ensuring that none of the passengers made a move toward the prisoner. If this was a planned attempt by the Elk Mountain Gang to rescue one of their leaders, they were going to find it difficult to pull off.

The train came to a halt as Jack saw two horsemen gallop past his window and his heart skipped a beat. In an instant, he recognized Lobo and Charlie Shields, and he knew it was his old gang. But they couldn't possibly have known that Jack was on this train. They had probably planned this as another long-distance robbery, completely unaware of the lawmen who were on board. Jack was understandably anxious; this could get dangerous quickly, especially with Morrison in charge.

Rick stood up when Morrison returned. The marshal handed his rifle to Rick, then knelt to unlock Jack's ankles from the leg irons.

"You two," he instructed his deputies, as he stood up, "take positions at the windows and be ready for a fight. Don't fire unless they come at us. We don't want an all-out gun battle here." He pulled out his revolver and grabbed Jack by his left arm. "Come on, Kiefer, on your feet. Now." Morrison hauled him up and hurried him toward the door.

It all happened so fast, Jack only had a vague impression of the scared eyes watching him scramble toward the exit. The boys, who had earlier been all excited about a possible outlaw raid, were now clinging to their mothers. They found the reality of such a raid far more frightening than anything they could imagine.

Then, the two men were out on the landing, just as the current leader, Gus Shaffer, and his lieutenant, Hank Wilkinson, trotted their horses past, on their way to the baggage car.

Before Jack could grasp what was happening, or even yell a warning to his former compatriots of the danger they were in, Morrison aimed his revolver and fired. Whether Morrison was really that good a shot, or he'd just been lucky, Jack would never know, but the result was that Hank's head jerked back and he fell from the saddle like a rag doll. He didn't move, once he hit the ground.

Jack gasped in shock. It was surreal; he couldn't believe this was happening. As soon as the shot was fired, Morrison pushed Jack forward, in front of him and, turning the revolver, pressed the still-warm muzzle against the prisoner's temple. Jack heard the hammer being pulled back, and he felt sick.

Gus pulled his horse up and aimed his handgun in the direction the shot had come from. Then he froze, hardly believing what his eyes were showing him.

"Kid. What the hell?" He trotted his horse closer to the two men standing on the car.

"Hold it right there, Shaffer," Morrison yelled at him. "Now that I have your attention, you and the rest of your men better back off. Your boss here is wanted dead or alive, and after all the problems I've been having, I'd just as soon blow his brains out, right here and now. It's up to you. Back off, or he's dead—and I mean it."

That got Gus' dander up. He took aim at Morrison, trying to look like he meant it, too.

"Well now, what makes you think that once you shoot Kiefer, I won't shoot you? We were just here pullin' an honest train robbery. Hell, we heard Nash and the Kid had been captured, but that ain't new, and it always turns out to be a false alarm. We didn't even know Kiefer was on board, and you go shootin' one 'a my men, and makin' threats. Maybe we'll just shoot you where you stand and take Kiefer with us."

Other members of the gang gathered around, drawn by the gunfire, and they all hooted and laughed, like they thought Gus had a great idea.

Meanwhile, Malachi Cobb, a scruffy little man with a terrible chawing habit, dismounted to check on the fallen Hank. When he looked up, his expression was none too happy.

Jack felt like a chicken caught between a hungry coyote and the chopping block.

Morrison pressed the muzzle of his gun harder against the prisoner's temple. "You best tell them how it is, Kiefer, or I swear, I will kill you, and Shaffer will be the next one to go."

Jack swallowed, trying to moisten his very dry throat. "Best listen to him, Gus." His voice sounded gruff, even to himself. "You got no idea what you're up against here."

Malachi remounted and approached his boss, looking pale and scared. "Gus?"

"Not now, Ky. I'm busy."

"But Gus, Hank's dead."

Gus shot a look at Malachi, who nodded solemnly. They both glanced back to where a couple of the other boys were heaving Hank up across his horse's saddle. Gus glared at Morrison, his expression livid.

Jack groaned. "Aww no, not Hank."

Morrison heard him and smiled. "You better tell them, Kiefer. I'm getting tired of this game."

Gus was about to explode.

Jack knew he had to stop it, and stop it, now.

"Back off, Gus."

"He killed Hank!"

"And he's gonna kill me, and then you, if you don't back off," Jack yelled at him, frustrated with the man's dimwittedness. "Do you really think he's alone here? You have at least three rifles aimed at your chest, right now."

Gus sat back and noticeably paled as he scanned the windows of the passenger car.

Out of the corner of his eye, Jack noticed four rifle barrels emerge through the windows, soon followed by five revolvers.

Gus chewed his lip and forced his gaze back to his ex-boss. "Well . . . what about you, Kid?" The outlaw's voice rose his anxiety. "It don't feel right, ridin' off an' leavin' you here."

Jack's temper threatened to take control. Why did Gus always have to be so damned stubborn?

Morrison got perverse pleasure out of the battle of wills between the two outlaws. Apparently, even a band of thieves has problems with middle management.

"Gus, please," Jack persisted. "Go. Just go and live to rob another train tomorrow."

"But Kid—"

"Go! And stop callin' me 'Kid'. Ya' know I don't like it."

"All right. We're goin'," Gus finally agreed, his stubbly chin jutting out in anger. "But this ain't over. What's ta' stop us from comin' at ya' again, further down the track, and takin' 'em by surprise?"

Jack groaned. "Maybe the fact that you just told the law, that's what you're gonna do. It kind'a ruins the surprise, don't it?"

Gus blustered, feeling insulted. "Fine then! We'll leave ya' to it. Just tryin' ta' help, and you get all uppity. We'll be goin', then."

"Fine. Do it."

"We're goin'."

"Go!"

With one, final exasperated snarl in Jack's direction, Gus signaled to his men, and they turned and galloped toward the nearby woods.

Before the small band of outlaws got more than a few yards, Morrison took sudden aim and fired at the backs of the retreating group.

Gus slumped forward, obviously wounded, but he didn't fall, and the gang of outlaws kept going.

Jack yelled in anger and rammed into the marshal, spoiling his aim for another shot. Quick as a snake, Morrison rounded on Jack and whacked him across the head with the side of his revolver.

Jack went down in the confined space, his back against the railing, as he tried to raise his shackled hands to protect himself from another blow.

Morrison moved to shoot him where he sat, but then Rick was there, knocking the marshal's gun off target.

"No Tom. Don't!"

"What do you think you're doing?" Morrison rounded on his deputy.

"There's no need to kill him," Rick tried to reason with his boss. "Leave him be. He did what you asked."

"What? Are you turning into a bleeding heart, too, Layton?" Morrison sneered at him.

"No. Just, everyone needs to calm down. Kiefer's not going anywhere, and I doubt that gang is going to come back, now that we're on to them. Just leave him be."

"Fine. You babysit him, then." And Morrison stomped down, off the landing, to join some of the other male passengers heading toward the engine to help get the train moving again.

Both Rick and Jack breathed a sigh of relief. "C'mon, Kiefer, on your feet." And, not thinking, Rick grabbed him by his right arm and started to pull him up.

Jack gasped in pain, and nausea swept over him.

Rick backed off. "Oh. Sorry." Stepping over Jack, he took hold of the prisoner's left arm and helped him to his feet.

They went inside the car and headed for their seats, making their way through the other passengers, who were up and excitedly discussing the day's events.

A few of the male passengers were still in the process of securing their own firearms, having pulled them in a show of support for the lawmen. The adults, at least, were getting fed up with the number of robberies that had been staged along this line.

On the flip side, the youngsters, now that the danger was over, were animated in their own re-enactments of the attempted robbery/rescue. Unlike earlier, their allegiances had quickly changed from the famous outlaw, to the heroic lawmen. Jack was no longer the man of the hour.

"Wow. Did you see that?" one child asked, needlessly.

"Bang, bang. I'm going to kill me some outlaws."

"We sure showed them."

"Wow. The Elk Mountain Gang."

Rick still had hold of Jack's arm as they made their way down the aisle, and Alex came forward to clear the boys out of the way. Their main priority now was to get the prisoner safely back to their seats. So much for using a passenger train as a ruse. All three men were aware of how much worse this whole situation could have been, if the outlaw band hadn't backed off.

Jack was pale and shaken up, as the deputies got him seated and secured again. Rick took a handkerchief and tried to dab away the blood on Jack's cheekbone, where the hammer of Morrison's revolver had split the skin. Jack flinched and drew back.

"Yeah," Rick said, giving up the effort. "You're going to have quite a shiner there."

Jack didn't respond but sat staring out the window as the train jarred slightly and then started moving again. Rick could see the cloud of pain settling over the prisoner, a pain that had nothing to do with the man's physical condition.

"I'm sorry," Rick said. "Morrison didn't need to kill that man. Was he a friend?"

Jack looked at Rick in a daze. Finally, he answered. "Yeah, he was. I've known 'im for years. He didn't deserve that. Hank Wilkinson didn't have a mean bone in his body."

"He was an outlaw."

"You don't have to be mean-spirited to be an outlaw," Jack mumbled, then looked pointedly at the empty seat in front of them, where Morrison generally sat. "Just like you don't have to be an outlaw to be mean-spirited."

***

Rocking M Ranch, Colorado

Cameron sat at the dining table, contemplating the piece of paper he held in his hands.

Jean had passed by her husband a couple of times, trying to get Eli settled down after his last meal. Being preoccupied, she hadn't paid too much attention to Cameron, as the baby was squirming and irritable. Finally, after patient soothing, she got the infant to sleep.

Coming out of the day nursery, she took note of her husband and realized he had been sitting there for a while, with neither his expression nor position changed.

"Is that a telegram?" she asked, by way of starting a conversation.

Cameron looked up. "Hmm? Oh, yes. It's from Peter's lawyer, Mr. Granger. He is politely 'requesting' my presence at the trial, to give testimony for the defense."

"Oh." Jean sat down at the table. "That's hardly surprising. After all, Peter is a friend." She noticed Cameron's concerned expression. "Do you have a problem with doing this?"

"No, no," he assured her. "I guess, I just never thought I would be asked. And the timing is not great. Miss Shadbolt can take over my teaching classes, so that's not a problem. But the fall auctions are happening right around the same time, and we have a lot of stock that's ready to go."

"I know. But Sam has been doing a good job, here," Jean smiled. "I think he's working extra hard now, to make up for past deeds."

Cameron chuckled. "Yes. A guilty conscience can work wonders. I know he has a couple of friends in town who could use the work. Maybe they would be willing to hire on temporarily, just for the season."

"I'm sure they would." Jean pushed herself away from the table. "Now, I better get started with supper. Do you know where the girls are?"

Cameron glanced at the front door. "I believe they went for a ride. They're getting so attached to those two horses, I don't know what we're going to do when the boys come back to get them."

Jean patted her husband's hand. "One thing at a time," she advised, then headed for the kitchen.

***

Conversation over the supper table, was more animated than usual. The girls returned from their ride, bubbling over with excitement about their two charges.

"And Karma is so fast," Penny said, for the tenth time. "She's wonderful to ride. I can certainly understand why Peter is so fond of her."

"Midnight may not be quite as fast, but he's very dependable, and always careful where he puts his feet." Caroline was not to be out-done. "He's a kind horse, and I'm sure, in his youth, he was just as fast as Karma."

"Keep in mind, those horses are on loan," their father reminded them. "I fully intend to return them to Peter and Mathew whenever they're ready for them."

"Yes, we know," both girls acknowledged.

They were torn between not wanting their friends to go to prison, but also, not wanting to give up some fine mounts.

"Have you heard anything, Papa?" Caroline asked.

"Yes. I received a telegram this afternoon, asking me to testify at Peter's trial at the end of August."

"Really?" Caroline's eyes widened. "Can I come?"

"I don't think that's wise."

"Why not? You know I'm interested in the law, and what better way to see how things work than to actually go to a real trial?"

"Wasn't going to your own hearing, education enough?"

"That's not the same thing." Caroline threatened a pout. "That was so long ago, I barely remember it. And I was too scared, I wasn't really paying attention. Besides, that was a hearing not a trial."

"I think you're too young to deal with something like this," her father reasoned. "This could get intense. You may not like some of the things you'd hear about your friend."

"I'm not too young, Papa." Caroline frowned in her frustration. "You keep saying that. I'm going to be nineteen in October. I'm a grown woman. And whatever I hear about Peter, he's still going to be my friend—nothing will change that."

"Let me think about it," Cameron glanced at Jean, then back to Caroline. "Your mother and I will discuss it, and then we'll see."

"Can I come, too?" Penelope asked, in a small voice.

"No," came the adamant response from both parents.

***

Cameron and Jean settled into bed for the night. Eli was in his night crib, already sound asleep, and the household was deceptively quiet.

"So, what do you think?" Cameron asked, as they sank into the pillows.

"About what?"

"You know 'about what'. Do you think Caroline is mature enough to go to Peter's trial?"

Cameron was met with silence. He waited to give his wife time to think about her answer.

When it finally came, it was an honest, "I don't know. What do you think?"

"I don't know. That's why I'm asking you."

Silence. Both parents lay in bed, staring up at the invisible ceiling.

"Well," Jean finally broke the stalemate, "she is nineteen, and an adult in her own right. Why are you against her going?"

"She'll likely be hearing some harsh truths," Cameron said. "The girls have only seen them when they're on their best behavior. It was a reality check for me, when I finally had to come to terms with whom and what they really are. What's that going to be like for a nineteen-year-old girl?"

"But she's not a little girl anymore," Jean commented. "She's a grown woman now, and it might be easier."

"Easier? How do you mean?"

"She's still young and flexible in her thinking," Jean said. "She knows what they are. Even before they'd met them, the girls had heard all about Napoleon Nash and the Kansas Kid. They also know about the war and the affect it had on many people—they learned that much in school. But hearing about history in class, or about people through dime novels, isn't the same as getting first-hand accounts. It might be difficult for her to hear the truth, but at least then, she would know the truth."

"So, you think I'm being too protective."

"I think you're being a good father," Jean countered, "but being good parents also means knowing when to let your little girl grow up."

Silence. Jean could hear Cameron's wheels grinding. More silence.

"We know she has a real interest in the law," Jean continued. "She's very interested in how the system works, and how she can use it to help people. This trial would be an education for her, in more ways than one. I guess the conclusion I'm coming to, is that we would end up with more regrets by not letting her go, than by letting her."

Cameron sighed. "The lesser of two evils?"

Jean smiled. "Or a blessing in disguise."

"Yes, I suppose." Cameron was dubious in his agreement, "and it's not like she would be there on her own. I can keep an eye on her, and if things get too difficult, I can pull her out." He lay silent again for a few more minutes. "All right, we can tell her in the morning that she can come with me."

"If I know our girls at all, she already knows."

They sent knowing smiles to one another, kissed goodnight and settled in to sleep.

***

In the next bedroom, Penny and Caroline sat on the floor, their ears pressed up against the adjoining wall to their parents' room.

"Can you hear anything?" Penny whispered.

"No, they've stopped talking."

"What did they decide? Could you hear?"

"I think they said I could go."

Penny sighed. "I want to go, too. It's not fair; you always get to do the fun stuff."

"I'm older," Caroline reasoned. "You're still just a little girl."

"I am not." Penny got up, in a huff, and went to her bed. "You're not that much older than I am, and a little difference doesn't make any difference at all."

"Look at it this way," Caroline joined her sister on the bed. "I'll smooth the way for you to go to Mathew's trail. If everything goes fine with me, there's no reason why you can't go next time."

"Yeah," Penny considered this, "but what if it doesn't go fine? What if it's really bad?"

Both girls sat quietly, contemplating that possibility.

"Peter will be all right," Caroline assured her younger sister, even though she no longer felt as confident about it, herself. "You'll see; they'll both be back here for Christmas."

But the looks they exchanged held a tinge of worry and doubt, and sleep did not come quickly for either one that night.

***

Cheyenne, Wyoming

"Hey, Taggard." Leon was off his cot in an instant and up to the bars to greet his old friend. "Sure is good to see you." Then he noted Taggard's solemn expression, and his own smile dropped from his face. "What is it? Is Jack all right?"

"Yeah, Leon. Jack's all right," Taggard assured him. "Morrison's got him secured in the jailhouse on the other side of town. But I do have some bad news for ya'."

"What Taggard? What is it?"

"Hank Wilkinson's dead."

The news hit Leon hard. He paled and looked like he was going to be sick.

"What? Why? What happened?"

"Your old gang stopped the train that Jack was being transported on. They were just gonna rob it. They had no idea there were lawmen on board. Then they came up against Morrison."

Leon closed his eyes and groaned. "Aw, no."

"Yup. Accordin' ta' Jack, Marshal Morrison didn't even give them any warning. Just shot Hank right out of the saddle, to 'get their attention'. Apparently, Gus was wounded, as well, but Jack doesn't know how badly."

Leon leaned against the bars, his forehead resting on his crossed arms. "Hank was one of the nicest fellas I've ever known."

"I know, Leon. C'mon. Let's get out of here, go for a walk."

"I don't feel like going for a walk."

"I know. But let's go, anyway." Taggard unlocked the cell door and snapped the handcuffs on Leon's wrists.

Leon went along with his friend, thinking maybe some fresh air would do him some good, after all. Maybe a stiff drink would help even more. He couldn't decide if he was more hurt or angry, but one thing was for sure: His hatred for Morrison was now locked in and solid. That man was going to get his own back. Leon didn't know when, where, or how, but a day of reckoning was coming.

CHAPTER SIXTEEN
THE TRIAL OF NAPOLEON NASH: THE PROSECUTION

Cheyenne, Wyoming. Summer 1885

Leon wasn't bored. If it weren't for the fact that he was a thirty-four-year-old male, a born leader of men, highly charismatic, and a confident, self-proclaimed genius, one might say he was weak in the knees, knot in the gut, scared to death. But since he was all the above, it would be safe to say he was extremely nervous. The date of his trial had arrived, and he felt a mixture of both relief and anxiety at what the future would bring to him.

Taggard showed up earlier than usual that morning to help the inmate get cleaned up for his first day in court. Taggard had also brought him a suit to wear. It wasn't brand new, but it had been washed and pressed, and it didn't have any holes in it. Napoleon Nash looked quite the clean-cut citizen, rather than the down-and-out prisoner, who'd been sitting and pacing in a jail cell for three months.

As the time of the trial drew near, the group of men assembled in the front office and prepared to go through the back door that Leon had only been through once before. It opened to a hallway that led them up the stairs and directly into the courthouse, which was where Leon had gone for his preliminary hearing. That had been three months ago, and now he was facing that same doorway again. This time, it was for the real deal.

He wasn't in handcuffs, as he was being allowed that small courtesy, but he still felt no less a prisoner. Sheriff Turner stood in the lead, with Mr. Granger on Leon's right, and Taggard on his left. Bringing up the rear was Mike, with the ever-present rifle. Leon swore that he didn't need to see the deputy, to know he was there. The man was so big, his very presence caused the air pressure to increase to where Leon could feel his ears wanting to pop.

Or was that just nerves?

Turner faced the group. "Are we ready?" Receiving an affirmative from the lawyer, he unlocked the door, and the small group of men started down the corridor.

Leon felt Taggard's reassuring hand on his arm.

"Deep breaths, Leon. Here we go."

"Yeah."

Though it only took a few minutes to reach the courthouse, to Leon, it seemed an eternity. Finally, they arrived at the second door, and Turner opened it. The group found themselves amid a flurry of quiet voices and an atmosphere of anticipation within the courtroom reserved for Napoleon Nash's trial.

Leon had been in Cheyenne before and, this being the capital city of Wyoming, it had always maintained an air of superiority over the rest of the territory. The courtroom was no exception.

The twenty-five-foot ceiling was adorned with large chandeliers casting light upon a large room that easily handled an audience of fifty people, more if they were willing to stand.

Tall, narrow, multi-paned windows bracket the judge's bench. The bench itself was set back in an alcove with another floor to ceiling window behind it, only this one was partially covered with long, flowing drapes that contributed to the imperial atmosphere of the room.

The furniture was all of dark, polished mahogany, and the hardwood floors were covered with plush carpeting that absorbed much of the noise that would be created by such a large assembly.

As soon as the five men entered, a hush fell upon the room, and Leon couldn't help but feel like a caged mountain lion on display. This was, by far, the largest, most impressive courtroom he had ever been in. But those had all been slapped together courthouses in small frontier towns that he'd been dragged into for some misdemeanor or other.

This, on the other hand, was the supreme court of Wyoming, and he wasn't here for some misdemeanor. What happened in this room was going to change his life, and he couldn't help but feel the weight of this powerful place settle upon his shoulders.

He scanned the occupants, wondering if he'd see anyone he recognized, but it was like trying to distinguish individual trees inside a thick forest. He gave up when he was abruptly ushered into the row of seats that he and his 'party' were to occupy for the duration of the trial.

Change of Leads: The Lost Shoe

'Oh, my God, why am I so nervous?' Leon couldn't remember the last time he shook with fear, and he hoped he'd calm down once the proceedings began.

He scanned the jury box, hoping to see some familiar faces. The players from the poker game would have been helpful, but the jurors were all strangers to him and probably had been brought in from out of town to avoid that very compromise from happening.

After what seemed another eternity, the bailiff entered the courtroom and stated the inevitable, "All rise. The Honorable Judge John W. Lacey, presiding." Everyone stood up, while the judge entered the courtroom and took his place on the bench. Leon's heart sank. It was the same judge who had refused to grant him bail. Leon had hoped for one who might be a little more sympathetic.

Initially, as the trial officially began, there was muted talking and paper rustling, while the legal necessities were dispensed with. Then the bailiff faced the assembly and everyone quieted in anticipation.

"I hereby declare the official commencement of The Territory of Wyoming vs. Napoleon Nash. The defendant has been charged with armed robbery, breaking and entering, and fraud. The defendant has entered a plea of non-compliance, due to extenuating circumstances. We will now begin."

Soft murmurings greeted this announcement as the bailiff took his place.

Everyone anticipated an exciting trial.

The prosecuting attorney, Mr. Harold DeFord, was confident the trial would be short and sweet, and he wasn't going to waste any time beating around the bush. The first witness for the prosecution was Tom Morrison.

***

"Marshal Morrison," DeFord began, once the marshal had been sworn in. "I understand that you were the arresting officer. Is this correct?"

"Yes, it is."

"And there is no doubt in your mind that the defendant is the outlaw Napoleon Nash?"

"No doubt about it. It's him."

"And why is it, do you think, that you were able to arrest and bring this man to trial, when so many others before you have tried and failed?"

Morrison snorted, making no effort to hide his disdain for the defendant "Because I know him. I know the way his mind works. I know the tricks he'll pull when given half a chance. I simply didn't give him that chance."

"Did he try to escape custody?"

"Oh sure, he tried. More than once. But he obviously wasn't successful."

"So, hardly the actions of a man anticipating a pardon from the governor, then."

The marshal shook his head at this idiocy. "He knows there's no pardon coming. I wouldn't be surprised if Nash and Kiefer started that rumor themselves, just to avoid prison time."

"Thank you, Marshal Morrison," said DeFord. "No more questions."

DeFord retreated and the judge nodded to the defence. "Your witness, Mr. Granger."

"Thank you, You Honor." Mr. Granger approached the witness. "Marshal Morrison, do you not think it unusual that Mr. Nash has not run with the Elk Mountain Gang for five years, now? And, indeed, cannot be directly connected with any crimes committed during those five years?"

"No," Morrison said. "If he hasn't been running with his old gang, it's only because he and his partner had moved on to other things. They simply got better at covering their tracks."

"So, you don't think it's more than a coincidence that the five years Mr. Nash claims to have been living an honest life, coincide with the five years he has not been with his old gang, and has no crimes accredited to him?"

"No. Like I said, he'd simply moved on to better pickings. He's an outlaw, and five years of discretion doesn't change that fact."

"Thank you. I have no more questions for Marshal Morrison."

"You may step down, Marshal."

Morrison left the stand and headed back to his seat. On the way, he caught Leon's eye and sent him a subtle, but triumphant, smile.

Leon bristled.

"Relax," Granger whispered to him, as he sat back down beside his client. "Don't let any of these people know they're getting to you. Mr. DeFord is looking for just that kind of response."

Leon sighed and tried to settle. He knew Granger was right, and he had to watch his own body language. But under these circumstances, it was proving to be harder than he imagined.

"Your next witness, Mr. DeFord," the judge said.

"I'd like to call Mr. Kenneth Roberts to the stand."

A middle-aged man came forward to be sworn in. He was bow-legged and walked like a man more accustomed to sitting in a saddle, than in a courtroom. His boots clunked loudly as he approached the bench and, in his nervousness, he forgot to remove his Stetson.

A pointed look from the bailiff reminded the witness of his indiscretion and he snatched the hat from his head. He sat in the chair and rolled the brim with his hands as he awaited his moment in the limelight.

Mr. Granger had been given a list of all the witnesses Mr. DeFord would be calling, but there were a few on that list whom Leon did not recognize. Mr. Roberts was one of them.

Mr. DeFord approached the witness. "Mr. Roberts, would you please tell the court what you do for a living?"

"Yes, sir. I have a small ranch here in Wyoming."

"And how is business on your ranch, Mr. Roberts?"

"It could be better," Roberts said as he stroked his handlebar mustache. "About seven years ago, we had taken some prime stock up to Denver and sold them to one of the ranchers up there.

"They were good breeding stock, and we got a fair price for them. We were counting on that money to upgrade our place and turn it into a real high-end cattle ranch. We were going to invest in even better stock and keep on building.

"Well, we deposited that money in the Merchants Bank, right here in Cheyenne, because they had a brand-new, state-of-the-art safe.

Both the bank manager and the local law assured us that it was fool-proof, and nobody could break into it."

Roberts stopped there, shaking his head with regret.

Leon had a sinking feeling in his gut. He already knew where this was going.

DeFord moved the witness along. "What happened, Mr. Roberts?"

"It got broken into." Roberts' nervousness disappeared into angry resentment. "Every dang red cent of our money got stole. Instead of bein' able to put money into our place, we ended up havin' to sell more stock just to keep our heads above water. Turned out to be a hard winter that year, too. We had a lot 'a stock die on us 'cause we had no money to buy extra feed. By the time we got back on our feet, the damage had been done. It's only been in the last year or two that we've finally started seein' some growth again. Yes, sir, it's been a real struggle."

"Do you know who stole your money, Mr. Roberts?"

"Sure do," Roberts answered. "When the detectives got through piecin' together how that safe got blowed, they said it would have taken a genius to 'a done it. Someone who had a real understandin' of calculatin' to figure out how to blow it like that without damagin' the contents. The only outlaw they knew of with the brains and audacity to attempt it, would 'a been Napoleon Nash."

Mr. Roberts sent an accusing glare toward the defendant.

Leon wanted to melt into the floorboards. He'd been so proud of himself after that job. He knew nobody else could've pulled it off, and he also knew that the Law knew it, too. He had taken perverse pleasure in rubbing their noses in it, not thinking, or caring, about the long-term effect his actions might have on regular, hard-working folk. Now it was all coming around to slap him in the face.

"So," DeFord continued, "how would the suggestion that Mr. Nash has been living an honest life, these past five years, change the way you feel about what happened?"

"Wouldn't change it at all," Roberts insisted. "I wouldn't care if Napoleon Nash risked his life to save a sack full of drownin' puppies. What he did to me and my family was devastatin'. Pardon be damned! He should go to jail."

"Thank you, Mr. Roberts," DeFord finished, then turned to Granger. "Your witness."

Granger smiled and stepped forward.

Leon groaned and ran a hand through his hair, an unfortunate nervous habit that Granger had already cautioned him about.

Apparently, it'd been to no avail. For a man who was so good at reading other peoples' body language, under this kind of stress, Napoleon Nash was oblivious to his own.

"Mr. Roberts," Granger began, "we are not here today to decide if Mr. Nash is or is not guilty of the crimes of which he has been accused. On the contrary, he openly acknowledges that he committed those crimes. What we are trying to determine, is whether his own acceptance of guilt, and attempt at reformation, should be takin into consideration in his sentencing."

Mr. Roberts snorted and sat back in his chair. He was not impressed with attempts at reformation.

"Him, decidin' ta' go straight now, don't change what he done ta' us."

"No one is denying that, Mr. Roberts. But, isn't it more the bank and the safe manufacturer, from whom you should be seeking retribution? After all, they are the ones who assured you that your money was safe with them."

"Well, I suppose." Roberts went back to fidgeting with his hat, his nervousness returning. "The safe manufacturer did pay us some back, but not all, and it sure took a long time to get it. The bank didn't pay us nothin'."

"Indeed. My point, exactly. And it was not Mr. Nash's intention to cause you and your family hardship. In fact, it was because of the way the banks treat hard-working citizens, like yourself, that prompted Mr. Nash into his unfortunate choice of employment. He came to realize the error of his ways and is attempting to turn his life around. Do you not think that this attempt is worth at least some consideration?"

"Well . . ." Roberts shifted uncomfortably. "I suppose. If a man realized he's done wrong and is tryin' to make it right, that should be considered—a little."

"A little is certainly better than none, Mr. Roberts. Thank you. No more questions."

"You may step down, Mr. Roberts," the judge informed him. "Mr. DeFord?"

"Yes, Your Honor. I would like to call forward Mrs. Joan Baines."

A young woman came up to the stand. She walked ramrod straight, and her chignon matched. She was dressed in dark, though not quite black, and gave the appearance of being forever in mourning.

Her complexion appeared pale compared to her clothing and her eyes stared straight ahead as though blocking out her surroundings was the only way she could get through this ordeal.

Though overwhelmed by the legal atmosphere, she was determined to have her say. Her voice was clear and strong, as she was sworn in.

Leon hated every moment of this. It was turning out worse than he'd imagined. He sank down even lower in his chair, again wishing he could simply disappear.

"Where is he finding all these people?" he whispered to his attorney.

"Unfortunately, Mr. Nash," Granger informed him, "as soon as word of your arrest and upcoming trial got out, they found him."

Leon glanced up at Granger and rolled his eyes. He then met Taggard's look and that didn't help him feel any better.

"Mrs. Baines," DeFord acknowledged her. "Would you please tell the court where you are living, and of your current circumstances?"

"Yes, of course," Mrs. Baines nervously cleared her throat, then continued. "I live in Wyoming, by Rawlins. Things are better for me now, since I met my husband, but up until that point, I was very hard pressed to make a living."

"And why was that, Mrs. Baines?"

"It was a little over five years ago that my dear mother and myself were traveling by train, to come and live with my sister. She had recently been widowed. We sold our house in Montana and had the money from that sale in a safe in the baggage car, along with some of our other valuables.

"We intended to use that money to set ourselves up here and live together. The railroad assured us that it was unusual for outlaws to stop the passenger trains, being more interested in the freights that would be carrying more cargo.

"We have since realized this was not entirely true. Indeed, we were stopped by a band of thieves, and forced off the train, while they rummaged through the baggage and helped themselves to all the valuables that were there."

"Do you know who the band of thieves was?" DeFord asked her.

"Yes, indeed." Her features tightened, and her back arched as she lifted her chin high. "They introduced themselves as The Elk Mountain Gang, led by Napoleon Nash and the Kansas Kid. They took a great deal of pleasure in making sure we all knew who we were being robbed by."

"Aww, Leon," Taggard whispered. "Couldn't you have been meek and discreet, just once in your life?"

Leon glanced at his friend, thinking how odd it was that this same question had just occurred to him, as well.

"What happened then, Mrs. Baines?"

"We lost everything," she said in a soft voice. "Mr. Nash had no problems at all, opening that safe and taking all our worldly possessions. It was extremely traumatic, and my mother, who, of course, was not young anymore, was devastated. We had intended on arriving in Rawlins to help my sister get back on her feet after the tragic loss of her husband, but after that, we showed up at her doorstep as paupers, ourselves."

"Did the railroad not cover your financial loss, Mrs. Baines?"

"Oh, some. Eventually. But nowhere near what we lost." She struggled to keep her composure but those sitting close to her could see her façade of inner strength begin to crumble, and she had started to cry. Very quietly, the tears ran down her face as she raised her hanky to hide them.

She bravely got herself under control, and then continued. "Unfortunately, the strain and anxiety caused by the robbery proved to be too much for my mother in her advanced years. She suffered a heart attack and passed away shortly after we arrived in Rawlins."

There were some gasps and sad murmurings from those in attendance, and Leon felt sickened.

They had always prided themselves on not hurting anyone during their robberies. But gradually, he had come to realize, even before the trial, that there was more than one way to cause injury to another person.

He felt his throat tighten and wondered if it were more for sympathy toward this young woman on the stand, or pity for himself. He didn't want to dwell too much on this question, and taking a deep breath, he sat up straighter and forced himself to remain calm and collected. There was going to be a long way to go yet.

"Thank you, Mrs. Baines," DeFord said. "I realize this must be difficult for you. I have no more questions."

"Mr. Granger?" the judge inquired.

Granger stood up and shook his head. "I have no questions, Your Honor."

"Thank you, Mrs. Baines. You may step down, now."

Mrs. Baines left the stand holding her head high and deliberately avoiding the defendant's dark brown eyes.

"Mr. DeFord, your next witness, please."

"I summon Mr. Nigel Snodgrass to take the stand."

Leon groaned. He hadn't been looking forward to Snodgrass getting on the stand. That man was such a weasel; he would hound Leon to his grave, just to get a dollar back on his losses. This was getting worse and worse. Witnesses for the prosecution were coming out of the woodwork, but witnesses for the defense were burrowing tunnels and disappearing.

Leon had given Granger something to counter Snodgrass with, but he couldn't give too much without implicating others, and that was something Leon wouldn't do.

Granger noticed Leon fidgeting and leaned in to whisper a simple, "Relax."

Mr. Snodgrass resembled a weasel as he strode purposefully to the stand. Snout in the air and a monocle in his right eye, he dripped with disdain for the average citizen and showed complete loathing for the man standing trial. Settling into the chair, he sent an accusing glare to the defendant as he took his oath.

"Mr. Snodgrass," DeFord said, "can I assume that you are familiar with Mr. Nash?"

"I most certainly am."

"Can you point him out, in this court room?"

"Certainly. That's him, right there." Snodgrass pointed an accusing finger directly at Leon.

"Can I inquire as to how you are acquainted with Mr. Nash?"

"Indeed. I am ashamed to say, I was scammed by Mr. Nash, and three of his cohorts, in a fake investment. I ended up losing a great deal of money. I also had to pay a small fortune to clear my name of the false charges that were filed against me, as a result of that scam."

"You said there were four people involved in this 'scam'?" DeFord said. "Do you know who the other three are?"

"I know one of them was Mr. Kiefer, but, unfortunately, I was never able to discover the identities of the other two. One of them was a young woman, and the other was an older, distinguished-looking gentleman."

"Unfortunate," DeFord sent a pointed look to the defendant. "Perhaps, with a bit of persuasion, we will determine the identities of the other two people involved." He then returned his attention to his witness. "When did this unfortunate scam take place?"

"Three years ago."

"Three years ago?" DeFord smiled, this was all coming easier that he could have hoped. "Well within the last five years, during which Mr. Nash was supposedly living an 'honest life'. You seem like an intelligent man, Mr. Snodgrass—a businessman aware of how contracts work."

Snodgrass nodded.

"How did Mr. Nash trick you into falling for their 'scam'?"

"Oh, he's a slick one." Snodgrass got on a roll. "I can usually spot a scam a mile away, but Mr. Nash is an artist. He's got a silver tongue that makes everything sound legit, and then keeps things moving so quickly, you don't have time to evaluate what's going on. He's dangerous. A thief and a swindler. All I can say is, thank goodness he has finally been brought to justice."

"Thank you, Mr. Snodgrass." DeFord nodded to the judge as he took his seat.

"Mr. Granger, your witness."

Granger rose and approached the stand.

"Mr. Snodgrass, if you were so badly misused by Mr. Nash and his accomplices, why were no charges ever brought against them?"

"I didn't know who they were, until later."

"But still," Granger pushed the point, "I would have thought, an honest businessman like yourself would want to come forward and inform the authorities that a crime had taken place."

"Well," Snodgrass flustered, "I was embarrassed that I had been taken in so completely."

"Naturally. I can believe there was a certain amount of embarrassment. But I find myself questioning the reasons for it. Was it for being taken in by conmen? Or was it for having your own 'slightly' dishonest business practices discovered? You mentioned having to quickly cover your tracks. Could it be you had been doing a little flimflamming on your own, Mr. Snodgrass?"

"No." Snodgrass sat up straighter, his face reddening. "I have never, ever, embezzled funds from my clients. Those accusations are the ones I mentioned right up front, that had been falsely brought against me by Mr. Nash and his cohorts, to make me look bad."

"Yes. And for which you paid a 'small fortune' for it to be swept under the carpet."

"Cleared," Snodgrass yelled. "I was cleared of those charges."

"Yes. My mistake." Granger smiled, knowing he'd touched a sore spot. "Cleared. No more questions, Your Honor."

"Next witness, Mr. DeFord."

"The prosecution would like to call Mr. Rolland Murdock to the stand."

Leon tensed. He was surprised to see Rolly's name on the list for the prosecution. He was an even bigger numbers player than Leon and could easily spend time in prison, if he was ever found out. Leon looked around, and sure enough, good ole' Rolly approached the stand and allowed himself to be sworn in.

The same age as Leon, Rolly liked to appear as more of a gentleman and suave lady's man than Leon ever pretended to be. He was a good conman, Leon wouldn't deny that, but though Rolland Murdock looked the gentleman on the outside, with his fashionable suit and slicked back hair, underneath all that suaveness was an arrogant man, who was not so much a fool, as he was an inattentive coward.

Leon had worked with him a few times but was never comfortable doing so. He was sure, sooner or later, that man would slip up, and Leon wouldn't want to be working a con with him when he did so.

Once Rolland Murdock had taken the stand, Mr. DeFord turned his attention to the jury.

"Gentlemen of the jury, it should be noted, Mr. Murdock is a confessed con artist himself and has agreed to give evidence here in exchange for leniency in his own case. What he has to say should be accepted as truth, based on his own experience."

Leon's brain spun. What was Rolly up to? What could he possibly say that would damn Leon even more than he already was?

"So, Mr. Murdock." DeFord approached the new witness. "Could you please tell the court, how it is you know the defendant, and whatever information you have that relates to this case."

"Certainly. I know Nash and Kiefer from way back. I first met them when we were in the care and employ of Mr. Fedamire McPhee. We realized, we had similar backgrounds, in that we were all orphans, and had found sanctuary with that fine gentleman. Although I did much of my training with another person, a Mr. Jonathan Redekopp, it's a small club and, eventually, you end up knowing most of the players. I knew Nash had worked mostly with Mr. McPhee, or 'Fingers', as he was known in those circles."

"And what circles were they?"

"Well, the con game. Flim flam."

Leon's teeth bared in anger and all decorum was forgotten. "You bastard."

The expletive caused a disruption in the courtroom.

The judge's gavel banged through the sudden commotion. "Mr. Granger. Control your client or he will be held in contempt."

"Yes, Your Honor."

But before Granger could address his client, Rolland Murdock over-ruled him. That unworthy gentleman snapped his attention over to Leon as soon as the insult had been uttered, and he was quick to defend himself.

"C'mon, Nash. They were going to send me to prison if I didn't agree to this. What else was I supposed to do?"

"Go to prison!" Leon shot to his feet, preparing to rip the man's heart out.

Taggard and Mike grabbed the prisoner and threw him back into his chair.

The judge's gavel banged out a staccato, while the house came abuzz with anticipation.

"Control your client, Mr. Granger." The judge scowled with indignation as he pointed the gavel at the defendant. "And you, Mr. Nash, another outburst like that and you will attend the rest of this trial in shackles. Do you understand?"

Leon's eyes were dark with anger, but with two lawmen pinning him to the chair, he could see the futility of his current stance. He forced the anger down and, using the well-honed skills of the conman he was accused of being, he enveloped himself in a demeanor of civility.

"Yes, Your Honor, I understand. I apologize to the court, and it will not happen again."

"Good. Mr. Murdock, if you will please continue."

Rolland kept a suspicious eye on Leon. He knew a quick cover-up when he saw it, and he also knew Leon was a master of the game.

"Yes, of course," he said in response to the attorney. "Ah, where was I? Oh, yes, Mr. Redikopp, I discovered he was a kind-hearted gentleman, who often took in ragamuffins as new recruits to learn the trade. Those whom he recognized as having special talent, he nurtured to be top players. Taught them how to sound and act like gentlemen, that sort of thing. I know Nash was one of his favorites. Kiefer wasn't bad, either, but he didn't have the same touch Nash did."

Murdock smiled. "Yeah, Nash was a real artist. Anyway, the last con I know of Nash pulling, was about four and a half years ago. He and Red were running a scam that involved setting up a fake gambling establishment, to entice a mark into betting on horse races that had already been run, with the results, therefore, already known. The mark was a very lovely young woman named Lilly Wilkens. Nash and Red took her for five grand."

Leon heard murmurings from the assembly behind him as many of those present voiced their opinion of such behavior. Especially toward a woman.

His jaw tightened, but he controlled himself, with the help of Taggard and Mike holding him down. The gavel was busy bringing everyone back into order again.

"Silence in the courtroom or it will be cleared."

Silence settled over the proceedings.

"Thank you, Your Honor," Mr. DeFord said and turned his attention back to his witness. "Are you certain this incident took place less than five years ago, Mr. Murdock?"

"Oh, yes, definitely."

"Thank you. Where does this Mr. Redikopp reside?"

"Last I heard, he was living in San Francisco. Mr. Fedamire McPhee, whom I knew personally, and who was also instrumental in teaching us young bucks the tricks of the trade, so to speak, I believe lives in Denver."

"Thank you, Mr. Murdock. I think the law might be interested in having a word with those two 'gentlemen'." DeFord switched his attention to the jury. "Again, so much for our five-year period of abstinence."

Taggard felt Leon trembling with anger, and he placed his other hand in a part-consolatory, part-restraining hold on his friend's shoulder.

"Take it easy, Leon. It could just be all bluff, trying to get a reaction out of you."

"Both Fingers and Red are old men." Leon barely controlled his outrage. "Neither of them would last six weeks in prison."

"Your witness, Mr. Granger," said the judge, then continued with an air of long-suffering indulgence, "and, please keep your client under control."

"Yes, Your Honor. Thank you." Granger approached the witness. "Mr. Murdock, you seem to be quite familiar with this crime, and who was involved with it."

"I was there."

"So you claim. However, as far as I am aware, there was never any crime reported to the authorities. No victim ever come forward to bring charges against either Mr. Nash or Mr. McPhee. I would think, if this Miss Wilkens had been swindled out of five thousand dollars, she would have reported it."

"Not necessarily." Murdock seemed to enjoy informing the court of these details. "Often the mark doesn't want to contact the law, simply because they would then implicate themselves in some unlawful activity. That's one of the conditions you look for, when choosing a mark. That way, when they realize they have been swindled, they won't go to the authorities."

"So, this Miss Wilkens was a thief herself, then?"

"I suppose she was, in a small way."

"A small way?" Granger cocked a brow. "What exactly was her small crime, Mr. Murdock? Do you know?"

"According to Nash, she wanted to leave her lover." Murdock chuckled. "That's not a crime, of course, but she needed money to do it. She secretly stole five thousand dollars from his safe and pinned the crime on Nash and Kiefer, then disappeared. The law believed she had become Kiefer's lover, and the two outlaws had put her up to the robbery. Nash claimed that this was a falsehood and put him and his partner in a difficult situation."

"Really?" Granger's brows went up. "Why? They were already outlaws. What difference would it make to them?"

"Well, Nash claimed that he and Kiefer were trying to . . . ah . . ."

"What, Mr. Murdock?" Granger prodded him. "Trying to what?"

"Well . . . go straight."

"Really?" Granger sent a satisfied smile to the jury. "Interesting. That would be a legitimate reason for Nash and Kiefer to attempt to get the money back, wouldn't it? To keep their names clear of the crime and protect their vested interest in attaining a pardon?"

"Well, yes, I suppose so."

Granger returned his attention to the jury. "Tends to make you wonder, doesn't it? No more questions, Your Honor."

Rolland Murdock left the stand, wondering if he would still get his reprieve, even if his information hadn't achieved the desired results.

Leon bore holes in that man's back, as he left the floor and disappeared among the spectators.

"Mr. DeFord," the judge said, "do you wish to call any more witnesses for the prosecution?"

"Yes, Your Honor. One more witness, if I may." Receiving affirmation from the judge, he continued. "I would like to call Mr. Brian Charles to the stand."

Again, Leon was curious about this witness. The name had not sounded familiar, and he hoped that once he saw the individual, it might ring some bells.

A clean-cut man, a little older than Leon, made his way forward and was sworn in.

"Do you know him?" Taggard whispered.

Leon shrugged and shook his head.

"Mr. Charles," DeFord said, "would you please tell the court where you spent your childhood?"

"Well, for the first twelve years of my life, I lived with my family on a farm along the Kansas/Missouri border," Mr. Charles said, a slight southern twang coming through. "Then, in 1860, raiders attacked our farm, killin' most of my family. My younger brother and I survived, and we were sent to an orphanage, where I stayed until I was seventeen."

Leon felt a chill go through him. Brian? 'Bratty' Brian? Leon would never have recognized the bully who had learned early on to leave young Napoleon Nash alone.

An excited murmuring rose from the assembly. Then, with a collective recollection of the threat to empty the courtroom, everyone quieted down.

"It has been suggested in some circles that Mr. Nash and Mr. Kiefer should be shown leniency for their lives of crime because of the traumas of their childhoods," Mr. DeFord continued. "What is your opinion of that reasoning, Mr. Charles?"

"Oh. Well, sure, it's rough losin' your family, like that. And things at the orphanage were always kind of tight—never enough to eat, really. But, if you behaved yourself, you were treated fair enough."

"And did you behave yourself, Mr. Charles?"

"For the most part."

Leon snorted and received a nasty look from the judge. He smiled an apology and the questioning continued.

"You appear to have done well for yourself, Mr. Charles. Did you ever feel inclined to follow the outlaw trail?"

"Oh, no, sir. When I was seventeen, I was set up in an apprenticeship and learned a trade. I'm married now and have a family of my own. I owe a lot to Blessed Heart Orphanage, and the Sisters who worked there."

"Was that a common occurrence?" DeFord asked. "For the young men, coming out of the orphanage, to be set up in an apprenticeship?"

"A' course. They wanted us to succeed. Not end up turnin' to . . . well," he darted a sheepish glance to Leon, ". . . to thievery, to survive."

"Indeed." DeFord smiled. "Wouldn't want that."

"No."

Leon sighed. What a pretty picture good ole' Brian was painting of that institution.

"So, Mr. Charles, do you remember Mr. Nash being at the orphanage with you?"

"Oh sure. I had already been there a while when Leon and Jack came in, but they made themselves known, pretty quickly."

"Trouble makers, were they?"

"Mr. DeFord," Judge Lacey interrupted, "you are leading the witness. Please keep your questions succinct."

"Of course, Your Honor. My apologies. In what way did they make themselves known, Mr. Charles?"

"Oh, well, Leon was a bit of a trouble-maker. Now Jack, he was kind of a sweet kid. Oh, but I remember one time, he—"

"Please keep your comments relevant to Mr. Nash," the judge interrupted. "Mr. Kiefer will have his day in court."

"Sorry, Your Honor. It's just kind a' hard to talk about one of 'em and not the other."

"Do the best you can, Mr. Charles."

"Yes, Your Honor."

"So," Mr. DeFord continued, "Mr. Nash was a trouble-maker, you say?"

"Well, yeah." Charles became reflective. "He was always gettin' into some sort of mischief. But he was such a charmer, he'd usually end up gettin' away with it. Irritated the rest of us to no end, I tell you. But we also learned real quick, not to tangle with him. Or with Jack, either."

"Really? Mr. Nash was a scrapper, was he?"

Judge Lacey rapped the gavel. "Mr. DeFord, I presume you have been in a court of law before. You will stop leading the witness or he will be dismissed."

DeFord smiled. "Of course, Your Honor."

Lacey rolled his eyes. He was hungry and in no mood for pushy lawyers.

DeFord returned his attention to the witness. What caused you to not want to tangle with him, Mr. Charles?"

"Well, he wasn't a scrapper, not normally. He'd just find a way to get you back. Especially if some of the older boys picked on Jack when Leon wasn't around. Leon was devious. Wouldn't matter if it took a day, a week, or a month, he'd wait for the perfect situation to present itself, and then he'd set you up to take a fall. And he always managed to do it in such a way, the evidence never pointed to him."

Leon sat in his corner with a reflective smile on his face.

DeFord cocked a brow toward him. "Indeed. Well, I can see how that would be irritating."

"Yeah," Mr. Charles nodded. "I tell ya', most of us were real relieved when Leon got sent somewhere else. Jack weren't happy about it, but you can't please everyone."

"So, Mr. Nash was taken out of the orphanage?"

"Yeah."

"Why?"

Mr. Charles shrugged. "Don't know. We all figured he'd been set up with a family or something. He was kind 'a young, but some folks, taking on an orphan, figure the younger the better. As long as they could work. It wasn't a surprise to none of us, that it didn't last, and he got sent back a year or so later. I don't know what happened to him while he was gone, but he sure was a mean son-of-a-bitch after that.

"It didn't matter much by then, 'cause I left shortly after. I must admit, I wasn't too surprised when I started hearin' about those two taking to the outlaw trail. It seemed to fit, you know?"

"It didn't surprise you when Mr. Nash ran away from the orphanage, before he could be set up in another trade?"

"Hardly. I mean, I was already gone by the time they ran off, but I heard about it, soon enough. I wasn't surprised at all. Leon would never have been able to settle into a trade. It always struck me as odd when they tried ta' set him up in one. He was too wild, always challengin' authority. He wouldn't have had the discipline. So, no, I wasn't surprised that he ran off. And I wasn't surprised Jack went with him, either. Those two were thick as . . . well, thieves."

"So, in your opinion, Mr. Charles, Mr. Nash was not forced onto the outlaw trail because of his life at the orphanage, but rather, he was already inclined to challenge authority."

"Mr. DeFord," Judge Lacey's tone rose, "You are putting words in the witness's mouth. Rephrase your question."

DeFord sighed. "Yes, Your Honor. In your opinion, Mr. Charles, why did Mr. Nash become an outlaw?"

"He was always challenging authority," Mr. Charles repeated what the lawyer said. "There were other options open to him, and he chose not to take them."

"Thank you, Mr. Charles. No more questions."

"Mr. Granger, your witness."

Mr. Granger pushed himself up and approached the bench. "Mr. Charles, do you recall any of the details surrounding the murder of your family?"

Mr. Charles shrugged. "The raiders hit our farm on a Saturday mornin', killed everyone and burned the house to the ground."

"That's all you can recall? How did you and your brother escape?"

"Oh. Well, we weren't actually there at the time."

"So, you didn't witness your parents and other siblings being murdered?"

"No," Mr. Charles bit his lip, sensing his validity being questioned. "Joe and I left early that morning to go fishin'. The first we heard of it was when the preacher found us. Then we went to stay with him and his family until we could be moved to the orphanage."

"I see. So, for a young child, say ten years of age, witnessing the brutal murder of his family . . . well, that could be quite traumatic, don't you think?"

Mr. Charles shifted in his chair. "Well, yes, I suppose."

"You suppose? I think it quite likely, Mr. Charles. In fact, I submit that by the time young Napoleon Nash was delivered to the Blessed Heart Orphanage, the damage was already done. A young boy, filled with pain and anger, was thrust into unfamiliar surroundings and then ignored unless he acted out in some way. Then to be forcibly separated from his only friend, to be whisked off to . . ." Mr. Granger shrugged, ". . . where? Now, I'm sure the people who ran the orphanage did the best they could under difficult conditions, but I think it safe to say, there was very little time to give any of the children individual attention."

"That's true," Mr. Charles nodded. "But many of the children there had similar experiences as Leon and Jack, and they did not become criminals."

"I'm sure. But, how many of them are leading contented lives, I wonder."

"That is all conjecture, Mr. Granger," the judge interrupted. "Please, try to stick to some semblance of the facts."

"Of course, Your Honor. My apologies," Granger acknowledged the bench. "I guess, what I'm suggesting, Mr. Charles, is that young children, experiencing such traumatic events in their lives, may react differently to them, depending on the extent of the trauma, and according to their own individual personalities. Some become extraverted and act out, while others may become introverted and shut down. Either way, anger can fester and then manifest itself, later in life, with behaviors the rest of us, who grew up in loving families, would find difficult to understand."

"What?" Mr. Charles looked confused.

"I'm sorry." Mr. Granger dumbed it down. "Witnessing the brutal murder of his family, may have been what caused Mr. Nash to become wild and 'challenging of authority' in the first place."

"Oh," Mr. Charles nodded. "Well, like I said, other boys went through similar experiences, and they didn't cause any trouble."

"Right. I have no more questions, Your Honor."

"Thank you, Mr. Granger. You may step down, Mr. Charles. Mr. DeFord, have you anything more to add?"

"No, Your Honor. I have no more witnesses at this time."

"Then I suggest we break for lunch. Court will resume at 1:00 o'clock this afternoon."

CHAPTER SEVENTEEN
THE TRIAL OF NAPOLEON NASH: THE DEFENSE

Back in his cell, Leon paced in anger while his bowl of stew and biscuits sat untouched on the floor by his cot.

'Damn that Rolly. How could he turn on Fedamire and Freddie like that? Both those men had a hand in saving our lives. Even Rolly's. Took us in off the street, gave us food and lodging, and hope. Treated us fairly, taught us a trade—so what if it was an illegal trade? It was a way to survive. Now, Rolly's turned on them just to save his own skin. Damn him.'

Taggard came into the block and approached Leon's cell. The other occupants darted anxious glances toward the outlaw, not trusting him while in this mood. But Taggard felt he and Leon had enough history to handle anything the ex-outlaw threw at him.

"You going to eat your lunch, Leon?"

"No."

"It's going to be a difficult afternoon. You should calm down and eat something."

"I don't want to calm down." He continued to pace just to prove the point.

One of Leon's neighbor slinked away from the bars separating them. He'd already had a taste of Leon's bite and preferred to keep distance between them.

"And who the hell can eat?" Leon turned on Taggard, but that worthy friend did not back down. "Except for Mike. It seems he's like Jack and can eat anytime. And speaking of Jack, why didn't Morrison just bring him here instead of taking him all the way up to Rawlins? We're in this together, aren't we? I should be able to see my own partner. Why are you keeping us apart?"

"Leon, calm down. You're ranting now, just angry for the sake of being angry, and that's not going to help either you or Jack. You know it's not me keeping you apart. There's nothing I can do about it, and believe me, we've been trying. Granger's doing everything he can to get Jack moved down here, but in the meantime, while you're complaining about only getting an hour a day out of your cell, he hasn't been getting anything.

"The judge in Rawlins refused him bail, and Morrison isn't giving him any leeway, so your partner has been stuck in a cell, day in and day out. Thank goodness, he's handling it a whole lot better than you are."

Leon continued to pace, his anger not abating. Then the real reason for it came out. "Damn that Rolly. Let me get my hands on him. I'll kill him."

Taggard's anger flared. "Leon, don't you dare make a threat like that in my presence. That puts me in a very uncomfortable position. You want me to keep helping you, do not make death threats in front of me. You are no longer the smartest wolf in the pack. These lawyers are just as intelligent as you are, and they know the law, inside out. Start showing some respect and self-control, or you will end up cutting your own throat."

Leon scowled at his friend and continued to pace, his face dark as a thunder cloud.

Another man whom Taggard did not recognize, approached the cell and, nodding a greeting to the sheriff, turned his attention to the prisoner's tense back.

"Well, is this your idea of 'dealing with things'?"

Leon spun around, preparing to chew the head off whoever dared speak to him in such a subordinating manner, and then, instantly, the fire went out of his eyes, and his aggressive stance softened.

"Cameron. I . . ." Leon dropped his gaze as embarrassment took over.

Taggard looked at the newcomer in amazement. He'd never known Napoleon Nash to defer to anyone so completely. The mere presence of this man had brought the outlaw out of his temper tantrum, to a point where he might start thinking more clearly.

Taggard extended his hand to the stranger.

"Sheriff Taggard Murphy."

"Oh, of course, Sheriff." Cameron accepted the hand shake. "Cameron Marsham. We've exchanged telegrams."

Taggard nodded acknowledgement. "Yes. Mr. Granger said you will be speaking for the defense. Good to finally meet you. Leon has a lot of respect for you. Perhaps you can get him to behave himself."

Taggard and Cameron both sent a questioning look toward the prisoner.

Leon sighed, feeling foolish now. Why did Cameron have such a disarming effect on him? The man was dominant, without being domineering; assertive, without being overbearing. And he could knock Leon down five pegs with no more than a look or gesture.

Leon sighed again. "All right." He threw up his hands in defeat. "I'll try to 'behave' myself in there. I'm not used to playing this kind of game."

"You better get used to it—fast." Mr. Granger approached the three men. "This afternoon isn't going to be any easier than this morning was. Actually, it's probably going to be a hell of a lot harder." He nodded a greeting to the two visitors. "Gentlemen, if I may speak with my client, in private?"

"Certainly."

"Of course.'

The two visitors left the cell block.

***

Client and solicitor approached their respective side of the bars.

Leon slumped against them. "It's not looking good in there, is it?"

"No, it isn't. The best chance we have is for a sympathy plea, but that means putting you on the stand, and I don't think that's a good idea."

"Afraid I'll attack the prosecuting attorney?"

Granger smiled. "Well, maybe. But I would need to ask you some difficult questions, and for it all to work, you'd have to be completely honest with your answers. It won't be easy for you. For one thing, you never told me that you were removed from Blessed Heart. Where were you taken?"

Leon shrugged. "Just to another orphanage."

Granger frowned. "Why?"

"I think they wanted to separate me and Jack," Leon said, then snorted. "Like Morrison; keeping us apart made us easier to handle."

"Hm. I suppose I can see their point."

"So, you think baring my soul to the court is our best chance?"

"Yes, I do. There's no doubt in anyone's mind that you're guilty of the charges brought against you. We've never denied this. We need to convince the jury you had good reason, and you need to be convincing."

"Hm." Leon nodded, but he didn't sound enthusiastic. He didn't want to go back to his family life, or that day in Kansas when that family life had ended so abruptly. Even he and Jack rarely spoke about it. Now, he was being asked to expose it all to a courtroom full of strangers.

"Also," Granger continued, "if I put you on the stand, the prosecution will have the opportunity to question you, and once you are under oath, Mr. Nash, you will have to answer his questions."

"Well." Leon straightened up and thought about it. "I don't think I have anything to hide at this point."

"Haven't you? What about the names of your two accomplices, the ones that Mr. Snodgrass referred to?"

"Ah," was all Leon had to say.

"Are you prepared to give those names?"

"No."

"You will be under oath, Mr. Nash. If the prosecution asks you for those names, and you refuse to give them, you will be held in contempt."

Leon nodded. "Then what's the worst that could happen?"

"I know this judge. If you are held in contempt of court, you can forget about leniency of any kind, forget about any chance at an early parole. He'll throw the book at you. He'll drown you."

Leon closed his eyes and groaned. "So, let me get this straight. If I don't take the stand myself, and we only go by what the witnesses say, I'll most likely go to prison, but, hopefully, receive a reduced sentence and chance of early parole. The only way I'm likely to avoid doing any time, is if I take the stand and really lay it on thick for sympathy, so I might, possibly, be pardoned. But if I take the stand and the prosecution asks me questions I'm not willing to answer, I'll be even worse off than if I hadn't taken the stand at all. Is that it, in a nutshell?"

"Yes. I believe you have the gist of it."

Silence ensued.

Leon pushed away from the bars. He ran his fingers through his hair and tried to think what the best option would be.

"Well, Mr. Nash? What do you want to do?"

Leon was at a loss. He wasn't thinking clearly, and he knew it. Why was his brain feeling so muddy at a time when he needed it to be at its sharpest?

He conceded defeat. "I don't know, Mr. Granger. What do you suggest?"

"I suggest we let our witnesses give their testimonies, then decide how we want to proceed," Granger said. "If I feel we have a good case without putting you on the stand, I won't call you. However, if things are looking dicey, I'll ask you again, at that point, what you want to do. There's always the possibility the prosecution won't ask you for those names."

"Hmm. How likely is that?"

"Not very

***

"All rise. The Honorable Judge John W. Lacey, residing."

"All right gentlemen, if we may proceed with the defense." Judge Lacey brought the afternoon session to order. "I have two depositions here that I will now read to the court. These testimonials should be taken as truths and with as much regard as though the individuals were in this courtroom and under oath.

"The first is from Mr. Maxwell Coburn. Mr. Coburn states:

> *I have known Napoleon Nash and Jackson Kiefer for five years, and I have never had any reason to not trust them. They have completed several jobs for me, all of which included entrusting them with large sums of money or valuable property. I have, and would again, stake my life on their integrity. Maxwell Coburn, Red Sands, Texas. P.S. By the way, Peter is the best damn poker player I have ever had the pleasure of battling with, over the same $20,000 pot."*

There were several chuckles from the gallery, especially from local poker players who could appreciate the joke.

Judge Lacey did not find it amusing. He sent a scathing look to the assembly, demanding silence, then carried on with the next testimonial.

"The second is from retired Judge Henry McEnroe. He states:

> *I became aware of Mr. Nash and Mr. Kiefer's quest for a pardon four and a half years ago, and I have supported them in their quest since that time. When I first became acquainted with Mr. Nash and Mr. Kiefer, they showed a willingness to risk their own safety and freedom, to do the town of Hidalgo a great service. These efforts on their parts, have not been forgotten, and I will continue to support them in any way I can in their quest for clemency. Henry McEnroe, Santa Fe, New Mexico."*

The judge returned the papers to their folders and surveyed the attorneys and the jury members. "Again, these depositions are to be taken as literal truth and be respected as though the witnesses had been on the stand and under oath. Now, Mr. Granger, will you please call your first witness?"

"Certainly, Your Honor." Mr. Granger stood up. "I call Sheriff Taggard Murphy to the stand, please."

With a sigh to calm his nerves, Taggard stood and took his place on the stand.

"Sheriff Murphy, will you please tell the court where you reside and hold office?"

"I live in Medicine Bow, and I have resided there for the last seven years."

"So, you are well established in that community?"

"Yes."

"Then, now is it, Sheriff, that you are acquainted with Mr. Nash?"

"Well, as many people here know, I used to run on the wrong side of the law. I first met Nash about fifteen years ago, before he took up with the Elk Mountain Gang. He and Kiefer weren't together at that time, so Nash and I partnered up. I'd say we got to be friends. We pulled several small-time heists together, then parted company for a while. But we always seemed to meet up again.

"It went on like that for a couple of years, until Nash got back with Kiefer. They were both in with the gang by then, when it was being run by Joaquim Cortez. I joined up with them for a while, and ran a few jobs, but I was losing my taste for the life by that time. I'd fallen into outlawin' by chance. Coming out of the war, jobs were scarce. Sometimes you make bad choices just to stay alive, much the way Nash and Kiefer did.

"But I was starting to feel it wasn't right, and I decided it was time to make a clean break from that life before it was too late. To make a long story short, I turned myself in to a lawman I knew. He brokered me a pardon from the then Governor of the Territory, and, much to my surprise, offered me a position as his deputy. He seemed to think that my experience would come in handy, and so I began my life as an officer of the law, rather than a breaker of it."

"That certainly would put you in a unique position," Granger said. "How is it that you continued to remain friends with outlaws, after you put on the badge?"

"I didn't. I broke all ties to that life. That is, until Governor Hoyt approached me with an interesting proposition. It seemed that Nash and Kiefer were causing concern to the banks and railroads, and they, in turn, were putting pressure on the governor to do something about them. No one had been able to capture them or even get close to their hideout, so Governor Hoyt was getting desperate. He requested I get in touch with Nash and Kiefer and offer them a deal. If they would be willing to stop all criminal activity and work undercover for the governor's office, then, after a few years, Hoyt would consider giving them a pardon."

"Interesting," Granger said. "And were you able to contact them?"

"Yes. I hadn't associated with them for some time, but I still knew how to approach the hide-out without getting shot. It was a risk, and they were pretty leery of me at first, but they heard me through and let me leave, unhindered."

"They didn't agree to it, right away?"

"No." Taggard shook his head. "In fact, at first, they were adamant that they weren't interested. They suspected a trap or some form of manipulation. It was at least a couple of months before I heard from them again, and then it was unplanned. They showed up at my home, late at night. They wouldn't come near the town or the jailhouse. They also remained skeptical about the legitimacy of the offer."

Granger nodded and glanced at his client. "I can understand their concern."

"Likewise. I had my doubts. I wouldn't put it past the governor's office to use me to lure them in, and then spring a trap. We spent the whole night discussing the issue. But they were beginning to think, just as I had, that the life they had chosen wasn't morally right, or self-sustaining. They decided they wanted to take the chance."

"They accepted the deal Governor Hoyt offered them?"

"Yes."

"And they have been true to the conditions for, what? The last five years?"

"That I know of, yes."

"And yet, Governor Warren still hasn't stepped forward to confirm this arrangement. Why would that be?"

Taggard's jaw tightened. "I don't know."

"And you've continued, all this time, to support them in their efforts?" Granger verified. "Even though the governor's office has not remained involved?"

"But all the governors, from Hoyt to Warren, have been involved," Taggard said. "They each accepted the terms of this agreement and have utilized Nash and Kiefer's expertise on many occasions."

"And yet now, the governor remains silent."

"Yes."

"And even with that silence, you continue to support your friends?"

"Yes," Taggard was adamant. "I was fortunate enough to have been given the opportunity to start over. I felt if Nash and Kiefer were serious about getting out of the life they were in, well, who am I to abandon them when the going gets tough?"

"That's very generous of you, Sheriff. Do you still feel that it was worth the risk?'

"Yes. I have no regrets about it, either."

Granger smiled. "Thank you, Sheriff. Your witness, Mr. DeFord."

Mr. DeFord approached the stand.

"Sheriff." He smiled, but there was nothing amiable about it. "You say the defendant and his partner were serious about going straight, and yet, per the testimonies from two different witnesses here this morning, this is not the case. That indeed, Mr. Nash and his partner continued in their previous line of work and scammed several people out of thousands of dollars. How do you account for this?"

Taggard cast a quick glance at Leon, then returned his attention to the prosecuting attorney. "I am aware of most of these incidents. I am also aware that there is more to them than meets the eye. Many of the jobs Mr. Nash carried out in the past five years have been at the request of government officials.

"They may appear to show Mr. Nash sliding back into his old ways, but it is more likely, they were legally sanctioned operations that may have been too delicate in their nature to go through regular channels.

"That was, after all, the reason Nash and Kiefer were offered this situation, to work behind the scenes. It could not become public knowledge that the governor's office had such high-profile criminals working for them."

"Really?" Mr. DeFord's brows rose with skepticism. "'Operations that may have been too delicate in their nature . . .' Would you care to elaborate?"

"No, Mr. DeFord. I am not at liberty to elaborate," Taggard said. "If you need further details, I suggest you subpoena the governor."

A wave of chuckling went through the courtroom, causing the judge's gavel to be banged again.

"Quiet in the courtroom, please" Judge Lacey looked to the prosecuting attorney. "I strongly suggest you abandon this line of questioning, Mr. DeFord. I believe you could be getting in over your head."

"Yes, Your Honor." DeFord backed off. "So, Sheriff Murphy, to the best of your knowledge, Mr. Nash has not broken any laws in the last five years. Is this correct?"

"To the best of my knowledge, yes, that is correct."

"Thank you, Sheriff Murphy. No more questions."

"Your next witness, Mr. Granger."

"I call Mr. Cameron Marsham to the stand."

Cameron and Taggard traded off, and Cameron settled in to answer questions.

"Mr. Marsham." Granger greeted the rancher. "Where is it that you reside?"

"My family and I have a ranch outside Arvada, Colorado."

"And how long have you lived there?"

"We've lived on the ranch for three years now. Before that, we lived in Denver. But we didn't stay there long. We prefer a ranching lifestyle."

Granger nodded. "And it was at your ranch where Mr. Nash and Mr. Kiefer were arrested, is this correct?"

"Yes, it is."

"And how long have you known the defendant, Mr. Marsham?"

"About four years."

"Four years. And you consider him to be a friend?"

"Yes, I do."

"And you trust him with your family, with your daughters?"

"Yes. Implicitly."

"Even knowing who he is, you have no concerns about having him in your home, interacting with your family?"

"That's correct."

"What makes you so confident this man is worthy of your trust?"

Cameron sighed and looked at Leon, gathering his thoughts. "We originally got to know Mr. Nash and Mr. Kiefer under their aliases. We were not prejudiced by stories and rumors we had heard about them. To us, they were Mathew and Peter—two fine young men who never gave me any cause for concern."

"But once you became aware of who they were, did you not have concerns about them then? After they fled your property, you still welcomed them back, knowing they were wanted by the law."

"Yes, I know," Cameron nodded. "I suppose it was a chance I was willing to take. I knew they were trying to turn their lives around, and I felt they had a good chance of being successful at it, so I chose to support them, rather than turn them in."

"Why would you consider notorious outlaws, like Nash and Kiefer, capable of turning their lives around?"

"By their very natures," Cameron said. "Neither of them is bad or malicious in character. They simply got off on the wrong track, became involved with the wrong people. They were aware of the mistakes they had made and were genuinely trying to make things right."

"So, in your opinion, Mr. Nash is deserving of a pardon. Is that correct?"

Cameron looked at Leon again. "Yes, I do. I believe Peter is repentant of his past crimes and, given the opportunity, would make a worthwhile citizen."

The judge intervened. "Refer to the defendant by his legal name, Mr. Marsham, to avoid confusion, if you please."

"Of course, Your Honor. My apologies."

"I have no more questions, Your Honor."

Granger turned the floor over to DeFord.

"Mr. Marsham." DeFord approached the stand wearing the same smile he had given Taggard. "You just stated that Nash and Kiefer never gave you any reason to be concerned about having them in your home. Is this correct?"

"Yes. That's correct."

"Even when a legal posse surrounded you and arrested them, right in front of your daughters?" DeFord was incredulous. "It seems to me that they put your daughters in an extremely dangerous situation, wouldn't you agree?"

"It was the legal posse that put my family in danger, at that time, Mr. DeFord," Cameron fought to remain civil. "Not Peter and Mathew. In fact, they surrendered themselves to that posse to prevent any possible harm coming to my family."

"And yet, it was your family that later helped the outlaws to escape," DeFord countered. "It appears that you are no more reputable than the outlaws, themselves. It is on record that you and your wife stood accused of aiding and abetting, and that your daughters would be better off in a reform school."

"Accused and acquitted, Mr. DeFord," Cameron said. "My wife and I made no effort to assist in their escape. As for my daughters' actions that day, they were simply trying to protect their friends. They were young. They had come to know Mathew and Peter very well over that winter and thought of them as brothers. The boys lived with us, shared meals with us, and worked the ranch with us. They had become family.

"At their age, my daughters did not view the posse as being representatives of the law, but as a gang of thugs who forced their way onto our ranch and were posing a threat to two members of our family.

"Fortunately, the judge who presided at our trial realized how difficult it can be for young girls to understand legalities, and that sending them to reform school would do them no good. Many in our community came forward to show support to our family over this matter, and it was decided the girls were better off staying at home."

"With parents who justified their behavior."

"We did not justify it, Mr. DeFord. There were serious repercussions for their actions."

"Yes, I'm sure. I also find it interesting that soon after the so-called acquittal, you sold your ranch and left the territory. Why would you do that, if the community had been so supportive of you?"

"Our ranch was for sale long before Mathew and Peter showed up," Cameron said. "We did not leave due to pressure from our neighbors, if that is what you are insinuating."

Judge Lacey interrupted again, "Mr. Marsham, please. Legal names, if you will."

"I'm sorry, Your Honor. Old habits."

"Time to break old habits, Mr. Marsham."

"Yes, you're right," Cameron looked, with some regret, at his friend, 'Peter'.

"Yes, Mr. Marsham," DeFord picked up the thread right where he'd left off, "I am insinuating that you were no longer welcome. I also suggest that you continued to have contact with Nash and Kiefer after they escaped the posse. That they did, in fact, give you money so you could leave the territory and set yourself up in a better situation here."

"Part of what you're saying is true, yes. But the money they gave us was not to help us leave, but to pay for the legal expenses that ensued from the misunderstanding. They felt responsible for it and wanted to make it up to us.

"We did not hear from Mathew . . . I mean to say, Nash and Kiefer again, until I ran into them a couple of months ago and invited them to come by our place to visit. And again, I emphasize, we did not leave due to pressure. That ranch in Wyoming had been a bad purchase; it had always been our intentions to leave once we found a buyer."

"A buyer who paid far more for it than it was worth."

Mr. Granger stood up, frustrated with what he considered to be bullying of the witness. "Your Honor, what does the sale of a piece of property have to do with the witness' relationship with the defendant?"

"My thoughts exactly," the judge agreed. "Mr. DeFord, where are you going with this line of questioning?"

"Excuse me, Your Honor," DeFord turned to the judge, "I am merely attempting to show that Mr. Marsham's testimony cannot be taken too seriously. That he, in fact, has been friends with the defendant for many years. That the outlaws, showing up at their ranch four years ago, was anything but coincidence, and that Mr. Marsham did, in fact, encourage his wife and daughters to assist in the prisoners' escape.

"That the reason the outlaws were welcome at the Marsham ranch is not because they proved themselves to be honorable and trustworthy men, but because Mr. Marsham was, in fact, well aware of who they were and was willing to harbor them."

"All these points have already been dealt with, Mr. DeFord," the judge said. "The trial at the time exonerated the Marshams from any intentional wrong-doing. It was shown, beyond a reasonable doubt, that the Marsham family had no previous connections to the Elk Mountain Gang or its infamous leaders.

"As for the most recent association, Mr. Marsham was pardoned from any retributions in exchange for his testimony. Mr.

Marsham is not the one on trial here. Please return to the matter at hand."

De Ford looked disappointed, but he conceded. "Of course, Your Honor." DeFord returned his focus to the witness. "As to your reasons for trusting these men, were you aware of Mr. Nash's abilities as a conman and a card sharp? That he is incredibly talented at creating and maintaining a persona, all with the intention of concealing his true character and identity?"

"I am aware that Mr. Nash is accredited with those talents," Cameron said. "I am sure, in his previous occupation, they were developed as a defense mechanism. It is probably what kept him alive. I was never aware of him playing 'con games' with me."

"I think that would constitute a successful 'con' Mr. Marsham," DeFord smirked, sending a smile to the jury, "in that the 'mark' is never aware he is being conned, until it is too late."

"I believe I have known Mr. Nash long enough by now, to see him for who he is," Cameron said. "He is, indeed, a flawed human being, like most of us. But he is hardly evil."

"No?" DeFord was skeptical. "You are aware of his prowess as a poker player. It even gets referred to in the deposition from Mr. Coburn: *'Best damn poker player I have ever had the pleasure of,'* Etcetera. We all know poker is a game of deception and bluff. To be exceptionally good at it, one must have a perfect memory, as well as a sharp and devious mind. Does that not make you the least bit concerned about his integrity?"

"I have heard much the same said about lawyers, Mr. DeFord," Cameron said, to the amusement of the spectators and the defendant. "Are you suggesting that you are lacking in integrity?"

"Hardly a fair comparison, Mr. Marsham," DeFord responded, once the courtroom had quieted. "I chose to put my talents into upholding the law, not breaking it."

"Of course." Cameron conceded the point, though he didn't appear contrite.

"So, Mr. Marsham," DeFord changed tactics, "you have heard the earlier testimonies from several individuals whose lives were forever altered by the actions of Mr. Nash and his partner. Do you not feel the victims of these crimes are deserving of some form of justice for their grievances? After all, Mr. Nash openly admits his guilt. Why should he be allowed to walk away from the consequences of his behavior, when his victims cannot do the same?"

Cameron hesitated. This question from the prosecuting attorney was so similar in its content to the discussion he'd had with Mathew concerning them facing up to their actions that he found himself momentarily at a loss for words.

"Mr. Marsham?"

"Yes. Sorry." Cameron came back to the present. "Certainly, I agree they do need to take responsibility for their actions, but I'm sure there are other ways for them to accomplish that without doing prison time. The injustices which they, themselves, suffered during the war and in the orphanage, should be considered when judging them on their later choices and behaviors."

"Perhaps." Again, DeFord was skeptical. "But, par Mr. Murdock, other boys suffered similar injustices and did not become outlaws. Why should Mr. Nash be so privileged to use that as his defense, when others in similar circumstances made wiser choices?"

"I suppose one would have to look at each situation to correctly judge the choices made," Cameron said. "We also need to keep in mind that Mr. Nash wasn't much more than a child, himself, when he faced those life and death decisions. If given the choice of starving or stealing, who here amongst us would choose the former?"

"But Mr. Nash chose to leave a safe haven, thereby putting himself in the position of having to steal to stay alive. That was hardly a responsible decision on his part."

"Again, he was little more than a child, and children do not generally make responsible decisions. They simply react to the situation they're in. And, I'm sure very few of us here can know what it must have been like, growing up in an orphanage, especially during those times."

The judge interrupted this battle of conjectures and pointed out an obvious fact. "Gentlemen, I hardly see the point of discussing assumptions concerning the defendant's past, when we have the defendant available to set the matter straight, himself. Mr. Granger, the next move is yours. If you desire a few moments to confer with your client, as to whether he chooses to take the stand, I will grant a fifteen-minute recess."

"Thank you, Your Honor. I would appreciate that."

***

The atmosphere in the courtroom lightened, as people got up to stretch and move around. There was a soft buzzing of voices, while everyone discussed their thoughts and speculated on how things would turn out.

Cameron stepped down from the stand and approached the defendant. "I'm sorry," he said. "I think I may have messed that up to some degree."

"You did fine, Cameron," Leon stood and shook his friend's hand. "Don't worry about it."

"Looking back on it, I think Mr. DeFord deliberately set that up, to push you into taking the stand." Cameron frowned. "I'm not sure if that was your intention or not."

"We hadn't decided yet, Mr. Marsham," Granger said. "But it would look suspicious now, if we declined." The latter part of this comment was spoken pointedly to his client.

Leon smiled, though his discomfort was obvious. His heart thumped against his chest, and his palms were sweaty. He didn't want to do this, but the way DeFord had set it up, he tended to agree with his lawyer. To back off now would look suspicious."

Leon nodded. "I guess we better do it, then."

Nobody disagreed with him, but nobody looked happy about it, either.

"Just to confirm," Granger stated, "you fully understand the consequences of refusing to answer questions, once you are under oath?"

"Yes, Mr. Granger. I understand."

A heavy sigh from each of his companions came in response to Leon's acceptance.

"I better get back to my seat," said Cameron, but first he put a hand on his friend's shoulder. "Good luck. Either way, I'll try to get in to see you, later."

Leon nodded. His mouth suddenly dry.

Granger turned and approached the bench. "Your Honor, we have come to a decision."

CHAPTER EIGHTEEN
THE TRIAL OF NAPOLEON NASH:
THE BREAKDOWN

The bailiff stood and faced the assembly. "Order in the court, everyone. Ladies and gentlemen, please return to your seats. Court is back in session."

A few moments of people shuffling back to their spots, and then the room quieted down. Anticipation mounted.

"Mr. Granger," Judge Lacey addressed the defence attorney. "What is your decision?"

"My client has agreed to take the stand."

"Fine. Have him come forward to be sworn in."

Leon couldn't take a deep breath; he felt like he couldn't breathe at all. He somehow managed to get to his feet and make his way to the stand. A Bible was thrust under his nose.

"Place you right hand on the Bible and raise your left hand. Do you solemnly swear to tell the truth, the whole truth, and nothing but the truth, so help you God?"

"I do."

"State your full name."

"Napoleon Nash."

"Please be seated, Mr. Nash."

Leon sat down, and, for the first time, surveyed his audience. It looked quite different from this perspective, and intimidating, as every set of eyes in the room were aimed directly at him. It was a full house, with every seat occupied and even a few people standing along the back wall. He scanned for anyone he might recognize and saw several familiar faces in the crowd.

There was a fair showing of the regulars from the weekly poker game, which pleased him. Betsy, from the café, was there. Morrison, whom he quickly passed over. *'There's Cameron getting settled and, who's that next to him—David? The doctor? Well, that's a pleasant surprise. Oh, and there's Jean seated on Cameron's other side. No, wait. That's not Jean. Caroline? Oh no. Why in the world did Cameron allow Caroline to come to this spectacle?'* Leon groaned. *'She must be so disappointed with all the things she's heard.'*

Leon never felt more ashamed of himself than he did at that moment. Now, the things he was going to have to dredge up from his past were going to be even harder to relate, knowing Caroline would hear them. For not the first time that day, Leon wanted to disappear.

Then Mr. Granger stepped into his line of vision, and all else became secondary.

"Mr. Nash, may I ask when you were born?"

"February 24th, 1851."

"And were you born in Kansas?" Granger deliberately asked non-threatening questions to ease his client into the harder ones that were to come.

"Yes, I was."

"There was a lot of unrest in that area, during the late '50's and early '60's. So much so, it became referred to as Bleeding Kansas. Were you aware of any of that?"

"To some degree," Leon said. "Occasionally, we'd pick up on whispered comments about certain locations being attacked by raiders or one of the older boys in the area going off to fight. There were no official accounts of farms being attacked, but we'd heard rumors, so my father never left the house without his rifle. We didn't think too much of it. To us, it was normal. In many ways, our parents kept us protected from what was going on, so we had a pretty good childhood."

"By 'us', you mean you and your siblings?"

"Yes."

"How many siblings do you have?"

"Ah . . ." Leon hesitated, an instant of blank confusion flitted over his eyes. Then he collected himself and carried on. "I had a brother and two sisters, all older than me."

"So, three siblings?"

"I think that's right. Yes."

"You think?" Granger cocked a brow. "Don't you remember how many siblings you had, Mr. Nash?"

"I had three; a brother and two sisters."

"You're sure about that?"

"Yes," Leon was adamant now, though he still appeared squeamish. "My father was married before he met my mother, so my three siblings were much older than me. The eldest, Louisa, married before I was born, and she and her family lived on a neighboring farm. My older brother, Frederick, left to join John Brown's following when I was seven. We lost track of Fred after Brown was executed. He might have been killed himself at Harper's Ferry. We don't know. If he did survive the Boarder Wars, he likely joined the army when the actual Civil War broke out. I haven't seen or heard from him since."

"I see."

Soft murmuring rose from the assembly. Considering the devastating casualties of the civil war, no one in the courtroom doubted the fate of the older brother.

"So, how old were you when the raiders attacked your farm?"

Leon's jaw tightened. "I was ten years old. My sister, Antoinette, who still lived with us at the time, was twenty-one."

"But she was a half-sibling, is that correct?"

"Yes."

"So, you had no full siblings? You were the only child from your father's second marriage?"

Again, Leon hesitated.

Granger waited, wondering why this question caused his client distress.

Leon answered the logical, "Yes."

"And this was during the Border Wars, before the Civil War had officially begun?"

"Yes."

"Did you witness the attack?" Granger dug deeper. "Were you at home when it happened?"

"Yes," Leon's expression become detached. "It was early morning, summer time. Pa had gone out to feed the livestock. My mother and sister were preparing breakfast. I was setting the table—I think."

"What was the first indication that anything was amiss?"

Leon furrowed his brow, thinking back. "Ah, horses galloping. Coming closer. I heard my father yelling but couldn't make out what he was saying. The dog was barking, he was frantic. Then gunfire, rifles. My mother and sister grabbed other rifles, and everything went crazy. My mother pushed me behind the curtain that led to the pantry and told me to stay there."

"And you did?"

"Yes." He frowned, remembering back. "I was scared. I think, I started crying—I think. I wanted to help, but Ma told me to stay there, so . . ."

"Then what happened?"

"Just—noise. Crazy. Couldn't keep track. Men yelling. Gunfire. I smelled wood and hay burning. My mother and sister were firing the rifles out the windows. My mother was screaming, but I didn't know why. Then men broke through the door and they . . . ahh . . ."

Leon hesitated. Memories he had long kept buried, now rose to the surface and his heart rate quickened with his distress.

Silence hung in the courtroom like a blanket smothering smoke.

"Take your time, Mr. Nash."

Leon took a deep breath and continued. "The curtain wasn't quite wide enough to close off the pantry, so I was able to peek through and see most of the kitchen. There are times . . . I wish I hadn't.

"My sister got in another shot and hit one of the raiders. He went down, but the others rushed in and got the rifles away from them. Two of the men grabbed my sister, and one man slapped her, hard—more than once. She went down behind the table, and they went down after her. She screamed, but I didn't know then, what they were doing to her."

Leon swallowed. He felt himself shaking with these old memories flooding back after all the years of keeping them buried. He had a difficult time with it, and this was obvious to everyone present.

Granger felt bad about pushing him, but he knew he had to if they were going to win over the jury on the sympathy plea.

"What happened next, Mr. Nash? When you're ready."

Leon looked up, the terror of that day, and the memories of people and events long past, haunted his dark eyes.

"My mother broke away from them, and she could have run out of the house, but she didn't." He hesitated, confusion in his voice. "Instead, she ran back to the pantry. Our eyes met for an instant, and she motioned for me to run, then she turned and deliberately drew the attention of the men away from me." Leon's voice shook, and his knuckles turned white from clutching the arms of the chair. "They grabbed her and hit her. I heard her dress tearing, and then I ran."

Leon stopped talking again. He looked like a small, frightened boy, and shame emanated off him in waves.

"You were only ten years old, Mr. Nash," Granger said, "you couldn't have helped her."

Leon looked at him. His eyes were dry, but the anguish in them was heart-wrenching. The only sounds breaking the heavy silence in the courtroom were the occasional, quiet sobs from some of the ladies who were present, and gruff coughing from the gentlemen.

"You got out of the house?" Granger asked.

Leon nodded. "Yes." It was barely more than a whisper. He coughed, trying to loosen his throat muscles. "Ah . . . I ran outside, and the air was filled with smoke. The barn was on fire, and the horses ran loose, in a panic. My father lay on his back, by the well; there was blood all over him. The dog was beside him, and he'd been shot so many times, he was hardly recognizable as a dog."

Leon stopped again, and took a deep, shuttering breath. He looked up, sought out and found Cameron.

The rancher watched Leon intently, his left arm around his daughter's shoulders.

Caroline cried softly, trying to hide it behind her handkerchief.

"Why would they do that, Cameron?" Leon asked his friend. "Spencer was a good dog. Why would they massacre him like that?"

A few heads turned to watch the man upon whom Leon was focused. All Cameron could do was shake his head. It was obvious to him that the painful question wasn't really about the dog.

"What did you do then, Mr. Nash?" Granger strove to keep his client from locking up.

Leon returned his attention to the lawyer. "Ahh . . . I ran." He shrugged. "My sister's farm was only a couple miles away, so I headed there. I heard screaming from my house, and more gunshots. The fires were crackling, and more screaming. I don't know if they were shooting at me, or . . . I just ran."

"So, you made it to the Kiefer place?"

"Yes. But before I got there, I saw smoke on the horizon and realized their place had been struck before ours. Dread hit me like ice water, and I ran even faster."

"What did you find when you got there, Mr. Nash?"

"Devastation." Leon looked down at his hands. This was proving to be harder than he thought. "The house and the barn had been burned to the ground and were smoldering, but there were small pockets of fire still burning around the yard. Two of the horses had been shot and were partially burned. I guess the others had run off. I came across parts of their dog, and then parts of . . . Jack's younger sister."

Groans traveled throughout the courtroom.

Leon coughed, then swallowed. He carried on, his voice monotone.

"I could see what was left of Jack's pa over by the barn, but I couldn't see his ma, my sister, anywhere. Then I heard sobbing, and I followed the sound around to the other side of a pile of burning wood. It was Jack. He was sitting on the ground beside his older brother, whose throat had been cut. There was blood all over them.

"Jack was sobbing, almost hysterical. He rocked back and forth, clutching his mother's dress—my sister's dress. It was the blue dress, the pretty one, with the blue and white lace around the collar, though you could hardly recognize it now, torn and tattered, covered in blood.

"Jack wasn't wearing any shoes, his hands and feet were burned, and his hair was singed. He was covered in soot and ash. He looked up at me as I approached him, and I could tell he was trying to say my name, but all that came out was more sobs. His younger sister was screaming, but I couldn't see her anywhere."

"So, Jack had two younger sisters?"

"No. Just the one."

"I'm sorry, Mr. Nash. I'm confused. I thought you said Jack's younger sister had been killed."

"Yes, she was."

"Then how could you hear her screaming?"

"Ahhmm."

A tingling chill went through Cameron. Something was wrong. Beside him, he felt David tense.

Leon sat with his mouth open, as though he expected to know the answer to that question, but nothing came to mind. His teeth chattered—just for an instant—then stopped.

David started to get up, but Cameron put a hand on his arm. Anyone approaching the defendant now, especially unsummoned, would surely cause guns to be drawn.

Leon's brain spun. His focus went inward as he tried to work this out. He knew the answer; it was obvious. But it was staying in the shadows just out of reach. Screaming. He could hear a baby screaming.

His gasp was audible even to those sitting in the back. His head jerked, as though someone had slapped him. He went white as a ghost, and his face shone with icy perspiration.

"Oh, God. Cameron." Leon's anguished eyes sought out his friend again and held onto him like a lifeline. "Oh, God, no. I left her behind." He could hardly breathe. His teeth chattered again and then stopped, again. "My sister. My baby sister. How could I have forgotten about her? Aww, Cameron, she couldn't have been much older than Eli. I left her behind, in the house, and they burned it down. She was burned alive, and I could hear her screaming, and I kept running away. How could I have left her? She was my baby sister, and I left her behind."

Caroline sobbed. Cameron felt sick. He wanted to close his eyes, to shut out this nightmare, but he didn't. He kept his eyes locked onto Leon's, trying, by sheer willpower, to keep his friend focused, to keep him from completely falling apart on the stand.

"Mr. Nash," Granger began in a tight, quiet voice. "Again, you were only ten years old. There was nothing you could have done. Your mother must have seen a way to save at least one of her children, and she did what she had to do, to give you that chance. If you had disobeyed her, and tried to get to the baby, you only would have been killed yourself."

Leon broke away from Cameron and stared blankly at Granger. The sensible words meant nothing to him.

"Mr. Granger," the judge intervened, "it's early in the day yet, but I suggest we adjourn until tomorrow morning. Give your client a chance to compose himself."

"Yes. Thank you, Your Honor."

"Court is adjourned until 9:00 o'clock tomorrow morning."

The gavel rapped loudly, and all hell broke loose.

***

The room erupted into a cacophony of noise, as people scrambled to their feet, everyone talking at once.

Taggard and Granger rushed forward and grabbed Leon. They hurried him to the side door and into the hallway leading down to the jailhouse. Deputy Mike and Sheriff Turner followed close behind them.

David also rushed forward, trying to catch up. He knew Napoleon was in trouble and needed help, but he was too late. The bailiff closed the side door, just as the doctor got there, and refused to let him through.

"But he's my patient. I need to get to him."

"Not this way, Doctor," the bailiff was adamant. "Only the defendant and officers of the court are allowed through here. You'll have to go around."

Frustrated, David turned and made his way back to the main doors of the courthouse. He tried to hurry, but there were so many people milling around, hindering his passage, that it took him a few minutes to reach the outside steps. Once there, he hurried down to street level and, with his long-strided gait in full swing, headed for the side entrance to the jailhouse.

Along the way, he passed Cameron and Caroline having a heated argument.

"But he's my friend, too," Caroline yelled. "I want to see him."

"A jailhouse is no place for a young lady," Cameron's voice hardened with authority. "You will wait for me at the hotel."

"I'm almost nineteen. I'm an adult. I can do what I want."

"I am your father, and you will do what I tell you!"

Having settled that, Cameron turned his back on his daughter and headed for the jailhouse.

David scooted past Caroline, not wanting to get assaulted in the aftermath. She was a picture of frustrated fury as she stood, with clenched fists, and stamped the ground with indignant anger.

David made it by her without her noticing him, and on the run again, he caught up with and past Cameron, in his hurry to get to the jail.

Inside the building, Leon got ushered back to his cell.

Leaving Taggard in the cell block with him, Turner and Mike returned to the front office to intercept anyone trying to get in to see the prisoner. They turned out to be David's second stumbling block.

"But I'm his doctor," David repeated the same argument. "He's in trouble, and I need to see him."

"He's fine," Turner said. "Besides, our own doctor has been seeing to him, so your services aren't required."

Then, from inside the cell block, came Taggard's urgent voice. "Turner. Get in here with the keys to Nash's cell. Now! There's something wrong with him."

***

Inside his cell, Leon started to pace. He was agitated, frustrated, confused—tormented. He repeatedly ran his hands through his hair.

"How could I have done that?" he kept saying, over and over, his agitation growing.

His teeth started to chatter again, and Taggard couldn't figure out why. It was a warm day. How could Leon be cold?

"Leon, try to calm down. You're working yourself into a state."

"A state?" Leon's mind was in turmoil. "A state of what?"

"Of nerves," Taggard said. "And you're not doing much for mine, either."

"How could I have forgotten about that, Taggard?" Leon's eyes glazed with confusion. He started to shake. He stopped pacing, then went and stood beside Taggard, holding onto the bars. His eyes became distant and his expression, blank. His teeth chattered.

"Leon, what's wrong?" Taggard was worried; his friend's behavior began to frighten him.

Leon shook his head, confused. His body escalated from a sporadic shaking to an all-encompassing tremble, and he leaned against the bars of the cell. Slowly, he sank to the floor, his body in a spasm of nervous anxiety.

"Turner," Taggard called. "Get in here with the keys to Leon's cell. Now! There's something wrong with him."

Turner came into the cell block and unlocked the door.

David followed close on his heels, and as soon as the cell was open, he sneaked in ahead of the lawman. Once inside the cell, he grabbed the blanket off the cot before anyone could stop him.

"Sheriff, do you have any strong liquor in your office, like whiskey or brandy?"

"Well, I have some brandy, but—"

"Good." David knelt in front of Leon and wrapped the blanket around him. "Get me two shots of it, will you please?"

Turner's brows shot up. "Hold on now. That's real good—"

"*Now*, Sheriff. If you please."

The two lawmen exchanged looks.

Taggard smiled.

Grumbling, Turner gave in and made his way back to the office to get the brandy.

Cameron passed him on the way. He stepped back from the group, not wanting to interfere with the doctor's administrations. Seeing his friend, who was normally so strong and confident, in such a state of collapse, was heartbreaking for him.

Leon was confused about his condition. Where had all his strength gone?

"David?" he asked, when he could get his teeth to stop chattering, "what's . . . happening? What's wrong?"

"You've gone into shock, Napoleon," David said, briskly rubbing his shoulders to get some heat generating. "We have to get you warmed up. You'll be all right."

"Shock?"

"Yes."

"Why would . . . I have . . . done . . . that?"

David gave an ironic laugh and glanced up at Taggard and Cameron. He was met with two concerned expressions.

Mr. Granger had also made his way into the cell block, but seeing how things were, he hung back, not wanting to interfere. There would be time later to discuss the proceedings.

Turner returned with a tin cup of brandy and handed it to the doctor.

Caroline glided in on the sheriff's wake, and stood quietly behind her father, watching the scene.

"Here, drink this." David offered the cup to Leon.

Leon took it with shaking hands and managed to get the two shots down his throat. He felt the liquor burn on its way down, then it hit his stomach, and its warmth radiated throughout his body. Gradually, the trembling subsided, and his jaw loosened, allowing the chattering of his teeth to ease.

David continued to rub his shoulders until Leon gave a deep sigh, and his body relaxed.

"There you go," David said. "Feeling better?"

"Yeah."

"Think you can stand up?"

"Yeah," then he added, "Doc, how's my nephew?"

"Who?" David frowned, confused.

"Jack."

"Oh. I'm sorry. This has all been over-whelming, and so much of it hasn't sunk in yet. Your testimony did pertain to this, didn't it? I guess I was too focused on other things. Anyway, he's fine. We're finally getting him moved into town. He'll be going to one of the other jails here."

"Good. Glad to hear it," Leon mumbled, but David couldn't decide if he was being sarcastic or not.

Leon pulled himself to his feet and seemed steady enough, once he got there, but he kept the blanket wrapped around his shoulders. He smiled at his two friends, and then his expression turned to mild surprise, followed by embarrassment.

"Caroline. What are you doing here?"

Cameron spun around. "Caroline. I told you to wait at the hotel."

The look she sent her father was one of pure defiance.

Leon couldn't help but smile. The girls had grown up.

"It's all right, Cameron," Leon assured him. "If she still wants to be around me after what she heard in that courtroom today, I have no problem with it."

Cameron sent him a look of paternal frustration, but Caroline wasted no time taking advantage of the approval.

"Of course, I still want to be around you." She slipped between the men, and entering the cell, she gave Leon a hug. "You'll always be my dearest friend, Peter."

Leon smiled. Caroline's hug did about as much as the brandy had done to help him feel better.

Turner was anxious about this young woman, not only being in the cell block, but now, also in the cell, hugging one of his most notorious prisoners. But since nobody else seemed to think this worthy of concern, he contented himself with simply keeping an eye on the situation.

***

The rest of the afternoon and evening went by in a blur for Leon. He was, understandably, disturbed by the revelations of the day, and continued to ask, "Why?" and "How?", yet was unable to process any answers presented to him.

Long after the others had left to carry on with their own evening affairs, Taggard stayed with his friend, for no other reason than to keep him company. They drank coffee together, and even had dinner brought to them from the café.

They talked about the old days, when life had been carefree and adventurous. Taggard even got Leon to laugh about some escapade they had pulled off together, or something that Jack had done, that had gotten everybody into trouble. But through it all, Leon had a cloud over him, and his hair suffered greatly with the constant attention it received.

As the evening shadows replaced the late summer sun, David returned to the cell block and smiled at the two old friends, who were doing their best to help one another get through a difficult time.

"Good evening, gentlemen."

"Doc."

"Hi David. Have you seen Jack, yet?"

David smiled. “Yes. He’s doing fine. Keeps asking about you, though, about as often as you ask about him.”

Leon nodded. He was glad to hear that Jack was all right, but knowing this didn’t ease the ache of missing his company.

David scrutinized his friend, noting that his complexion was back to normal. “How are you doing, Napoleon? Any more chills?”

“No. I think I’m all right now.”

“Good. I’ve brought you some medicine to help you sleep tonight. Tomorrow will be another difficult day, so you’ll need your rest.” David sighed and mumbled to himself, “I seem to be handing out more sleeping aids than anything else, these days.” He perked up and handed the small pouch to Leon, through the bars. “Here. Take this with water and get some sleep. Try to stay warm. If you get the shakes during the night, have one of the deputies come and get me. Okay?”

“Yes, David. I will.”

“Good. Gentlemen, goodnight.”

“I better be going, too, Leon,” Taggard said as David left. “I’ll see you in the morning. I’ll bring some breakfast over with me.”

“Can’t we just go to the café?”

“Nope. Your hour a day has been rescinded while the trial is going on. Wouldn’t want you inadvertently mingling with the jury members. Would create a conflict of interest. Sorry.”

“Oh.” Leon was disappointed. “I guess that makes sense. Goodnight, Ty.”

***

Leon slept well that night, considering his situation. But he awoke early, before dawn, and his mind took over again. He lay on his back, staring up through the dim light at the barely visible ceiling, allowing memories—and non-memories—to take control.

‘How could I have done that?’ His mind went right back at it. *‘How could I have forgotten about little Janelle, my baby sister?’*

Angry remorse washed over him. He reflected on the life that could have been—should have been—his, if not for those damned marauders.

‘How could men do that? Butcher young children? Babies, literally in their cribs. How could they do that?’

Leon groaned, then stretched. He tried to think of something else. He could kill for a cup of coffee.

Leon's thoughts turned to the Pandora's Box that Murdock had opened. *'What am I going to do about that? Just hope DeFord doesn't ask me about it? If I were to give up those names, I'd be no better than Murdock, but if I don't . . .'* He sighed, rubbing his eyes. A shiver of fear ran through him as he pushed those thoughts from his mind. He groaned again, then sat up, keeping the blanket wrapped around himself against the early morning chill.

'Oh, when is Taggard going to get here with that coffee? Hmm, and breakfast. Not sure if I can eat, though.' With the thought of food, his stomach tightened, and he felt nauseous. He sighed. *'I suppose I should try, or David will be after me. That man is such a nag.'* He scratched his chin and grimaced. *'I need a shave.'*

Leon missed Jack, and he resented the fact that they were still being kept apart. He looked around the cell block and felt even more irritated. There were only two other occupants, and they, by their request, were housed in cells as far away from him as possible. The cells right next to Leon, were empty, and so was the drunk tank. There was no reason why Jack couldn't come here.

'Oh yes there is. We're partners, and the law knows that if we get together, we'd be trouble.' He smirked at the thought. *'Yeah, we're dangerous.'* He laughed out loud, and his fellow inmates flashed anxious glances at him. He ignored them. *'I suppose they have a point. Together, we could make plans and work out a strategy. That bastard, Morrison, knows it, too. He's not going to let us get together, and he has enough clout to make sure it doesn't happen.'* Unfortunately, being logical and understanding the *why* of it, didn't keep Leon from missing Jack.

'Come on, Taggard. Let's get this day over with, one way or another.' Leon released a heavy sigh, ran his hands through his hair, then stood up and began to pace.

CHAPTER NINETEEN
THE TRIAL OF NAPOLEON NASH: THE VERDICT

"All rise. The Honorable Judge John W. Lacey presiding."

The formalities were quickly taken care of and everyone settled. The courtroom was more packed than it had been the day before. Standing room only was the billet for the day, with people crammed along the back wall and overflowing into the outer hallway.

Judge Lacey looked over his glasses at the defence attorney. "Mr. Granger, is your client able to continue?"

"Yes, Your Honor."

"Fine. Mr. Nash, will you please take the stand. I remind you that you are still under oath."

"Yes, Your Honor. I understand."

Leon moved to the front of the courtroom and sat down, facing the assembly. The crowd was intimidating, but he shut them out and focused solely on what needed to be accomplished.

Mr. Granger stood and faced him. "Mr. Nash, if we could carry on from where we left off yesterday. You had arrived at the Kiefers' farm and found Jack to be the only one left alive. Is this correct?"

"Yes."

"Please continue."

Leon took another deep breath, then started. "We headed toward town. I had to carry Jack, piggy-back, as he couldn't walk with his feet burned the way they were. He wouldn't let go of his mother's dress, and he wouldn't stop crying, even though I kept talking to him the whole time."

"How old was he?"

"Eight."

"Eight years old?"

"Yes."

A wave of sympathetic murmurings went through the courtroom, then everyone quieted down, already enthralled.

"How far was it to town?"

"Ten miles. But we only had to go about half way. Some neighbors had seen the smoke and came to investigate."

"So, you carried your nephew for five miles?"

"Yes," Leon didn't see anything remarkable about this.

"Then what happened?"

"Well, when our neighbors found us, they had a buckboard with them, so they got us into town. They tried to take Jack to the doctor, but he wouldn't let go of me, and he wouldn't let go of that dress. I wanted to go with him, too, as I didn't want to let him out of my sight.

"Eventually, we both went to the doctor. Turns out, he wanted to see both of us, anyway, so it all worked out. Fortunately, the burns Jack had suffered weren't too bad, and they healed all right, but they must have been painful at the time."

"Yes, I'm sure," Granger said. "Do you know how he received those burns?"

"No," Leon shook his head. "Jack and I have never really talked about that day."

"Never?"

"Well, not of any significance."

Granger nodded. "All right. Then what happened?"

"We stayed with our neighbors for a while, then they moved us to the Blessed Heart Orphanage." Leon heard small gasps and disapproving murmurs from the assembly, and he felt the need to justify the act. "Those were hard times for everyone. It was difficult enough for families to keep themselves fed, so taking in orphans would have caused quite a hardship. We didn't expect anything different."

"What about family, Mr. Nash?" Granger got him back on track. "Did you not have aunts and uncles, or grandparents, who could have been contacted?"

"My father and his first wife were Huguenots and emigrated here from Europe. There was bad blood between my father and his family. He never had much good to say about them. Jack's father came from England, so, again, pretty hard to track them down."

"And what of your mother's people? Are they also still in the old country?"

"No." Leon frowned. "Her people are here, in Wyoming, up by the Yellowstone, but no one seemed interested in contacting them."

"Why not?"

Leon simply shrugged, so Granger moved on. "How was life at the orphanage? Were you treated kindly there?"

Leon snorted. "I'm afraid I must contradict Mr. Murdock in his opinion of that institution. The only thing he said that had a ring of truth to it was that there was never enough to eat. We learned, right off, what to expect from the people running the place. While we were staying with neighbors, nobody could get Jack to let go of that dress. Even when he fell asleep, he clutched it so tight, nobody could get it away from him. I suppose they felt bad for him, and they didn't really try very hard.

"But when we got to Blessed Heart, the Mother Superior literally tore it away from him, calling it disgusting. Jack started to scream, and he wouldn't stop. They locked him in a room by himself and wouldn't let me stay with him. They told him, he could come out when he decided to 'behave himself'."

Leon went quiet for a moment, his jaw tightening in anger at the memory of the abuse. "It took two days for Jack to finally give in, and then it was only because he was hungry.

"Neither of us forgot that introduction to Blessed Heart. It turned out that 'hungry' was the normal condition there. We learned early that stealing was the only way we'd even come close to getting enough to eat.

"Jack was small for his age, so he got picked on a lot, and what food was given to him often got snatched away by one of the bigger boys. It seemed like I was always stealing food from the pantry for us.

"Despite Mr. Murdock's opinion that I usually 'charmed' my way out of trouble, unfortunately, the exact opposite was generally the case. The whip and the cane were a common punishment for boys who stole food, and for the years we were there, I usually sported a fine collection of bruises. The Mother Superior even broke my wrist, once."

Silence weighed heavily in the courtroom.

"What about apprenticeships or trades?" Mr. Granger asked. "Per Mr. Charles, you were placed in a situation. Is this correct?"

"No, it's not. I suppose they thought I was a bad influence on Jack, because they separated us and sent me to another orphanage. They didn't even give us the chance to say goodbye." Leon's jaw tightened, as his resentment of this situation took hold. "They distracted Jack just long enough to grab me and get me on a train heading west. It was two years before I saw Jack again."

"Yes." Mr. Granger nodded. "You were eventually returned to Blessed Heart. Why was that? Why did they not keep you at the other orphanage, or set you up in an apprenticeship? You would have been old enough by then."

"There were a lot of boys left homeless in that war, Mr. Granger, all of them looking for a way to survive. An opportunity would present itself occasionally, and the boy who seemed best suited to it, would be placed there. But that only happened for a very few of us. There were simply too many boys and not enough work. When things got over-crowded, many of the children, boys and girls alike, simply disappeared.

"Then I became one of those who disappeared. It must have been hard on Jack, not knowing. They never told him where I was, just that I was gone."

"So again," Mr. Granger said, "I ask why you were sent back. If there was no position available to you, why not simply keep you at the second orphanage?"

"It burned down." Leon shrugged. "They had to put us somewhere."

"So, you were returned to Blessed Heart," Mr. Granger stated, "only to run away. Why?"

Leon's smile was cynical. "Nothing had improved over the two years I was away, in fact, with more children coming in, things were getting worse, not better. On top of that, we were both afraid we would be separated again. So, one night, we'd had enough of going to bed hungry and getting punished for it. An opportunity presented itself and we left. Nobody came looking for us, so I don't think we were missed too much."

"How old were you, when you left?"

"I was fourteen."

A murmuring rose up from the assembly, but quickly dissipated.

"So, that would make your nephew twelve."

"Yes, that's correct."

"Awfully young to be on the streets. Did you fare much better, on your own?"

"No," Leon's lip curled in a sarcastic smile. "No. It was a tough go. Again, we found ourselves having to steal, just to eat, and sleeping wherever we could find shelter. I tried to get us to my mother's folks, but they were too far away. And there was no guarantee that they would take us in, anyway. Life wasn't easy for them during that time, either."

"Did you ever consider going back to the orphanage?"

"No." Leon actually barked a laugh. "No. As bad as it was on our own, it was better than that place."

"So how did you survive?"

"I don't know. I look back on it now and marvel at the fact that we did survive. For a couple of years, it was tooth and nail, always living on the edge. I don't think we would have made it a third year.

"Then, by happenstance, we tried stealing from a master, and got caught. But, instead of turning us over to the law, the gentleman took us in and gave us a home—and food, and a place to sleep. Gave us a family, of sorts." Leon smiled, briefly. "Jack, well, he did a lot of catching up in the eating and growing department."

Granger nodded and smiled. He could understand that. "And this man who took you in, can I assume that it is the Mr. Redikopp, whom Mr. Morgan has already mentioned?"

Leon visibly bristled. "Yes."

"So, I take it you feel a certain loyalty toward this man?"

"Yes, Mr. Granger. I think it is safe to say that I do."

"Even though the trade he taught you was illegal and eventually set you up on a life path that brought you to this court?"

"He saved our lives, Mr. Granger," Leon said, with some heat. "It's kind of hard to push that aside, even though Mr. Murdock seems to have had no trouble doing so."

Not to Leon's surprise, the gavel banged out a warning, and brought tempers down to a simmer.

"Calm yourself, Mr. Nash," the judge warned him. "Please keep your answers direct to the questions."

"Yes, Your Honor." But Leon's mood didn't soften. He found Roland Murdock in the crowd and glared at him, until he squirmed.

"All right, Mr. Nash," Mr. Granger got Leon's attention focused back on him. "You and your partner were obviously very successful in your careers. I take it, you were living a reasonably good life, especially when compared to your childhoods."

"Yes." Leon had the good graces to look ashamed of this fact.

"What was it that made you decide to change? To take the governor's offer of a pardon, if you went straight?"

"Well," Leon pondered a moment, "it was becoming obvious, even to us, that we were on a dead-end path. We were also beginning to realize the harm we were causing people, even if that wasn't our intentions in the first place. We had just never considered it before.

"The way we grew up, Mr. Granger, even before our folks were killed, we'd heard about raids all along the border, people being killed, homes burned to the ground. Seeing homeless people walking past our place wasn't unusual, and they'd beg for food, or steal it, if they got the chance. Our families would often take these people in for a few days, whether they were black or white.

"My pa and my brother-in-law did a lot to help the black folks who came to our door. Often gave them what little food we could spare, and even get them connected to others who could help. It was a difficult time for many. If you had to steal to eat, you did.

"Then, at Blessed Heart, stealing became second nature. We had to steal food to survive. By the time Jack and I settled in with the Elk Mountain Gang, stealing was simply what we did. It was a way of life. We never thought anything of it.

"But, like I said, we started looking around and realized that things weren't right. Our friend, Taggard Murphy, had turned his life around and was doing okay for himself, so when the offer came our way, we thought maybe we had a chance, too."

"And that was five years ago?"

"Yes. Five years ago."

"And you have been working toward that goal of receiving a pardon, since then?"

"Yes."

"Thank you, Mr. Nash. Your witness, Mr. DeFord."

***

Mr. DeFord approached the witness, a look in his eye that made Leon's skin crawl.

"Mr. Nash, I realize you already stated your name at the time of your swearing in, but could you please state it again, for clarification."

Leon frowned, but complied. "Napoleon Nash."

"Is it?" DeFord pushed. "Keep in mind, you are under oath, Mr. Nash. Your full legal name, if you please."

Leon hesitated. This was not something he had wanted to get into, but he could see no way to avoid it. "Napoleon . . . Navarre Nash," he stated.

DeFord looked smug. "Yes. Navarre," he said. "Interesting that you would attempt to hide that name away. I have done my research, Mr. Nash. I thought you would be proud to have come from such a noble family. Within the Huguenot society, are not the Navarres considered royalty? Are you not descended from a line of kings?"

"As I stated before, my father was . . . estranged from his family. He had been sent to Philadelphia to manage the family's businesses. But his first wife died, and he left the city, leaving his sister to care for the children. Two years later, he summoned his sister to come to Kansas with the children. He had bought land and was settled again. He had also married a second time. His new wife, my mother, was considered beneath his station, and his family would not honor it."

"Ah, yes. The second wife. That must stick in your craw, Mr. Nash," DeFord said. "Your father came from an extremely wealthy and noble family, and yet, there you were, on a dirt farm in Kansas, living in poverty, being denied your birthright. I can see where that might fester into feelings of resentment, and even entitlement. Did not the Nashes and the Navarres add to their combined fortunes through the financial and transportation industries in Philadelphia? In other words, banking and railroads?"

Leon's lips tightened. He felt an anger that he couldn't explain.

"I never knew my father's family," he stated. "They mean nothing to me."

"They must have meant something to you, Mr. Nash, since you have gone to such length to hide it, even to the point of lying under oath. Your father gave you that name. Why would you not honor it?"

"Like I said, I feel no connection to that family. I never knew them."

"I think there is a lot more to it than that, Mr. Nash. I think you were an angry young man. First, your father was disowned and ostracized from a wealthy and influential family. He changed his name to his mother's maiden, but felt enough connection to the Navarre's to keep the name going. And yet, when your parents were killed, no one from that family came forward to acknowledge you. You were sent to the orphanage, where resentment grew into a festering need for revenge."

"No."

"I remind you again, you are under oath, Mr. Nash."

"I realize, I am under oath, Mr. DeFord. I felt no resentment toward my father's people. They were not my people. I did not know them."

DeFord smiled and nodded. "But you knew your mother's people, didn't you?" he pushed. "And, from what I understand, her family was just as honored and influential in their own society, as the Navarres and Nashes are in theirs. And again, circumstances deprived you of that prestige. Yet, considering your maternal heritage, I can understand you being ashamed of it."

"My mother was a decent woman." Leon's fist clenched. Fortunately, it was hidden from the assembly. "I had no reason to feel ashamed of her or her family."

"And yet, again, you hide the connection so well. If you were not ashamed of it, why hide it?"

"I object, Your Honor." Granger stood up. "What has the defendant's heritage got to do with these proceedings?"

The judge nodded. "Explain this line of questioning, Mr. DeFord."

"I am merely trying to establish the probability of both an ingrained hostility toward the industries Mr. Nash took such pleasure in attacking, and a genetic predisposition toward thievery and deception." He paused and looked back at the defendant. "Add these two tendencies together, and we have a solid template for the outlaw that Mr. Nash has become."

Taggard frowned. He had no idea what the prosecuting attorney was getting at, but one look at Leon, and it was obvious that Mr. DeFord had hit upon a well-kept and guarded secret.

The judge also looked confused. "A genetic predisposition? Please clarify, Mr. DeFord."

"Certainly. Mr. Nash's mother was a full-blooded Shoshone woman. Apparently, the daughter of the medicine man, who, in that society, is considered very prestigious. But as we all know; the Indian culture is a far cry from anything civilized. They are a nation of savages, liars, and murderers. They'll cheat their own family just as quickly as they will a stranger.

"We already know Mr. Nash is a liar. Now we can see he was denied the status and prestige that was his by birthright on both sides of his family, and he grew up in poverty. He came into adulthood carrying a grudge, supported by feelings of entitlement and justification. The only thing to be said in his favor is that by the savage influence of his mother's blood, he comes by it naturally."

The assembly burst into conjecture, and the gavel banged for order.

Taggard met his friend's eye, but couldn't hold it, as Leon turned a defiant glare toward the prosecutor.

Mr. Granger, still on his feet, yelled out his protest to be heard over the cacophony behind him. "Your Honor, you cannot be taking this seriously. A man cannot be judged by the blood that runs in his veins. This is ridiculous."

The gavel continued to pound out its staccato. "Order," Judge Lacey boomed his command. "Order in this court. Mr. DeFord, you will cease with this line of questioning immediately. The members of the jury will discount everything that was said here concerning Mr. Nash's heritage. Is that understood? Order! Quiet, or the courtroom will be cleared."

The verbal onslaught from the assembly quieted, and those who had risen from their seats, now hastily returned to them.

The jury acknowledged the ruling, but everyone, including Mr. DeFord, knew that once those words had been put out there, it would be impossible to ignore them.

"Your Honor," Granger remained standing, waiting for the room to quieten. "I submit that the jury has been tainted. I request that this trial be postponed until a new jury can be instated."

"Request denied, Mr. Granger," the judge snapped back. "The jury has agreed to disregard those last statements. We will continue. Mr. DeFord, do you have more questions for the defendant, or was that all you had to offer?"

Mr. DeFord looked pleased with himself. He knew his line of questioning would not be accepted, but he had planted the seed of prejudice, and he was content to back off that track.

"Oh, I have more questions for the defendant, Your Honor. I'm not done yet."

"Fine." Judge Lacey still huffed with the indignity of the outburst. "Carry on."

Granger sat down, frustrated over this turn of events. He tried to meet his client's eye, but Leon avoided him.

Mr. DeFord approached the defendant, and the look Leon sent him was anything but friendly.

"Mr. Nash, as stated earlier, I have done my research." DeFord smiled. He knew his case was progressing as planned, "and, I find it disappointing that you insist on lying under oath. Are you sure there is nothing more about your childhood years you wish to declare?"

"I don't know what you mean."

"Then allow me to clarify. The truth is, Mr. Nash, that you were not sent away to another orphanage, were you? You were sent to a Residential School in South Dakota; a school specifically for Indian children. Is this not closer to the truth?"

"I don't see the importance of it," Leon fumed, but he kept his anger under control. "To my mind, it was simply another institution. The only difference was that my stay there was worse than my time at Blessed Heart."

"I'm sure," Mr. DeFord gave a knowing smile. "You didn't fit in, did you? You weren't really one of them, were you? And yet, apparently, the officials at Blessed Heart didn't think you fit in with them, either. Perhaps they felt that the Residential School would have more success in educating the Indian out of you."

"Beating it out of me, you mean," Leon snapped. "There was no love lost when that place burned to the ground."

"I'm sure. Which brings up another omission in your previous testimony. You weren't returned to Blessed Heart because the school burned down. In fact, you used the fire as a diversion, allowing you to run away, didn't you?"

Leon sat silent, his mouth a hard line of resentment.

"No comment?" Mr. DeFord raised a brow. "Well, then I also suggest that it was you who set the fire, wasn't it, Mr. Nash?"

"No." Leon was adamant. "Even at that time, I would not put other people's lives in danger for my own benefit. I don't know how the fire started, I simply used it to my advantage—"

"To run away."

"Yes, all right. To run away. I still ended up back at Blessed Heart, I don't see what difference it makes how I got there."

"Don't you?" DeFord said. "You swore to tell the truth, the whole truth. So help you God. What that means in a court of law, is that by the deliberate omission of facts, you are, indeed, lying. Lying under oath, Mr. Nash. And this is all on record. You were caught stealing, weren't you? In the same town where Blessed Heart was located. You were stealing everything you thought you would need to make a go of it on your own. The only thing missing was your nephew. You found your way back to Blessed Heart with the intentions of getting him out, didn't you?

"In fact, I put it to this court that you deliberately set yourself up to be caught so you would be sent back there. Why break in, when you could get in legitimately? You had a stash of supplies hidden, so all you had to do was wait for the opportunity to break out with your nephew, and then you'd be on your way. Isn't this a truer reckoning of what happened, Mr. Nash?"

Leon couldn't bring himself to make eye contact with anyone in the court. The only untruth in Mr. DeFord's surmise was the origin of the fire. Leon had not set it, but the rest, he could not deny. He had buried all this so deeply in his psyche, that now, hearing the truth of it sounded foreign to him. He could not bring himself to concur, and so he remained silent, and he felt the mood in the courtroom shift against him.

Not expecting an answer from the defendant and hearing no objection to his line of questioning, Mr. DeFord continued. "Mr. Nash, do you know what a psychopath is?"

Leon bristled at the double insult; insinuating that Leon was a psychopath, and that he was ignorant enough to not understand its meaning. "Yes, Mr. DeFord, I am aware of the word's meaning."

"Good." Mr. DeFord turned to face the assembly. "But, for those of you here who have no reason to be aware of this condition, in a nutshell, it refers to a person who has no social conscience. They take what they want, when they want, and without remorse or consideration for the effect their actions may have on others. They are often highly intelligent, charismatic, and manipulative. They see themselves as above the law, sneering down at us mere mortals, who are restricted by our own moral code. Does this description sound familiar to you, Mr. Nash?"

Leon did his utmost to remember Mr. Granger's advice to him, about not allowing Mr. DeFord to push him into a reaction.

"As I have stated," his response was a sneer, "I am aware of its meaning."

Mr. DeFord nodded. "Is that the only connection to this description, you can think of, Mr. Nash? Here you have, by your own admittance, spent most of your life stealing from others. Indeed, to the point that it became 'second nature', and you saw nothing wrong with it."

"We stole to survive," Leon said. "Once on that path, it is very difficult to get off it. As I stated, we came to realize it was wrong and have spent the past five years trying to turn that around."

"Yes, 'so you stated'." DeFord agreed with that much. "And Sheriff Murphy, per his testimony, also states you have remained law-abiding citizens during these past five years, and, therefore, should be considered for the pardon."

"Yes, that's right."

"And yet, it has already been shown that you have no problem with omitting certain truths. It makes me wonder what else you are not telling the court. Also, if I understand previous testimonies correctly, both you and your partner have, on at least one occasion, broken legal custody, and, per Marshal Morrison, you tried to escape from his custody after being legally arrested. Is that not considered 'breaking the law'?"

"Marshal Morrison may be of the opinion that I tried to escape from his custody, but the truth of the matter is, I had decided to see this matter through and face trial. If I had intended to escape, I would have done so and not be here in this court, today."

There came a loud *'Ha'* from the assembly, and Leon could only assume it was Morrison, giving his honest opinion of that statement. This was followed by appreciative chuckling from others in the room, until the judge brought everyone to order, again.

"Indeed?" DeFord cocked a brow. "You are that confident of your abilities?"

"Yes."

"Well, how good of you to join us," DeFord stated, then continued. "Per previous statements, you were involved in several scams, or con games, during the past five years. Now, your friend, Sheriff Murphy, suggests these acts were sanctioned by legal authority, and, therefore, you were not breaking any laws. Is this correct?"

Leon forgot his anger over the previous insults. DeFord was leading him into dangerous territory now. He would have to keep all his wits about him to stay ahead of the lawyer.

"My partner and I did a few jobs for government officials, yes."

"And these officials were happy with the results of your efforts?"

"Yes. I believe they were."

"Odd then, that none of them are here to support you now."

"Yes, it is, isn't it?"

"So, if these operations you were involved with, in the last five years, were legal, then you should have no qualms telling the court who else assisted you in these endeavors."

Leon felt a tingle of fear go down his spine. There it was; decision time. He needed to stall, to give his brain a chance to work this out.

"My partner, Jack Kiefer, assisted me."

Mr. DeFord smiled. "Yes, we are well aware of Mr. Kiefer's involvement. I am, of course, referring to the two people whom Mr. Snodgrass mentioned as being part of that particular operation."

"Which two people?"

"The two who are not Jack Kiefer," Mr. DeFord said. "What are their names, Mr. Nash?"

"I'm not at liberty to divulge that information."

"Why not?" DeFord pressed on. "If that was a legal operation, they are in no danger of prosecution. Indeed, we should be thanking them for being so helpful."

Leon felt the trap door snap shut. Fear, like a vice, took hold of his chest, and he found it hard to breathe. He looked at Taggard, his eyes desperately asking for forgiveness, knowing that what was going to happen next, would cut that man to the quick.

Taggard was confused and anxious. Leon and Jack had not told him anything about the scam to trap Snodgrass. When it had been brought up in court by that gentleman, Taggard hoped it had simply been another classified job through the governor. Now, though, seeing Leon's distress, Taggard began to have his doubts.

"No," Leon's heart lodged in his throat. "I can't give you those names."

Audible groans traveled throughout the courtroom. Leon wasn't sure who they came from. He only knew that he was lost.

"Why not, Mr. Nash?"

Leon's brain spun. Should he lie? Insist that the information was confidential? That it was too sensitive to be revealed here, in an open court? But then, he would be supporting the very things that DeFord had accused him of being: a sociopath and a natural born liar.

Plus, he was under oath. He had omitted certain truths, mainly because they were buried so deeply in his sub-conscious, they had lost all meaning to him. But he never out-right lied. Could he, in all honor, disrespect the court and his friends in this manner?

No, he could not.

He drew in a deep breath, then slowly released it. "Because that was not a legal operation," he forced the reply. Again, he looked to Taggard for forgiveness, but he didn't find any there. Taggard was angry.

DeFord's smile was smug. "It was not a legal operation. Hmm. You have claimed that you and your partner have been law-abiding citizens for the past five years, and yet now, you openly admit to having pulled a confidence game that was outside the law. Why would you do that, Mr. Nash, if you were hoping for a pardon?"

Leon felt sick. How could he say that a prostitute, high-class that she was, but still a prostitute, had come to them for help? How could he explain that they had tried to stay true to their goal, but she had used her knowledge of them to pressure them? She had one of the few photographs of him and Jack and had threatened to hand it over to the law, and even allow word to slip out to their fellow outlaws concerning their link to the governor's office. They would have been doomed.

Thinking back on it, they could have resisted her, that if push came to shove, she would not have put their lives in danger, simply to get what she wanted. But instead, they choose to jeopardize their pardons to help a life-long friend who was being blackmailed into the ground by Snodgrass.

Josephine had too many 'friends' in high places for her to be able to withstand questioning in a court of law. Just as Leon was experiencing now, it is doubtful that any of her clients would own up to the relationship and come to her assistance. If the law found out that she had that photo and held it back, she could be in serious trouble. Even if she didn't end up going to prison, herself, for being involved in the con, and withholding evidence, she would likely lose her livelihood.

No, Leon wasn't about to turn her in. And he sure wasn't going to turn on Freddie Redekopp.

Silence weighed heavily in the courtroom.

Leon had been expertly backed into a corner. He had nowhere else to go.

"We did it to help a friend." He was willing to admit that much.

"And what is the name of this 'friend'?"

"No."

"Mr. Granger," the judge interrupted, "is your client aware of the consequences of refusing to answer a question posed to him while under oath?"

Mr. Granger looked regretful. "Yes, Your Honor. He is aware of the consequences."

"Mr. Nash," Judge Lacey turned to the defendant. "I will give you one more opportunity to answer the question, or you will be found in contempt. Do you understand?"

"Yes, Your Honor. I cannot answer the question."

"Then I find you in Contempt of Court, Mr. Nash. Mr. DeFord, do you have any more questions for the defendant?"

"No, Your Honor. No more questions."

"Fine. Mr. Nash, please return to your seat."

Leon somehow managed to get to his feet and walk back to his place. He tried to connect with Taggard, but his friend refused to meet his eye.

Taggard was furious. As far as he was concerned, Leon had betrayed his trust. Everything he had done, supporting them in their efforts to stay honest, putting pressure on the various governors to honor the agreement, even putting his job on the line to press their case, had all been for naught.

Maybe it was too late. Maybe Leon was simply an outlaw, through and through, and there was no changing him.

Silence reigned over the courtroom.

The closing statements by the two attorneys went by in a blur. Leon hadn't even listened to them. What was the point? All he could do now was wait for the verdict, and hope that Mr. Granger's assessment of the situation had been overly pessimistic. Maybe he still had a chance at some leniency.

Maybe.

***

Taggard helped escort Leon back, but didn't say a word to him the whole way down to the lower floor. Once in his cell, Leon tried to get Taggard to stay, to talk to him, to please, let him explain. But Taggard was too angry, and he turned his back on his friend and left.

Mr. Granger came into the cell block to stand by his client at a time, he knew, would be difficult for him. Leon sent him a weak smile, as the lawyer came up to the bars.

"Well, Mr. Nash. I have to admit, it does not look good."

Leon simply nodded and slowly paced the cell.

"Is it truly worth your freedom to hold back that information?"

Leon stopped pacing and faced his lawyer. "Despite what Mr. DeFord would have the jury believe, I am not a psychopath. Nor am I genetically predisposed to turn on a friend. I will not betray a confidence or stab a friend in the—" and there, he broke off and glanced toward the cell block door. He had stabbed Taggard in the back, even though he had not meant to. Knowing what that friend was now thinking of him, made Leon heartsick. He wanted, desperately, to make things right between them, but he didn't know how.

Granger nodded, knowing there was no point in pushing the matter.

"If it helps," Granger said, "the longer it takes for the jury to reach a verdict, the better it could be. If it takes them a long time, it means they are undecided, and they may have to compromise. What you went through in your childhood should count for something."

"Hmm." Leon went back to pacing. He knew the prejudices against Indians. And it was even stronger against half-breeds. It was a secret he had kept well hidden, that only a handful of trusted, childhood friends knew about. Until now.

Cameron entered the block and approached the two men. Mr. Granger nodded a greeting to his patron, and then, with another glance at his client, left the two friends alone to talk.

Cameron stood quietly at the bars, waiting for Leon to make the first move.

Leon continued to pace for a few more minutes, not sure if he wanted to talk, but also knowing he didn't want to be left alone, either.

Finally, he approached his friend and mentor, and stood silently before him, unable to meet his eyes, and not knowing how things could be worse.

"Well, Napoleon, that was quite an eye opener, in there."

Suddenly, Leon knew how it could be worse. He looked at Cameron with disappointment in his eyes.

"It's 'Napoleon' now, is it? No longer 'Peter'?"

"Yes," Cameron's tone was regretful. "I think it's time to let go of old habits."

Leon slumped. "The promise you made was to Peter."

"The promise I made was to you," Cameron said. "I won't abandon you. I question some of the choices you've made, but I trust you have your reasons. Whatever the verdict is, whatever happens in there, you are still family, and we won't abandon you."

Leon clutched the bars between them, his knuckles turning white with the pressure.

"Cameron," his whisper came out as a strangled plea. "I'm scared. I'm so scared. I'll die in prison."

"You will if you keep telling yourself that. You're a strong man, Napoleon, stronger than you think. No matter what happens, don't give up. Will you promise me that?"

"Another promise, Cameron?"

"Yes. Will you promise?"

Leon sighed and leaned his forehead against the bars. He was no longer confident; he didn't think he could do it.

"Napoleon, if not for me, then for the girls?"

Leon sighed. That wasn't playing fair. He looked up at Cameron, meeting his eyes.

He nodded. "For the girls."

The door opened, and Mike came in with the keys to the cell. "Jury's back."

***

"Gentlemen of the jury, have you reached your verdict?"

"We have, Your Honor."

"And what say you?"

"We find the defendant, Napoleon Navarre Nash, guilty of all charges."

Reaction swept through the assembly like a wave, and the chorus of relieved jubilation competed with anguished disbelief.

Even though the verdict was exactly what Leon had braced himself for, nothing prepared him for the reality of it. He went numb, his heart pounding so hard, he was sure it would burst from his chest. He couldn't breathe.

"Napoleon Navarre Nash, please stand and face the bench."

Leon complied, feeling like he was in a nightmare.

"Mr. Nash," Judge Lacey looked down at him, "I must agree with the jury. Though I do not contend that you are a psychopath, nor even genetically predisposed toward thievery, perhaps the choices you have made, and the life you continue to embrace, would be more understandable if you were. But on the contrary, for all intents and purposes, you are a sane and intelligent man, who simply chose to live outside the laws of this land.

"You came into this trial insisting you had led a law-abiding life for the last five years, and yet, it has been shown, beyond a reasonable doubt, that this has not been the case. You have lied to your friend and supporter, and you have shown contempt for this court.

"Indeed, I feel that you are a very dangerous man, and have no true intentions of reformation. I, therefore, sentence you to twenty years to life at the Wyoming Territorial Prison. Sentence to commence immediately. This court is adjourned."

And the gavel came down.

Leon's groan would have been audible, if it hadn't been for the uproar of the assembly.

Everyone started talking at once, and someone, somewhere in the hubbub, was crying.

Mike snapped the handcuffs on Leon, before the prisoner regained his equilibrium and attempted something desperate. Leon was then dragged, unhindered, through the side door and, for the last time, down to the jailhouse and back to his cell.

He was uncuffed and left alone.

CHAPTER TWENTY
THE GAME PLAN

The silence in the cell block was suffocating, its other occupants acutely aware of the storm brewing. The rage came upon him gradually. Beginning in the pit of his stomach and the back of his throat, then spreading, until it engulfed his heart, his mind, and then his very soul.

Napoleon Nash screamed his anguish to the world, and not a single item in the cell was safe from his assault. No one dared approach him while he was in this mood, because for the first time in his life, his emotions were out of control and his mind engulfed in a blind rage.

***

The atmosphere inside the office of the main jailhouse, was electric. as though a thunder storm had blown in and smothered the whole building with a dark, ominous cloud, crackling with lightening.

Determined not to be left out of anything, Caroline quietly entered the office in the wake of the men, but the sounds of her dear friend, in the throes of a nightmare, echoing out from the cell block, assaulted her heart, and before she knew it, she was crying again.

Her first move was a bee line toward the heavy wooden door, insisting she wanted to offer some comfort to her friend. But she found herself blocked by every person in the room.

"But I want to see him," came her wailing protest.

This was met with a resounding "No!" from several male voices, not the least of which, was her father's.

The sheriff positioned himself between the young lady and the cell block door. "No, Miss, you can't go in there," Turner insisted, much to Cameron's relief. "He's not rational right now, and he wouldn't hear anything you had to say, anyway."

"I could try." Though she already knew it wasn't going to happen.

Turner shook his head. "No one's going back there. Not even you, Doc. I've seen men go like this before when they're been hit with a hard sentence. The best thing to do, is leave them alone until they calm down."

At this point, an exceptionally loud bang came from inside the block.

Turner sighed. "There goes the cot against the bars."

Then a crashing followed.

"That was the chamber pot. I hope it was empty."

"Well," Taggard sighed, "there's no point in hangin' around, listenin' ta' this. I'll give 'im a couple of hours, then see if he's worn himself out enough to hear reason."

"Good idea," Turner agreed. "Why don't you folks head over to the saloon or . . . oh, excuse me, Miss. I mean, the café, or something. Let things calm down here, a bit."

"Actually," Mr. Granger turned to the group. "I'd like to speak with you gentlemen, if I may. Over a cup of coffee sounds just as good a place as any."

The group agreed, and they all headed to the café, Caroline taking comfort from her father's arm around her waist. Cameron had resigned himself to the fact that Caroline was whole-heartedly in on these events, now. There was a determination about her that was not going to be denied, and even her father was finally ready to accept that maybe, his little girl had grown up.

***

Having seated themselves at one of the larger tables in the café, they caused Betsy a minor stab of disappointment, when all they ordered was coffee all around. Unfortunately, nobody was particularly hungry after the judgment that had been brought down. Even coffee was pushing the limits.

"I'm sure I'm not the only one here who feels that the sentence handed down to Mr. Nash was extreme," Granger began, and was met with several emphatic nods. "Unfortunately, I knew the judge was going to do this. He doesn't take contempt of court lightly.

"As a lawyer, I'm not supposed to take sides. I should be able to go into the courtroom and argue both the defense and the prosecution of any given case, with equal conviction. However, in this case, I'm finding it very hard to walk away and leave a man to basically die in prison, especially when he has never killed anyone, himself.

"I believe he is genuinely sincere in his efforts to reform, despite that unfortunate backsliding. In dealing with Mr. Nash, I was surprised to find him to be an honorable man, who is obviously loyal to his friends and benefactors. Indeed, the fact that he was willing to accept life in prison rather than betray a confidante, in my mind, speaks admirably for him."

Granger stopped speaking to allow his words to sink in and to permit anyone the opportunity to disagree with anything he had said. There was no dissension in the group. In fact, if he had been paying attention, he might have noticed a young woman's eyes intent upon him, and a heart, warming in his favor.

"I think we are all in agreement with you, Mr. Granger," Taggard spoke for the group. "What did you have in mind?"

Granger smiled. "Apart from the usual appeal that I will put in through the courts, and which will be ignored, I do have another idea. But it's going to take a lot of commitment and perseverance from those of you who may choose to accept the challenge."

"I'll do it," Caroline chimed in. "And I'm sure Penny will want to help, too."

Mr. Granger took note of her. "You don't even know what it is, yet,"

Her eyes were alive with excitement and the eagerness of finally being able to do something. "Whatever it is, we both want to help." And she sent the young lawyer a huge smile, full of brightness and hope.

Mr. Granger felt his heart do a somersault, and he smiled back at her.

Taggard and David were contemplating the lawyer's words and hadn't noticed the electrical exchange pass between the two young people.

Cameron, however, did notice.

Granger hesitated. "Ahh, yes . . . well," suddenly the lawyer found himself momentarily at a loss for words. "Umm—actually, Sheriff Murphy!" He was relieved to get his mind focused again. "Your comment to Mr. DeFord is what got me thinking about this."

"Oh yes? Which comment was that?"

"You suggested that he subpoena the governor," Mr. Granger reminded him. "We could do this, but it would be too time consuming, and we can't afford that. I have an idea of how we can bring him to account in another way."

"How?" Taggard asked. "I've been tryin' for three months ta' get him ta' respond ta' me and I keep gettin' shut out."

"That's because you have been respecting the promise to keep the arrangement a secret."

"Of course."

"But the governor's office has not kept its end of the deal," Granger persisted. "I assume each governor, upon appointment, had been made aware of the agreement made with Mr. Nash and Mr. Kiefer?"

"Yes. Every one of them was informed of it, and agreed to it."

"And yet, when push came to shove, the office closed the door and ignored the deal," Granger leaned forward in his enthusiasm. "I'd even go a step further and suggest that it was Governor Warren who hired Sheriff Morrison to clean up the outlaw mess in this territory. Once Nash and Kiefer were arrested, all deals were off. The governor reneged on it first, therefore, we are under no obligation to remain bound by it."

"What are you suggesting we do?" Cameron asked. "Storm the governor's office?"

"Yes," Granger smiled. "But not with people, and of course, not with guns. But with paper. We get in touch with as many newspapers in Wyoming that will take the story, and let the people know exactly what the governor's deal was, and that it was ignored in the end."

"But would that work?" Cameron was skeptical. "Most of the people in Wyoming with any kind of clout, are the big ranchers and railroaders. Not to mention the bankers. I think they would be more interested in seeing Nash and Kiefer behind bars, and not be too concerned about the governor breaking a promise made to outlaws."

"You underestimate the power of the average citizen, Mr. Marsham. Even though the governor is appointed by the president, if every person in Wyoming who has the power to vote, were to be convinced that their governor does not keep his promises, well, that's a very powerful tool."

Silence surrounded the table as this idea settled in. Caroline was already wrapping her brain around the possibilities, and was suddenly very antsy to get home and bring Penny up to speed on what was in the works.

She turned her big, brown eyes to her father. "We could do it, Papa. Penny and I could do this. We'll get in touch with all the newspapers in Wyoming, and in Colorado as well. And the sooner we get started, the better, because Mathew's trial is going to start soon, and maybe we can make a difference in time to help him."

"How are you going to manage that from home?" Cameron was skeptical of his daughters getting involved in such a scheme.

"I'll help them get it set up, as much as I can," Mr. Granger offered. "A lot of it could be done through the telegraph system and the mail service. I'll cover the cost of that."

Cameron sent Granger an exasperated look, but Caroline sent him one of open admiration.

Cameron frowned at his daughter's enthusiasm, but shook off his suspicions as he looked at the doctor. "You've been awfully quiet throughout all this, David. What do you think?"

"I think, I'm not really qualified to have an opinion here," David sighed. "There is not very much I would be able to contribute to the effort, though of course, I'll help out where I can. Personally, at this point I feel anything is worth a try."

"I'll do what I can," Taggard offered, "but, bein' a Wyoming Territorial Law Officer, I would not openly be able to do much. Just as you, yourself, Mr. Granger, cannot show involvement in this, as I'm sure it could cause you to be removed from the case."

"Hmm, perhaps. Once a case is closed, I am expected to go through the courts for appeals, if I so choose. Going directly after the governor might be frowned upon. Which is why I have presented it to you people who are their friends and supporters. I think it safe to say Miss Caroline has made up her mind, but if you gentlemen wish to think on it further, I understand. As I said, it will take commitment and perseverance, once it gets started. But please, don't take too long. The lives of two young men could very well depend on it."

'So, no pressure then,' was the prevailing thought going around the table. The man wasn't a lawyer for nothing.

Caroline smiled at him.

Cameron looked worried.

David and Taggard considered their options.

***

It took two hours for the prisoner to wear himself out to the point where he was rational again.

Only officers of the law were allowed near him, now that he was convicted, and Taggard knew that of this select group, only he would have any chance of reasoning with the man. He swallowed down his own anger and feelings of betrayal and entered the cell block. He realized, when all was said and done, that Leon was still his friend, and he would continue to fight for him, and for Jack Kiefer.

Leon snarled when he saw Taggard approach his cell.

"What was the point, Taggard? All those jobs we did for the governor, and for the governor's friends. What was the point? Where are they, now that I need them? Huh? Where? Hiding in their offices, behind their big, mahogany desks, that's where.

"Do you know how many times Jack and I could have hightailed it to Mexico? How many times we were in Mexico and came back. We could have gone to Canada. We were close to the northern borders so many times. It would have been easy.

"I bared my soul out there, and for what? I had forgotten so much of that bloody nightmare, and I had to dredge it all back up. Now I have to live with it all over again. *For nothing.* You may as well put a gun to my head and shoot me. I'm going to be just as dead, anyway. Damn promises.

"And that DeFord. Bringing my family heritage into this. What's that got to do with anything? I should have lit out for Mexico. Or gone back to my mother's people. I learned early; watch your own back. Me and Jack. I don't owe anybody anything. I shouldn't even be here, dammit. This is what I get for developing a conscience!"

Taggard stood quietly, accepting the onslaught.

Leon paced the cell, furiously hitting the bars with his fist, kicking the already-overturned cot, letting his anger run wild. But at least it was just anger now, and not blind rage.

Taggard waited.

Eventually, Leon calmed down, even to the point of realizing he had bruised his hand when hitting the bars. He stopped pacing and stood facing away from Taggard, his hands on his hips and his respiration heavy. He dripped sweat. He finally gave a huge sigh and turned to look at his friend.

Taggard looked back.

"I'm sorry," Leon said. "I'm sorry I let you down."

Taggard didn't respond. He was sorry Leon had let him down, too.

Leon shook his head as though in a debate with himself.

"We had to do it. I can't explain why. You'll just have to accept that we had to do it. And Snodgrass—that weasel! He's more of a scam artist than I'll ever be. He's the one who should be going to prison."

"And that other crime?" Taggard asked quietly. "The one that Rolland Murdock accused you of?"

"We told you about that one," Leon reminded him. "We had to get that money back from Lilly Wilkens, to clear ourselves. We returned the money to the authorities, you know that."

"Yeah, I guess I do." Taggard sighed. "Unfortunately, in the eyes of the law, all the good things you've done were cancelled out by the bad things. And your refusal to give up those names sealed your fate in the eyes of the judge."

Leon came over to the bars and leaned his forehead against them.

"Is Judge Lacey right, Taggard?" His tone begged for reassurance. "Am I beyond redemption? Beyond hope of a decent life?"

"No, Leon," Taggard had changed his own mind about this, now that he'd had a chance to calm down. "The judge was wrong. He doesn't know you. He was just going by the evidence. Your friend, Mr. Marsham, and I, have been talking with Mr. Granger. We have a plan. We're not going to give up, so don't you."

"Okay, Taggard," Leon pushed himself away from the bars, looking exhausted and burned out. "I won't give up."

***

Two days later, Leon found himself shackled to that damn belt, again. He had developed a healthy dislike for that contraption. The prison coach, which was to transport him to his new 'home', was outside the jailhouse, waiting for him. Mike was there, with his ever-present rifle, while Sheriff Turner made some last-minute inspections of the prisoner before they took him out and turned him over to the prison guards.

Everything was made satisfactory, and the group of lawmen escorted the prisoner out the back door and into the side street, where they expected the coach to be waiting for them.

No coach.

"Oh, for goodness sakes." Turner was disgusted. "They must be around front. Come on. We can just walk around. Better than trying to explain to everyone why we came back in."

The group headed to the front of the building, and as they came out onto the main street, both Leon and Sheriff Turner groaned. The coach had attracted the attention of passersby that now stood around the vehicle in hopes of one final glance of the infamous outlaw.

Turner growled under his breath. "Dammit. This is the very reason I wanted this coach on the side street. What the hell were they thinkin', parkin' it out here?"

All eyes turned, as the procession came into view.

With a rush, the crowd came at them.

Mike stepped between the prisoner and the onslaught, using his rifle as a barrier, but even he couldn't stop a select few from getting passed.

"Hey, Nash, I'm with the Daily Tribune. What do you think of the sentence? Did you expect it to be that harsh?"

"Nash, are ya' gonna try and escape?"

"Yeah, what about your gang? Are they gonna put up with this?"

"Do you think the Kansas Kid will be joining you . . .?

Leon jumped when he felt a hand tug at his shirt sleeve. He turned dark eyes upon the intruder, then frowned with mild surprise.

A lad, no more than twelve, stared up at him with eyes wide with fear and admiration. When Leon turned on him, he jumped away, then ran toward his friends.

"I did it," he was jubilant with his task accomplished. "I touched Napoleon Nash. He even looked at me . . ."

The boy's friends gathered around him and congratulated him on his courage.

Leon shook his head. *'What the hell?'*

More people crowded in on the group, throwing questions at him and reaching in for a touch of the celebrity.

Leon bumped into Turner, in his efforts to avoid them, but his movements were heavily restricted. Hands pawed at him, and he felt an insurgence of panic. *'Is this a lynch mob? Did my years of outlawing created this much anger?'*

The assault only lasted for an instance, as Mike became more aggressive in his defense. His bulk paid off here, as he cleared the way to the coach. One shove from his hand sent the average man stumbling into the background. A shove from his rifle knocked them on their butts.

It didn't take much for the crowd to get the message, and they backed off, but they did not disperse. They wanted to see the final walk of a dime novel hero heading toward his fate.

The procession carried on toward the heavy, black iron coach. With bars on the windows and locks on the doors, Leon thought it was the most intimidating vehicle he had ever seen. 'U. S. MARSHAL TERRITORIAL PRISON' was painted in brazen white letters on both sides of the coach, and it stood there, like the harbinger of doom, awaiting its next victim.

Leon barely noticed another small group of men that were going to the front doors of that same building. That is until he spotted Morrison in the group. He seemed to be able to sense the very presence of that man, now, and his anger toward him started to rise. He pushed it down, knowing that this was hardly the time to exact revenge upon the marshal. That little bit of retribution would have to wait.

Leon's entourage continued toward the coach, and Mike was preparing to assist Leon up the steps and into the vehicle, when Leon heard it.

"Leon!"

That voice. That voice was more familiar to him than his own. And his heart leapt to his throat.

Leon's head snapped up and he spun around, desperately searching for the source of that yell. His eyes focused on the other group of men who had just arrived at the front door of the jailhouse.

"Jack? Jack!"

TO BE CONTINUED

Coming soon.

Book Two: Ties That Bind

Leon wasn't long at his book when he felt the presence of someone at the open door of his cell. He looked up and saw Carson. When their eyes met, the guard beckoned him over, and Leon, feeling like this was the last person he wanted to deal with, none-the-less closed his book and approached. He stood quietly, avoiding direct eye contact, as this would be taken as a challenge, and he waited for whatever Carson had up his sleeve.

"Evenin', Nash," Carson greeted him. "I hear your partner's not going to be joining you here, after all."

Leon was startled into locking eyes with the guard. His heart leapt. Did that mean Jack had gotten his pardon? Was he a free man? Was he going to join the fight now, to get Leon out of here?

"Yes siree," Carson enjoyed himself. "They done found the Kansas Kid guilty of cold-blooded murder, and at 11:00 o'clock this morning, the law went and hanged him by the neck, until he was dead. Hanged him, Nash, like the filthy, thieving, murdering, gunslinger that he was."

Then Carson laughed; a loud raucous laughter that followed him as he disappeared from the doorway and continued his way down the corridor.

Leon's body turned to ice. He gasped and staggered backward as though Carson had just punched him in the stomach. He stood there for a full thirty seconds, his eyes staring straight ahead at nothing, until his knees gave way beneath him. He went down hard, landing on his rump, upon the cold floor. His body heaved, and he made a desperate grab for the wooden bucket, as he began to retch.

List of Characters

- Bains, Joan: Witness at Leon's trial
- Betsy: Waitress, Cheyenne, Wyoming
- Bill: Bartender, Arvada, Colorado
- Carlyle, Frank: Rocky Mountain detective
- Charles, Brian: Witness at Leon's trial. Fellow orphan
- Clayt: Telegrapher in Arvada, Colorado
- Cobb, Malachi: Shaffer's partner. Member of the Elk Mountain Gang
- Coburn, Maxwell (Max): Texas rancher. Friend of Leon and Jack
- DeFord, Harold: Lawyer for the prosecution
- Gibson, David: Doctor in Arvada, Colorado
- Gibson, Tricia: nee Baxter: David's wife
- Granger, Steven: Lawyer for the defence
- Jacobs, Carl: Sheriff, Arvada, Wyoming
- Jansen, Josephine (Josie): Childhood friend
- Jefferies, Merle: Sam's mother
- Jefferies, Sam: Hired hand at the Rocking M
- Jefferies, Tom: Sam's father
- Kiefer, Jackson (Jack. The Kansas Kid). Alias: Mathew White. Ex-outlaw
- Lacey, John: Chief Justice, Wyoming Territorial Court. 1884 - 1886
- Layton, Richard (Rick): Rancher, part-time deputy, Rawlins, Wyoming
- Lobo: Member of the Elk Mountain Gang, Wyoming
- Shaffer, Gus: Current leader of the Elk Mountain Gang, Wyoming
- Marsham, Cameron: Friend to Leon and Jack. Rancher, Rocking M Ranch, school teacher. Arvada, Colorado
- Marsham, Caroline: Eldest child of Cameron and Jean
- Marsham, Elijah (Eli): Youngest child of Cameron and Jean
- Marsham, Jean: Cameron's wife

- Marsham, Penelope (Penny): Middle child of Cameron and Jean
- McEnroe, Henry: Judge, New Mexico. Knows Leon and Jack. Friends
- McPhee, Fedamire (Fingers): Con man. Leon and Jack's benefactor during the early years
- Morrison, Tom: Sheriff. Rawlins, Wyoming
- Murdock, Rolland (Rolly): Witness at Leon's trial. Early acquaintance of Leon's
- Murphy, Taggard: Ex-outlaw. Former Elk Mountain gang member. Sheriff. Medicine Bow, Wyoming
- Nash, Antoinette: Leon's half-sister
- Nash, Edward: Leon's father
- Nash, Frederick: Leon's half-brother
- Nash, Janelle (Jenny) Leon's full sister
- Nash, Louisa: Leon's half-sister. Jack's mother
- Nash, Napoleon (Leon). Alias: Peter Black. Ex-outlaw, former leader of the Elk Mountain Gang, Wyoming
- Palin, Ben: Deputy, Arvada, Colorado
- Redekopp, Jonathan (Red): Con man
- Roberts, Kenneth: Witness at Leon's trial
- Shields, Charlie: Member of the Elk Mountain Gang, Wyoming
- Shoemacher, Mike: Deputy, Rawlins, Wyoming
- Snodgrass, Nigel: Witness at Leon's trial
- Strode, Alex: Deputy. Rawlins, Wyoming
- Tanguay, Gabriella: Actress, former undercover agent, Leon's ex-lover
- Turner: Sheriff, Cheyenne, Wyoming
- Wilkens, Lilly: one of their marks
- Wilkinson, Hank: Member of the Elk Mountain Gang, who was murdered by Morrison.
- Willis, Maribelle: Sam's girlfriend

Wyoming Governors

In order of term

- Hoyt, John Wesley: 1878 – 1882
- Hale, William: 1882 – 1885
- Morgan, Elliot: 1885.
- Warren, Frances: 1885 – 1886
- Baxter, George: 1886
- Morgan, Elliot: 1886 – 1887
- Moonlight, Thomas: 1887 – 1889
- Warren, Frances: 1889 – 1890
- Barber, Amos: 1890 – 1893
- Osborn, John: 1893 – 1895
- Richards, William: 1895 - 1899
- Richards, DeForrest: 1899 – 1903

About the Author

April Brauneis has always been a cowgirl at heart even though she has lived her whole life on the West Coast of Canada and the USA. Road trips always draw her and her husband, Paul, east and south. Montana, Wyoming, Colorado; these are places where her imagination, for both writing and artwork, is inspired and encouraged to run free.

Brauneis has been an artist/writer all her life, painting and writing about her first passions; the West, horses and an open range lifestyle. She also found a niche with painting pet portraits and animal studies. Now that she is retired, she can indulge in those things she loves the most: her husband, her animals, her art and her writing. She's busier now than she has ever been before, and she wouldn't have it any other way.

Visit her website at: www.twoblazesartworks.com

Visit her Facebook page Two Blazes Creations

Made in the USA
Middletown, DE
21 February 2019